Summer Madness

Morwenna J Holman

Published in 2015 by FeedARead.com Publishing

First Edition

A CIP catalogue record for this title is available from the British Library.

To all my cats, past, present and future, and my father: I affectionately dedicate this book.

Other books by Morwenna J Holman

Westerdale
Heaton
Rainharrow
The Calling
Bleak Spirit (about the Brontes)
Split Moonbeam (the story of my great-grandmother)
The Awakening (animal rights novel)

CHAPTER 1

The dazzling brilliance of the summer sky became shrouded in a little cloud, rapidly losing colour and pronouncing itself to be one of those lingering, hazy evenings that could be close to sunset or sunrise. A few flickering candles graced the window sills of the thatched cottages, which together with a stately mansion, partially concealed behind hedges of yew entwined with ivy, formed all that could be seen of the tiny village of Ardle. Further away a line of straggling houses breasted a hill, where two ploughed fields and another even smaller dwelling raised its head. It was isolated and removed from the rest of the habitations, its position being that it turned away from the rest and faced east, the others all inclined to the west where the dying sun was now sinking.

It was almost eight o'clock on a certain day in August and near the end of the 1820s. An auditory cacophony of regular and irregular sounds now arose, the former being the striking of the village clocks, others starting as the first ones died away confirming there was a great variance of time in Ardle. The latter sounds were the clip clop of a horse's hooves and the tuneful whirr of carriage wheels. Presently the aforementioned vehicle could be seen descending the far hill and making straight for one of the outlying houses which was painted tastefully in pink. The driver drew rein by the gate post and the little vehicle stopped. From the vehicle stepped a tall, fairly handsome gentleman of around the age of twenty five, carrying a leather holdall. He alighted slowly, went around to the driver and handed him a single coin after much deliberation. The carter surveyed the piece in disappointment, dropped it into his breast pocket and clicked again to the horse, who responded at will.

"'Tis just like a Scotsman," he murmured.

The addressed individual did not hear the whispered comment but regarded the dimming scenery with interest, his young eyes having been used to the lofty contours of mountains and the wide curve of the glens. He shaded his eyes from the dying sun and flung his bag into the rough grass.

"'Tis as different from home as chalk is from cheese!" he cried in a voice that spoke of the soft accent of a Highlander. "I wonder if I can come to terms with it?" As this was impossible to tell and needed to be deliberated on with judgement and in time he lowered his blue eyes a little, picked up his bag and walked on.

It was soon clear that his destination lay within the walls of the pink house and to this the Scotsman now headed, crossing the garden threshold and approaching the evening tranquillity of the building. He raised his gloved hand and knocked once, twice, thrice upon the cherry stained door. A knot of birds twittered sleepily on the dark thatch and a chained dog barked from the deepening shadows of a shed. The Scotsman contracted his brow and waited.

3

The dying sun slipped a little lower on the horizon and the high cascading clouds assumed an ominous grey colour which the man, who was no stranger to storms, now became aware of. A drop or two of rain tested the air. He knocked again.

After another minute or two of boot tapping and sighing he went a little way down the path and paused in silent deliberation. Eventually, deeming it possible it could rain harder, he decided to seek solace in the nearest inn which could, at least afford him a night's shelter. Having decided on a plan of action he was not a man to dither so he shouldered his bag and marched into the growing twilight of the road.

He had only gone a hundred yards or so when rapid steps behind him announced the presence of another person, travelling at a much faster pace than he. The Scotsman waited, turned about and peered a little nervously into the gloom. A dozen or so stunted poplars to his left rattled their leaves warningly and, as if in answer, the distant roar of thunder broke upon the air.

A man appeared along the dusty margin of the road, his dress being that of a simple farm labourer now at ease in the comforts of his home; that is his shirt was thrown open as far as the waist and the latter portions of his trousers were rolled up to reveal a length of woollen sock. He wore no belt or kerchief and had removed the heavy outdoor boots of his trade so that now he was forced to run in knitted wool.

"Mr Straeton!" panted the labourer. "Mr Straeton! Wait a minute! I was lost in sleep when you came knocking, and my wife was in the hives till almost too late to wake me! Will you return now – us being of the same flesh and blood so to speak?" The words smacked of a rich rural accent of Dorset influence.

The gentleman held out his hand and smiled.

"Penlow! 'Tis good to see you again! I was sad that our last meeting was at a funeral but this is much better!"

That the two men who were facing each other were actually second cousins, it was hard to believe. The younger bore the natural charms of youth, his fine Northern skin being completely covered with auburn brown freckles which inclined to ginger on the forearms and hands. His hair, when revealed, was cut in a straight, universal style of medium length and it wavered uncertainly between brown and chestnut. Blue eyes windowed the pallid background of his face; eyes full of keen feeling and knowledge that were often dark as seawater when he was pensive. His height was upwards of a good six and a half feet, his figure was robust without possessing a pound more of flesh than it ought. Altogether he approached the borders of male beauty without quite touching the centre. And before him stood a short, balding yokel of perhaps forty years of age who inclined towards portliness as much as the former inclined to slimness.

4

Shirley Penlow was then thirty one and, in short, not quite nine years younger than her husband whom she had married in a rash moment, believing him to be moneyed after witnessing the lavish funeral of his first wife. Too late she perceived her mistake. Her world was not to be one of luxury but the hard-working world of a labourer's wife where every penny counted. But she was as cheerful as she was wise, and Damion was reasonably kind to her and generous when he had some money so she regarded her lot as bearable but not happy. Thus she inherited a moderately pretty eighteen year old daughter with whom it was a joy to walk round the village and snatch comments that the two were uncannily like sisters.

The clocks of Ardle were striking ten when the lights in Russet Cottage flickered and went out. By then the storm had rolled away far inland where it could be heard but faintly, like the distant roar of the tide.

In the little market town of the area, known hereabouts as Stackhouses, the frequenters of the only inn called appropriately the World's End, were engaging in a topical discussion the subject of this being soundlessly asleep about a mile distant. The World's End was an ugly little house of resounding ill-repute where the slatterns, labourers and fly-by-nights gathered every evening to stretch out their beer money. In architecture, it was a mixture of all the dubious features of every past age and by daylight it appeared dirty, dark and primitive. At dusk all these deformities were covered up in the night's essence and everyone was so busy savouring the beer that there was no time to notice that the tankards were usually unwashed.

The interior of the inn was simple and almost basic which made even the wandering vagabonds feel at home. There was a much told tale in the 1800s that one old tramp resting there, evidently having seen better days, had complained that it was too dirty for him and had accordingly gone out to sleep in the surrounding fields. Low benches skirted the sanded floor and rickety stools stood among them and the landlord, who was as fat and jolly as he was lazy and dirty, served behind the bar with welcoming civility.

On this particular evening the talk ran almost as freely as the ale.

"Ah! He is a gentleman, a rich paying gentleman who thinks nothing of giving a farthing tip for a favour!" cried the carter who had driven the local carriage not five hours ago.

"Do ee tell it, Mr Sims!" mused another, characterised by a red face and vivid blonde hair. "I've heard he's a Scot!"

"He is! 'Tis all ochs and ayes, neighbours, and perhaps one day he'll show us the tartan of his kilt!"

There was much general laughter at this and the landlord indulged himself freely in their gossip, which he always did when there were no empty glasses to fill up.

"Ah, could be he's a Royal Stuart or something of the like, with ancestral houses in every glen!" suggested the man behind the bar, when the raucous laughter had died down.

7

"And me, worth only a farthing tip!" cried Sims bitterly. "Ah well, I cannot think him above me, as he's only one of them newfangled horse doctors who thinks he has a calling in the world!"

A short silence fell as they were all judging it time to take a swig of beer, which they did gladly, rolling it round their mouths speculatively before swallowing, although most had drunk here for nigh on twenty years. There were few young men amongst them and scarcely any women but a gnarled hag and a widow.

After they had all cleared their throats a timid little lady of around forty-five asked,

"And is he handsome?"

"'Tis fair tolerable for you, Mrs Dowley, now your Cecil is cold in the earth. Yes, fair tolerable!"

At these words a flagging form, who had been leaning heavily upon the narrow window sill stood upright and pressed an ear to the partially open window. It showed itself to be a woman in silhouette, although it was dubious if any lady would frequent the outside of an alehouse at this hour.

"And how is he formed?" asked the widow from within the inn walls. At this a general chorus of laughter and whistles arose and the listener leant back and waited for the noise to die down.

"Faith! His hair is chestnut and as I recall it he has a score of freckles and ee is so tall ee could touch the sky if ee had a mind to!" replied the carter with another wink to the male company.

"How do you reckon his height then, Mr Sims?" cried the red-faced individual. "'Tis surely no taller than I?" And standing he revealed himself to be a little over six feet.

"'Tis half a foot above ee, Trent! Half a foot!" cried the carter, delightedly, waving his mug about and then setting it down on the bench with a deliberate rap. The angry Trent sat down again sulkily, all the rest laughing heartily at his discomfit.

"Come on then, landlord!" yelled the merry Sims. "Let us be having a flow of spirits to the drier regions. Ah, neighbours, I be a-parched in my throat almost to my innards with all this talk. A good drop and a song, eh?"

The others assented willingly and the general interest in the stranger died down. The silent listener, perceiving this, moved away from the window and edged out onto the narrow roadway which ran past the back entrance of the inn. As she walked a gleam of moonlight fell onto her dark features and revealed them to be those of a young woman little more than twenty years of age. She walked briskly, rather too fast and slovenly for a lady, and it could be noticed every now and then by anyone whom chose to observe her that she murmured short phrases in the sing-song voice of one who quotes. She seemed completely unperturbed by the darkness she encountered, the only noise that slowed her rapid progress being the tone of passing voices. Then she would flatten herself against a wall or glide into an alley, there being

8

"Well, well," murmured the Scotsman broadly. "I am not a man to stand upon the idle branch of ceremony when I believe her to be unnecessary. I would choose to be John and you...?"

"Damion."

"Good."

They turned back to the charms of the pink cottage, a definite chill now wandering through the once balmy air. The evening thunder sounded nearer and, spasmodically, a few more drops of rain fell.

"We are in for a soaking, John," cried the farm worker who possessed the countryman's eye of reading the weather. They both turned their heads upwards where several huge black clouds climbed the heavens. A distant sobbing in the trees announced the downpour and soon flashes of blue lightening graced the zenith. Thor sent out his thunder bolts to shake the earth. Meanwhile the two men had reached shelter and the dark interior of the cottage soon became lit with electric flashes, their power somewhat diminished by the light from an oil lamp.

"There – we are saved!" cried the labourer, thankfully shaking a few drops of water from his shirt and wiping his bald head. "'Tis said all our storms; and there have been many of late, are due to a witch living at Fern Cottage, but I cannot believe it of an innocent young girl! I cannot!" He echoed it sorrowfully as if he wished a good few more did not believe it either.

The Scotsman shook his head knowledgeably.

"I have heard such nonsense before," he admitted.

"In your home country?"

"Aye, something of the like."

"And you have wolves there and goblins and will o' the wisps rising from every marsh?"

"No, no, I'll not say that. 'Tis a might lonesome at times but canny fair if you were born there and raised in the glens!" As he uttered these words a slight air of melancholia came over him and his eyes glazed in awe as he viewed the flickering pictures in the light of the oil lamp. The ageing labourer was impervious to the romance of his visitor.

"It must be mighty cold there in the winter," Damion ventured.

"Aye, snow from November till March and water frozen solid in the burns."

"Ah! That is a sore trial for a man; so it is! Hopefully you will be happier now you have come south."

The young Scotsman suspended judgement on this, as if expressing by his silence, that he thought it impossible. Both men went forward through a low wooden door, of equal hue to the exterior, where they found themselves to be in a small whitewashed room with a bare wooden floor covered in a profusion of rugs. It was sparsely and even poorly furnished, the chief component, apart from a big, scrub down table, being a long aperture that was once possibly a settle. It stretched from the doorway to the opposite wall diagonally across the floor, which gave it the appearance of great length, several, leading off the street she now journeyed on. She was tall, rather above the height of the average woman, and although thin, she was well-formed. Her dress was a simple dark silk and that in turn was covered by a flowing black cloak which at present she drew tightly around her, the gaping hood hiding all but the bare outline of her face.

Presently she passed the last house of the market town and here she stopped to indulge in a curious action that would have bemused anyone who had come across her. But tonight there was no one but the wind sobbing quietly and the gentle rhythmic sound of silk rustling as she walked. The woman had raised her hands in the air and formed a strange figure with her long fingers. It was something like an upside down cross and when she had done this to her satisfaction she uttered thirteen jumbled words, her performance being finished with a much practised spit that reached a good three feet. After this she flung back her hood revealing tress upon tress of golden ringlets that soon hung silkily to her waist. She pulled up her skirts with one hand and began to run, the silence of her running footsteps being accounted for by the fact that she wore no shoes. Yet her total indifference at running over grass, stones or thistles could only be explained by the fact that her feet had acquired, by degrees, a thick layer of skin on her soles due to this habit.

Within a quarter of an hour the running form descended a long, curving hill past the first stone cottages of Ardle. She sprinted silently, her wet feet barely leaving any impression in grass or mud and soon it became apparent she was heading for the lonely little dwelling that stood back from the fields in isolation. In another minute or two she struck the path, waded knee high through nettles that left no stings upon her white flesh and went quietly through the unlatched gate. At the front door she paused a moment, listened hard and then lifted the handle to enter.

Inside a light burned dimly which revealed itself to be an almost spent candle. The girl went to this and nipped it out without wetting her fingers, she then turned to the narrow stairway and once at the top she paused cat-like and listened to the rustling approach of another figure which held a taper.

"Well?" said the dark figure, who revealed herself by tone to be a woman.

The girl hung her head sullenly and traced out the pattern of a backward cross upon the landing rug with her long toes but she never said a word. The woman raised the taper higher and revealed herself to be a small middle-aged lady with deep auburn hair and a much wrinkled skin.

"Where have you been?" she asked angrily.

There was no reply for a moment then,

"To Stackhouses," murmured the addressed one.

"Why?"

"To see if they spoke of HIM, who I knew was coming by the evening star, Hesperus."

The woman grew more and more irate but she held her temper, although the taper shook and her lips grew thin and creased.

"Well, and did you learn anything of him?"

"He has come. Out of wishing wells and fountains the lustre of my youth has arisen to greet him. He is the one who comes with cures for those who cry out in their misery to me as mother! It is enough for tonight that they have spoken of him, for I stood at the window and fed on flies whilst I listened!" She grew excited as she spoke, her huge, azure eyes dilating wildly and her hands beginning to tear at the edge of her dress which she had gathered up in her passion.

The woman looked distressed. She waited until the fire had died down in her daughter's face and then she whispered,

"Well, are you coming?"

An expression very like fear crossed the young girl's face and her tongue fell out of her open mouth like a dog's. She suddenly bounded forward on her knees and cried,

"I am, Mother!"

The older woman took her thin arm and led her forward to a door which was concealed beneath a rich fall of arras. Five minutes later the mother reappeared with the flickering taper, a number of small cuts being visible on her face and forearms, some of which bled profusely. Behind her came a low laugh that soon ended with the slamming of the thick door and the drawing down of the heavy arras. No one, on reaching the top of the stairs would have supposed anything like a cupboard, let alone a large bare room, led off from here, but would have concluded that the tapestry covered only bricks. It could be seen now that the woman bent quickly to lock the door and carried the key with her to her nearby chamber which she also locked. Then, flinging off her robe, she climbed into a small narrow bed and proceeded to fall into a deep dreamless sleep that so often marks complete physical and mental exhaustion.

The young woman did not sleep so soundly in the locked room, although the only sounds she emitted were a low whine and the strange rattle of metal which sounded hollowly whenever she moved her arms or legs. A casual observer coming into her bedroom would have discovered, to his utmost horror, had he light in the eerie gloom, that in the windowless room the young woman was gagged and she slept in heavy iron chains.

CHAPTER 2

A low, fiery glow in the east at the hour of six o'clock marked the first birth pangs of the morning sun. The night, which had been moonlit and warm after the full power of the rain, now receded to make way for a loud chorus of cocks greeting the dawn.

In the tiny pink cottage signs of stirring greeted the new day and the sound of water being poured alternated with doors banging and stilted conversation. At half past six a motley figure left the dwelling, carrying upon his back a wicker basket from which protruded the ends of several tools and the corner of a lunch box. The man walked down the path, went through the gate and was soon swallowed up in the thick canopy of bushes which all but covered the track at this season.

The wife of the afore mentioned man scalded the milk pan and took grain to her dozen fowls, collecting the eggs with gentle fingers and smiling gratitude to those who had laid them. Presently her tiny basket was full; she covered it with a little straw and made her way back to the house through the beehives and vegetable garden. For some reason she raised her eyes to the window of her cousin's room which looked over the back fields and perceived him to be drawing up the blinds. Soon he flung open the sash and saw her down below, their eyes met and the more tenderly disposed of the pair smiled.

At breakfast John found her attentive and attractive to a degree that he had never beheld in other women. It puzzled him a little but he did not possess the foresight to realise she had thrown herself away on a man far beneath her and one, who furthermore, had few physical attractions to strengthen the knot.

She asked him what he proposed to do now.

"Tomorrow," he answered, observing the careful way she watched him, "I shall move to my new residence in Stackhouses so I am afraid I must trouble you for one more day's shelter."

She affirmed that he was no trouble at all but she did not say what she truly felt which was that it was a pleasure to be in his company. Yet he seemed to read the words in her and she blushed a little and gazed downwards.

"Is your husband always kind to you?" he asked, suddenly curious.

She stopped playing with a quantity of salt spilt on the table cloth and looked up.

"He is not…very attentive," she admitted. Then her heart swelled within her and the true Shirley emerged. "But oh, what is the use in bewailing it! I married for no honest thing such as love but for monetary comfts of which I discovered, too late, my husband lacked!"

"That is very sad," he murmured and felt for her.

11

About seven o'clock there was a gentle tapping on the back door and then it quietly opened. John, who was drinking a basin of coffee, barely perceived it but his companion flung down the dishcloth and rushed forward.

"Connie! I am glad to see you. Have they been working your pretty fingers to the bone?"

The addressed person came forward now and took off her simple bonnet which she laid upon a nearby chair, unbuttoning her cloak meanwhile and, at length, sitting down.

"No, Mother, I am fairly well, just a little tired, that's all. Till yesterday we had a shooting party at the Hall and there were hunt breakfasts to prepare. But today they are gone by the morning carriage and my lord and lady are off to Banstead for a week so they judged I could be spared for a day, especially as it was more than time for my holiday!"

By then Connie, who was a girl of very simple intellect, had perceived the tall pleasant-looking gentleman at the table and she raised her eyes a little bemusedly to her stepmother.

Shirley took her hand and led her forward.

"John Straeton, this is my stepdaughter Constantina. Connie, meet a third cousin...or some such of yours." The man and woman locked hands, one at least a little awkwardly.

"So," said he, in his broad accent. "I have another beautiful cousin to befriend!"

They all felt this was not strictly true as the girl's looks fell nondescript beside her good-looking stepmother. Her hair was a mousey-red which changed colour in the light so that sometimes it was straw and sometimes almost auburn according to sunshine or shadow. Her sallow skin looked a little unhealthy, as though she had been ill recently, and her features were very ordinary although her eyes were comparatively large and fine. They darted nervously from one face to another, never still but restless in strange company. John felt she was afraid and shrank from contact with his person but that seemed preposterous and, at length, he dismissed it.

The young girl sat down to breakfast, the mother rather speculatively leaving the couple alone whilst she performed the drudgery of housework. Leaving the sitting room door open she was able to hear large part of the conversation and she observed John spoke first.

"Well, Connie, if I may call you such, where do you earn a living? Your father is my cousin in a distant sort of way so we are related."

"Yes," replied she, a shade nervously. "I am maid at the Hall."

"The Hall? You must remember I am not of your country, nay, a Scottish stranger, and treat me to more detail."

"Very well – at Porleau Hall," she acknowledged, keeping her eyes bound to the circle of her plate.

"Ah, I think I observed the building, a little, when I alighted. But you seem very young to be maid at such a place?"

"Not at all, Mr Straeton, I am eighteen."

"Really? You do not look it! Please call me John as I do not stand on ceremony – so unnecessary!"

She raised her eyes as he said this for he spoke gently but with feeling and, for the first time she looked at him properly.

"Ah-ha!" mused John, thinking to catch her off guard and tease her, "You are wondering how old I am and expecting an answer since you have disclosed your years!"

"On no account am I thinking any such thing!" cried she, looking away in embarrassment. "The revelation of my age was my own idea – I would not have said it unless I was comfortable with it!"

"Oh, aye, aye, I am sure, of course!" he replied, a little bemused, staring out of the window at a heap of rotting cabbage leaves. "Well, at eighteen I would have probably disclosed my age...but now...well, I chose to keep it secret."

There was a long uneasy silence and then the gentleman rose and gave a small bow. Connie perceived how very tall he was and how freckled were the broad backs of his hands. She did not think him handsome, as he did not think her pretty, but afterwards she chose to label him as interesting whilst he could not make her out at all. Yet her naturally reserved manner was lifting and at their next meeting she felt she would be able to look at him without qualms.

He took his leave of the two women on the excuse that he wanted to see his nearby lodgings although in truth he felt they wished to be alone. Picking up his hat and the simple leather case he always carried he let himself out through the front door and made his way across the wet fields.

As soon as the outside gate had slammed Connie abandoned the remains of her breakfast and went through to find her stepmother. Shirley was down upon her knees brushing the scanty material of the rugs from which rose a cloud of dust and numerous crumbs together with dried flakes of mud.

At the sound of feet she ceased, sat back upon her heels and swept a few locks of hair from her face.

"Well, Mother, how did you happen upon him?" asked her stepdaughter.

Shirley shrugged her shoulders and replied in as casual a tone as she could muster.

"He came last night by carriage. Damion did mention something about meeting him at the funeral he attended a little while back but...oh...I don't know...'tis your father's relation."

"Which by choice would be yours too! Mother, I saw the way you looked at him; the way you look at every man of pleasant disposition. Why, when you are a married woman? If I perceive it do you not think John does, and it is only fatigue that clouds the eyes of my father?"

Shirley flung her brush down on the floor and stood up.

"Connie - I think you have said enough!" Her tone was cold and angry, her beautiful eyes possessed of an irate power that made them sparkle and flash.

"You have no right to criticise me so hold your tongue and control your imagination!"

"Oh Mother, I mean no harm by my words but I do not like to see my father duped. I heard a strange tale of you before you met Father but I do not like to believe or repeat it!"

"Now - now! That is enough! I'll not be debased in my own home and that's an end to it!"

The young girl became a little uneasy, fetched her bonnet and cloak and let herself out of the back door, whereby, in a few minutes she could reach her tiny room at Porleau.

Shirley heard her go and was much grieved by it, and the harsh words she had uttered, but she would not be spoken to like that by someone she regarded as her junior. She could not go after her stepdaughter and offer apologies because the tale Connie spoke of that had circled Ardle was not entirely fictional. Two years before her rash marriage to Damion she had been briefly involved in the life of a famous doctor who had since departed to the high life of London, leaving her broken-hearted and desperate. Thus she had rushed into the union with Damion as a solace to her loneliness and to give her some new-found respect. But, alas, the much repeated phrase "Marry in haste, repent at leisure" became fact to her and many was the time she contemplated leaving. So far, since she became a wife, three men worthy of her deepening affection had entered her life but two had deemed her unsuitable for a dalliance. One, however, had returned her love and for four wonderful months she had bathed in the light of true passion so that leaving Ardle became a reality. But, sadly, it had burnt out and that was now behind her. In front there was another temptation that at present she would struggle to find the strength to resist – if the chance offered itself. She was too flighty, too young, too driven by romance and all the material things of life to settle down.

John Straeton reached the centre of Stackhouses, turned back a little and found himself in the very street where the accused witch had listened outside the inn, not ten hours ago. He gazed up at the sign reflected deeply for a moment and then pushed open the narrow back door.

Inside a few weary travellers were resting, two or three reading journals and others enjoying the dubious culinary dishes of the place. There was quite a few turned heads at the stranger's entrance, some even whispering rashly to their neighbours,

"Do you know him? Have you seen him afore?" And the neighbours in turn wrinkled up their foreheads, screwed up their eyes and shook their heads perplexedly. The stranger stepped up to the bar, rapped his knuckles upon it and asked of the landlord behind the counter in his best Scotch accent,

"Can you be telling me the way to an area called Fourcrosses and a house by the name of Fourbridges?"

14

The landlord put down the empty beer barrel he was moving, eyed up the questioner a little suspiciously and dusted his hands upon his white apron.

"Are you a foreigner here?" he asked, rather unnecessarily.

"Aye."

"A Scotsman?"

"Aye."

At this a few ears pricked up and several pairs of eyes were turned in his direction, two voices whispering loudly," 'Tis the new horse doctor."

"Aye," said the named one who was possessed of keen hearing. "That's my profession and Fourbridges is my business after today so I'll trouble you for directions and then I'll be off."

"There, there," soothed the landlord, coming round from behind the counter. "You'll drink a sup with us, sir, before you go, just for a welcome then?"

John frowned a little, then answered hesitantly,

"Aye, well, just a drop then."

The barman obtained a clean glass for the occasion and opened a bottle of Scotch whisky which he affirmed was nearly as good as the worst of the English ale. There were a few half-hearted laughs at this but the stranger was determined not to be riled and kept silent.

"Cheers to you, Mr Straeton! It may be early but it's never too early for a good malt!" cried the barman raising his glass cheerfully.

John returned his salutation, drank the tot down in one and felt instantly warmed.

"Well, landlord, if that is your nightly offering you can take it from me I shall be here very frequently so I'll not be a stranger long, faith, will I?"

"No one is stranger here for many days, sir," called a local, warningly.

John paid no heed to this but gazed at his watch, placed it back in his pocket and reminded the landlord of the directions he required. When these were furnished to his satisfaction he put on his hat, wished them good day and took his leave.

"Ah, so that is John Straeton," murmured the landlord as he put the whisky away. "I cannot say he has a pleasant face or manners but that must come from all that mist and heather!"

"Well, he is a Scotsman," replied the stock man who was rolling barrels behind the counter. "And surely neighbours that's enough to say of any man!"

The portion of the town called Fourcrosses was situated on a hill in the northern part, the latter slope of this forming the pathway to the first houses of Ardle so it was hard to ascertain where one place left off and the other began. In reality it was a lonely, barren district where only the doctor and farrier resided, the frequent clop of hooves being the sole noise that broke the silence. The few houses there were comprised of some of the oldest in the neighbourhood, all uncannily dark with large spidery rooms that often remained shut up, the dwellers only inhabiting the front rooms which were smaller and looked out over calm cornfields which lessened the solitude. At the back was a sluggish little river, huge beds of dry osier reeds and dark water meadows that lowered under darker skies and were only just tolerable in summer time. The houses were well known for being damp and for frequently flooding, a pervading air of rotting stagnation hanging over them. Thus they were cheaply sold and often remained empty for many years. In short they were a bad investment.

To one of these John Straeton now paced, his keen eye noting the wide variety of colour in the morning sky and the golden fields that fell about him. In many men and teams of horses worked as it was nearly harvest and the farmers prayed desperately for fine weather. The horse doctor reached the foremost house, gazed at its name plate, observed it was Fourbridges and stood watching his surroundings. The house proved to be the first in the small row and the only one with the provision of a large garden.

"How fortunate!" he murmured to himself and moved round the outside of the crumbling walls. Soon he had circled the house as best he could and seen much to invoke his pleasure and little, as yet, to disappoint him. Accordingly he wished to get a better view of the place from a higher elevation so he crossed one of the narrow bridges behind the garden and paced up the slightly inclining bed of reeds. When he reached the top of the small summit he gazed down at the flat water meadows beneath him and back at the outline of his house. A spasmodic noise caught his ears and he descended the bank, observed it to be the splash of water and went onwards till he reached the edge of the river. Tall reeds, some above his head, blocked his view and he perceived the splashing to be close at hand now so he peered cautiously through the dry stems. He blinked his eyes and stared again.

In the rather miry waters a naked girl was swimming strongly, the blonde ringlets of her hair tied up with a piece of brown twine. She inclined her head away from him and paddled to a halt then she stood up and the water reached a little above her waist. His eye caught the glare of white clothing draped over a rock nearby and, concluding she was about to come out and not wishing to be seen, he set off at a fair pace along the bank, the reeds hiding his presence. He stopped, sat down quietly on a raised grassy bank and waited. Presently he heard the rustle of clothing and then a soft voice singing, not far off from where he rested. He parted the reeds slightly and observed her to be fully clothed now and in the process of combing out the ends of her hair, which had been dampened by the river water. He waited a few minutes for propriety's sake then stood up and came forward with the air and gait of one who takes a leisurely morning stroll, his eyes diverted upon the water meadows or on the lofty houses opposite. He pretended that he did not see her until he was almost level with her and then he looked down and smiled, raising his hat in politeness.

"Good morning," he said in his fine clear Scottish accent.

She looked up at this, heard his words and ceased combing her hair.

"Good morning," she replied. "Have you just come by?"

"Yes," he assured her, not liking to mention he had viewed her indiscretion.

She seemed relieved at this and uttered a deep sigh. Presently she stood up and he observed her to be tall and possessing the most angelic features he had ever seen in a human face. Her eyes were cornflower blue and bore a sparkling power as they focused on him; her nose was small and chiselled whilst her lips were full and ruby red. If any fault could be found with her form it was that she inclined to boniness with narrow shoulders and a tiny waist, now elevated by the simple tie-in gown she wore which clung in places to her damp body. It was her hands and bare feet that intrigued him for each digit was double jointed and very long, finished with ivory white nails. She was beautiful, she was perfect and he was mesmerised. His thoughts strayed to the water nymphs that lured men to their deaths in whirlpools and eddies. What a way to die in the arms of such a beauty! After he had stared at her for full on five minutes she, who did not seem to be in any way embarrassed, commenced conversation.

"Are you John Straeton who has come here to treat sick beasts for the farmers and gentry hereabouts?"

"I am he, aye," he answered. "But at the moment I rest in ignorance of your name?"

"Ah, then I must give it! My name is Cannetta Hardy and I live at Fern Cottage in Ardle."

He started at this and his mind raced as he remembered the words of his cousin.

Cannetta narrowed her eyes.

"What? You have heard bad things of me already?"

He shook his head.

"No, only some fairy story that said a witch lived in Fern Cottage. A black ugly witch with huge talons, a hooked nose and a crystal ball which she gazed into to raise every storm that raged over Ardle!"

The young girl laughed, throwing back her head in a powerful display of energy.

"And does she resemble me?"

"Only as far as an angel resembles a devil!"

She paused to consider that and the smile faded from her lips.

"But they may, in time, come to sully my name and try to poison my friends against me. If you hear these tales remember I am purely her you see before you."

"How can they be so mistaken?" he asked, a shade angrily.

"I am something of a recluse here and I take no part in village gossip and little interest in my fellow man. Indeed, I avoid most people who are ruled by greed and selfish urges."

He felt her desire for solitude as it was written on her face and he asked anxiously,

17

"Then shall I leave you now?"

"Oh no!" she stated vehemently. She came a little closer and smiled at him. "I love those who help my fellow beings who are the animals of the fields and the birds of the air. No snake will ever leave his poison in me and even the winged creatures of the night avoid me. Animals are much maligned in our society and abused. I seek to end that abuse and I know you do too by your profession."

John considered that quietly and then nodded his head as if he understood. "Miss Hardy! I must go now but I enjoyed talking to you and, unlikely though it is we will meet again as you rarely go abroad, I will remember your beauty. A face such as yours should be seen; it is wasted, hidden away in Fern Cottage."

"I may go out more frequently now," she asserted. "But, seeing as you must go then I bid you good bye for the moment." She gave him her hand which was very soft and white apart from the extremely long nails. He kissed it dutifully, retired a few steps and called, "Goodbye!" Then he disappeared behind a brake of fern and she heard him crossing the bridge where his tall form was swallowed up in the houses opposite.

She flung herself down on the grass and lay on her back, long arms above her head and her blue eyes on the slowly shifting sky. At length she smiled.

Two days of rain and tempest followed; such storm and wind never having been felt in the vicinity of Ardle before at this time of the year. The ripening harvest was dampened, sodden and finally some of it began to rot before the labourers could wield their sickles. Every eye was turned to the menacing sky in the hopeful sign of a white cloud or a small square of blue but none came. Darkness fell upon the earth by day and night and candles were scarcely snuffed out before it was time to rekindle them again.

John saw no more of Cannetta but she was often in his mind as a pleasing thought or a tender fancy when time allowed. He remained at his cousin's for a few more days until his house was ready and he was able to move and progress with his profession. During that time he felt that Shirley was becoming more and more friendly, which was awkward for him as he did nothing to solicit her affection, and he feared Damion would notice and break off the newly-established kinship.

Yet, in the evenings when he and Shirley sat, sometimes side by side on the settle or close at hand by the fire seats, he was conscious of her looking at him in a way he could scarcely ignore. Her eyes said too much about the state of her heart whilst her husband snored his way through the evenings, totally oblivious to his wife's flirting. There were times when John was tempted to take her hand or plant a kiss on her cherry lips but the picture of the swimmer returned to him, as if in reproach. He determined to find out a little more about Cannetta and satisfy his curiosity.

18

On his last evening at his cousin's house, some five or so days after his arrival in the district, Damion was called away suddenly to visit his mother who had had a serious fall and broken both hips. The doctor's lad came running to the cottage requesting Damion's presence as Mrs Penlow was very poorly and unlikely to last the night. The labourer flung on his coat and hat, imparted the sad news to his wife and then sprinted off across the fields to his mother's bedside.

Shirley, who had just sat down upon the settle, got up and went to the window where she observed her husband to be mounting Grey's stile whereupon he turned left and disappeared.

"Yes, that is the way I am treated," she cried to John, who sat quietly on the settle. "Hardly a word and then off he goes! You asked me if I was happy and if he was a good husband? Can you now form your own answer?"

"Yes," replied John, vaguely. "But he is still my own flesh and blood so I will not air views that debase my cousin."

"True, true," she acknowledged turning away from the window. "But flesh and blood, unless it is warm and passionate, is useless and may as well be cold and dead."

He gazed into her tired and unhappy face and saw the pain that had grown in her since her rash marriage.

"You feel bitter?" he asked.

"Yes!"

"And you wish for things that cannot be?"

In answer to this she knelt down upon the hearth rug and, putting her arms about his neck, kissed him in a way that suggested she saw him as more than a cousin.

"Sometimes," she murmured, drawing away a little and letting her eyes grow misty, "I crave for a touch of love and affection. Just for someone to treasure me for a few hours...someone to make my blood hot and my passion rise again and now...you."

She stood up uncertainly whilst he savoured the sweet touch of her lips and felt unable to meet her eyes.

"Shirley," he said simply. "You are very beautiful..."

"And of what use is that to me here?" she cried angrily. "When my husband regards me as a faceless machine to do his housework and his cooking? I tell you truly, John, that since our wedding night he has never laid a finger upon me! But I cannot endure this forever...things come to tempt me. John, are you married?"

"No."

"And do you see my vows as binding and lifelong?" she asked in a desperate tone, flinging herself at his feet in her despair.

"Vows are only as lasting and binding as the people that make them."

"And MY vows?" she enquired. "Am I allowed to break them?"

She fixed her beautiful eyes upon his face but his heart could not furnish her with an acceptable answer. At length she shook her head.

"It is no matter," she muttered. "He will not be home tonight which is one blessing."

Eventually he perceived she was crying and being tenderly disposed towards her, though not actually feeling the emotion she emitted, he took her up in his arms and held her.

The long summer evening wore on till the hour of nine o'clock and there was no Damion or message from him. Presently it grew dark in the small room and Shirley, rising to light the lamp, heard footsteps approaching the front door.

"Hush- hush! It is he," cried the guilty Scotsman, jumping up but Shirley, who was more familiar with his gait, shook her head. A little rap sounded upon the wood work and she raised her eyes to him.

"Who can it be?" she asked.

The rap came again, somewhat louder.

John felt no fear, bade her stay where she was and opened the door, whereupon a young boy thrust a piece of paper into his hand, raised his lantern by way of salute and ran off into the darkness.

Back in the sitting room Shirley sat down upon the settle and tried to still her wildly beating heart. To have him that close, and be in his arms...

Presently John came back with a folded slip of paper which he handed her silently, kneeling by her side as she read it with her bright eyes.

I shall not return tonight. Expect me about six tomorrow.

D P.

He reached out a cautious hand and caressed her bare arm.

"He will not be back tonight," she quoted, mechanically, flinging away the note as if it had served its purpose. "In fact I do not care if I ever see him again."

John kissed her fingers, she putting an arm round his shoulders and moving in to his embrace.

"I have given him every chance!" she bewailed, as if pleading her case. "I have loved him, worked for him, cried for him! John – I am a passionate woman and I cannot live with this starvation in my soul any longer!"

He looked up from caressing her and nodded.

"You have done your best for him," he replied. "The vows bind you no more as he did not fulfil them so therefore they do not exist. You are a strong temptation, Shirley, for any man! A temptation that cannot be wasted! A flower that will not stay forever in a sleeping bud, but seeks to burst out and flourish!"

She perceived the beautiful romance of his words and her head was turned.

"Oh my love, my love!" she breathed. "I married the wrong cousin! But I did not know of your existence then. Why does HE possess me when he only

20

hurts me by his behaviour? But, no, for tonight I am yours, I am yours! John, we are alone and need fear no interruption now! I need you!"

She fell into his arms and he felt the power of wanting her take over so he knew nothing but her and her alone, in his embrace.

A little before the hour of six o'clock a man appeared in the morning fields with a cheap, worsted jacket slung over his shoulders. The first thin blankets of mist were dispersing as a prelude to the rising sun which at this moment was just a red glow in the east. As the man walked he wept and frequently wiped his rheumy eyes with a large spotted kerchief. He kept his gaze upon the ground and occasionally murmured low words to himself. Eventually, whilst climbing the slight rise to his home, he encountered an elderly man walking with a stick.

"Good day to you, Mr Penlow! I was much grieved by the sad news so please accept my sympathies."

"Yes. Yes, thank ee," replied Damion, somewhat awkwardly. "It has been a night of suffering, Sullivan, a dreadful night of suffering but it is over now and I pray she is at peace."

"Perhaps it will help ee to talk about it," said Sullivan, sensibly. "For when I lost my Olly 'twas natter, natter, natter all the time with me till I slept for sheer exhaustion of talking!"

They continued conversing in this vein until they stood right outside the front walls of the tiny pink dwelling which was cloaked in silence. After a little while their voices became louder as the old man was somewhat deaf and this raised volume was carried through the thin walls of the house to the parlour. It entered the brain of one of the sleepers lying there and reminded her of time and occasion. She sat up. The clock on the mantel piece had stopped at two o'clock and for a moment she thought she heard its rhythmic tick so she lay back idly. Then she noticed the light creeping through the small dirty windows and rising she crept to the nearest lattice and peered through. Her eyes took in the scene outside with fear and horror and she rushed to her lover, coupling her cries with gentle shaking. John lay as dead on the settle, in a deep dreamless sleep.

"John! John!" she whispered, as loud as she dared. "Quick! Wake up! My husband is outside talking but he will come in any time now!" John came too gradually but did not seem to heed her words as he put his arms round her and tried to kiss her.

"No, no!" she cried. "Did you not hear me? My husband is here!"

The words had the desired affect and John jumped up, gazing around him. He put a protective arm around her shoulders.

"No, no, my love, not here but outside the window. Quick, he is coming in!"

He took in the meaning of her words and heard the murmur of voices so he crossed to the window and looked out.

Returning to her side he whispered,

"I shall be upstairs," and he picked up his clothes and withdrew.

She nodded.

"Last night, John, I..."

"You do not have to say anything."

"No," she smiled gratefully. "I do not regret last night...not for a minute."

He pressed her fingers as he passed her then mounted the stairs quietly and she heard his bedroom door shut. She sighed aloud with relief and as she tied her dress she heard Damion wish good day to his companion and make his way to the cottage door. Shaking out the tangled tresses of her hair she went into the kitchen, trying to calm her racing heart and mind. For the next few hours she would play the dutiful wife just as she had been excited, during the night, to play the passionate lover to someone who was far more than a cousin to her...

CHAPTER 3

John Straeton left the cottage of his cousin at twelve o'clock that day. Damion, who was exhausted and still very tearful, resolved not to work but rested in the back bedroom, from where he had his wife running with requests for food, drink and writing implements in between his naps. People came freely to the door to express their sorrow, enquire for Damion's health and make other comments befitting a recent death. John remained in his room for the first two hours, at last venturing out to speak to Shirley, who he chanced to meet in the kitchen where she was preparing breakfast for her husband.

She looked up at his approach, evidently marked his pensive mood and gave a small sigh.

"You are regretting what occurred last night?" she asked.

"No."

"But you have pondered on it whilst in your room?"

"Yes," he admitted. "I can't deny it – I have. And some thoughts have not been pleasant."

"Ah! You blame me!" she gasped, believing, at last, she had hit on the truth. He shook his head strongly at this.

"And yet," he continued coming round to face her as she sliced bread. "I cannot think about it as a grave step directing our future life! It was for the moment and the moment was last night and last night alone. Now it is another new day. Do you understand me?"

"Yes," she replied, laying down the knife with a heavy heart. "I understand. You want to forget it."

"Not entirely. The feeling is more that I do not want to remember. I shall continue to see you, Shirley, of course, but you are married. Nothing can change that."

"No, I suppose not," said she quietly, lowering her eyes. "I acknowledge what you say but I do not regret what happened. Not for one second. No one has touched me in the way you did! Last night I lived so do you blame me for snatching at some happiness, transient though it was?"

"Blame you? No, how could I Shirley? We were together and whatever happened we took that step together! But it is over now and we must part. Yet our friendship remains and I shall think of you fondly as I move on with my life."

She smiled at these words and he perceived that she viewed him in a different light since their indiscretion.

"We part friends?" he asked, anxiously, turning to her and holding out his hand.

"We part more than that," she whispered, kissing his offered fingers.

Upstairs there was a long, loud tapping and she, to whom the knocking was directed, continued with her preparations and left the room silently. After five minutes John followed and left the house several hours later without another glimpse of her.

From Ardle he travelled on foot to the nether regions of Stackhouses, encountering no one in his journey for the dull, dark nature of the day had kept many indoors. Those who had gone out were busy, by and large, in the fields, it wanting another hour till the lunchtime break. Thus he reached his destination unseen and observed his house was finished and the key left hanging in the porch with a note from the builder who stated he had mended the roof and squared the chimney. John took the heavy piece of metal and unlocked the front door which shuddered violently for half a minute when he entered. It was not a good sign. He walked into the living room, where he saw most of his furniture had been placed haphazardly, the majority of it having belonged to his late parents.   Although his eye was not over-critical he managed to move his bits and pieces to create a more pleasant atmosphere where comfort reigned. The rooms were still lofty but felt more like home with his familiar property in residence. Here and there some damp remained and it was dark due to lack of sunlight. Only three of the downstairs rooms were prepared for use, the others being shut up and smelling of must and rotting beams. He wrinkled his nose at these but left them and climbed the stairs to the two bedrooms that had been furnished and the tiny dressing room that led off the largest one. It seemed stifling and stale on the upper floor and he threw open a window and leant out, looking far over the water meadows where a sudden movement caught his eye. The girl he knew as Cannetta, the naked swimmer of his dreams, was striding across one of the bridges from the opposite bank. Instantly she looked up, saw him and raised her hand in salute, he returning the wave immediately.

He was not aware that she had come here on purpose of seeing him and that she carried in her arms a ginger kitten, which nuzzled fondly against her. She chattered brightly to the little animal, much as a young mother would to her child and striding round the side of the house, where she observed there was a gate, she whispered,

"Soon he will help you, tiny one. Did I not tell you of his coming by the blue light in the north star which shone for twenty days last month?" The kitten made no struggle but a calm look of resignation shone in his green eyes and he uttered a small mew.

Cannetta ducked through the overgrown gateway where the tall, green nettles left no trace on her bare legs, her feet being covered by a pair of simple brown sandals. She crossed the pathway, stepped up boldly to the door and knocked, a low echoing boom sounding through the building. She waited. The kitten cried again but was comforted by the gentle rocking motion of her arms. She knocked again.

Presently a hurried step approached the door, struggled with the stiff bolts and at length managed to open the barrier so that the man she had come to see stood before her.

24

"Mr Straeton!" she breathed gently. "Oh Mr Straeton, I have come to plead for your help. Not on my account but for a life I deeply cherish. Do you know anything of domestic animals?"

"Aye, a little," replied he, surprised at her warmth to one who was scarcely more than a stranger.

"Then I beg leave to trouble you and ask for your assistance."

"Please, Miss Hardy, do not be so desperate! How could I refuse such a plea rung from the heart nor such a face as yours. Come in!"

She assented, bowed her head and stepped across the threshold, finding herself to be in a long, dark corridor of considerable height and flanked by an interesting stairway and a maze of doors. Her overall impression was of cold and dampness, a picture of dripping water on castle walls or the smell of age.

John led the way forward to the further most of the doors, opened it and motioned her in. She found herself to be in a large chamber which was simply but perfectly furnished in a style of some fifty years ago. A fire was laid in the cold grate but not yet lit. Three pictures piled against a chair awaited putting up, the top one, which was visible, showed a smeary oil painting of a loch surrounded by heather and trees. She looked critically but did not think it good.

The kitten now reminded them of his presence with reproachful mews as if he sensed he was merely an excuse for attaining some end. Cannetta brought him forth into the light and put him down upon the floor where he attempted to walk on three legs, the other limb being held aloft.

"There," murmured she as if to qualify her visit. "See the twist of bone above his thigh? I cannot make it out, Mr Straeton and Mother only wishes to drown him till I talked of you. Even so she was very reluctant to let me bring him but you will not fail him, will you? We – all of us – have waited so long for your coming!"

He did not understand her last words but knelt down to examine the kitten who mewed piteously and continued limping.

"How did it happen?" he asked simply, staring up at her in interest.

"A dog attacked him outside my cottage and before I could get there the damage was done! Oh Mr Straeton, please say you can save him!" And she reached out her long fingers and touched his hand whilst her eyes grew wider and wider with distress. Her touch was like feathers on his skin and he relished the sensation but she withdrew her hand and gazed at him.

"The bone has moved a little," replied he. "But I can see to that easily and the wearing of a splint such as I have in my bag will help." He began to work gently, talking all the time and manipulating the bone with his large, firm hands, she watching him intently. Eventually the bone was set and the limb dropped so John was able to splint it. Cannetta's sparkling eyes missed nothing.

"I have never seen such skilled hands before," cried she, taking one of his in both of her hands. "Such power to heal in them and what magic to end pain and suffering!"

"But what about doctor's hands?" John asked.

"No, no," she replied, caressing his freckled skin. "It is not the same thing at all! Curing the dumb creatures is the greatest gift life can bestow on a man!"

"Well, animals are my vocation," he acknowledged, stroking the kitten. "It would be a sad and empty world without them."

"Indeed it would, Mr Straeton, and I should not want to live there at all."

Her tone was very emphatic and her flushed face was serious.

"You must call me John," he corrected and handed her the kitten which nestled fondly against her.

"You don't like people in general do you, Miss Hardy?" he commented plainly. "I have heard talk in the village that you prefer your own company and that of your animals."

"Have you heard anything else?" she asked quickly, tucking the kitten in her cloak.

"No," he replied. "Should I have?"

"People gossip constantly here and embroider tales so that it is hard to form any friendship but with the animals. I do not trust people, I do not like them and, indeed, sometimes I am moved to hate them!"

"Everyone?" he asked. "Does that include me?"

"Hate you?" she cried, immediately. "No never! I admire you, John. I am in awe of your skilled hands that work for us and your selfless inspiration that motivates you to strive to save a single life – as you have just done."

"Oh, it was nothing," he murmured.

"Maybe not to you!" she cried. "But to me it was everything. John, I believe the kitten was hurt deliberately. I had thought not to tell you but 'tis the truth." A slow tear coursed down her cheek and her eyes became sad and misty. "A man I dislike very much set his dog on the poor little thing knowing him to be mine and doing it to upset me. Faith, I would rather he had set the dog on ME, yes, that I would!" and she raised a sob or two from the memory.

John was extremely moved. He put a caring arm about her shoulders and bade her compose herself, assuring her he would see her safely home. It was a tender little scene, she leaning against him and John with his arms round her in a protective silence. A loud bang at the front door woke them from their reveries: she lifting her head directly and he withdrawing his arms. He guided her into a chair and bade her wait.

"I shall not be long," he affirmed, hopefully.

The great door creaked inwards and emitted enough light to reveal a small boy of eleven or twelve who held in his left hand a piece of blue paper.

26

"Mr Straeton?" he gabbled as soon as a face became distinguishable in the gloomy air of the hallway.

An affirmative was the reply.

"Then, please, you are to come to the Hall, not far off, to cure a horse fair dying of colic. Here is some instructions for yer." And he handed John the piece of paper, prepared to wait and leant against the wall.

"I shall not be a moment!" cried John, disappearing into the gloom again.

Cannetta had remained motionless in the chair, hugging the kitten and talking to the little creature.

"I am called upon," he said simply as he approached her. "A horse needs my help. I hope you understand?"

She rose immediately.

"Of course. You must be off at once!"

"Not until I have extracted a promise that you will have tea with me at four o'clock tomorrow here?" he replied, not wanting her to go now he had found her again.

She assented at once, gave him her hand silently and then descended the stairs with him after which he showed her out of a side door. John fetched his bag and then went out to the waiting boy.

Walking along with his young companion the flexible contours of the Scotsman's face remained puzzled and slightly confused. He swung his bag as though angry and gazed out over the untroubled sea of grain fields. At length he ventured a question at his guide who was obliged to jog to keep pace with him.

"Tell me, lad," said he, in his fine Scottish drawl. "Do you know of a lass by the name of Cannetta Hardy in the village?"

"Cannetta!" exclaimed the young boy, somewhat breathlessly with his exertions. "Oh, yes, sir! Everyone do know of Miss Hardy!" He blew out his cheeks and wiped his moist forehead.

"And what do they say of her? Do they like her?"

"No, no," replied the lad. "Master, if I must speak I need to slow down my pace!"

They slowed so that the boy was now able to walk rather than run and he resumed the interrupted conversation.

"Some say she is mad, sir, some say she is a witch and others say she is in league with the Devil to fill the oxen with gargut and the like which we has no hope of curing, even with moth mullen, sir. Then there are the rest, sir, of course and...well..."

"Yes? What do the rest say about her?"

"They say that she is a poor ill-wished maiden who wants to be left in peace with her animals." John was a little heartened by this last remark and asked the boy if he knew how many were in the latter group who thought good things about Miss Hardy.

"Why, yes, sir, I know the exact answer to that one as it is myself sir!"

27

"Just you?" The tone of surprise and disgust struck the boy immediately and John realised he had been very rude.

"Yes, sir," replied the lad in hurt tones.

"Definitely you - and only you alone? No one else thinks well of Miss Hardy?"

"No sir."

"By Scotland!" swore the horse doctor. "What can she have done to get such a name?" The fact that a twelve year old boy praised her had no significance at all in John's eyes.

"Well, sir," cried the boy. "They is old fashioned hereabouts and as she do not go out much and never attends church on Sundays nor speaks to people and shows more love for creeping things than folk so they name her as odd! But I know her different, sir, as she is my friend and if you mention my name she'd tell you so too!"

"Well, laddie, how come you came to be friends with Miss Hardy then? For I see the Hall approaching and I would fain know before I begin my work there."

The young boy was glad to tell the story as he was the smallest in a big family and was rarely accredited with sense enough to be listened to.

"This happened only a month ago, sir, whilst I had gone walking over Dalbury hill on Fenlough's estate, some three miles from here. It was the time of dusk and I was hurrying on my way when my foot struck upon something in the gloom and bending down I could see it were a leveret struck down by dogs and left for dead. At first I was planning to leave it but then, it had such a nice gleam in its eye that I could not and so I picked it up and put it in my coat for 'twere bloody and sick."

"I knows," says I to myself. "I'll take it along to Miss Hardy for folks do say she cures God's creatures with the black arts but as for the last bit, sir, I never did believe it. So I went to her cottage and it were quite late at night but she was up and her mother came for the door but Miss Hardy got there first and begged me to come in. So I sat down upon a stool and showed her this baby hare and when she saw it almost dead she cried real tears and so did I! But she dried her eyes and took it gentle-like and said,

"Johnny, you have done very well and I will always be grateful to ye for bringing my sick brother to me. Now, never fear lad for he shall be mended wholly and returned to the wild where he belongs but here's something for your trouble." You must pardon me, sir, for her being something of a lady she never said quite those words but more refined as it were. However the meaning is the same and that's what I wanted you to learn!

Anyway, her gave me three pence and a kiss, both of which caused my tears to dry immediately and then she told me to come back at noon the next day to free it and then she went away and I never did see her any more as she said that it was not seemly for me to remain any later."

"And you went back?"

"Yes – though Mother tried to stop me! And the creature were whole and well so that I freed it in Gant's Meadow and it ran off hearty-like. But when I thanked her she said it was her life I had saved but I never did understand that so I went home and did not see her any more though she told me before I left that we would always be friends!"

The vague outline of Porleau now arose from the green honeysuckle hedges and the red bricks of a wall which ran round the perimeter of the Hall and contained a pair of wrought iron gates nearly seven foot in height. John, though very intrigued by the tale young Johnny told him, could come to no firm conclusions about she who he deliberated on. Accordingly he shelved it until such time as he was alone and at leisure to peruse it further. Going through the gardener's gate at the side their arrival was announced by the peal of a bell and John stared in amazement at the rich generous   layout of the flower beds and green lawns, the abundance of herbs and sweet-smelling blooms broken here and there by the glassy surface of a pond.

The boy ushered him through a narrow path of pennyroyal and tansy then past high plants of marjoram and the essence of flowering celandine. They skirted a gravel track, crossed a small, earth-beaten yard and climbed two or three steps to the stables which stretched back almost to the windows of the Hall itself as the Langtons often kept seven pairs of horses or more.

A short, thin man stepped forward from one of the stables and eyed up the stranger cautiously. In his hand he carried a hunting whip and his thick, cord breeches were of good quality.

"Mr Straeton?" enquired the man of the stranger. "I trust you are he?"

"Aye."

"Well I am Rivers, my Lord's head stable groom. We require your services for a colicky horse that has, so far, conquered all efforts to cure him."

John lay down his bag and opening it took out a large glass bottle with a long neck and enlarged mouth which was at present stoppered.

"What has been done?" he asked, briefly, setting to work to fill the bottle from various other corked containers.

"He has been bled and then watered with boiled dill and fennel; lately I gave him fenugreek and garlic but even that has failed to help."

"Hm...Is he staled? I have some styptic liquor with me."

"No."

The Scotsman was silent then and finished mixing the potions in the drenching bottle whereupon he called for the help of two strong lads and proceeded to the stable. The horse had been tied shortly, his black coat flecked with white foam and he nervously kicked a back leg whilst glancing towards his flank.

John checked him over carefully, pronounced it to be the colic and asked for a rug to be wrapped round the creature's loins. One was brought and John spread a thick layer of straw underneath it and then began to wipe off the sweat with the simple twist of a home-made wisp. The horse was restless and almost wild; he trembled considerably at a stranger's touch, his eyes rolling in pain whilst the foam flew from his nostrils. The three stable lads, all apprentices, stood morosely nearby staring at the stranger but never saying a word. At length John called them forward, bade each hold a different part of the horse so that he could thrust the drench bottle between the animal's teeth.

"A switch!" he called. "Have you a switch?" as he pinched the horse's nostrils to prevent him from taking his head higher. Johnny was sent to fetch one and John applied it so they could try again, success naturally following as the horse swallowed the long draught. Presently the bottle was empty and John placed it back in his bag.

All eyes were turned upon the animal who suddenly dropped his head wearily and staggered a little, content to rest his quarters upon the nearest wall. Straeton picked up his hat which he had flung to the ground in the essence of emergency and turned to the head groom.

"The medicine will work quite swiftly and he will recover in a few hours or even less but it is important I remain nearby in case of any relapse. So I shall stay for a while and just observe him."

He folded his arms across his chest, was deserted by the stable lads who, finding it was the hour for their luncheon, drifted hungrily away. A little watery sun pierced the zenith and the breeze dropped. John experienced considerable hunger pangs himself, having eaten nothing since the following evening, and coming out of the stable he leant against the door and closed his eyes. The stark details of last night rose up to throttle him, reminding him all too clearly of his weakness leading to the indiscretion. The incident seemed suddenly like a garish nightmare and he felt the familiar stab of guilt assailing him. Therefore it was a joy to hear, as he rested his weary eyes, a light tread approaching and a woman's soft tone calling his name. He returned to the world and saw, before him, the very picture of innocence in the form of Damion's daughter, Connie. Yet the connection with the stepmother caused him a painful shudder and he felt flushed and half-turned away from her.

"Mr Straeton!" she cried again. John turned back to her, stood up straight and greeted her distantly yet politely, wondering of her purpose here. Then he remembered that she was maid at the Hall and that her starched uniform spoke of her work here. In her hands she carried a tray cloth around which her nervous fingers played as she waited for his full attention.

"Mr Straeton, the housekeeper here would be glad if you would take luncheon with us as we have learnt you need to remain here for a while to keep an eye on your patient. Will you come in?"

He considered this offer and then regretfully declined because he did not want to venture indoors and leave the horse.

"Can we not get a stable lad to do that and relieve you? He could call you at the first sign of trouble."

John shook his head but continued gazing at her because in some strange way she reminded him of her stepmother. Whether this was good or bad he could not decipher.

"Please tell your housekeeper that I am very grateful for the offer and that on any other occasion I would have been glad to accept it!" He seemed crestfallen at having to give up the chance of a good meal and it showed in the disappointment in his face.

"Forgive my intrusion, Mr Straeton, into your affairs but do you have a housekeeper to prepare and cook your food?" she enquired, turning towards him again.

He shook his head.

"No,"

"And not even a daily help to leave cold dishes?"

"No."

"Then surely you have a woman coming in a few hours a week to do your washing, mending and so on?"

"I do not hae one, no," he returned a little sadly she thought for his good-natured smile faded from his lips and his forehead became lined with worry.

"You have not had time to hire one yet?" she continued.

Again a shake of the head.

"In truth, Connie," he admitted, looking up at her with wistful eyes. "I do not think I hae the money to pay one. Ah! Times are hard until I get set up in my work!"

She blushed guiltily, thinking she had caused this revelation of his poverty by her questioning and that he would think her too inquisitive.

"Oh, forgive me!" she cried. "I did not mean to pry."

"Have no fear of that," he replied. "I should not hae told you if I did not want you to know. Do you recall saying those words to me in another conversation, Connie?"

"Yes," she mused, the rather stilted conversation of a former day returning to her mind.

"Now, if I tell you my age, cousin, we are on equal terms are we not?"

"By no means!" she retorted in alarm. "You must think me very forward and rude."

"By no means," repeated John smiling. "Since, I mean to tease you a little first. Of what age would you think I am?"

"Well," and she hesitated. "From here you might be one and twenty or even less but up close who knows?"

"Then come closer and observe me. Do!" he cried playfully turning his face to the light. She did as she was told and after gazing at his fine, unlined skin which was hardly wrinkled on the forehead or round the eyes she became pensive. That he was rather good-looking in a rugged way she did not deny now and he felt her admiration of his features. If he had been vain he would have swelled with conceit at being thus regarded, but as it was he just smiled and murmured,

"Well, does what you see support your earlier guess?"

She was silent for a moment and then a loud, rasping voice interrupted her thoughts

"Connie! Connie! Where have you got to?"

"Oh!" she cried. "'Tis Mrs Newbury! I must away, John!" The shout had broken the spell, Connie said nothing more but turned and ran through the stable yard and disappeared into the house.

CHAPTER 4

The next day saw the arrival of yet another tempest which sent the despairing harvesters scurrying from the scarcely touched fields. To the farmers, as they traversed the perimeters of their land, it seemed the smell of rotting wheat was already pungent in their nostrils. Everywhere dripped freely with water.

About midday it cleared a little and a faint but hopeful gleam appeared in the corner of the dark sky where previously storm clouds had congregated. The sodden harvesters returned to the fields and picked up their abandoned sickles. Never before had the wheat dropped so late and in such a state of unsuitability for human stomachs, hardly even palatable for bovine creatures. After a while the aching workers rested from their useless labours and stood in casual groups amongst the rows, awaiting the arrival of the farm bailiff with fresh orders. The wheat squeaked eerily in the rising wind then fell silent.

Just before twelve o'clock a small but lithe figure appeared along the footpath that ran parallel with the large grain field on such a level that meant a six foot man passing by was viewed from the waist up only. Young children had been known to creep by unobserved and women returning from the local market town were characterised by a bonnet on a shawled pair of shoulders. The labourers were well used to this natural phenomena yet it still interested them, chiefly due to the varying complexity of heights among the passers-by that always revealed a new level of anatomy.

The figure who now walked the path was dainty, graceful in gait but without any pretensions to vanity, and definitely ladylike. Her light flaxen hair fell thickly about her face which was, as yet, untarnished by the passage of time. In her open arms she carried a basket almost hidden beneath a red and white kerchief and in the crook of her elbow a large earthenware flagon rested, topped by a dark cork. A few of the men gazed appreciatively, narrowed their eyes to recognise the features and prodded one of their group to point out who the body was.

"'Tis yer wife!" cried one. "And as such she has brought the missing fodder! A fine woman, Damy, a fine woman!" The owner of this admired body did not seem particularly pleased with her journey but rather suspicious of her motives. Accordingly he flung down his tool, left the gawking collection and crossed to the high bank where he helped her through the hornbeam hedge and onto the outer portion of the field.

"I have brought your meal," she observed, handing him the basket and the none too light flagon.

"Yes, yes," murmured he. "It is kind of 'ee but I should get along home now. 'Tis gonna rain."

"It has done so already," she replied in a flat tone.

"Well, well! Yes! Are you wetted?" he enquired, without a trace of concern in his voice, attempting to feel the dampness of her coat.

She sprang back as though he had burnt her and cried, "No, no, I am perfectly dry, Damion. I shall go to Stackhouses today – indeed I am on my way there now."

"Oh," he replied, stung at the reserve of her manner.

"Yes, I thought to call on your cousin if there is time and he is at home, of course!"

"You had some special reason for seeing him?" he enquired, innocently.

"Not really," she gasped, emitting a certain surprise. "But he is a relation and as such a stranger in our midst whom we should guide and help..."

"Ah, yes! Well, you must do as you think fit!"

She lowered her eyes to the ground and wondered at his extreme simplicity which saw no hidden meanings in her visit to John. She doubted that Damion was even capable of feeling jealousy for a fellow man and he certainly gave no signs that he thought her relationship with John was anything but that of cousins by marriage.

"Have you any message for him?" she asked now, suddenly anxious that she obtain a reason for her journey.

"Nay – well – yes, tell him I should like to stand him a whisky if he can pick a night. Name him the Resort and a suitable time when I can go. Faith, sometimes a blood tie gets awfully strong in a man!"

She nodded silently, bit her trembling lip and turned back to the hedge, he tramping carelessly across to the group.

Shirley retraced her steps, ascended the hill to Stackhouses and looked back across the golden fields to her husband. She arrested her progress and gazed down at the red drops of blood in the corn, which were really flowering poppies, blurring the sea of yellow haze.

"You fool," she uttered through clenched teeth, in a bitter tone. "Oh you fool, Damy, you are losing me and you do not even have the perception to realise it!" Then, with an angry toss of her head, she continued up the hill and onto the outer districts of the market town.

John Straeton had, all that morning, been bothered by calls of the most trifling kind, chiefly from the outlying farms of the area requesting his presence. Accordingly he had tramped a good few miles to inspect healthy stock and receive the keen-eyed scrutiny of the hill farmers to whom he felt he was fast becoming a spectacle. Eventually at one he had finished with them, retraced his steps to the mildewing mansion and discovered he had scarcely enough food to feed himself let alone a guest. He sat down upon the sofa, pulled off his boots and leant back with a reclining air that saw the nightmare scenario of the morning settle into something more bearable.

Presently there was a loud knock at the door, followed by one of a gentler nature, as though the knocker was apologising for the first harsh outburst.

John jumped up a little guiltily, peered at the clock then went to the door with an element of fear that she he had invited was unaccountably early.

The light soon revealed that the visitor's face was not the one he desired to see and, in some way here, he felt himself to be impolite.

"Shirley?" he almost gasped. "Is owt amiss? Has something happened?"

"No," she replied with a sense of calm that he did not possess. "Do I need a reason to call upon you?"

"Of course not and yet I see by your face there is a reason!"

She bowed her head to acknowledge this fact and stepped past him into the darkness of the hallway.

"So this is your dwelling." she murmured in not altogether appreciative tones.

"You do not care for it?" he asked quickly.

She wrinkled her nose and replied languidly that it was the damp she did not care for.

"Have you dined?" she asked. "I should hate to interrupt you if you are eating."

"I must admit I have not," he declared, rather sadly. "But at present I do not even have the provision of a housekeeper or maid. Och! I am no cook!"

"You have food in then?"

"Well – I am hardly well-stocked but – aye - I think there is sufficient."

She loosened the cord of her coat and gazed at him boldly.

"Then I shall prepare a meal for you."

"Nay!" he retorted immediately. "Act as my maid? No, Shirley, that is not right."

"Why not?" asked she. "I am in no hurry to return to the emptiness of the cottage. Oh John, I know you said that what occurred was momentary but the place is empty since you left. It is a desert!"

"Has your husband been cruel to you since I went then?"

"No, but his very silence and indifference is cruelty to me! Oh John...No, no, I must not…" and she checked herself by tapping her chest briskly and moving away. "Let it be as you say. I am a fool to dwell on it!"

"You do not have to rush back you say?" he enquired gently.

"No, I am not needed till later. In fact sometimes I do not think I am needed at all!"

She turned to him, her eyes questioning his thoughts but he felt deeply embarrassed as his idea had been for her to prepare some dishes for his tea party at four o'clock.

"I am already beholden to you for my board and lodgings but I could pay you for the cooking and give you some independence with your own money." he continued.

She considered his idea, took it a step further and coloured it nicely.

"I could be your housekeeper!" she mused in delight. "It would give me a valuable few pennies of my own. Do you agree then, cousin? Is the deal struck?"

"Aye! We must shake on it!" he enthused holding out his hand towards her.

She declined to take it but instead stepped up to him and kissed him full upon the lips, winding her hand in his and revelling from the contact. He did not respond to her passion but drew back and she felt it and moved away.

"What has happened?" she asked. "In faith it was only a kiss to seal a bond. We are cousins – do you not remember?"

"Yes, yes," he murmured. "But lovers - no! That cannot be Shirley. Whether you love your husband or not is not the issue. Damion exists and maybe I am not as free as I once was!"

She gazed at him quizzically, her eyes dilating with tears. He, however, made no further comments and she, though it pained her, asked no more questions.

"You wish me to cook," echoed she. "And so I will. I am the servant now and you the master. Let what went before be dead and buried. I shall never mention it again!"

He did not reply to this and chose not to meet the pathos of her eyes which filled him with a mingled sense of love and guilt. But what he had said was undeniably true: she was not a free woman and his heart was ensnared by another.

A few minutes later she commenced her duties in the kitchen and when she was alone she allowed the tears to flow, some of them falling into the dishes as she prepared them. The pain of wanting what she could not have drowned her in hopeless sorrow but she knew his words as truths and there was nothing she could do.

A premature darkness seemed to roll over the silent earth and the clock on John Straeton's mantel piece struck four in a precise, calculated way, the notes of its timekeeping flying through the house and waking the dozing occupant of the sofa. He rose slowly and rubbed his weary eyes.

Outside the room the indecisive ring of footsteps sounded and a small tap came upon the door. Shirley entered, somewhat awkwardly, and tried to smile upon her cousin as he stood, tall and silent by the fireplace.

"I have done all you asked me to, sir, "she murmured. "So I will remove myself." She bowed her head.

"Now, now, Shirley," he scolded gently. "There will no more sirs or any curtsies. You are my relation by marriage and as such my blood so we do not stand on formality!"

She acquiesced readily.

"And your husband will not mind?"

She shook her head dolefully at the memory of Damion.

"I shall tell him all tonight," she replied.

36

"Aye. That is best."

There was a moment's awkward silence, each casting their eyes upon the floor in the effort to avoid temptation but Shirley felt it more acutely than her cousin. Neither had the courage to face the pervading eyes of the other.

At length Shirley shook herself from her reverie, walked over to the door and opened it with a click which roused her cousin.

"All is ready in the dining room. John – do you expect a guest?"

"Aye."

"And is it – I mean she – is a woman?"

"Aye."

"But you are not at liberty to name her?"

"I would rather not. Shirley, you are very good to me!"

She gave a bitter little smile at this.

"Tomorrow at twelve?" she enquired. "I do not yet know what hours you need me or quite what you expect of me?"

"Come when you are ready, Shirley. Faith, I will be pleased to see you whatever the hour. I know I have wronged you by my reckless behaviour but I shall make it up to you; that I swear!"

"Good God, John, I do not blame you at all. Do not reproach yourself. It must be as you said earlier. We can have it no other way." She spoke with a bitter sadness which brought tears to the eyes of the speaker and also affected the listener.

Upon saying this she wished him goodbye, quit the house and made her way back to Ardle and the futility of her life.

He sat down, feeling surrounded with guilt and sorrow. He sensed that one day he would have to pay for his rash behaviour and it saddened him that Shirley had planted seeds of love from that one night which were already growing into flowers. To him it had been an intense physical pleasure which had fled with the morning light, never to be resurrected. He hoped one day she would come to understand that.

A little after quarter past four another knock came at the door and he jerked himself back to reality from his painful thoughts. His guest had arrived. He hurried to the door, trying to shake off his sombre mood and let her in with a polite bow, taking her dark cloak and showing her into the room where Shirley had laid up for them. There he found all to be perfect and beautiful, the crowning glory being a huge bunch of roses, wild daisies and green leaves as the centre piece of the table. It was laid up for two by loving hands and John felt his heart wincing. Two or three plates of cakes and sweet treats graced the damask cloth and the bread and butter was cut daintily thin. Even the chairs they were to sit on had been polished and he smelt the homely aroma of beeswax. John was surprised but delighted and his guest showed her amazement in the time and trouble taken over the meal with a loud gasp.

"Is this your work, Mr Straeton?" asked Cannetta with a gleam in her blue eyes that implied she doubted it.

"Nay," he replied honestly. "Another hand has created this splendour – one far more artistic than mine! Please sit down."

She did as she was bade, casting an eye over the perfect feast and unwilling to break the spell by moving a single item.

"This has a woman's touch," she murmured, knowingly.

"Aye," he agreed with a quiet sigh. "It has, and, faith, it's a touch I would like in every one of these dark and lofty chambers. Cannetta, if I may call you such, it is a dreadful thing to be lonely!"

"Are you really so rejected down here because of your nationality?" she enquired, staring into his face as if to trace any suffering there.

"Nay – not rejected. Isolated seemly and yet I find some hearts here curiously warm! But I am a stranger in an even stranger land than the one I was born in! Happen one day I will go back but until then I must shoulder the burden of loneliness and move on."

"Do not make light of your qualities here," she pleaded. "To have the power of healing in those hands is the greatest gift that you can possess. And if you went back tomorrow you would be judged by the great works you have done here!"

"Great works?" he queried in surprise. "Cannetta – I have done nothing good or great in my entire life! I am just a Scotsman who pines in other climes for a touch of his native soil!"

He sighed afresh at the thought, unfolded his serviette and took the bubbling kettle from the fire where he had placed it when they entered the room. Pouring tea for her he felt his hands shake under the powerful flash of her eyes and when he passed her the cup their hands touched and sparks flew.

When in his presence Cannetta noticed she could ignore the deep turmoil of her mind and the urgent and insistent voices that had troubled her since childhood. For four years now she had lived with her mother's ignorance of her mental condition and borne the cruelty such ignorance necessitated, such as the indignity of sleeping in chains. Mrs Hardy told no one of her struggles to control her daughter and, at times, desperation had made her forge shackles to imprison Cannetta when she became frantic. In many ways it was her mother's fervent desire to control her daughter's insanity that had seen its survival.

After tea a long, gentle evening spread out its lengthening shades by which the two sat and talked, Cannetta reclining in a low chair and he seated upon a wicker stool that was drawn up close to his companion. At last it began to darken slightly as that mysterious hour called dusk approached – the hour of lighting candles and oil lamps plus the drawing down of blinds to prepare for night's pervading hues. Cannetta began to grow increasingly restless. She turned and twisted in her chair, plucked in distress at her hair and clothing and finally announced she would have to leave.

"Your mother will wish me to see you home safe?" he enquired, rising from his stool.

"Mother will be anxious, yes," cried Cannetta. "'Tis almost black and I promised I would be home before the light left the sky!"

"Do not be alarmed!" he soothed, going to find her cloak. He believed, like many women, she was frightened of the dark and had not noticed the rapid change in her face as evening fell. "I will see you to your door, never fear!"

"No, no," said she, trembling profusely. "Please you have troubled yourself enough for me already. I am happy to go alone!"

"By no means!" insisted John, shaking his head. "I will see you to your gate, if no more."

She bowed her head in acceptance of this, flung on her cloak and, at his invitation, took his arm, the two plunging into the deepening twilight where a chill little breeze had sprung up.

"One day, if our friendship blossoms, I will ask you something that I hope you will furnish a positive answer to. Cannetta, I need a wife, not as a housekeeper you understand as I have hired one of those, but oh! I am so lonely at times! It is fitting for my age and occupation that I marry soon so remember my words."

She was struggling to cope with her racing brain and the voices which were beginning to shout at her. She felt like banging her head on the ground and giving into them but she controlled herself with great difficulty and bit her lips so that the physical pain drowned out the screaming of her mind. They descended the hill that led from Stackhouses, turned off into the fields and slowed down.

"Listen!" cried she stiffening visibly and refusing to move. "Do you hear noises?"

"No," he replied. "I don't hear anything at all apart from the small whisper made by the breeze."

"It is there again!" she whispered, cowering. "Hark it begins once more! Is it in the air I wonder?"

He remained perplexed at this, could make no sense of what she heard or said and, at last, urged her on by gentle persuasion.

They hit the path that she pointed out led to her cottage and she felt able to relax a little due to his comforting presence. At the garden gate they paused.

"Shall I leave you now?" he asked, fondly. "You will be quite safe to go in from here?"

"Oh yes," she cried though her eyes seemed to roll from side to side as if she saw visions rising out of the darkness. "John – I thank you for the lovely tea and your kindness this evening. Pray do not wait but return home with my gratitude. I shall go in now!"

He nodded silently and, at length deemed it proper he might kiss her which he accomplished by simply placing his lips on top of hers. She yielded immediately and slipped an arm round his neck.

"I will see you again?" she asked in a half-whisper.

"Oh, yes, yes! Go in now, Cannetta, I will contact you very soon!"

She drew away from him, tried to quieten the rapid beating of her heart and unlatched the gate, he slipping away silently on the path so that in a minute a brake of stunted trees took him from view. Cannetta waited a few seconds then, instead of entering the dwelling, she rounded the far end of the cottage and struck a narrow track.

Here she paused, felt in the deep pocket of her cloak and brought out a shiny, silver object which caught the light of the waxing moon in profusion. Approaching a small tumbledown building that did office as a shed or outhouse she applied the shining object to the lock, gained entrance and stepped inside.

Her hands fell upon a candle which she kindled and then placed in a grotesque holder, representing a combined griffin, gargoyle and Medusa all rolled into one and calculated to give nightmares to those of a nervous disposition. Other maliciously carved faces leered out of the darkness, some of them with twisted features, others represented by triple faces of hideous caricature showing bloody teeth and protruding tongues. The girl ignored these monstrosities, her attention being focused on the black cover of a calf bound book that stood behind the masks. She picked it up, drummed her fingers upon it and then began thumbing through the well-worn pages, her eyes searching for some item concealed within. She turned the page to the candle light and perused it then flicked the page over. In the light the book professed itself to be "The Book of Spells and Chants Pertaining to the Art of Black Magic."

At length the girl found what she was looking for within the volume and gave a satisfied smile. She laid the page next to the flaring candle and began to read. The page was headed-

"Recipe and spell for the quickening of a loved one unto tying the knots of marriage."

She read the full page until a gleam of inspiration and a new light of understanding shone on her face and in her eyes. Then she closed the book and placed it back on a convenient ledge before going over to the far corner of the shed where a myriad of drawers presented themselves. She opened one or two of these and took out a number of objects which comprised of a large pack of marked cards, a white crucible, two carved wooden sticks and a small pointed fruit knife. She took these back to where she had left the book, took it down again and opened it at the dog eared page she had lately read. She then arranged the objects on the page, paused a moment as though in silent deliberation and then opened the door, ducking out again with easy stealth, the only sound being the scratch of her long skirt over the uneven ground. Several dry twigs rattled against her feet as she walked and made her start from her inner reflections. The night had drawn on a little since her parting with John and a gleam of moonlight now lit her way although the path was very familiar to her and she could have traversed it in her sleep. Eventually she came to the side of the cottage, reached up her hand and plucked a spray of ivy leaves from the top portion of the wall where they grew thicker and in greater size. Then she turned, knelt on the ground and brought forth two white pebbles from her pocket. These she spun round and round seven times then she picked them up and returned to the shed where she laid the white pebbles on the book with the other objects. After this she froze whilst uttering a strange jumble of words which were too low for clarity. Next she took up the knife, made a small incision in her left thumb, without even a flinch, and from the V shaped wound let the blood run into the crucible until the white bottom was stained red. She then nipped the oozing wound to stem the flow, after which she began chopping the ivy into small pieces that she mixed with the blood. She stirred it seven times one way and seven times the other way. Her spell was interrupted by a sharp knock at the shed door which did not frighten the girl as she had marked the approach of footsteps.

"Yes?" she said.

"Are you coming in, Cannetta? Are you coming in? It's very dark now!"

"Soon, soon," she replied, still stirring the hideous concoction.

The steps receded at this and Cannetta carried on her chanting undisturbed.

At the end of some thirty minutes she took up the smooth white pebbles and dropped them into the weird mixture; then she resumed her frantic chanting, taking it up an octave and getting louder and louder. Her blue eyes dilated, her nostrils flared and she became comatose with the power of the spell she was weaving.

"Let him who has me in his heart,
Show full royal blood to witch's curse;
Let him who loves me love me true
And take for better, leave for worse."

She was then silent, her fingers counting out the seconds with regular beats until she could suppress her feelings no longer and, flinging back her head, she cried,

"It is done!"

Trembling with anxiety she picked up the topmost card in the pack and all but fell back in shock. It was the card of death.

"No!" she cried. "That cannot be! The stones do not lie! Take it back, take it back!"

She picked up the full crucible, dug her nails into the pot and by degrees hoisted out the two stones, laying them next to the other objects as though they were some precious jewels. Her eyes narrowed to perceive, by the dying light of the candle, their true colour. Then, at length, she flung back her head and laughed.

"It is ended!" she shouted. "The stones cannot lie but the cards are past their usefulness! He will be in my grip – at last, at last!"

In another few minutes she left the shed, locking the door on yet another grim secret. The stones had turned bright blue.

When Mrs Hardy returned to the cottage, after finding her daughter in the shed, she was in a state of alarm as she knew, all too well, that Cannetta was casting her spells again. Moreover it was twilight and she was forced to admit to herself that she was scared of her own flesh and blood once night had darkened the sky. An inborn fear of anything to do with the black arts and witches had prevented Mrs Hardy from investigating what the shed contained and as long as her daughter was in by nightfall she was content to leave Cannetta to her own devices during the day. She knew that the girl had books on spells and used them periodically to obtain her own way but she turned a blind eye to it in case her concerns inflamed her daughter's moods. Yet, recently, it had been later and later before she had coaxed her daughter in. Rose felt little love for her offspring and had but a limited understanding of Cannetta's problems, preferring to keep silent about the severe mood swings and periods of insanity that plagued the girl. Valiantly, as though her life depended on it, Rose strove to keep her daughter's strangeness from the outside world without caring about the lengths she went to achieve this.

A little after ten the widow rose from her seat by the dying fire and took a candle to the window to search the garden for movement. There was no sign, as yet, of her daughter and no feet crunched on the gravel path. Rose listened for a moment, went to the door and after opening it called Cannetta's name into the darkness. No reply, save the shrill whistle of the breeze. She returned to the fireside, sighing anxiously, and regarding the stern face of the timekeeper, she picked up her sewing and attempted to continue with the embroidery but her mind was elsewhere. After a few minutes the clock struck the half hour reprovingly and Rose got up, lit the little oil lamp and putting another shawl round her quit the cottage.

Taking the path from the side of the building she hurried in the direction of the shed, suddenly frightened what she would find there. The deep aural roar of the rising wind alarmed her as Cannetta was affected by such things and often unmanageable in gale-force conditions. As she neared the outhouse she heard the familiar dry scratch of a skirt over rough ground and knew that her daughter was approaching. Rose reached her, raised the lamp to stare at the girl's wide, mesmerised eyes and perceived that her daughter was in the grip of the nightly demons that haunted her. She tried to grab the girl's hand and shake her.

"Well?" the mother asked angrily. "Are you coming in at last, Cannetta?"

The tall, lithe figure did not appear to hear her but walked past, throwing off her mother's fingers and heading for the cottage which she entered, her mother following in concern.

"Cannetta!" scolded the widow. "What have you been doing?"

The girl paused on her ascent to the landing and gazed down at her mother but she did not say anything until Rose reached her and took her hands.

"Yes, Mother," she whispered, putting up no resistance but holding out her arms in submission.

"Come and imprison me, do! But it may be one of the last times you do it! Do you realise that, Mother? It will not be long before I leave this place and rise up in the world! What you thought would never come to pass will be! The stones do not lie!"

Rose was mystified.

"I do not understand you, Cannetta. What are you ranting about now? It grows very late! There is no time for any more of your nonsense! Do you not see how high the moon is in the sky?"

Cannetta stared at her mother and shook her head.

"The stones have told me," murmured she. "I am to be a wife and he who was forecast to come has arrived to take me in marriage. Do you hear that, Mother? He has come for my hand! We are to be joined together for life. Soon he will come and see you. It has to be yes, it has to be yes! He is mine, mine and I am his, his!"

Rose took these words and sentiments to be another sign of her daughter's impending insanity and sighed. She grasped Cannetta's arm again and urged her forward.

"Come now, come now! It is almost eleven. No more talking! Are you coming? You must be locked away for your own safety and for my peace of mind, too."

The girl seemed as one resigned to her nightly imprisonment and bowed her head, ascending the rest of the stairs to stand in front of the pulsing arras whilst her mother thrust the tapestry aside and unlocked the door beneath. It fell inwards with an eerie groan and swallowed up the two entering forms. After a few minutes only one figure emerged, drawing down the arras in mingled guilt and fear, after relocking the door. Rose hurried to her own room, stunned by the silence that followed her and all through the night only the timekeeper stirred the heavy trance-like state of quiet that enclosed the dark cottage.

CHAPTER 5

As soon as her husband had departed for the fields next day and she had prepared the luncheon snack, Shirley threw on her best lace-trimmed shawl, took the papers out of her hair and left by the back door for Stackhouses.

It was another cool day with visible signs of rain apparent in the cloudy sky and no glimpse of sunlight. The treetops were heavy with water: small bushes and shrubs bent down with the weight almost fit to snapping and the few flowers of the garden encrusted with drops like icicles. All this Shirley perceived but dimly, her mind being upon loftier topics, the weather comprising the least of her troubles at present. Even when the sharp rap of falling raindrops sounded upon her bonnet or the gossamer, spun with dew, clung to her face, she was only abstractedly moved to brush it away. She walked briskly for one of her height, fast for a woman, and the creeping things of the fields ran from her path. Her skirt rustled upon the nodding grass heads and, by degrees, became sodden with cold dew which she felt transiently as a physical discomfort.

Traversing the hill to Stackhouses she took a long, sweeping glance down over the settlement of Ardle, thought it beautiful then turned her praise to scorn. Her husband was there. A vague, grey mist still hung over the cornfields, dense in places where the ground was boggy, gathering thickly over the course of a small stream. At this very moment her tired bedfellow would be yawning as he wielded his sickle or sat in miry mud in a furrow consuming the hastily thrown together breakfast she had prepared for him. She wrinkled her nose at the idea of him, turned her sad eyes away from the scenery and rounded the hill to hit the outer districts of Stackhouses.

Here all was denser with water and a small rill of it trickled down the hill slope its very colour and smell showing it was anything but pure. At the top she paused for breath, then hurried on and entered the district of Fourcrosses, her eyes alighting eagerly on the house where her cousin lived now. She turned in at the gateway, grasped the handle of the door firmly and marvelled that it was open at this hour. The water meadows behind the house were a mass of grey mist through which no reed or rush was visible.

Once inside she heard the heavy tread of footsteps on the stairs, raised her eyes and beheld John descending with a light summer coat over his arm. "Good morning!" she breathed. "What? You are abroad already?"

"Aye – yes - almost!" he replied, coming down to her level and placing the coat across the hall chair. "Mr Weber has a sick cow to be attended again first thing in the morning but it seems hardly fitting to call upon the man afore he has breakfasted!"

She took off her bonnet, shook the water from it and hung it upon one of the nearby hooks, doing likewise with her shawl.

"Well!" she exclaimed. "I think I shall prepare you some food first as doubtless you have not eaten."

44

"No – no – I have not!" he cried in his fine Scottish accent. "Will you do me the honour of eating with me? Faith – I am not one to dine alone and I have something to talk about if you'll hear it?"

She affirmed she would and wondered what news could cause such a light in his pensive blue eyes, causing her to make for the kitchen with a heart not entirely glad. He, after smiling to himself dreamily for some seconds, ascended the stairs once more and entered his bedroom. There he repaired to a small padlocked chest which he now opened, delved into the contents and brought forth a tiny exquisite wooden box. Turning to the window he freed the clasp, raised the lid and caused a gentle refulgence to rival the brightness of the daylight as a delicate diamond set with a sapphire in a gleam of spun gold was revealed. John gazed at it with love, polished the stone with the sleeve of his shirt and stowed the ring away until it was time to bring it forth to fulfil its purpose in life.

Eventually he descended, rejoiced in the hearty smell of food and observed his housekeeper (for so he vowed to think of her) to be then in the act of serving the breakfast. They sat down. She seemed ill at ease and very restless, as if pre-empting his news.

"John," she begged, at length. "What has occurred that you need to speak to me so urgently? Have I displeased you already? Did your tea party fail on account of some culinary error on my part or did the lady not turn up?"

"Fail?" cried he, in amazement. "Fail? Due to all your hard work? Good heavens, Shirley, it was quite the reverse and it blossomed! Are you not pleased?"

"Yes." But she dropped her eyes to her scarcely touched plate and was evidently speechless.

"Shirley," continued he in as gentle a manner as he could muster. "I must inform you that soon I shall not need your services. I hope then to have another to replace you, though doubtless in the cooking department she will not rival you!"

"So I have displeased you!" she cried, in real distress. "Come, tell me of my faults and I will change them so you will be happy with my work and not decide to dismiss me. In all honesty you have given me no time to prove myself but if you do I will not be found wanting!" She was almost in tears as she said this.

"Now, now, now, Shirley!" he scolded gently. "'Tis not as you perceive it to be. Faith – I am not replacing you in that sense! But I am all but engaged and shall be bringing a wife here soon to do for me!"

She gave a startled exclamation of surprise and shock, froze in her movements and remained staring at him fixedly.

"It had to be, Shirley!" cried he, abandoning his meal for the important news. "I need a wife – I need a companion in life. This is a dark, drear place to be alone in with night after night stretching into oblivion!"

"Was I not enough?" she reproached. "Was a cousin not what you wanted? I am here now and your meal is cooked and soon your house will be cleaned. Even my husband approves of my work. No one knows of us, John. Are WE not enough?"

"Don't plead so desperately, my dear," he murmured. "I don't like to see you so upset and lachrymose. You cannot keep two houses pristine. Do not forget you have a husband and your first duty is to him."

"Then what about his duty to me?" she cried bitterly, flinging up her hands in despair as she realised she had lost her new love. "Oh John...I thought, yes, I did at first but.no."

She burst into tears, flung them away as useless comforters and looked up at him. "John, I would do anything for you...anything...I even thought of leaving HIM but I see it is too late for that now. I am recovering. I am nearly myself I am resigned. Come tell me of your love, I wish to know! Was she your guest of yesterday?"

"Aye," he replied, evincing a pang at her obvious pain. "It was she. This evening I must go to her mother and then we shall arrange the day. Can you not see, Shirley, that what we had was doomed from the start?"

"Yes. I was foolish for I vowed never to speak of that again! Oh John, I am sorry. Let me be happy for you and pray your love is more lasting than mine was."

"Yes, yes, I thank you," he smiled, returning to his cold plate and endeavouring to eat a little of what she had laboriously prepared. She pushed hers away, in distaste, attempted a weak smile but her eyes remained misty and sad.

A moment's silence ensued and then she asked, gently,

"Am I allowed to know the name of she who will soon be Mrs Straeton?"
He continued eating, flung down his knife and fork and shook his head.
"Not quite yet my dear, not yet. Let me do the honest thing and tell her mother first. Let me ask for my love's hand in marriage and then you shall know, cousin. I shall publish the banns at once and then the whole world shall know and be glad!"

She nodded carelessly, swallowed hard and left the table in haste as if the news had suddenly overpowered her and she could stay to hear no more.

About half an hour later he gathered up his things and went out, she marking the slamming of the door with a loud sigh from her kitchen retreat. Accordingly she went through the hall and on into the dining room where she cleared away the scarcely touched meal with a heavy, painful heart. It was not, she told herself, the bitter emotion of jealousy or the stifling vice of envy but true, unadulterated love that filled her being and that love had been forcefully rejected. There was no hope now of these idle seeds she had planted growing into the flowers she had imagined at the start of their affair. Rank weeds they would become if they germinated at all and the pain of uprooting them was almost physical. She threw herself into her work and

46

gained an element of relief from the routine of cleaning and tidying. Here, at least, she was close to her beloveds' chattels and her flesh touched things he would lay his hands upon. It was not enough but it was all that life could offer at the moment. She shelved all plans as to a future and struggled on.

By one o'clock John had accomplished his round of calls which, he found to his relief, was steadily increasing as word got round as to his prowess. He had travelled over six miles on foot that very morning, had had two lifts on wagons and had been offered a five year-old black gelding for a song. His savings, coupled with those of his father's, had been eroded somewhat by the purchase price of the dwelling but there was still sufficient for the outlay of a horse. Accordingly he had given the equine a clean bill of health, clapped hands with the farmer who owned him and deferred settlement until he had sorted out stabling for his newly-acquired mount. Returning to Fourbridges he remembered Shirley, felt an air of awkwardness at facing her again, and was heartily relieved when her bonnet and shawl were missing from the hall stands when he entered. In the dining room he spied a folded note which he picked up and read-

John.
        Forgive me! Your luncheon is beneath the cloth and your house is cleaned. Somehow I am called away but I will return tomorrow. Your secret is safe with me meanwhile and I hope to hear good news of your union very soon.
                                        Shirley.

He let the words flow over him, screwed up the note but felt unable to throw it away. Poor Shirley! He perceived as if for the first time her deep affection for him and the complex situation she found herself in, bounded one side by the prison walls of marriage and the other by a hopeless love. "I should have married her by rights if she was free after what we did!" he murmured to himself. "But she IS wed and I must have a wife so seeing as she is the mate of another, let things be as they are for my mind is set on Cannetta."

The evening sky darkened in preparation for the hues of night to sweep across the horizon and a sultry batch of black clouds graced the zenith. Despite the dullness it had been a warm afternoon but not one illuminated by sunlight as the greyness of February had prevailed although it was August. In many fields the harvest was tied in sheaves, some stalks remaining to rustle and provide shelter for the small animals of the field who had fled from the harvesters in droves. A few adders emerged from the sodden fields, rats and mice sought the spilt grain and rabbits thumped the ground in warning signs to their fellow kind. The clouds began to gather more densely.

Just before dusk took hold a tall, very erect man appeared by the side of the wheat fields, paused to regard the state of the harvest and crossed the meadows on his way to Ardle. John was on his way to Fern Cottage with the notion of arranging the day that, he judged, would make him the happiest of men. He swung his arms, powerfully strode up the next incline and presently reached the gateway of his love's cottage. There was a great air of peace about the silent dwelling and no murmur of voices reached his ears, whilst no sign of habitation reached his restive eyes, making him wonder if anyone was home. He pushed up the latch of the gate and went in. A small roost of sparrows departed from the thatch at the echo of his footsteps, some squabbling crows on the topmost branch of an elm tree fell silent, spread their wings and flew off into the dying summer evening. Somehow John felt vaguely uneasy and the bubbling confidence he had left home with evaporated into the chillness of the location. He felt it was not only dismal but lonely too, as the habitation bathed in its seclusion and delighted in its own desertion.

The blank squares of the windows shone as empty faces and he could perceive nothing stirring within. Summoning up his flagging spirits he rang the old fashioned bell which hung low on a rusting link chain. For a moment there was nothing save the vague reverberation of the chimes then the rustling of a stiff dress and finally the front door opened before him. The woman he regarded was a small, auburn-haired lady in her early forties, her pale freckled skin heavily lined but she bore a strong resemblance to Cannetta in her face and the doleful shape of her eyes. She was evidently ignorant of him, gazed at him somewhat blankly and asked in a rather harsh voice,

"Can I help you?"

He thought he caught a grate of fear in her tones but he could ascertain no reason for this.

"Mrs Hardy?" he asked politely, donning a pleasant smile and making a small bow.

She looked surprised he knew her name, assented she was the person he mentioned and seemed to wait for him to explain further.

"Mrs Hardy, I am John Straeton. Your daughter has doubtless spoken of me?"

She shook her head, seemed startled at the mention of Cannetta and then recovered sufficiently to ask him inside. The door was shut and she ushered him into the untidy coldness of a back room, lighting an oil lamp as she did so and drawing down the blinds.

"Please sit down, Mr Straeton," she murmured when she observed he stood rather awkwardly in the doorway. "In truth I did not expect anyone this evening so you must excuse me."

He begged her pardon for disturbing her unannounced and gazed round at the unfamiliar surroundings he found himself in. Taking a deep breath he plunged into the reasons why he had travelled here.

"Mrs Hardy, I gather from your daughter that you have no husband and therefore Cannetta no father to whom I can properly apply. I am sorry for this, and to trouble you but I have come to ask for your daughter's hand in marriage. In short I wish her to be my wife."

When he had concluded the receiver of this news was smitten into shocked silence. She held onto the back of the settle as if her life depended on it. Her lips twitched uncontrollably but she said nothing.

John became a little alarmed, rose as if to go but was motioned to stay by a wave of hand which seated him again and then his audience walked over to him.

"Mr Straeton – I cannot comprehend this! Cannetta! My Cannetta! Why, you cannot mean this? You cannot be in earnest surely?"

He gazed up at her dark, troubled face and affirmed strongly that he meant every word he had uttered.

"But you do not know her!" gasped she. "Oh Mr Straeton – wait – consider – do not be rash in marriage!"

"No, no, I hae not been – I mean we have not been," he murmured. "Cannetta feels as I do. It is mutual. Mrs Hardy – I originate from the wilds of Scotland and I have recently lost my father. Being motherless anyway I felt my lot was through with Gaelic charms. The glens seemed empty to me and the burns full of polluted water, even my ain folk cold, nay distant. I desired to wander, to move but where was I to go? By chance I met my only distant relation at a funeral and he lives but a few yards from here! 'Twas he gave me hope for a decent future. Mrs Hardy, I am a trained horse doctor and it is a hard but thriving life for although I shall never be rich I shall always be comfortable and my savings have lasted well. I have secured myself everything but a wife and that I want more than life itself! My house is not far from here and although run-down it is roomy, oh too roomy for me and lonely too. But Cannetta can end that. Mrs Hardy, you must believe me when I say I love her and she, in turn, loves me!"

The widow shook her head vigorously, sat down beside him and bit her thin lips.

"Mr Straeton – you do not know what you ask! I tell you – it is impossible! How can you think you are acquainted with Cannetta after only days in her company? Have you not heard what the village people say about her? Do you not know that she is thought of as mad, insane, and she is named as a witch, sorceress by all around?"

"That does not affect me!" he declared vehemently. "She told me everyone has turned against her but I will not! That is not how she appears to me! What do I care for village gossip, idle chat?"

"Oh sir, but if you could see her at... If I could take you up the narrow twist of my dark stairs and...but, no, no, I cannot and will not do that to her. No! Not by my hand shall she be condemned! Perhaps I have sheltered her for too long! It is time for me to make way for another – that person being yourself sir!" She jumped up in a state of agitated excitement and walked to the door. "You have beaten me into submission, Mr Straeton. If that is your wish and Cannetta desires it too then so be it. So be it! But remember, in your sorrow, if such sorrow ensues, and I believe that it will that I warned you, repeatedly and steadfastly and you did not heed me. Remember that, sir, and do not reproach me after....after trouble comes from this union."

He did not altogether understand what she was saying but he could see she was upset and a violent emotion seized her so that her hand trembled considerably on the door handle. She avoided his eye and seemed to desire his departure.

"I will fetch Cannetta," she murmured at length when she had recovered a little. "She is an adult now and as such no longer in my care. Mr Straeton – you may have her! Would that I had the strength to put a stop to this marriage but it is beyond me!" He felt the despair in her tone and was under the mistaken concept that it was a mother's grief at losing her only daughter to a man so he went over to her and put his hands on her shoulders.

"Mrs Hardy – I do not seek to possess her. Cannetta is a person in her own right and I would never stop her from seeing her own flesh and blood!"

"Ah," replied his future mother-in-law gravely. "But do you know what kind of person Cannetta is?"

As he believed he already knew the answer to that question he remained silent and turned away from Rose. She saw he was totally committed to the purpose of his coming and gave up any hope at all of dissuading him from his plan. In her head she was already planning a life on her own, a peaceful life as it had been before Cannetta's insanity had taken a hold.

She bent her head and gave a small bow.

"So be it," she repeated. "I will send her to you."

"But we part friends, do we not, Mrs Hardy?" he cried, holding out his hand towards her. "Faith, I should not want to distress one who I shall come to regard as a mother! Do you hate me?"

"Hate you? No – why should I? I see only foolishness in you and impetuosity but also the love of which you speak. If you are so dedicated to my daughter you will suffer enough without the weight of my feelings dragging you down!" Her eyes flashed at him but she dropped their powerful gaze to the ground and went out, leaving the door open and John alone with his thoughts.

The conversation had bemused, frightened and shaken him to the very core but he clung to his feelings and tried to still his mind-numbing fears. Had he not spoken to his love in depth about the village's spite against her and had she not explained herself clearly and lucidly so that he understood why they

50

slated her? So, she was not as other young girls. Was that not why he loved her? She preferred the company of animals to the villagers so why should she be criticised for that? And these stories of witchcraft and insanity? Nothing more than evil tittle-tattle banded about to do harm to her he loved. Well, let them say it when she was his wife! Let them say it to his face and then he could do something about it! The nonsense of it! He only saw the beauty, tenderness and kindness that had enthralled him; to every other conceivable fault she possessed he was blind.

In a moment or two he heard the light tread of footsteps approaching the room and he stood up, eager to take his darling in his arms and tell her to name the day. His eyes dilated in readiness, his cheeks flushed, his chest heaved and his heart raced. Cannetta came through the doorway and flung herself into his waiting arms with breath scarcely less rapid, her rosy cheeks as flushed as his and her eyes glistening. She was radiant, beautiful, perfect and any nagging doubts that still assailed him fled and were replaced by overwhelming joy and pride. His bride-to-be kissed his temples and he felt her long fingers spanning his back as she hugged him.

"Oh John..."

He kissed her fondly and caressed her flowing hair till everything around him was misty with tears.

"My Cannetta!"

"Mother has just told me! Oh John, John, can you really mean it? Is it true?" Her clutch of him was almost wild and would have pained him had he been in the real world but the digging depth of her nails did not touch his senses so drunk was he on love.

"My darling!" he breathed. "Cannetta – will you have me? Will you take me as your husband? Will you marry me, my angel and be mine for eternity?"

"And is Mother reconciled to the union? And will you love and care for her too, John, in her old age for I cannot leave her!" cried she, in a frenzy, grabbing at his wrists and leaving marks on them.

"Yes, yes, darling, of course I will! Come, bonny lass, say the words and be mine! Say them, my sweet!"

"John – my own love – I will marry you! But let it be soon, my darling, let it be soon!"

"As soon as I can make it, my angel, that's when it shall be and not a day longer!"

Cannetta put up her mouth to be kissed and her frenzy seemed to diminish a little.

Within another half an hour all was settled and John felt he was the happiest man alive. Her soft skin, her wistful face and her sweet manner were all that lingered with him as he left the house. How bound he was to her side and how empty he felt now she was no longer in his arms! By half past eight he had departed across the wet fields where the first drops of rain were once again testing the air. The fading image of her form leaning over the cottage gate stayed with him as he traversed the paths between their dwellings and the warmth of her caresses took him home as though on a magic carpet. He felt his feet scarcely touched the ground and the fields flew by as though in a paradise-filled dream.

As he turned up the hill to the first districts of Stackhouses he encountered his cousin, now making his way to the Resort for a nightly pint of ale. John hailed him and slowed his gait to walk with Damion for the worker was but ambling after his hard day in the fields.

"Come hither, man," cried Damion. "And I will stand you a drink for 'tis the cousinly sort of thing to do when meeting a relation. I don't seem to have seen you many times since you moved here, John!"

"Very well," returned the Scotsman neighbourly. "In truth I am exceedingly dry and I would fain speak to some one of my good fortune and the person I would most like that to be stands before me!"

"To be sure," replied Damion eagerly. "I am all ears and kindness when it comes to good fortune!"

They strolled on a little further and passed the quarter where John's house lay, remarking on the flat, misty water meadows that seemed sinister and louring in the moonlight.

"To be sure," continued Damion. "I am convinced I would be in fear to live there on my own, especially when darkness covers those lonely marshes. Does it not strike you that way cousin or are you reconciled to the fact?"

"At one time I was, surely, reconciled to it...but now...well, Damion, I shall not be there on my own for long!"

"Oh, what is the meaning of that then, cousin?"

John's eyes gleamed in the moonlight and his breath came loud and deep.

"My meaning is that I have this very night made plans to take a wife and that wife is none other than the so-called witch of Ardle. How shallow and narrow minds can taint a life! Why, Damion, I vow the very first person who speaks ill of my beloved shall feel the full force of this fist!" He clenched it and struck the air. "And this one!" Doing the same with his other hand. "Even if he is the king of England himself I will not rest till he is beaten into submission!" His eyes sparkled with ire and he turned on his cousin in righteous anger, falling silent when his outburst brought only a clap of hands.

"Well done, cousin, well done! You have spoken powerfully enough to hush all the gossips of Ardle and Stackhouses in one breath! Brave words! In faith I like a man who sticks up for his kin! Blessings to the both of you and long-lived happiness to the union! Come, the inn is in our sights and you shall drink a pint of the best before you utter another word!"

The pair entered the public house in high spirits, one amazed and the other delighted with the recent news but the latter still bore the deep crescents of his beloveds' nails on his wrists and he should have remembered that skin wounds heal but bleeding hearts do not...

CHAPTER 6

When Damion arrived home after a lengthier bout of drinking than usual, due to the presence of his betrothed cousin, his wife, who often waited up for him, had locked the door and gone to bed. Damion tried the door uselessly, went round to the back of the house and attempted throwing stones at the bedroom window where he knew she was sleeping. After a while he saw a subdued light flare up in the room which he judged to be a candle and then a protesting squeak from the window frame told him she was up. She shone the light out into the darkness, perceived his face looking up at her and gazed down sleepily at her husband.

"Shirley! You little fool!" he fair yelled at her. "The door is barred so get down here and open it!"

"You should have been in sooner," returned she angrily. "It is past midnight, Damion, and no time for you to be abroad!"

"That is my business," he retorted, coldly. "Yours is to do my bidding as my wife. Now get down here and unlock this door before I lose my patience!"

"You are drunk!" cried she withdrawing the light and shutting the window. He heard her descending the stairs and ran round to the front door, almost knocking her over as he burst in whilst she was unlocking it.

"Now, my lady!" shouted he. "What do you mean by keeping me out of my own house? Damn the time! You are at fault here!"

"Yes," replied she, in tears. "I am. It is my fault for ever being foolish enough to marry you in the first place. Now, hit me if you wish – I do not care! It is too late for us and I am a fool to put up with you!"

She smelt something more than beer upon his breath and, in his mood, something more belligerent than usual and suspected that he had been consuming spirits in large quantities. He seemed beside himself with fury, rolling his eyes at her and clenching his fists churlishly at her words. At length he could control his temper no longer and commenced slapping her savagely about the face and neck.

"Don't you dare to cheek me! By right I am your lord and master and you should grovel before me for your daily bread! Get down on your knees now and beg for mercy!"

"Never!" cried she trying uselessly to cover her face as he hit out at her. "You will have to kill me first!"

"Then take that!" screamed he, rushing at her and striking her three tremendous blows on the back, after which he rapped the full force of his knuckles against her nose which bled freely. Another huge blow to the chest dropped her to her knees and another felled her completely so she became insensible to nothing but the intensity of the pain. For a few minutes she lost consciousness and could no longer feel the kicks he administered to her prostrate body but, at last, he became aware of what he did and drew off.

Shirley came to and found herself alone, covered in blood and aching from head to foot. She sat up with difficulty, perceived her attacker had returned and was in the act of rinsing out a cloth to clean her wounds.

"It is too late for that," she whispered, for her lips were torn and sore. "You should have killed me, Damion, and saved my worn out body the trouble of healing itself!"

He murmured he was sorry and that he did not know what had come over him. Shirley turned her face away.

"Keep off me," she warned. "Don't touch me again. You have frightened and shocked me! I cannot trust you anymore and, as such, cannot have you anywhere near me. I have long ceased loving you and now that indifference is turned into hate and fear. Well, I hope you are happy with this night's work! Leave me now – leave me and by and by when I recover strength I will take myself up to the spare room to rest."

"I will help you," he murmured, feeling thoroughly ashamed at the sight of her injuries. He handed her the cloth and she began dabbing her wounds.

"Keep away from me or I shall scream!" she cried when she saw he tried to approach her. He jumped back and spread his hands out in regret.

"Shirley, I did not know what I did and an angry red mist clouded my mind. It was the whisky in me doing that. I would never hurt you."

"Sober maybe not," she replied, still attempting to dab away the blood from her eyes. "So, did you drink alone or is some other poor labourer's wife getting beaten as we speak?"

"I drank with John," Damion said simply, still feeling deeply ashamed and rueful.

At this she looked up and started, seeming surprised at his words.

"Ah, that has caused you to jump!" exclaimed he, mystified as to her reaction.

"It is nothing," she muttered. "Why did you drink with him then?"

"Why, I met him ascending Longman's Length and invited him to the Resort. On our way there he gave me some very strange news!"

"Oh!" cried she, unable to contain herself any longer. He observed she shook and looked horrified but he put that down to shock from his unspeakable behaviour.

"John is to marry very soon and the amazing thing is that his wife to be is no other than Cannetta Hardy. Do you hear that, Shirley, the acclaimed witch of Ardle? Shall I call the doctor to you as you seem visibly worse?"

"No, no, it is nothing, nothing but the pain of the attack and extreme tiredness. Will you leave me now, please?"

He nodded his head slowly, agreed to her demands and went upstairs to his bed, leaving her in the darkness to recover her strength. But unconsciously he had hurt her far more by his news than by any of the blows he had struck to her person and her mind, racing with anxiety and upset, eclipsed her physical pain. She had lost John and another had claimed him.

On the following morning both the drinkers of the night before rose later than was their custom, the elder of the pair suffering a considerable headache due to the strangeness and quantity of the spirits he had consumed. John was more or less his usual self but he rarely succumbed to the effects of liquor and despite drinking half a bottle of best Scotch whisky he felt nothing but a little weary.

On studying his reflection in the shaving mirror he suddenly became aware of some long, red wheals, a few of which were encrusted with blood on his neck and presently, in dressing, he spied more on his wrists and on the fleshier parts of his arms. They were the marks of Cannetta's nails.

Outside it was blowing to a fair degree though a watery sun had, at last, pierced the thick array of dark cloud which covered the firmament. The harvesters were collecting in the last of the crop and dreaming of the great supper to follow culminating in the Festival itself on the next Sunday.

Shirley did not stir until her husband had left the house and he, suffering from overwhelming guilt, was glad his injured wife did not appear to make him feel worse. Shirley had dragged herself up to the spare room by two o'clock in the morning and managed to get into bed but sadly not to sleep. Accordingly Damion had left straight for work, forgotten to prepare any food to take with him and just swallowed a few mouthfuls of water from the ewer in the kitchen. He was already a good half an hour late for his toil and he knew he would have to make this up if he were not to have his wages docked.

Shirley rose with difficulty as she was stiff and sore. Her face in the mirror appalled her. One eye was a mass of dried blood and blue bruising whilst her cheeks were swollen and black to the very ridge of her nose which looked flattened and yellow. Her other eye was half shut and she could not open it so her view of the world was rather restricted. Her lips were almost purple, the upper one scabbing nicely while the lower one still dripped blood from a long wound. On her neck were the clear signs of pinching and finger marks where his digits had dug into her ivory skin and bruised it badly. She stared in horror at her own tarnished reflection and thought of the scars that would ensue from this battle.

Leaving the house somewhat later by the back entrance she wondered what John's reception of her wounds would be when he saw her. It was partly his fault that she had suffered as Damion was never moved to cruelty when he returned with a full belly of beer but whisky...well that was a different matter. His meagre wages allowed no purchase of spirits and only a pint or two of ale so the generous flow of whisky had completely changed his character and resulted in the fury of temper that had thrashed her almost to the door of death. Only John could have provided such money to buy spirits in that quantity as to intoxicate her husband so he knew not what he did and now she was paying for it. But the information of last night, when it returned to her, was far more lasting and painful than anything she had ever borne in her life so far. That had permanently damaged her heart and troubled the once tranquil nature of her mind. Was John blind as to his choice of bride...or had Cannetta bewitched him as she had once bewitched the entire stables at Porleau with poll evil? The farmers often blamed her for the failure of their crops, for the death of their livestock and even for the recent tempestuous weather. Yet it could not be proved and was all hearsay so maybe she had talked with a silver tongue to John and she was definitely a beauty who would turn any man's head.

She drew near to Stackhouses, entered the long avenue of Fourcrosses and went to the door of her cousin's house, thinking he would be up or even abroad at this hour, attending to his calls. The hour was later than when she had arrived yesterday yet the chances were John would be suffering like her husband from the excesses of last night too.

She went in. The door was again unlocked and she spied John's light summer coat on the hall rack, together with the black case he used for his patients. From the dining room she could hear the sounds of eating, coupled with snatches of song interspersed with tuneful whistling. Clearly he was not suffering from any sort of hangover from his drinking of last night. She untied the strings of her bonnet, deposited it with difficulty on one of the hooks, for her arms were sore and stiff, and then tried to get her coat off. As she struggled to remove the article she heard John come to the door, perceive the dreadful state of her face and hurry across, taking her coat off her with extreme gentleness.

She wished with all her heart that he would not look at her with those eyes or stand so close to her that she could hear his breathing.

"Och! Shirley! Whatever has happened?" cried he, in horror, regarding the ugly bruises on her person.

"It is nothing," she murmured, turning away from him. "I am quite well, thank you."

"But your poor face!" he retorted. "I have never seen such wounds on a woman! At whose hands did you receive those blows? He must have been a madman to inflict such injuries on you! Time he tried it on a man and learnt a lesson!"

"In a way it was YOU who gave me those blows!" she returned, angrily, choosing not to look at him.

He drew back in amazement.

"I?" cried he.

"Well, John, you were the means of inspiring another to do so! By your hands the whole thing began! Next time you drink with my husband do not give him spirits. He was as drunk as a lord and with such a temper that I have never seen in him afore! Thus it was the whisky that beat me and not Damion as he was not of sound mind when he did it, fuddled as he was with liquor. You must have bought those spirits for him as he could not afford it on his money!" Her tone was very bitter and she touched her face softly as though it pained her even to talk.

The accused party was silent for a moment then he spoke slowly.

"Oh Shirley! I would not hae had this happen for the world! I did not realise your husband was like that when he drunk as he appeared very jovial to me and I stood him a few whiskies to celebrate my engagement and future happiness. I suppose by the time he became morbid in his cups I was too drunk to notice! Oh, my poor bonny lass. You shall do no work today."

She attempted a weak smile and announced she had come to offer congratulations on his intended union.

"Not that I am altogether happy in your choice of bride, John, and I cannot understand why you would fall for such a girl as Cannetta but I abide by your choice and honour it. Do you not know about these tales that are widespread of her conduct and behaviour?"

He seemed a trifle angry at this and grew sullen at her words.

"I am not one for tales, cousin! I make my own mind up about people! Cannetta - a witch? I have never heard such nonsense. She is all gentleness and sweetness to me, anyway."

"Ah," breathed Shirley. "But can you shake off the story of insanity in the family so easily?"

"I see no madness in her behaviour, only a little eccentricity and she has talked to me far more lucidly and kindly than most in this village."

Shirley was still very suspicious.

"But she affirms she detests people and keeps her own company! Her eyes start from her face when she beholds strangers in her walks and she never speaks to anyone!"

"Well, at our first meeting she spoke to me with a soft sweetness I have long been starved from," replied he, growing angry again. "She told me she is shy of folk and prefers the company of animals and that explains her conduct completely. Why should she socialise with those that condemn her for her way of life? I see no wickedness in this at all. And I know her, whilst your views are based purely on gossip!"

Shirley thought for a moment and then acquiesced.

"Perhaps there is truth in what you say," she acknowledged. "And as I have never spoken to her I will bow to your greater experience with the lady concerned."

He nodded at this and replied,

"Remember, Shirley, your own reputation is hardly stainless is it? How would you feel if someone condemned YOU with no proof?"

She flushed at this and asked quickly,

"What then have you heard of me?"

He smiled, assured her that it was nothing serious and that he had chosen to disregard it because, on acquaintance, he had found a totally different person.

"If they paint such a wicked picture of you, cousin, then what do you think they are doing to my Cannetta? And who does she have to refute it but me? No one really knows her!"

Shirley agreed with this, wished him luck and dropped the subject.

"If Cannetta has found just what she is looking for in you then she is steeped in great sensibility. John, sometimes you are too good and you deserve success. Will not you and your wife, when you are wed, come and visit us so we may come to know and love her too?"

He affirmed it would please him to do so, kissed her in a gentle cousinly way and showed her out, declaring that she must not come again until the wounds were healed.

"And do not blame me for intoxicating your husband," finished he. "Faith, I have made you suffer so much for my behaviour and I cannot bear that you think badly of me! One day I am sure that all this will be made right – I am certain of it, though how it will all draw together I cannot comprehend as yet." He did not know the irony of his words and she, who could see no way this would happen, heard and forgot his sentence instantly as the pain of losing him took over.

On arriving back at her own cottage she found the door open and realised, in her haste to see John this morning, she had forgotten to lock it. Someone was within and at first fear overtook her but then a familiar voice hailed her and she entered to find her stepdaughter in the kitchen.

"Well, well, Connie, dear, how are you?" Shirley echoed as she shut the door and turned to her relation.

The young girl looked up from her study of the wooden table, coughed loudly and replied,

"I am tolerably well, thank you, Mother." then catching sight of Shirley's face, "Oh my God, whatever has occurred to leave such marks?"

Shirley turned her face away.

"They are nothing, dear," she murmured. "Visible wounds will fade in time and very likely leave no scar or trace but those of a deeper kind, invisible to our outward eyes, will never go! Connie, your cough does not seem any better. Have you a day's holiday?"

"Not as such but the doctor did not like the sound of my chest. He was summoned for my lady's cold and noticed me so cook and the housekeeper judged I could be spared for a day or so to rest."

"Did the doctor say what was causing the cough, dear?"

"Yes," replied Connie. "He called it inflammation of the left lung – nothing serious so you need have no fear and I do not want to tell Father as he fusses so! He advised a few days' rest and has applied a blister which was dreadfully painful at first! I also have some medicine to take which is foul-tasting but may do me some good. Now, mother, you will not escape so easily! I have told you of my illness so what is the cause of your suffering – mine has been explained!"

Shirley sat down and took her stepdaughter's thin hand.

"Do not be alarmed by it, my dear, if I tell you the truth for it looks worse than it is. It was your father. Last night he came home in a furious temper, very much the worse for drink, although I hesitate to say intoxicated but he is not used to hard liquor. Need I say any more? The results are what you see lingering on my face this morning, the occasion of the drinking was John's engagement which he has just announced."

Connie ignored the last sentence and stood firm.

"There is no excuse for it, hard liquor or not," she said, angrily.

"Well, no, but John did all the plying of drink!"

"Father should have known better and I shall tell him so when I see him," Connie cried. "As to the other matter - who is the woman then, Mother?"

"I can hardly say it but 'tis Cannetta Hardy who has bewitched him although HE says she is innocent and suffers from nothing more than shyness in the presence of strangers and a liking for her own company and those of her animals! Her reputation he refutes utterly and sees only her physical beauty, sweetness and gentleness! Thus he speeds ahead with the wedding and will hear nothing against the girl. Should we be concerned for him do you think, my dear?"

"No," returned Connie thoughtfully. "It is his life and, as such his to do what he wants with including making mistakes and misjudging people!" After this she indulged in a long, drawn out fit of coughing which ended all conversation and so alarmed Shirley that she insisted Connie go lie down at once in the spare room. Looking at the pallor of her stepdaughter's skin and the black marks under her eyes Shirley felt a stab of pain. The girl was worryingly thin too and seemed to constantly lose flesh so that every time she visited her face was more drawn and her frame frailer. Sleep soon overtook the coughing and Shirley, having watched her stepdaughter until she fell into slumber, left her with the silent vow that Connie should not return to the Hall until she had gained weight and was strong again.

Directly the news became known that Cannetta Hardy was engaged to marry John Straeton talk that would have been best silenced circulated Ardle and Stackhouses, almost to the point of slander. All Cannetta's old spells, potions and curses that she had apparently used to blight the last three harvests, bring potato famine to several springs and give the year-old calves the staggers on every farm within a mile of her dwelling were recounted in elaborate detail with many additions. The spreaders of this malicious gossip were very careful who they told and thus these tales did not reach the ears of either party in the engagement, mostly because the perpetrators feared being cursed by Miss Hardy or getting a sound beating from Mr Straeton, their apprehension of Gaelic tempers holding true.

Thus, although John was vexed by the gossiping groups he saw on every street corner in Stackhouses, he could not prove their talk was malicious or

59

even about him and his love. By degrees he learnt to ignore these whisperings and pass by without a glance. He yearned for this marriage as a starving man yearns for the splendour of a laden table or a traveller in darkness yearns for the return of light. In his heart all seemed smooth and easy; he had no worries that he would find in Cannetta as a wife anything but what she appeared to be. And if he did notice, late in the evening, a restless tendency in her he defined it only as premarital nerves, dismissed it and forgot it in the throes of her beauty.

The following week saw the last details of the wedding arranged to everyone's satisfaction and all went smoothly with the banns. He was not at all surprised that Cannetta shunned going to church as he knew she suffered in company due to her extreme shyness and the anti-social element of her character. John had been brought up as a strict Protestant and was somewhat shocked at his love's lack of religion in her life but he was too infatuated with her to take this any further. Therefore he blamed Cannetta's mother and left it at that.

After another week he received no news of Shirley, gave up expecting her to come and worried transiently that her injuries had proved to be more serious than first surmised. Accordingly, as he was riding passed his cousin's cottage after a lengthy consultation with a pig farmer, he decided it was seemly to call and see how she was so he tethered his horse to a stake of beech hedge that rambled along the north border of the property. The cottage seemed bathed in silence, almost a deathly hush, and he observed the top blinds had been drawn down as if to keep out the light for the afternoon was reasonably bright. His first thought was of illness and he stepped up to the door and knocked, waited briefly and then knocked again.

A hurrying step descended the stairs, unlatched the door and pulled it open. He was face to face with his old lover and he saw both fear and anger residing in her surprised eyes. Her face was more or less healed and her untarnished beauty had returned although she bore the kind of dejection apparent after too little sleep.

She invited him in, apologised for the confusion that reigned and felt like breaking down and weeping on his shoulder. Her eyes, he noticed, were red from recent crying and black shadows flitted around them from sorrow or illness.

"Oh Shirley!" he cried, in concern. "What has happened to bring you so low? You look like death itself!"

At first she was unwilling to tell him, then she tried and finally she broke down completely and leant against him, so overcome was she with grief. He put his arms around her, lifted her up and carried her through to the front room where he laid her gently on the settle. Bidding her compose herself he wiped her eyes with his handkerchief and asked, again, what troubled her so deeply.

"It is Connie, John that I weep so freely for," cried she, dabbing the corners of her eyes with the sleeve of her gown.

"Surely she is well?" asked he.

"No, no, she is not. She is very ill with a severe stagnation of the lung that the doctor cannot seem to allay. He is afraid it will spread to the other lung and it will turn into consumption! She does not seem to get any better, even after all the treatment. And I have no one to turn to for a sympathetic touch, apart from you and you, by rights, now belong to another."

"You will always be my cousin, no matter who I wed," he said, gravely, stroking the fingers of her hand. "Why should I not comfort you? But where is your husband? Why is he not here to help and console?"

She bent her head and sobbed deeply again. Then she shook her head and shivered.

"He is immuring himself in his work as usual and he comes home exhausted, always meaning to be caring but never succeeding. Do you think I want the kind of attention he brings? Were my cuts and bruises of former days not proof of his worthlessness? He is worse than nothing to me and my marriage is the heaviest burden I have ever carried!"

"But, surely as her father, he must care?" cried John, incredulously. "Come, I hate to see you so upset!"

"And because I am only her stepmother, and not truly her mother, I should not be so devastated?" asked she. "John, Damion is nothing to me anymore but Connie...she seems all my heart has to hold onto now. And death wants her more than me and seems set to take her!" She dissolved into tears and leant against him for support. She felt he pulled away from her slightly so she sat up, drying her eyes.

"I should not be troubling you so," she murmured. "You have your own life which is just beginning and is not overshadowed by grief or sorrow but rests in happiness and joy. Oh, John I envy your carefree spirit! Yet not so long ago you lost a loved one so you, too, have suffered. What, if anything will prepare me for this loss, or see me through this tragedy?"

John thought deeply for a moment, gazed down at the rough floor beneath him and then replied slowly,

"Your own good sense and judgement will see you through this Shirley! You will survive because there is no other way. Every day in passing affords a little more relief and strength because time is the greatest healer. Yet, can it really have gone this far and sweet Connie be within grasp of the Grim Reaper?"

"The doctor holds out little hope for her. He expects her suffering to be over in another few days, maybe even today! Oh John – I hate to ask you but will you look in upon her just once more? I am sure it would comfort her as she seems strangely distressed at times when I am there and I do not know what to do to ease this agitation. I know she enjoyed meeting you and she has asked after you several times. I told her of your wedding and she was happy for you, believing that she would be well enough to attend it with us."

John nodded silently and stood up. Shirley dried her eyes hastily and took his hand in her cold fingers, leading him up the familiar stairs to the spare room. As he climbed he became conscious of a peculiar smell that had a kind of sweetness he could not place as belonging to any herb or flower. The fragrance lingered thickly around one particular door which Shirley opened slowly.

"That smell," he mused. "Can you tell me what it is?"

She replied that it was merely some sort of antiseptic spray to guard against infection spreading to the healthy and that the pine oil and spruce it contained would help the invalid to breathe easier.

They went in. An ashen grey face graced the pillows, huge staring eyes that were full of fever and at her cousin's approach Connie tried to pull herself up, could not gain the strength, and rattled up the breath in her throat. John was appalled at the noise and sat down gingerly on the bed, as gently as he could. "Hello Connie dear!"

The invalid attempted a reply, evidently found it impossible to speak and could only murmur a whisper of recognition. Her stepmother bid her lay back, remain silent and merely listen to the words of her cousin without thought of framing any answers. Her bright eyes seemed to take it all in and follow the lips of the speaker but John found it distressing to talk to one so gravely ill. A few minutes later he left, his face dark and drawn, his voice offering no comfort to Shirley who clung to his arm almost desperately. One thing he promised faithfully,

"I shall come again tomorrow," murmured he. "I can give you no false hopes, Shirley; she seems very bad. There is nothing left to do but pray for her and I shall pray for you too – almost as much as I shall pray for her."

"Prayer?" echoed she. "And my sole thought has been to damn God for blighting her and torturing her to death! God? I have not thought of His presence for years so what relief will that afford me? You are more than He is to me and my one salvation is the knowledge that you will come again. Goodbye for now, John!"

He went out sadly into the afternoon, untethered his dozing horse and swung easily into the saddle. For a moment he paused, gazing back at the silent exterior of the cottage as if he dreaded leaving it and the bleeding heart it contained. Then he tightened his lips, wrinkled up his forehead and drove his steed onward.

The longer he meditated upon it the more tragic it became and he could hardly believe one so young was doomed to die. It pained him deeply to dwell on it and he felt shocked by the picture he had beheld. Consequently he was unable to concentrate on work for the rest of the day and evinced considerable relief when five o'clock came and his love arrived for tea.

Yet even in the warm, gentle glow of her presence, which usually filled him with joy and hope, he felt totally uninspired and remained brooding and silent. Cannetta, observing he ate no tea and scarcely swallowed a mouthful of liquid, sat by him after the meal and took his hand in hers.

"John," she whispered. "John, tell me what is the matter?"

"I can't," replied he, stroking her hair absent-mindedly.

"Why not darling?"

He shook his head.

"It does not concern you," he murmured.

"John, if it concerns you then it concerns me," she retorted. "I do not like to see you so silent and withdrawn! Can I help at all?"

Again he shook his head.

"No, that is impossible."

"We should not have any secrets from each other," she breathed. "Come – there is so much pain in your blue eyes and I hate to see it!"

He paused, looked deep into her caring face and at length replied,

"It is my cousin's daughter, Connie, who is very ill, maybe even dying. She is suffering from some kind of consumptive disease of the lungs and is nothing but a child. I saw her today and it haunts me, Cannetta, it haunts me! I cannot forget her bright eyes, so full of pain and her dreadful rattling breath. She is unlikely to last the night, put out like a recently lit candle dying in a powerful breeze! It is wrong, so wrong!" He threw his head into his hands and wept.

Cannetta seemed thoughtful and pulled a strand or two of her hair in contemplation.

At length she spoke.

"John – is this person important to you?"

"Yes, very. The ties of my family are deep and binding. I feel broken at the notion of losing her, even though we have only just met."

Cannetta bit her lips in silent reflection and then stood upright in a single graceful movement. She walked over to the door and opened it, after which she returned to John's side. Kissing his hand she murmured that she was very sorry but she would have to go.

"What? Already?" cried he, waking from his deep reverie. "It is only six o'clock! Oh Cannetta! I am so sorry if I have been withdrawn and distant. Come let us forget about my poor cousin and talk of us! I will try to be gay and charming! Stay a little longer with me, darling, and forgive my mood!"

"I have forgotten that, John, so pray don't worry about it," replied she. "But Mother wishes me to be in early tonight and I am keen to oblige as I realise I shall not be with her for much longer. I will see you tomorrow, John!"

She kissed him lovingly, collected her cloak and left by the back door, skirting the garden with a watchful eye and at length crossing the bridge to the water meadows beyond. In the space of another ten minutes she had gathered in her arms vast quantities of marsh-loving plants, particularly those pertaining to the marshmallow family which she wrapped in her cloak. The sky was beginning to reflect the first dull shades of evening and the glimpse of sunlight from the west weakened slightly. Cannetta held up a moist finger to the evening breeze, established its direction and then ran briskly passed the group of houses, out of Fourcrosses and down the long curving hill towards Ardle.

By the time she had reached her narrow lane all traces of sun had vanished behind a dome of grey cloud which slowly rolled across the sky from east to west. Cannetta paused to gaze up at it, shook her head somewhat angrily and hurried on.

"It must be boiled before daylight leaves the sky!" cried she. It was soon obvious that her destiny was yet again the interior of the tiny shed and that stealth in passing the open windows of the cottage was needed if she was to remain undisturbed. She rounded the bend, traversed the side of the cottage with ease and left her mother sewing peacefully, unconscious of her daughter's close proximity.

In Penlow's cottage all was not so peaceful. As the hours wore on and midnight drew closer Shirley became more and more conscious of the heavy and deathly silence that pervaded the entire dwelling and the frightening fact that she was totally alone. A little after eight her husband had retired to sleep in the main bedroom, a gentle drift of breath assuring Shirley that he was oblivious to the suffering so close to him. She, herself, had never felt so far from slumber. Frenziedly she paced the landing, listening to her husband's small snores and the dreadful rasp of her stepdaughter's breath. Returning to the sickroom she saw Connie was sinking fast and wrung her hands in misery.

"What can I do?" she cried, in desperation. "Oh God – what?" She flung away her bitter tears and felt softened by the image of her cousin as it rose to comfort her. What had been his words to her?

"I will pray," said she aloud.

She knelt down by the bedside, placed her trembling hands together and closed her weeping eyes. Her lips moved fractionally and words, cut deeply by sobs, were eventually framed.

"Dear God," breathed Shirley.

"Thy will be done – take thee the soul of this poor, suffering child to thy bosom. Into thy gentle hands I commit her spirit..." She did not know how to pray and she fell against the side of the bed and wept, covering her face with hands that shook uncontrollably. It seemed the last hope she clung to and the means of relieving the dreadful ache of loss, through prayer, was futile.

About eleven o'clock, as Shirley sat up watching over her dying stepdaughter, a strange change crept over the sleeping girl. Gradually Connie, who had been deeply unconscious, seemed to come to, stir and move despite her rattling breath and sinking frame. Shirley was too exhausted by now to stir from Connie's bedside and she was even too tired to weep any more. She sat, utterly dejected, pulling around her a rough, plaid shawl as the night was chill. The candle flame flickered incessantly, spinning giant shadows on the opposite wall and its colour changed to a deep violet. Shirley watched it in dread.

Suddenly the invalid began to tremble, her whole body vibrating so that Shirley, who was watching this spectacle, flung herself on her knees and clenched the bedclothes between closed fists.

"Oh God!" she cried. "Don't let it end! Don't let it end! No, no, I can't bear it!"

Momentarily the trembling ceased then restarted with greater violence as though some invisible force shook the sleeping girl, waking her from slumber. In another few minutes the eyes of the invalid flickered, opened and she drew a long, sharp breath.

"Mother?" cried she. "Is that you?"

"Yes, dearest, it is," came the eager reply.

"Oh Mother! I thought I was back in my tiny narrow bed at the Hall but, no, no, I am home!"

"Please do not talk, dearest! Try to rest!" called Shirley, coming to the side of the bed.

After another few minutes of observing her stepdaughter, who seemed wide awake and lucid Shirley observed,

"Connie – what has happened? How do you feel?"

"Very weak," affirmed she. "But I am conscious of where I am and who you are, Mother dear. Have you sat with me for days?"

"Don't worry about me, my dear. Just rest and be silent for you need to keep your breath. Sleep now, my love, and close your eyes. I cannot tell what has happened tonight but if I had to describe it I would say a miracle has occurred. I do not care what it is to be sure, all I know is that it has happened and for that I am thankful, very thankful!"

Shirley watched over the girl until sleep came, gentle and insistent, but her breath in that sleep was slow and rhythmic, free of any rattling or rasping. Her forehead was dry and cool, her brow unmarked by any fever and her cheeks seemed to lose their blanched colour. The candle flame still burnt with a violet hue, now blue, now green then back to violet again. Shirley stared deep into its translucent light and felt mesmerised. How could this be? Her lips moved silently with prayers, grateful thanks in her racing mind, and when she had finished she observed Connie was sleeping peacefully, covered her with another blanket and then left the room.

Ere the first signs of dawn appeared in the sky the sound of a horse's galloping hooves broke the silence of the lane by the cottage and before long an impatient rap came upon the front door. The visitor rapped again, in great urgency, and the lady of the house descended the stairs to let the guest in.

"Shirley!" cried the caller in his beautiful Scottish lilt. "I have lain awake all night, worrying about you and Connie and I could wait no longer so I saddled up Grenadier and here I am!" He marked the worn expression of her face and the darkness that haunted her eyes which told of days with no rest to refresh them.

"Oh, John!" she replied. "Miracles are still exist I believe. I am stunned after the events of the night and hardly know what to say to you."

"What do you mean?" he asked his face deeply troubled. "Is she better then?"

"Yes, she is. Lucid and talking…conscious of where she is and what surrounds her. In truth I cannot make it out at all! The doctor came half an hour ago and was as amazed as I! He cannot explain it at all but murmured of wonders beyond his control. He thought to come and lay out a corpse and yet he finds a living, breathing girl getting stronger by the minute! John – the disease is receding and her lungs breathe fully and freely with no trace of pain. She is still weak at present but that is to be expected after the seriousness of her condition. I pray she will make a complete recovery."

"So that frail body I saw yesterday, slipping in and out of life has not succumbed to the sting of death! Quite frankly I am speechless, my dear, but speechless with joy!"

"Yes, I feel the same," replied Shirley. "Come in, John, do! My husband is still asleep and I have not called him so please be quiet but you must see Connie just to tell me I have not imagined it all. I will see that she does not work for many a week but is waited on, hand and foot until she has recovered flesh and become strong and hearty. God has seen fit to spare her, John, so maybe your prayers have worked!"

They ascended the stairs, side by side, her lovely though sad eyes lingering upon him so that he felt their power. He returned her gaze and she, carried away with relief and her blossoming feelings, kissed him tenderly and taking his hand led him forward into the sickroom.

John observed the curtains had been tied back and the top window opened a little to allow a small amount of fresh air to circulate around the room. A smell of lavender, briar rose and balsam lingered around the bed and he saw a couple of bunches of dried herbs hanging from the headboard. The bed itself had been changed and refreshed with clean pillows and a pretty checked coverlet. A low stool stood by the bed and Shirley bade him sit and talk to his cousin while she made tea and woke her sleeping husband.

"They do not expect him at his work till later," she whispered to John, observing Connie was still slumbering. At the noise her eyes opened and she gave a yawn.

"Well, Connie," murmured John, in wonder. "I am overjoyed at the speed of your recovery. Are you in pain anymore? I declare you will be your usual beautiful self by the time my wedding day dawns!"

66

"Thank you for your good wishes. Yes, I am feeling much better, cousin, and your news inspires me to be up and about to greet your new wife. I still feel very weak and somewhat numb but no longer in pain. I felt like a mighty hand had me in its grasp and was shaking me from the stupor I had fallen into. Everything was suffused with a pink light and when I opened my eyes from this trance I beheld a violet candle flame and saw Mother sitting there with tears and love in her eyes. It was a truly magical experience. I feel I have returned from the jaws of death! John, my life has been spared and I am exceedingly grateful." He kissed her thin hands and observed a new light in her eyes and a flush on her hitherto pale cheeks. After a while he saw she was drifting back into sleep and he kissed her once more and left the room.

Shirley met him on the landing. In the next room sounds of Damion dressing were audible so she beckoned him downstairs and when they were in the hallway she cried,

"Well, John, can you explain it to me? Just how the disease has flown so readily? The doctor could not understand it and neither can I unless a miracle has occurred? It seems she has been turned away from the very doors of death. It is just like magic!" cried she, with unintended irony.

He shrugged his shoulders.

"Maybe we are not meant to search too deeply for meanings or explanations," he replied. "Perhaps this time we must accept it without question and just rejoice in its existence. And be grateful, of course," he added. "Shirley, I prayed for you both last night. What time did you perceive this improvement?"

"I also tried to pray," she admitted. "But it has been such a long, long time that I could not find the words and they would not come to me! About half past ten I could see she was sinking fast and I could find no comfort! I waited for the end and wished you were with me. Then, at eleven, as I sat too worn out and exhausted to cry I perceived a violent trembling coming over Connie which I mistook as the rigidity of death. But, no, death did not arrive, just more trembling after a brief silence and this time the shaking seemed to wake Connie and she stirred herself as if returning from sleep instead of sinking into the finality of death. The candle flame burnt violet and then I heard her speak to me...lucidly and calmly without any struggle for breath...I could not believe it! John – that was the turning point and from then on she grew constantly stronger. Her cheek is cool, no fever burns her brow and no infection corrupts her lungs. And, as you say, I shall question it no longer but just accept that miracles do occur and save us from the despot of tragedy!"

CHAPTER 7

Rose Hardy was instinctively an early riser, her hour for her morning stroll being fixed at six o'clock, regardless of season or weather. At that time she would emerge from her cottage door, walk round to the back gate, past Cannetta's shed and take the lonely track which led down to the fields of Ardle. Here she was occasionally seen and enjoyed playing the role of impoverished, lonely widow upon whom the years had been less than kind. Clad in a thick shawl and bonnet in winter and dressed in a lighter coat in summer she wandered for half a mile or so, never turning her eyes to other walkers; indeed, she avoided people in general and rarely replied to any greetings. With her eyes low upon the ground she was seen as being almost as anti-social as her daughter and it was remarked that no wonder Cannetta resorted to witchery when her mother was so aloof. Rose rarely entered the village itself and paid the carrier to deliver her food and other wares, persuading him to leave them in the tiny porch and take the money from there so that she was not disturbed. Yet, in reality, she was not as poor as people surmised as her husband had left her a tidy sum and she spent very little on living expenses. Her stranglehold on her daughter had only exacerbated Cannetta's madness and left the girl no hope for a fulfilling future. Thus Cannetta sought to escape from her mother's clutches, even though these desires resulted in considerable guilt and heartache.

On this particular morning, which had already seen a miracle performed in its early hours, Rose unchained her drowsy daughter, led her into the girl's actual bedroom and put her to bed, then left for her walk. It was somewhat darker on this day than usual as the month of August was almost spent and the sun rose slightly later although Fern Cottage was always the first in the district to receive the early light. In the evening it was also the first to take on the hues of night and become swallowed up in the shades of dusk.

As Rose passed the tiny shed she was curious to see a number of objects reclining drunkenly in the grass that proved, upon inspection, to be a pile of stripped woody stems, a huge earthenware container and a large, jewel-encrusted knife whose blade was heavily stained. Besides this Rose could see the ashen remains of a fire, the broken statue of a cross and a dark trail of liquid that had stained a great many of the stones around there with its deep, red hue. The container still contained a quantity of the liquid which was of the consistency of treacle but smelt much less pleasant, several flower heads remaining infused in its volume. The whole effect was rather grotesque and the woman hurried by after peering into the jar's depths; perhaps she would not have looked had she known the deep red hue was that of blood from the veins of a human. She went through the far gate and turned upon the familiar track.

A few harvesters were already in the fields, whistling merrily as they tidied the meadows after the grain had been gleaned and leaving them ready for the onset of autumn and then winter's whiteness. The tall grasses by the track's side and the contours of the path generally hid the woman and she continued her walk with no interruption.

Presently, however, she heard the sharp rattle of hooves approaching her from the opposite direction and, in fear as to who it could be, Rose pressed herself into the bank and waited. Soon a deep voice assailed her and steadied the frisky horse; the accent she recognised as being that of her future son-in-law so her anxiety was allayed and she stepped onto the path once more. That she thought him foolhardy and his love doomed to disappointment she still believed but what could she do in the face of such devotion?

"Good morning, Mrs Hardy," cried he, raising his hat and controlling the dancing equine at the same time. "'Tis almost like coming from darkness into light for the rest of Ardle is terribly black by comparison to these skies here. The sun hits you earlier!"

She acknowledged that it did.

"You are about early, sir!" returned Rose. "My daughter still sleeps if you are craving her company?"

"No, no," returned he, shaking his head. "I have been visiting my sick cousin who we had almost committed to eternity but, lo, miracles do transpire and from the gaping jaws of death she has returned and is recovering nicely. Now I am required to attend a different invalid in the shape of a bovine on Mr Taylor's farm, far less pleasant but my bread and butter nevertheless. Good day to you, Mrs Hardy!" He let out the rein slightly, allowed the horse to increase his pace and scarcely moved in the old dark leather saddle.

At about this time Cannetta was waking up, conscious of a throbbing pain in her left arm from where she had extracted about a pint of blood last night. The wound was healing but her arm felt stiff and sore and the knife had left bruises as well as cuts. She felt weak and slightly dizzy due to the complexity of the ritual she had performed. The spell had taken not only her life blood but a great deal of nervous and physical energy which she felt amounted to her magical power. In return she had received energy from the invalid, the sick corrupted energy of disease, which she had diluted in her shed blood. Never before had she attempted the restoration of a dying body - and succeeded.

The spells in Cannetta's life had begun, on a very small scale, concerning the perfecting of her beauty or the diminishing of blemishes and had moved, very quickly, to the curing of sick creatures of the fields shot and left for dead by poachers or gamekeepers. Of late she had enchanted her loved one, put an idle curse on one or two farmers who she knew were ill-treating their stock and now, for the first time, she had restored life to the dying by draining away bad blood in exchange for her own. Cannetta rarely felt it necessary to curse her fellow humans, her attitude being that as long as they left her alone she was content to ignore them and let them get on with their own lives. Her mother she felt a mingled regard of love and hate for, which tortured her at times, and the ghost of her suicidal father kept the fear alive in her mind. She could still remember finding him hanging, cold and lifeless, from the oak tree by the farm gate where she had wandered at the tender age of twelve. Despite her horror, her mind had wondered at the strange physical distortions his body had gone through when he was cut down and the stone-like grimacing of his features as he lay in his coffin. She had been made to kiss him and the putrid stench of death had filled her nostrils for many months, leading to nightmares and finally the deepening insanity that enveloped her at night. The mother believed the daughter had inherited her father's madness.

Soon Cannetta heard the heavy tread of her mother's feet upon the stairs so she opened her eyes fully and stretched her aching body.

"Cannetta!" called the widow as she climbed the last few stairs. "Cannetta! Have you risen yet?"

"No!" called the daughter. "Mother – I do not feel well today. I feel drained and tired."

Mrs Hardy entered the bedroom and gazed at her daughter anxiously. The girl was very pale and her pulse, when felt, was alternately fast and slow.

"I have just seen John," Rose informed her daughter. "He was full of joy at the miraculous healing of his cousin who was destined only for certain death. Well, Cannetta, there is a considerable mess by your little hut this morning! There is a strange red liquid there that looks like blood mixed with God knows what. Do you know anything about this?"

"No," replied Cannetta, turning her face to the wall. "Mother you had best leave me to rest for I shan't be up this morning!"

"Dear, dear and you normally so strict with locking your shed! Who has got in to ransack it I wonder? I heard nothing last night, did you?"

"No, but you know how the village people gossip about me. They may have damaged my hut and thrown the contents around. I will clear up later when I feel better, Mother."

Rose left the room with considerable suspicion that the mess was of Cannetta's own making and it pertained to some weird spell the girl had been performing. She had seen the scabbing wound on her daughter's arm which she knew meant the girl had been blood-letting and the weakness definitely accounted for it. There was some link with John's cousin too but Rose did not want to know what rituals her daughter had been invoking so she said nothing more and tried to dismiss it from her mind. It only reminded her that Cannetta's illness was getting worse.

The rest of the day passed away peacefully and by the evening Cannetta had recovered enough strength to rise. She disposed of the remnants of her spell secretly and revelled in her success despite her weakness. The long month of August was ushered out with grey skies and rain to make way for the colder month of September. By now the workers were rising in darkness, breakfasting in gloom and going afield as the red skies of the season greeted the advent of dawn. Rain still fell in profusion and darker evenings sent the cottagers scurrying to their store cupboards for candles whilst larger fires were lit to warm the colder nights. Harvest supper came and went with the traditional feast; the church was decorated with the splendour and plenty of the season and the children tied sheaves to the pews as they rejoiced in the full bellies that the celebration brought.

John found himself increasingly busy in his job so he had very little spare time but every minute he set aside for his Cannetta, therefore he was a rare visitor at his cousin's. He gleaned news of Connie's health and felt relieved that she continued to get stronger with no relapse of condition although her parents kept her at home and cosseted her. He knew that Shirley would be the one doing the cosseting and that Connie's father would be the one immersing himself in his work to forget the sad state of his marriage.

The night before the wedding arrived; a cold Friday evening within the second week of September which had, so far, proved to be a tempestuous month of wind and frost. John left his dwelling at Fourcrosses a little before the hour of five and travelled on foot to the cottages of Ardle. Once there he directed his steps into a familiar path and knocked upon a door stained the colour of ripe cherries. It was the last time, he reflected, he would walk down this lane as a single man. Tomorrow would see a Mrs Straeton created - the very picture of wedded bliss he had been dreaming of for a long time.

After a few minutes there was still no answer to his knock, though he repeated it louder, and concluding all were out he was about to withdraw when the sweet echo of singing drifted to him from the direction of the garden. He listened for a moment, recognised the familiar tune and rounded the side of the house in time to see his cousin coming through the hives with arms full of linen on her way to the back door. And as she went she sung sweetly -
"I lost my love and I care not,
I lost my love and I care not,
I'll soon have another that's better than 'tother,
I lost my love and I care not."

He stopped to mark the beauty of her voice and pondered if the song were really a reference to him and how she now felt about the two of them. She had not seen him so he was able to wait for the back door to shut before returning to knock again on the front.

After a few seconds she answered, seemed surprised to see him and invited him in with her usual warmth and politeness.
"My husband is still at work, my daughter gone to the Hall to collect more of her belongings seeing as she will reside here a little longer. Was it her you wished to see or Damion?" asked she, with a newly-found coolness.

"Please do not talk to me like that, Shirley. You were warm when you saw me and now you are frosty but it does not suit you. Besides you know there is only one person I have come here to see and that is YOU!"

"Then I wish you wouldn't!" she burst out, her blue eyes welling up with tears. "You are as good as married and I already have a husband!"

"And have you forgiven Damion and taken him back in your bed then?" he asked.

She shook her head.

"I can never do that," she replied.

"Then why do I feel you are spurning me?"

"Oh John – you know I could never do that! Have I not suffered enough for your sake already?"

"Then why this coolness now, Shirley?"

"John, I am trying to get over you as you suggested after...our indiscretion. What else can I do? And then just when I believe I am succeeding you walk in and scatter my efforts like dust in the wind!"

"But you would have seen me tomorrow!" he cried.

"Yes, yes, with another woman on your arm. A beautiful, desirable one who you love and wish to marry! Oh, John, I should not be alone with you – you have heard what sort of woman I am!"

"You are a very mesmerising woman," he said with complete honesty.

She smiled and turned to look at him, having previously tried to keep her eyes from his face.

"And that has finished it completely. Any pretensions that I was over you are now shattered into a thousand pieces! You are a constant temptation, John Straeton, and you will be till the day I die. Do not blame me for my feelings since you ignite them by your flattery and Gaelic charms!"

They entered the parlour together and sat side by side on the settle.

"It seems no time at all since you came here and yet it must be several weeks!" she murmured, feeling a little awkward by his close proximity.

He acknowledged that it was.

"And yet, Shirley, it is the last time I shall sit here as a free man talking to you..."

"Who is not a free woman," she interjected.

There was a moment's silence then he asked, in a hurt tone,

"And did you really mean to forget me and reject your only cousin, even if the kinship has been forged by an imprudent marriage?"

"In truth I did – at least at first," she admitted. "I knew it was best as we both have other mates. But, sadly, I could as soon as forget you as I could forget to breathe. Perhaps I could have succeeded a day longer if you had not called!"

He smiled understandingly.

"And did the almost attained victory bring you any pleasure or satisfaction, cousin?"

"No, it only brought a twisted kind of pain and a certainty that I was doing the right thing but...well...it is over now with a few words from you and one glimpse of your face! Come, talk of it no more, but tell me if you are ready to receive your wife on the morrow?"

"I am," he replied. "But sadly Cannetta has been ill with the same symptoms that Connie had but milder and more transient. They passed in a couple of days and her strength returned. We shall not see each other tonight and will not touch again until we hold hands and are joined as man and wife in the church. You will come won't you?"

She affirmed she would and told him Damion planned to attend as well as her stepdaughter.

"It is very strange," he mused. "But I feel very restless tonight and from tomorrow I am sure that my life will change radically..."

"It will certainly be very different," she agreed.

"Yes, I know it will take some adjusting to even though my love for Cannetta grows constantly. What thoughts did you have the night before your wedding, Shirley?"

She smiled at the memory and replied,

"Lots of vain hopes lived in my mind that night, mainly the belief that I would be leaving a life of poverty for one of graceful ease and money! Instead I left home for... this which was, in many ways, worse! Oh John, it is a terrible thing when all your hopes and dreams crash around you and you are left with paper and ashes! I would love to walk out of here tomorrow and throw off the tattered robe of my marriage but it is not possible! I am not the person you should be talking to about wedded bliss so maybe I will remain silent."

Her words deeply moved John and flung him into a reverie which was interrupted only by the striking of the mantel piece clock.

"Well, Shirley," he declared, after perceiving the time. "I must go!"

"What? Already?" exclaimed she, rising with him so their bodies brushed together.

"Yes, I am afraid so. Please be at the church by half past ten and pray for fine weather."

"I will," murmured she. "Well, John, your last few hours as a single man fall upon you. The next time we talk you will be endowed with the responsibilities of a wife and perhaps later a family. The single phase of your life is over and another approaches. Do you not feel that?"

"Aye but it does not stop the fact that you do not approve of my choice of mate does it?"

Her eyes belied her words but she swallowed hard and replied staunchly,
"I approve."

She did not add that she would dislike anyone that he wed because it meant she was replaced in his heart and that by being married he was removed a little further from her reach. And, of course, as a single man there was still the hope that if she left Damion she could be with him. But she wished him luck, kissed him as coolly as she could and then saw him out with good wishes for the morrow.

When Connie came in about twenty minutes later with a small bundle of clothes under her arm Shirley, who had not expected her to be back so soon, jumped up guiltily from the settle and wiped her eyes. Connie came through to the parlour, announcing that she had removed all her belongings from the Hall and that she had told Mrs Newbury she would return to work in three weeks' time.

Shirley did not look at the girl but gazed down and replied with a nod. Connie could see the traces of tears on her stepmother's face and felt sorry for her.

"Are you still very unhappy, Mother?" she asked. "It seems months since I have seen you cry so much and so frequently! Can you not tell me what the matter is? Is it my father; has he been cruel to you again?"

"No, no," replied Shirley. "It is nothing, Connie, nothing at all. John called a few minutes ago to say we must be at the church by half past ten tomorrow."

"Ah!" murmured her stepdaughter perceptively. "Then that is it!"

Previously such accusations would have sent Shirley into a defensive rage but her heart inclined more to sadness concerning John so she tried to smile and taking her stepdaughter's hand she confessed,

"Am I really so very wicked, Connie, to love another man who can never be my husband? Moreover a man younger than me and one who is taking a wife tomorrow! And worst of all a man who is a blood relation of my own husband!" She hid her face in the folds of her voluminous gown and sobbed, Connie stroking her hair and trying to soothe her.

At length Shirley raised her wet face, sat back on the settle and dried her eyes.

"Oh, Connie, you must laugh at me and feel our roles are reserved with you the older, wiser mother and me the young foolish girl! How you must despise me for my weakness!"

"Despise you? Oh, no, Mother! How can I?" acknowledged the girl softly. "My needs and wants in life are very different from yours and duty bounds me in all my thoughts. I have never entertained romance or been driven to flights of fancy. My feet are very firmly planted on the ground and will remain there all of my life I am certain!"

"Then seeing you are so wise and sensible what is your advice to me in my predicament? Whatever it is – however harsh – I shall try to take it!"

"Mother, I appreciate your feelings cannot be turned off and on and furthermore we cannot help who we fall in love with! I believe it is partially Father's fault as if he had been a better husband then you would not have an open heart ready for romance with any decent man you come to know. I am not condemning you or calling you a philanderer but you have fallen in and out of love many times have you not?"

Shirley sighed.

"Before I met your father I had several romantic dalliances and one after we were wed, when I realised my mistake in taking Damion as a husband but since then I have vowed to be good and stray no more! And I kept to it until.....that man crossed my path! Somehow with him I feel totally different and my heart is pulled constantly in his direction. I have tried and tried to stop it," here she put her hand on the offending organ, "but it defies me and only pours out more love in response to my attempt to stifle it!"

She rose and began walking around the room in a state of agitation, trying to calm her racing mind and emotions.

"Oh, what can I do?" she cried, wringing her hands. "It seems everywhere I turn...there he is..."

"You must forget him," said her advisor gently.

Shirley stopped in her perambulations and turned to her stepdaughter.

"Connie, you are young and innocent. You do not know what you ask! I have never felt like this before!"

"You must think no more about him except as a married man who is out of your reach."

"But, Connie, he is always in my mind and I cannot get him out. Waking and sleeping he appears to me and my mind does not rest..."

"You must come to regard him entirely as a relation."

Shirley nodded dumbly whilst the tears ran down her cheeks in profusion.

"Yes," she ventured at last. "Yes, I know you are right. But you will say nothing to anyone of the temptation that I strife to resist, will you Con?"

"What has passed between us, Mother, stays between us," replied Connie, earnestly.

There was a long silence broken finally by the chiming of the half hour by the clock, as though it alone remained dedicated to duty whilst all around it neglected their tasks. The noise seemed to rouse Shirley and she perceived it was getting darker and that her husband would be home shortly. Accordingly she set about preparing the evening meal aided by Connie who reproached herself for being too harsh with her flighty stepmother. Whilst they chopped vegetables for the meal Connie put an arm round her parent's shoulders and whispered fondly,

"Mother, if your feelings are true and you are prepared to wait and be constant then all hope is not lost. Remember that in your hour of despair. Everything comes to he who waits."

Cannetta spent her last night as a spinster at Fern Cottage clearing out her belongings and packing clothes and valuables. In reality she possessed precious little and it did not take a full evening to gather up and secure her few chattels. Rose helped her at first but Cannetta's mind was wandering and she became very sharp with her interfering mother so Rose descended and finished altering the white silk gown which had proved a little too full for

Cannetta's lithe form. Kindling a candle Rose pondered on future nights when she would sit here alone and the prison upstairs would remain cold and empty. She bent to her needle again and finished the small seams with near perfection.

A few minutes later the girl came downstairs, took a seat opposite her parent and watched her mother tidying over her work. Rose looked up.

"'Tis all but finished!" she cried, holding up the gown for Cannetta's approval.

The daughter nodded and kept her eyes on the white splendour of the dress. "You would curtail this, would you not, if you could, Mother?"

"Yes, Cannetta, and you know why," replied Rose staring at her daughter.

"Do you not think I have a right to some sort of happiness?"

"Yes but not at the sacrifice of another's sanity!"

"Mother!" cried the girl, in horror. "You sound deeply pessimistic about my union! Is my husband not a fine man? He is HE that was forecast to come and take me away from this drudgery of an existence! Do you not perceive that destiny is fulfilled and it will all be smooth and even from now on because it is meant to be?"

"Your husband rests in ignorance of your true character, Cannetta, but when he endures the mad episodes that come over you at times he will throw you off like an ill-fitting shoe!"

"He will endure my indiscretions at times, Mother, because he loves me and that conquers all!"

"Do not be too sure on that, daughter. I loved your father when I first met him but did I not endure years and years of his insane behaviour until finally he ended it on a tree? Is that what you will come to, Cannetta – a corpse, a body hanging from a branch?"

The girl shivered violently.

"You may indeed achieve your happiness," the mother continued," but at what price to your husband's health? Do not forget that!"

"Be silent!" cried Cannetta, becoming angry at Rose's words. "You are rid of me tomorrow – is that not soon enough? And I am free from your cruelty! Yes, I rue leaving this house. I think a part of me shall always wander round these rooms but I go to a better life. Since you have finished, Mother, let me have the gown."

Rose folded the dress up with infinite care.

"No," she returned, firmly. "You shall have it in the morning as tonight you may harm it. Do not try to snatch it! Cannetta, it grows late! See it is nearly eleven! How he will manage you tomorrow night I do not know! I pray he is strong both mentally and physically but your behaviour may make him cruel after a while as I have had to be to preserve my life!"

She went to the door followed by the girl who growled and tried to jump high enough to reach the gown but Rose was used to her ways and evaded her completely. She locked the dress away and hid the key in the folds of her gown.

"Now, now, Cannetta!" cried she as the tempestuous girl remained growling, standing transfixed at the bottom of the stairs. "Now, Cannetta, for the last time in this house, are you coming?" At first there was no response. The mother repeated her request and, at last, after much coaxing, the girl ascended the stairs on all fours, snarling like a dog and nipping her parent's ankles. The arras was drawn back, the key applied and for the final time Cannetta allowed herself to be chained, locked up and humiliated. Her groans rang out with the nightly chiming of the hour and then, at last, sleep overtook her and silence reigned.

A gentle, somewhat muffled sound of bells tested the fresh, morning air, increased in power and informed the people of Ardle that a ceremony was about to commence. The tiny church was almost empty, the bride's side of the building a line of deserted pews save for where a lone figure drooped, a dejected woman who kept her eyes on her folded hands and bathed in an air of sorrow. On the other side four or five small groups sat which amounted to the entire Penlow family, two well-wishing farmers, an elderly couple who liked to attend every church ceremony and lastly, the frail form of a small boy.

The little collection at the altar seemed strangely joyless for a wedding and even the vicar, as he conducted the ceremony, paused dangerously long between his words as if he expected someone to curtail the marriage and halt the proceedings. He fixed his eyes on the tall, elegant woman who stood before him but she did not return his gaze, preferring instead to look at her bouquet which she held in trembling hands. Her soon-to-be husband seemed more at ease but even he picked up the doubt and incredulity of the vicar's tones and his spirit felt awed by his unfamiliar surroundings, his attention resting on the gleam of copper plate that caught the late summer sun in refulgence. When addressed he answered firmly in a low, strong voice but there was a grave and serious edge to it although the lilt of his Scottish accent diminished it slightly. His wife-to-be beside him answered in mere whispers and most of the listeners heard nothing of her, tapped the people in front of them to find out if she had declined the vows and found she had uttered them perfectly.

Cannetta's dress had a full, long skirt topped by a tight lace bodice trimmed with silken ribbons which also took precedence in her train. Her blonde hair was curled and had been brushed till it gleamed like spun gold. It fell in profusion to her waist and the yellow splendour was only broken by a spray of red leaves which were weaved into the ends of her tresses. On her head she carried a circular halo of spun lace from which her veil fell, gathered at the sides but full in front. Her long, thin fingers were encased in white gloves that were considerably too small for her lengthy digits and her sharp nails had cut the ends of the material already. Her feet were invisible but they bore silver slippers under her full dress which rustled slightly in the breeze from the partially open door. She, herself, never moved and her face, under the veil, was emotionless and drawn as she felt a strong unease in the present strange company. In many ways she was a lost soul thrown into a pit full of unpredictable devils who she knew stared at her and imagined many things. She felt exposed and vulnerable to their curiosity.

John did not suffer such discord of feelings but he felt the grave importance of the vows which weighed heavily upon him as he uttered his responses. He was conscious of the family he loved behind him and their regard flowed around him as he stood, tall and erect by his silent partner. He knew this was killing Cannetta but he could not protect her from the speculation of the guests. Only time would do that when he proved the rumours to be untrue as the Cannetta he knew came into existence as a loyal and faithful wife. In some ways he felt deeply happy and at peace but the element of fear remained to spoil the experience.

The service ended, the vicar pronounced them man and wife and as he turned to kiss Cannetta his eyes caught Shirley's wistful gaze and he shivered. Cannetta's lips were like ice and her hands, despite the gloves, were cold and lifeless as he grasped them. They walked down the aisle and as he passed the Penlow family he saw the tears rising up in Shirley's eyes. As they brimmed over Shirley dropped her hymn book and knelt to retrieve it, glad she could take her eyes off the couple but especially John, who mesmerised her.

Outside John shook hands with a few well-wishers, noticed that his wife totally ignored these people even though their good wishes included her, and knew she would have backed off instantly had he not had hold of her hand firmly. He announced that anyone who wished could accompany then back to his dwelling where a simple spread had been laid out with a few drinks in honour of their union. Eventually he found himself with only his new mother-in-law, Connie and Shirley surrounding him, the rest having drifted away as no scandal presented itself.

"Well!" cried the bridegroom, with a determined effort to be cheerful although his heart sank within him. "Will you three not join us to celebrate in our festivities? My wife and I shall be delighted to receive you I know!" His wife, however, said nothing but remained motionless on his arm, her face turned away from the little group.

They walked slowly and somewhat solemnly from the churchyard and ascended the incline known locally as Longman's Length, Shirley and Connie walking side by side dressed in matching turquoise and far behind them Rose tottered, as though in a trance. The wedded couple strode off a few paces ahead of all but he, annoyed by Cannetta's silence and aloofness with his family, chose not to look at her but marked the passing scenery instead. The sun was shining in her noontide glory, infusing the remaining sheaves of corn with a tantalising gold and the breeze whispered to the stalks of winter's advent and the return of cold. Further on the cropped stubble became a patchwork of squares of rich brown clod across which pairs of horses were working with encouraging shouts from the drivers.

Cannetta, who was quick to notice her husband's apparent absorption in every fold of the scenery except her face, asked him candidly,

"Of what are you thinking, John, and what worries furrow your forehead? Are we not man and wife and as such joined together in a new life that stretches away from us?"

"It is nothing, angel," he replied. "Just a faded hope and an unrealistic dream – that is all!"

"Ah! You expected there to be a greater turnout at the church!" guessed she, cleverly.

"Yes, I can't deny that I did but the most important person of all was there and that, of course, is yourself!"

She smiled sweetly at this and squeezed his arm, likewise turning her head to the scenery.

"It is beautiful, is it not?" she returned. "I think at times that I shall never look upon anything else finer. Oh John! I should hate to leave here!"

"Ah! But you have not seen Scotland," enthused he. "Nothing is as fine as a Scottish glen, my bonny lass, with the sun rising in glory or else sinking down behind the hills! When you have seen Scotland you have lived!"

"You sound clamorous to be back," she observed, somewhat crestfallen.

"Ah! Who can tell? Scotland is deep in my blood and the wanderlust strikes me at times, deep in the south as I reside. Yes, I am tolerably settled here at present!"

"So you do not want to return to the land of your birth?"

"Nay – och – well you can never be sure but I am very content to stay at present!"

They turned into the row of houses that was Fourcrosses, waited for their guests who had fallen somewhat behind and then marched up to the house, John carrying his bride over the threshold as was the custom.

During the celebrations it became painfully obvious that Mrs Straeton spoke to no one and avoided the eyes of her guests and, at last, when she could take no more she excused herself to John and left the room. Shirley felt rather embarrassed and deemed it was time they left. She motioned to her stepdaughter to wait for her and then sought her old lover for a quick word.

"Well, John," murmured she quietly, so that Connie and Mrs Hardy did not hear. "I toast your health and happiness!" She drank the last of her wine and put the glass down on the nearby table. He, likewise, drained his whisky tumbler and gave thanks for the pleasure of her company.

"Oh John," she whispered. "You knew I would have come whatever has passed between us."

He nodded thoughtfully and she, perceiving he was in no mood to talk, called to Connie and left without a backward glance at her cousin.

Once they were outside Connie took her stepmother's arm and they walked slowly home, side by side.

"Well, daughter," began Shirley. "I have seen it through and I am glad I came and overall I feel impassive and calm."

"Yes," replied the younger woman. "He is married now and legally joined to his love. You must see him no more on his own. He is a husband and has the responsibilities of a wife."

"Yes," whispered Shirley, a slow tear drop descending her pale cheek.

"Come!" cried Connie, shaking her stepmother's arm. "It is for the best, Mother!"

They passed the last houses of Fourcrosses and descended the long sloping road back to Ardle.

A few minutes later Rose Hardy also excused herself and left just as Cannetta returned to her husband's side. John saw her out, attempted to kiss her as his mother-in-law and was cut short by her manner as she turned away.

"Mr Straeton – I wish you joy of Cannetta. I have struggled to control her for several years and have not succeeded so now it is up to you. Perhaps you can achieve things with love that I could not! I wish you luck. You will certainly need it!" And the tall houses that surrounded his dwelling swallowed her up.

He went back to his love who, he observed, was greatly agitated so that she wandered restlessly round the room snatching things up and almost throwing them down as though they did not prove to be what she was searching for. At length he turned towards her, called her name and asked,

"Why did you feel it was necessary to leave the room when our guests were here? I would remind you, Cannetta, that they were OUR guests! Could you not have stayed or were you suddenly ill?"

She stopped in her tracks and murmured simply,

"No."

"What does that mean, Cannetta?" he asked.

At this she began to sob and shake.

"Oh John, John, I can't help it, I can't! I am frightened, so frightened of people I don't know. And I have been thinking that maybe you should not have wed me after all as you have a family. Yes, yes, that is what makes me cry so!"

At her tears and lamentations he melted instantly, took her in his arms and murmured,

"No, no, darling, do not say such things. Think no more of it. Yet your mother was greatly troubled by something."

"She was – I own it!" wept his wife. "But she was totally against the union. She did not want me to leave her. Do not trouble her with questions, John, but leave her as she is."

"Yes, yes," he replied vaguely.

"And everything is all right now between us?" she begged anxiously.

"Yes, of course, my darling. Let no more be said and dry your eyes. How terrible that you should cry on your wedding day!"

He observed her fearful agitation passed off a little and the remainder of the day unfolded peacefully but towards evening, when a squally shower called them home early from their walk, he noticed a feverish excitement rising in his wife which he could not attribute to any circumstances she had encountered. Later still, after nightfall, she became more and more distressed, her beautiful eyes widening dramatically and shadows flitting over her face so she turned constantly from light to dark. When he did manage to persuade her to come and sit by him she was stiff and taut and when he took her in his arms she did not move or show any sign she recognised him. He wondered if she was afraid of him as every limb seemed ready to spring on command and her breath came in gasps. When he spoke to his wife her lips twitched with words too low for him to hear. He perceived her eyes were glazed and although she looked upon him she did not see his face. At length he put it down to over-excitement and tried to forget about it.

But later, as they lay in bed together, he found something wild and desperate in her lovemaking and the way she clung to him. There was an animal-like fierceness in her caresses and she cut him with her nails and only laughed when he rebuked her. Her mouth frequently bit him too and he was glad when, exhausted and replete, she eventually slept with deep groans and murmurs. He lay there watching her by moonlight, filled with horror that this was the woman he had married and, for him, bemusement and shock kept sleep away for the remainder of the night.

CHAPTER 8

The next morning dawned fair. Cannetta unaccountably woke early, gazed at her husband with mingled love and respect and remembered nothing of her behaviour of last night. She was unaware that John was feigning sleep as he was too confused to face her until he had sorted his feelings out regarding what had occurred. As yet he could make no sense of it all. To Cannetta last night had brought the consummation of her marriage and the sealing of a union she regarded would last for the rest of their lives. Feeling happy and content she kissed her sleeping husband, slid out of bed silently and moved to the window.

A profusion of golden light was touching the dullness of the water meadows, driving out darkness and illuminating the stubble fields beyond with dancing yellow sunbeams. The higher ground to the front of the house was already radiant, occasional shadows skimming across the wet grass. Cannetta dressed, left the room and descended the twisting stairway, unlatching the back door with stealthy fingers. Outside the dark forms of swallows swept the eaves in constant flight, chattering as they fed on the wing and planned their vast migration. Further up in the heavens the last swifts screamed and darted but they would be on their way before the swallows gathered in the treetops.

Conscious of her new husband Cannetta did not go far but wandered out to the borders of Stackhouses where the lanes of Ardle began. She picked a large, fragrant bunch of windflowers, ragged robin and heart's ease that grew in profusion by the cart tracks. The sharp smell of crushed stalks brought back memories of collecting plants with her father and how the two of them had spied on the minutiae of life in the hedgerows and fields. Then, later after his death, she remembered going alone as a weeping child receiving little or no comfort from her mother. Did this parent really grieve when her father killed himself? She could not recall any weeping or sadness but more a sense of relief and a new enthusiasm for life. Her favourite haunts were still those that her father had showed her and they had changed but little since he walked them with her. She shed a tear at the loss of the man and turned back to Fourcrosses.

The sun had risen a great deal higher than when she first came out and anxious that John might be abroad and searching for her she ran the last quarter of a mile to arrive breathless and laughing. She danced into the house, called his name, perceived he was not yet downstairs and began to lay up the table for their breakfast. Cannetta was reasonably skilled in the kitchen having looked after her mother for a short while in her childhood when Rose was ill and her culinary knowledge, though not vast, was certainly adequate for a husband. She kindled up a fire, set the kettle upon it and mixed up some simple cakes from flour, butter, eggs and milk which she set upon the large griddle. Presently she heard John descending with many a stifled yawn and looked up from her flower arranging as he entered the room.

"Why, darling," she cried in amazement, coming forward to kiss him. "You seem very tired. Is it possible you slept badly?"

"I did not sleep…well," murmured he, surprised at her spontaneity and innocent tone.

She kissed him very gently in a way that he could not doubt her deep affection for him.

"Come, dismiss those clouds from your brow!" laughed Cannetta, taking his hand. "There, I can make you smile again!" as John tried to brighten his mood and look happy. But confusion still remained in his mind. This beautiful, radiant creature before him was so far removed from the biting, snarling, clutching harpy of last night as to render them two completely different women.

At her urgings he sat down at the breakfast table, spread his napkin and waited, she flitting over him like some bright, captivating butterfly. With every word she uttered and every look she gave it was obvious last night was totally forgotten by his wife and she was now the angelic and loving Cannetta that he had been mesmerised by.

"Does anything ail you, my darling?" asked she when she had served the cooked dough cakes and he still never moved.

"No, my love, what could trouble me so soon into our marriage?" cried he, staring into her eyes and seeing nothing there that clouded their purity.

"Then you must eat up before I defeat your paltry appetite and clear the table!" she enthused. "Do you not like the wonderful flowers that grace our table?"

"Yes, darling," he replied, smelling the sweet perfume of the windflowers that cascaded from their vase near to him. "I fancy I have seen their colour before. Where did you find them?"

"Ah," returned his wife. "I was abroad very early before you were awake and I journeyed to the borders of Ardle and found them growing in the lanes there. It was the same lanes that I traversed with Father many years ago."

"You have lost him since then?" asked he, interested in her history.

"Yes, many summers ago," sighed she.

"It is a loss you find hard to bear?"

"I did once. Now the happy life I find myself leading with you eclipses such pain."

John watched her closely.

"How did he come to die?" he enquired, never taking his eyes off her face.

Cannetta could not meet his gaze and cast her orbs downwards to her plate. Her face rouged slightly and she turned her food round and round in her anguish. After a while she replied in a confused voice,

"It is not important. It does not matter...now." She poured her husband more coffee with a shaky hand but her face cleared.

"No," he mused. "Time heals the most gaping wounds and only leaves the smallest of scars. The scabs of past battles become so thick and impervious that not even the strongest passions can penetrate them!"

"Ah, then you have suffered, too," murmured she, all sympathy and concern, glad to turn the subject away from her father's death.

And her husband could only wonder on her genuine love and devotion to him so that the snarling woman of last night lost her power and slipped into oblivion...

In the afternoon John was obliged to go out and attend a sick calf at Thurlow Farm which was some three miles distant from Fourcrosses. He left his beautiful bride with deep regret but she encouraged him to go, realising that an animal was in need of his professional skills and he would return to her within an hour or more and gladden her with the news that his hands had bought healing to a suffering soul. John saddled his black gelding ready for the journey, clattered past the house and waved to Cannetta who held up the window sash in order to salute him and blow kisses. He noticed the soft light of love in her eyes and reproached himself for ever having had an ugly thought about her. Promising to be back as soon as he could he gave his horse his head and cantered off to his patient.

Passing through the lanes of Ardle and taking the twisty hill path to Thurlow, which was little more than a hamlet, he overtook a female form that came forward from the hedge, raised her hand and bid him stop.

He did so with difficulty as the horse had other ideas but when he observed the woman was Cannetta's mother he flung himself from his steed and approached her.

"Mrs Hardy," began he.

She gave a small bow and begged leave for interrupting his journey. He brushed her words aside instantly.

"I am off to Thurlow Farm, ma'am but can surely spare you a minute's conversation seeing as you are my relation now."

Rose seemed very confused and embarrassed by his jovial tone. She remained silent and the growing breeze blew some of her shyness away, ruffling up the gelding's black mane and flapping the edges of her cloak in a noisy dance.

At length Rose spoke.

"I am sorry, John," she said at last. "I have nothing to ask you as such. I stopped you only on a whim." She did not say she had called to him because she thought he was fleeing from one of her daughter's insane moods.

"You wish to know if Cannetta is well?" he asked gently, noticing how hesitantly his mother-in-law spoke to him and how she averted her eyes from his person.

"Yes, of course," Rose returned, glad he had spoken and moved the situation on from her embarrassing disclosure. "And you, too, now we are related by marriage. I trust you are happy and well?"

He smiled at this. "We are both in very high spirits and our health, likewise, is good today, thank you. But you need not take my word for it; you know you are always welcome at our house."

She murmured she was grateful for his kindness and generosity but she did not deem it necessary to visit as she did not want to trouble them so soon into their marriage.

"It is no trouble at all!" denied he. "Faith - come as you wish but if I can help you no further I shall go on and complete my call."

She bowed her head in acknowledgement of this and wished him good day.

"Goodbye," replied he, springing into the saddle whereupon the restless horse bore him away at a considerable speed.

The woman continued in her walk with a grave shake of her head and a troubled mind. Would he still be so happy in a few weeks when Cannetta's condition was revealed? She was besieged by doubts that swarmed around her like black crows, restless, predatory, forbidding...She forged on.

"There, there, Mr Haverly 'tis done and I'll wager a ton of oats that you'll not find further cause for alarm. 'Twas a bad case of the scour but he's steady now."

The dark-haired farmer he addressed just scowled and replied,

"Well, most days I'll not have anything to do with any horse-leeching doctors and the like but beggars cannot choose. I suppose this is going to cost me a pretty penny?"

"Not a great deal, sir," affirmed John civilly. "Here is my bill. I think you'll find it very reasonable and will have no cause for complaint."

The taciturn farmer took the piece of paper but gave no comment on it. John took a last look at his patient, gathered up his implements and closed his case.

"Well, Mr Haverly, I would recommend you keep him on a bland diet for a few days. That should be sufficient to settle him and very likely you'll not need my services again."

"Hopefully not, judging by this," and Haverly shook the bill in his hands. "But wait a minute, young lad. You are quick to give me advice on my stock so happen I have some advice for you before you leave. Lately married are ye?"

John affirmed he was and picked up his case for departure.

"And to Cannetta Hardy so 'tis flung about this hamlet!"

John nodded in reply.

"Then, lad," continued Mr Haverly with a strange twisted look of dread and foreboding on his face. "Before the corn ripens again I think you'll wish you'd embraced the single state and not become joined to the local devil

85

worshipper! Ah, she's witched you it's certain and she will doom your soul next once she's cursed your body!"

John was furious. He could not even frame an answer though his lips twitched with anger. He flung himself out of the shed and yanked the reins of his waiting horse. The farmer's eyes followed his tight-lipped face in concern.

"'Tis only a warning!" shouted he. "But one you'll wish you'd listened to in a few weeks' time!"

Flinging himself into the saddle John pulled his horse's head over to the left in preparation for leaving.

"I'll harken to none of your nonsense – I'll not hear it! Next time your stock gets sick, Mr Haverly, you can go to the Devil for assistance as I'll not come! Good day!"

He applied his heels to his mount's side and sped away from the abuse he considered he had suffered.

The farmer removed his hat in a gesture of respect for a doomed man.

"Ah, my lad, next time my calf gets sick happen you'll not be here to see it," he whispered.

As the alternating fields of green and gold flashed by him in a blur of colour John felt the essence of his rage cooling and diminishing. The rhythmic sound of his horse's cantering hooves soothed him and a few scattered raindrops refreshed his hot forehead after which the gentle breeze then came in to dry him. After a mile he was annoyed, after another vaguely disturbed and after the   third he was remarkably careless. He pulled the sweating horse into a walk and patted his wet neck as he entered home territory.

"Damn them all, by Scotland, damn them all!" he muttered, entwining his fingers in his mount's thick mane. "What do I care for their shallow views and biased opinions? Aren't I the fellow to prove them all wrong?" He gave a loud laugh, dismounted and loosened the girths on his horse in preparation for removing the tack once he had finished his ride.

When he reached shelter it was raining again in large, cold drops that clung to his coat and hat. He led his mount into the stable he had rented near his dwelling, rubbed him down and fetched a rug as Grenadier seemed chilled from the journey. Tying him a hay net and replenishing his water bucket John left the small yard and walked the few yards to his house, picturing the clamorous reception from his Cannetta.

The kitchen was silent and empty although it was clean and tidy. On the scrubbed wooden table lay a tea tray upon which stood two cups, two saucers, spoons and two plates with a tea pot residing nearby. He picked it up and noticed that it held a teaspoon or two of strange smelling leaves, unlike the tea he normally drank. He put it down, carefully opened the door and then heard the tinkling notes of a piano accompanied by a sweet voice singing an old country song he had heard in Scotland. In a flash he was back in his father's parlour in Wickso with his mother's high tones filling the room and his father's fingers moving over the keys in military precision. Tears rose to his eyes as he listened to the words his wife sung

"As I was a-walking one morning in May

I spied a young couple a-making of hay;

The first was a young girl and her beauty shone clear

And the second was a soldier, a bold grenadier."

Ere this verse ended he noticed his hair was dripping onto the hall carpet where he had meandered; he made a move to fling the water away and in startling the player he was forced to come forward and reveal himself.

"John," cried she. "How you frightened me! Why were you lingering there? Do I displease you with my recital?" She left the piano and came forward. Looking in his eyes she sensed his confusion and asked,

"Has anything happened? You seem distracted! Your face speaks of trouble."

"No, no, nothing has occurred apart from a difficult patient and a cantankerous farmer who did not want to pay his bill."

"Have you heard anything?" she continued. "Has anyone spoken of me? Have you been told bad news? Come, you can tell me the truth!"

He observed her keen eyes were following the contours of his face as he spoke and she appeared to read him like a book. He shuddered.

"No of course not. Why do you ask?" he lied.

"It was just a picture I had in my mind and I felt you were angry with someone," she finished, returning to the piano and shutting the lid.

"I was angry," he admitted. "But only because the farmer refused to pay my bill after an hour's hard work. Now I do not care – my ire has flown as soon as I heard your beautiful rendition!"

He smiled at her and she felt at ease again after her fears.

John sat down and begged her to return to the piano.

"Cannetta, play for me! A melody of my homeland, please, for sometimes I am wild to be there!"

She handed him a book of music and tunes and he picked out a Scottish lullaby which he affirmed she could play and he would sing.

Returning to the keys she began tinkling away and presently he joined in with his fine deep voice. She played the song through twice at his request and on the second rendition she noticed his eyes were misty with tears.

"Oh how that moves me!" he declared, passionately.

Cannetta closed down the piano, folded up the music and asked,

"Does that inspire you to leave England and go back then, John?"

"To Scotland? Aye – there are times I'll not deny when the call of the glens is loud and fierce," he admitted, dreamily.

At this Cannetta rose, moved to the door and murmured that she would now serve tea it fast approaching the hour of five. When the laden tray had been carried through and she was allowing the prepared brew to strengthen he returned to the former subject.

"Are you not anxious to see the land of my birth?" enquired he with a jovial air.

She stared at this and asserted that she did not think that very likely.

"Och, we will not always be resident here, Cannetta! Faith, I could not stand a lifetime of hours in this house! Do you not agree?"

"No," she returned with direct frankness. "John, I am totally happy here. This is my ain land as you would call it. These fields that unfold before you are my life blood, be they your prisons." She handed him a full cup. "So if you talk of leaving then you must plan alone and leave your wife behind you. I'll never go!"

She seemed steadfast in this and he, who had mentioned it as a shadowy future idea, dismissed the topic immediately and turned the conversation back to the present.

Presently it grew darker and John, who was ever anxious to please his new wife, asked her if she would like to go a short way with him before night eclipsed the sky. At this she seemed pleased, affirmed she would enjoy some fresh air before bedtime and departed to fetch her coat and bonnet. He, in the ensuing interval, filled it with a mournful tune on the piano, a propensity to sadness always striking him when he had been particularly sanguine or gay.

They went out together arm in arm, she walking very close to him, so that she touched him at every opportunity and often leaned against him when the path was narrower. Soon they observed the rising of the full, round moon, it still being harvest time, and the light thrown off was considerable, easily powerful enough to effectively block out the blackness of approaching night.

"'Tis only half dark!" cried he in amazement, gazing up at the huge lunar apparition.

"Yes," murmured she vaguely, her eyes fixed on the planet too, her limbs trembling with the power given off by the full moon.

"Cannetta! How your fingers shake in mine! What can ail you?"

"I am cold, that is all," she stammered. "Do you not feel the rising chill?"

"No darling. To me it is a moist, sweet night! The wind of earlier has dropped its pensive whine and become a gentle sigh and the last fragrance of the summer honeysuckle graces the air! It seems all the evil has gone out of the world tonight!"

"No, no, no!" cried Cannetta, desperately in frenzied alarm. "Do not say that – it cannot be - I am cold - so, so cold!"

"I have uttered nothing to alarm you surely?" he enquired, endeavouring to calm her but her tortured expression continued and the terror on her face brought memories of their wedding night back to him vividly.

"Oh, John, if you love me get me inside, please!" At her insistent clutching he led her blindly through the garden and in by the back door. In the dark passageway she leant against the wall and by degrees recovered herself, eventually lifting a more composed face to him. Slowly her breathing returned to normal and the shaking of her limbs ceased.

He affirmed his concern for her and asked for permission to fetch a doctor but she was resolute she did not need or want one. It was not, she explained, any physical illness but a nervous dread that lived in her mind at times and now she was indoors the terror would dispel. He asked if she were afraid of the dark; she replied she did not think so and then entered the parlour, fully recovered.

John shut the door, came to sit opposite her and took her hand.
"See," murmured she calmly. "I am myself and it is forgotten. My fingers scarcely move – my brow is cool and my thoughts collected. It will not reoccur, darling, do not look so worried. Ah, I see I perplex you!"
"Then enlighten me!" begged he, turning his face to her as if pleading. "Cannetta – I love you dearly. Yet, at times, you are distant and not the vibrant woman I married."

At this she cast down her eyes and at length whispered,
"John – I cannot explain it any better than I have. I am still your devoted wife no matter what moods overpower me."

He wondered at the strangeness of her words but she said no more and he was anxious not to press her and cause any further signs of confusion or fear to make themselves felt. She had been through enough, regardless of what had brought it on. There was still a pained expression on her beautiful face but that was lifting and she seemed recovered. The clock ticked away. Cannetta took up some sewing and John began to read one of his veterinary journals. For over an hour silence reigned.

John was engrossed in his study when a succession of noises entered his brain and caused him to look up and observe his wife. She seemed to be suppressing violent, conflicting emotions which caused her body to jerk and a mumble of obscene words were forced from her lips. Her head was hung low and she dug the needle into the work in a good many places but never actually sewed a stitch. Occasionally he saw she stabbed the needle into her hand or finger but she exhibited no signs of pain when she did this and, at last, she folded the work away and stretched her arms over her head, yawning as she did so. As the clock struck ten Cannetta rose, stumbled to her husband's side and put her arms around his neck, kissing him passionately and murmuring, "Sorry," in his ear. Instantly he was won over, returned the caress and took her in his arms whereupon she melted into his body. But his eyes lightened upon the bleeding fingers and pierced hands and, try though he might, he could not shake off his fear of her…

Later, in bed, she was tender and loving so that he rebuked himself for his doubts and whilst she slept he stroked her soft hair whilst all seemed as gentle as a dream…Hours after this he stirred, put out a hand for his love and found she was not there. He felt he had been asleep for ages but his pocket watch, by the bed, pronounced it to be ten to two. A long shaft of pale moonlight fell across the bed and lit up the empty space where his wife should have been lying. The pillow was hardly dented and the sheet cold when he leant over to touch it. John sat up, flung away the bedclothes and wiped away the last film of sleep from his mind and eyes. Where was Cannetta? The fact that she had gone spurred him into action and he pulled some clothes on and moved over to the window. Nothing was visible save for the strong almost icy glare of moonlight which flooded the sleeping garden glinted further away on the river and lit up the dark water meadows. He pulled up the sash and called her.

"Cannetta! Cannetta! Where are you?" There was no answer but an echo mocked him momentarily and then faded. He gazed over the brightly light scene below him but saw no movement and for a moment the sleepy twitter of birds above him sounded like her voice. Then reason asserted itself and he called again. Nothing. He pulled down the window, left the room and ran down the stairs to the kitchen. The back door was wide open.

He hurried through, cast his eyes this way and that in desperation to seek her out.

"Cannetta!" he called again. A gentle wafting breeze fluttered his open shirt and teased his hair. He ran to the nearby bushes and began to search them for his wife, his mind racing. After a while he realised she was not in the garden, which glowed as bright as day, so he left by the side gate and went round to the front of the house where a small copse stretched along one part of the slope beyond the building. Here he knew his wife loved to wander and accordingly he crossed by the dyke path and hurried into the centre of the wood. She had told him she came here before he moved to the area to observe the birds and animals in their habitat but now not a sound was audible save the harsh rasp of his own breathing and the throaty shriek of an owl which died as the bird passed overhead on swift wings. The atmosphere was almost suffocating, and John felt paralysed with fear trapped as he was within the branches of the gaunt elms. Immediately he broke free of the copse ran further on, away from the haunting shadows of the trees and took note of his position. To his left the huge, pale face of the moon gleamed like a lantern and to his right the slumbering stubble fields fell in a never-ending line of light and shade according to how the moonbeams hit them. And there, not so very far ahead of him, was the silent, dark figure he quested for.

"Cannetta!" he screamed, cupping his hands together to intensify the sound. She made no movement at his call and he wondered if her mental state prevented her from hearing outward noises. Was she immersed in her inner world of terror and fear? A bitter barb snared his heart. Is she really going insane, he wondered? But then, perhaps after all she was only sleepwalking and was unconscious of her surroundings and the fact that he called her. She was in her own dream or nightmare and he, he was now part of it.

He ran lithely across the grass, observed her full attention was on the power of the moon and her arms hung uselessly by her side as though she was

90

unaware of her body supporting her. Coming round to face her he could see a wild but glassy stare in the depths of her blue eyes and that her lips were parted slightly as though in pain or surprise. Joyful though he was to have found her something prevented him from reaching out to touch her and apart from a regular flicker of her eyelids she stood as though a statue. Her breath was very shallow and spasmodic and only the breeze moved her golden tresses, a fact she was totally insensible of. Her full, long nightdress was twisted round her thin legs and her feet were visible, several scratches upon them bleeding profusely. He knew she felt no pain from this, nor any sensations of cold despite the lack of cloak or coat. He called her name again, once, twice, thrice, in varying tones which in the end were desperate and pleading. She acknowledged nothing and never a muscle twitched or pulsed. He stood back at a loss as to what to do next, for his heart quailed at the thought of actually touching her white skin and though he tried his hands recalled from contact with her. If she really was sleepwalking then it must be her, and her alone who would move and come back to reality.

Suddenly he could bear the eerie scene before him no more and he stepped up to her, flinched considerably, but managed to slap her hard on both cheeks, resulting in colour flooding into her face. His rough fingers grazed her delicate skin and the effect was instantaneous; she drew a long breath as though waking, puffed out her cheeks and turned to him in a heightened state of alarm.

"John...I..." she mumbled, clutching at him as he stood before her.

"What, Cannetta? What do you see?" he asked softly.

"I see men coming...one, two, three, running as though they are in pursuit of something. They have stopped under my window and they call me...no...it is stronger than that...they command me and I am summoned. They have chains for me and handcuffs to shackle me...They are set to trap me with their queer sulphurous lights and I have nowhere to go to flee from them! You, in ignorance of them are asleep and then - I cannot even scream - and I am gone! Oh. John...don't let them take me!!!!"

"Hush, hush, darling! 'Twas only a bad dream!" he cried, horrified at her words. But was it a dream or, to her, a constant waking nightmare?

He led her back through the sleeping trees at which she trembled and emitted little cries of fear but when they reached the dyke paths she seemed to recover and know where she was.

"We are near the house are we not?" she murmured, as though to soothe herself. Then she went rigid as she saw the shine of the naked windows.

"No, no, no, "she suddenly screamed, pulling back with such power that John almost fell over. "They are within aren't they?" and she cowered on the ground trying to cover her head with her nightdress.

John tried to pick her up but she slithered away from him.

"There is no one there, dearest," he tried to convince her. "Your dream is over. Feel me! I am flesh and blood and stand before you as your husband.

There is nothing of nightmare about me! You have been sleepwalking and I have come for you to get you back to bed. It is after two o'clock."

"No," she denied, shaking her head violently while her teeth chattered loudly.

John felt completely out of his depths and did not know how to control her. She remained slumped on the damp ground, pulling at her hair as if for comfort.

"They are still calling me!" she affirmed. "So you are lying to me."

"No," he replied. "It was ME calling you, no one else. There is only you and I here, Cannetta."

She turned and looked at him as if she did not know who he was and he felt terrified.

"Look, look, I am your husband, John Straeton! I am no enemy to you. Cannetta – you are my wife. Do you not know me? Think carefully!"

She stared at him and her eyes were glassy but the dazed look was lifting from her face.

"Oh John," she cried, as if the nightmare had fled and released her from its power. "Oh John – yes, yes, you are my husband and we were married a couple of days ago!"

He gave a huge sigh of relief that she remembered him and standing up she took his hand and walked with him to the back door. Passing through it she began to tremble and cry but he assured her that it did not matter; she was safe now and with him.

Gathering her in his arms he carried her up the stairs and back to the bedroom where, exhausted and confused, he tucked her into bed and then watched over her until she drifted into a peaceful slumber. And only when he was sure that she would wander no more that night did he give up his vigil and climb in beside her, shaking and bewildered...

CHAPTER 9

As his strange, new wife lay in his arms during the remainder of the night, peaceful now yet as ominous as a silent volcano, John knew sleep would elude him however much he wished for its oblivion. Despite locking every door in the house that possessed a key he could not rest and every time Cannetta stirred in her sleep his heart raced. He tightened his grip upon her as though by holding her firmly he could keep her sick mind from wandering.

A faint gleam of dawn brightened the room at last, giving him a glimmer of hope in a largely black world. Counsel and reason returned to him as he lay there turning over the night's events and trying desperately to find excuses for Cannetta's behaviour. He had only been married a couple of days to a girl who had led a very sheltered life with a tyrant for a mother who ruled her with an iron will. That much he had surmised from Rose's reaction to the wedding and his wife's constant desire to please her lone parent. Thus Cannetta had left her home and the strict discipline she had lived under all her life in order to set up house with her husband, possibly her first and only love. Would her mind not rebel under such circumstances and induce confusion and sleepwalking until it had come to terms with the major changes? Was this not the culmination of twenty-two years of being misunderstood and abused? And what of her father? What strange mysteries surrounded his death that his daughter did not want to talk about? Surely this still affected her and in her subconscious mind, hidden during the day by routine and duty, periods of incoherent excitement reigned resulting in vivid dreams and nightmares that she acted out and believed as real. So all he faced was a time of adjustment from a restricted lifestyle to one where her freedom was her own. John felt comforted by these thoughts and snuggling into his wife's back he slept lightly now that the nightmare of the previous night was explained by his deliberations.

When he awoke it was much later and the sun had climbed halfway to the zenith whilst the mists of the approaching season of autumn had been burnt off by the golden light. John sat up, looked at his pocket watch and perceiving it was five to eleven he woke his wife gently and murmured to her that it was time to be up.

"I have an appointment with Mr Manderling at eleven!" cried the harassed husband, leaping out of bed. He commenced dressing with speed. "I am sure he will excuse my lateness when he knows I am newly -wed!"

"I do not see why that should concern him," Cannetta replied, sounding somewhat annoyed. "You are late for his appointment – nothing more!"

He recognised anger in her tone and did not take the conversation any further. Buttoning his coat he commented softly,

"Well, it is not so very late after all and I am ready to leave."

"What, you still mean to go with no breakfast inside you and no wash? Don't! Stay here with me – stay with your wife and let him think what he likes!"

John approached her and gave her a goodbye kiss. She tried to put her arms around him and pull him back to bed but he disengaged her eager hands, kissed her again on top of the head and quit the room.

"Farewell!" called he, from the hallway. She waited until she heard the back door shut and the rattle of hooves sounded on the track and then she rose hastily.

She began to dress, putting on her auburn gown and was in the act of brushing out her hair when a sharp tap upon the front door sent the comb crashing to the floor. The knock was repeated – decisive, bold and urgent, commanding the hearer to hurry and answer but Cannetta felt unnerved and anxious at the intrusion to her privacy. She rose, descended the stairs, and with shaking hands opened the door.

"Who is there?" she cried, in hesitant tones.

"Mrs Straeton?"came the high voice of a woman. "Mrs Straeton – may I speak with your husband?"

Cannetta opened the door a little wider, gazed at the young, slim form of the girl who stood before her and stared as her mind worked on the pale complexion and mousey coloured ringlets. Suddenly she remembered where she had seen this girl before....and Cannetta's suffering that night came back to haunt her.

"Be still! I know you!" she cried. "You are she I bled for that night. Did you not think your recovery remarkable? But for me you would be beneath the sod! Are you not grateful to me for my kindness? In faith you should be as I have the means to reverse the spell and remove my blood from your veins!"

"I know nothing of what you say and neither do I understand it," replied Connie, bemusedly. "I am John's second cousin. Does the name Connie mean anything to you?"

"Yes, I remember your name but what do you want?"

"To see your husband please as I have some urgent work for him to undertake."

"John is not here," returned his wife, somewhat haughtily. "He has just left for a lengthy appointment and will not be back for hours. He cannot help you. Good day!"

"Then our dog may die!" burst out Connie, in real anguish. She turned away from the door.

Cannetta was about to shut the barrier but comprehending the last words she flung it open wider and recalled her visitor.

"Quick! Take me to the animal! Waste no idle words in chatter."

Connie turned back to the girl.

"You?" she queried. "What can you do?"

"Trust me, trust me," urged the witch with a flash of her powerful blue eyes.

94

Connie felt the power and shrugged her shoulders.

"Come then," she replied and hurried away from the front door, Cannetta following with an anxious face.

They arrived at the cherry pink cottage which seemed silent, as though devoid of any human inhabitant. Connie passed through the side gate, hesitated a moment and then warned,

"Don't be afraid if he barks as Father keeps him mostly as a guard dog though, faith, I remember he had no bark in him a few minutes ago before I ran to find your husband."

"Think nothing of it," returned her companion. "Lead on and waste no more time with warnings. This is my mission – do you not realise that?"

Connie did not reply but crossed the rough path by the side of the house and opened the door of one of the tiny sheds.

"Here," she called to Cannetta who followed a little way behind. "He is within."

Cannetta ran forward eagerly, saw the huge grey dog, in breeding possibly part Irish wolfhound, and knelt down by him, observing the froth at his mouth, the laboured breathing and the weak pulse.

"He has taken poison!" cried she, at length. "Now, fetch me a knife then get gone and leave me. It shall all be done."

"A knife?" said Connie, in horror. "What can you want with such a weapon?"

"Do not linger. Every minute the dog grows worse and it makes my task harder. Can you not understand that?"

The young girl stared incredulously at her companion and then fled in the direction of the house, returning swiftly with the desired utensil.

Cannetta took it without thanks, shut and barred the door, then knelt down beside the sinking victim and began her work. Connie, left bemused and worried outside, could only sit on the cold damp step of the next shed and wait.

Ten minutes passed; the listener heard an eerie howl from within the outhouse but whether it was from Cannetta's lips or the dog's mouth she could not tell. Next there came a jumble of words that Connie could make no sense of apart from that they sounded like a curse said with some venom. Then a deathly silence filled the air and Connie was just berating herself for allowing a woman that all of Ardle knew as a witch to be alone with her father's beloved dog when the shed door flew open.

Cannetta appeared in the doorway looking extremely pale and drawn, her frame shaking as if with exhaustion or fear. Connie ran to her side and made as if to help her but Cannetta held up her hand to warn her rescuer off.

"No, no, do not touch me," she panted, evidently having trouble in breathing. She could hardly stand and held onto the shed door as if her life depended on it. Her lips were vividly dark against her pallid face and one arm hung uselessly by her side as if it were paralysed.

95

"It is all done," she murmured, recovering a little strength. "Yet most of my power is gone. His life was in threads and it took much to restore him but it is done, it is done!"

Connie looked on with horror, unable to say anything or even move.

"Is he…?" she stuttered to Cannetta pointing to the mound of dog visible in the doorway of the shed. At this Cannetta shook her head and uttered a faint whistle, turning to the hound as he lay, seemingly prostrate at her feet. Instantly the animal bounded up, licked his rescuer with a healthy, pink tongue, his eyes now full of life and sparkle. Connie he ignored completely as his whole attention was on Cannetta's face and when the girl smiled at him he barked and whined in delight.

"There!" enthused Cannetta, raising herself up and regaining her feet. "You doubted me. In fact you worried what I was doing in the shed alone with your dog. You are just like the rest of Ardle, condemning me and pointing the finger! You came to find my husband's skills but have not mine been adequate? Have they not exceeded his? Yet it has cost me dearly." She reeled back against the shed, the dog jumping and bounding around her feet. Connie observed a large gash upon her companion's wrist which still dripped blood occasionally and, instinctively, she shivered.

"What can I do to help you?" she asked, suddenly concerned for Cannetta's well -being.

"Feed him some bread and milk every few hours," replied Cannetta, "He is totally empty but I am drained."

"I meant to aid you," continued Connie, feeling very anxious. "What can I do to help you?"

"Nothing, nothing, I do not want your hands upon me. Please leave me now. I will get myself home by and by as my strength returns." Cannetta clung onto the shed wall, managed to support her weight and began to totter shakily along the track that led, ultimately, back to her house.

Connie could only watch her slow and painful progress in amazement. She did not know what to think but she grabbed hold of the recovered dog who would have fain gone with his saviour, and led him back to the shed which doubled as his kennel on cold and wet days. Bedding him down and fetching food for him she noticed the carelessly left knife and picked it up. It was covered with a darkening liquid that was just beginning to congeal and another pool of the same liquid was drying on the shed floor. To Connie it was painfully obvious the congealing liquid was blood – human blood.

John arrived home sooner than expected, was shocked to find no one there and took a turn or two about the surrounding fields without finding anything more human than a gathering of migrant swallows. They twittered at him from their elevated position, as if warning him winter would soon cover these meadows with snow and ice. He stared up at them, suddenly envious of their departure to pastures new while he was left here, immersed in a marriage that

96

was fast becoming a nightmare. Where was Cannetta now? He circled the stubble fields calling her name but only the crows replied to him and then flew off like ominous black harbingers of doom. Fear now rose unchecked in him and stifled him with its grip. He felt he could not breathe and leant against a tree to recover. Where in God's name had she gone? He searched the garden and the lanes that she loved to wander in and at last concluded she must have gone to Ardle to visit her mother. He aimed his footsteps that way and prayed she had come to no harm.

Descending the long, twisting hill path he caught sight of another female figure climbing upwards which the regular turn of the track and the overhanging branches frequently hid. Realising this could be his wife he hurried on until the woman came into sight but, to his dismay, he discovered it was his cousin Shirley with a wicker basket upon her arm.

"Why, John!" cried she, in delight. "How happy I am to see you! Is all well at Fourbridges?"

"We are...quite well, thank you," returned he, with some difficulty in a tone that completely belied his words. His eyes did not look at her but gazed over at the confusion of green fields that presented themselves from their elevated position. She dropped her stare to the grass beneath her feet, feeling awkward as her heart raced at his close proximity. A brief silence fell then John asked in as casual a tone as he could muster,

"I don't suppose you have seen...Cannetta?"

"Why, yes!" acknowledged Shirley, seemingly surprised that he did not know where his wife was. "Connie came running after me as I left Ardle to tell me of the strangest thing involving your wife and our dog."

John started and clutched at his cousin's arm in desperation.

"Oh my God!" he groaned. "Tell me, what has occurred? What has she done and where is she now?"

Shirley raised her eyebrows and looked at his hands which still held her arm in a strangle-hold that was almost painful.

"John...whatever has happened?"

He turned away and tried not to look at her. It seemed he was too distressed for words.

Shirley struggled to reassure him.

"After I left for market our dog was taken sick – at death's door apparently. Connie was very upset and ran off to find you to see if you could help him. Sadly you were out on a lengthy call but she raised Cannetta who was very keen to come back with Connie and cure the animal!"

John shook his head incredulously.

"Cannetta?" he gasped.

"Apparently so! She went into the shed where the dog lay and affirmed he had eaten poison so she asked Connie for a knife and after shutting herself into the shed began some sort of ritual. Connie waited outside but could not make out what happened except that Cannetta emerged drained and exhausted."

John swallowed hard.

"And the dog?" he asked.

"The dog fair bounded out, returned to rude health but Cannetta was listless and pale, hardly able to stand, so Con said."

"Then where is she now?" cried John, feeling alarm returning to his tone.

"Connie told me your wife refused all help and began to direct her step towards Fourbridges. But here is the weirdest part of the tale! John, our shed is full of drying blood!"

"Blood?" cried he, breathlessly.

"Yes, and there were traces of it upon Cannetta too, from a gaping gash on her wrist. Connie was fair put out about it and did not know what to think. Has your wife not returned home yet?"

John shook his head, his eyes full.

"Good God!" he burst out. "Oh Shirley – I – no, no, I must keep silent! No, Cannetta is not back."

"Maybe she has taken the longer route across the fields seeing as she likes to avoid folk. You should turn around and retrace your steps in case she has eclipsed you!"

He stood in ghastly silence, his face grave and sombre his blue eyes dark with tears.

"John," whispered Shirley, squeezing his hand in concern. "How is your marriage?"

He jumped at her touch and even more at her words but shook his head as if dismissing any outburst that threatened to leave his lips.

"Oh, Shirley, I am not at liberty to tell. That I have been deceived by flaxen hair and blue eyes is no secret. She flew to me as an angel but she leaves me, it seems, as a devil!"

Shirley perceived the stilted pride in his tone but could see through the bravado and her heart ached for him.

"I do not think she is as mad as the rumours make her out to be, John," murmured she, gazing at him as if pleading with him to break down and tell her all so she could comfort him. But John's sole attention was on the fields around him and he did not reply to her words. In the end he began to wander off as though in a trance and Shirley said goodbye to him and continued on her way. She waited until he had disappeared round the next bend before she moved.

"Oh, cousin," soliloquised she, her eyes full of tears. "If you had not seen Cannetta and I had been a single woman how different life would be!" But the thought of a better future was but a fleeting one as she was grounded in reality, so she swore to forget it and walked on.

At this moment the subject of several thoughts – not least of all her husband's – was letting herself into Fourbridges with a stealth that implied she expected to find another being already there. Thankfully her search proved otherwise and she dragged her limp form into the kitchen where she dug out a large lump of cheese and a hunk of bread (she had for years refused to eat meat), ate them ravenously and perceived, in a few minutes, its good effects. Receiving strength from nourishment she stood up, moved into the hallway and was diverted by a small sound at the window. It was a large blowfly buzzing frantically at the glass. Cannetta crossed the hall, swept up the insect and popped it into her mouth.

"Blood for blood," she said.

Her deep love of animals had never extended to the world of insects and she had, from a very young age, enjoyed repasts of bees, wasps and gnats, none of their stings having any effect on her mouth or system. She was able to pick up adders without fear of their bite and in her presence the majesty of the lion would assume the gentility of a kitten. Now, low in blood, and craving more live food she scoured the other rooms and gathered a few more trapped insects which served to replenish her veins. Instantly she felt stronger, was about to descend the stairs when she heard her husband come in through the front door. Instinctively he raised his eyes to hers, as she stood at the top of the stairs, and she saw, in his face a furious anger he made no effort to conceal. She froze.

"Cannetta, come here, NOW!" cried he.

She did as she was bade but seemed as though she was going to walk past him so he grabbed her arm to arrest her progress and twisted it cruelly.

"What the hell have you been up to?" he spat.

She struggled furiously to get free.

"John," begged she. "Let me go! You are hurting me!"

He flung her off with a curse, watching her rubbing her wrist and shedding tears with an impassive face.

"How can you be so cruel?" she sobbed. "What have I done that has caused such venom in you? I would be safer facing a raging lion than you! And so my husband has a temper that he uses against me after – what is it? Four days? Too late have I discovered this – I am married to him!"

"Do not talk of repentance," replied he, bitterly. "I have thoughts on that subject that would shock you could you hear them! Cannetta – do not lie to me! I have just met my cousin."

"Then why do you attack me? The mission of curing sick animals calls me as much as it draws you! Can you not understand that? The dog was poisoned! It was a build -up of bad blood in the stomach. Therefore, using the knife I freed it but the stench made me powerfully nauseous but cured him in an instant. The blood was not hard to stem – the bad stuff came out easily. Have you no faith in the medicines of the fields and hedgerows?"

He stepped back a little at this to ponder on her words which had taken him totally by surprise.

"Well?" asked Cannetta pressing home her advantage. "What was I to do? Let him die? The person who could have helped him was out so why could his wife not do her best instead? If I have done wrong then you must tell me so! How would you have cured the poisoning had you been there?"

"It must be let out in the form of bad blood from the stomach whereupon the poison will come out too," he replied, almost mechanically, perceiving that what she had done was exactly what he would have performed on the dog, although with more sophisticated tools than a knife.

"Oh, my angel, I am so sorry," murmured he, turning to her and holding out his arms. "It makes sense – of course it does! Can you forgive me and my harsh words?"

Cannetta smiled in triumph and let herself melt into his open arms. And as he caressed her John felt a sharp twinge of pain, regret and shame as he remembered his rash words of despair to his beautiful cousin...

The early evening darkness had come, brought down prematurely by the stifling power of a rainstorm. In the cottage at Ardle Shirley and her stepdaughter sat by the remnants of a fire, which they had raked together more for comfort than actual warmth. Damion had gone to Stackhouses for his nightly drink, not spurned by the bitter twirl of rain and wind. Connie, whose convalescence was nearly over, sat on one end of the settle sewing a pillowcase and her stepmother sat at the opposite end mending one of her husband's shirts. The lamps had already been lit, the meal eaten and cleared away and the dog fed. With a deep sigh Shirley lay down her work and gazed deeply into the dying fire.

"You sound very tired, Mother," observed Connie, pulling the tension of her thread.

"No, no, not really," replied she, with another sad sigh.

"You are unhappy then?"

"No."

Another long pause during which Connie carried on sewing but Shirley regarded her stepdaughter as she bent over her work, her hair shining in the light from the oil lamp.

"Con," she said, suddenly. "Are you really cured?"

The needle stopped for a moment and then the girl said,

"Yes, I believe I truly am, Mother. But it is not my illness that troubles you, is it?"

Shirley shook her head and her eyes took on a wistful glow.

Connie took up her needle again and commenced sewing.

"I saw John this afternoon," volunteered Shirley, at last.

"Ah," murmured the girl. "Then that is it!"

"Yes," admitted her stepmother, languidly. "I must be honest that that meeting has caused my numerous sighs this evening. I am ashamed to admit it, however. The feeling still hits me hard when I behold him!"

100

"Well at one time you would not have revealed it, Mother, so I am glad it is no longer hidden. Things are much easier between us lately, aren't they?" Shirley acknowledged they were.

"Connie – I was a simpleton and a fool and still am to some degree but since my secret is safe with you I will hide nothing. And by admitting everything maybe the feeling will fade."

Shirley picked up her work again and commenced sewing.

"Did John seem in good spirits when you met him?" asked Connie, without looking up.

"No," replied Shirley, with a worried frown, throwing down the shirt again. "I must say he was fair down in the mouth."

"You told him of his lady's triumph then?"

"Yes – he seemed very upset by it for some reason. His face told of sorrow and trouble and he more or less admitted his marriage was not happy. But that fierce Scottish pride would not let him break down and reveal all. Yet the blinkers have fallen from his eyes and he no longer sees his wife as an angel!"

"She said things this morning I could not understand at all," replied Connie with a puzzled expression on her face. "Poor John – do you not feel a little pity for him mixed in with your love?"

"Yes," returned Shirley with another sigh. "Yes, at times I feel despair that he should be within such clutches as Cannetta's. Yet some of it is for purely selfish reasons, I can't deny. But I must learn to control myself and, in time, I will forget him."

Connie gazed at her in disbelief.

"This time, Mother, you really believe you will?"

Shirley sighed deeply, nodded her head as though to a promise and picked up the shirt again.

"Yes," she murmured. "For certain – yes - I will do it this time."

Even before John mounted the stairs to bed he was aware of a great, feverish restlessness in his wife which had been gathering pace all evening as he watched her. From dusk she had wandered sullenly round the room as though pursued by something she wished to evade and his remonstrations to come and sit by him were met with a chilled silence. At times he doubted she heard him at all, so immersed did she seem in some inner world far from reality. When she turned her dilated eyes to him she appeared not to see him or even be conscious of his presence but rather she looked beyond him at apparitions that were not of this earth. Eventually he managed to urge her to bed but she went rigid in his arms, began to bite him about the neck and then laughed raucously when he pushed her off. She bounded out of bed on all fours and he was quite at a loss to know how to deal with her. Dragging her back to bed he felt her tear at his naked flesh again and revulsion hit him.

"Cannetta!" he scolded. "What the hell is wrong with you?" But she did not answer, just began picking and nipping him then biting him with her sharp white teeth. He perceived his neck was bleeding profusely but she just laughed and began to lick the blood from the wounds with great relish. He pushed her away and with some force held her down until her lust had abated and then, suddenly, she fell into a doze and from there to a longer, deeper sleep. John stared at her in the pale moonlight and wondered, yet again, what sort of monster he had married...

CHAPTER 10

Next morning John woke from a shallow sleep that afforded little physical or mental refreshment and turned to observe what kind of demon he had spent the night with. Cannetta had turned towards him, her arms folded on her chest and the sweetest of smiles on her sleeping lips. John evinced a considerable distaste for her company and, not wanting any contact with her he rose as quietly as possible, dressed and descended the stairs with slow steps.

Outside a beautiful, gentle September mist graced the water meadows and spun up high to decorate the distant treetops, hanging in viscous veils over the river and coiling itself among the reed beds. A light dew was beginning to dry upon the grass and the sun escaped from her bath and rose as a hazy red ball, breaking free from the fluffy white clouds that gave her birth. The last few swallows twittered mournfully as they skimmed the meadows searching for the last flies of the summer to give them strength for the migration ahead. John left the house, let himself out of the garden gate, turned across the field path and was lost in the white mists, unaware that two piercing blue eyes were watching him from an elevated position.

The observer flung off the sheet she had hastily wrapped around her, pulled on her gown and without stopping to put on shoes or stockings ran lithely downstairs and out into the September morning.

By using the maze of lanes between Stackhouses and Ardle a walker could, if he wished, reach any dwelling in either place and avoid the steep gradient, although it would take him a good ten minutes more to do so. Women returning from market in the town and bearing heavy and full baskets very often chose this route so they could avoid the hill and could also indulge in gossip and a reviving rest at the cottages scattered about the lanes. John, feeling exhausted after his poor quality sleep, chose this route but hoped he did not meet anyone as he felt unable to converse or even be civil to another human being. Presently he reached the most outlying dwellings of Ardle, turned down a smaller side track and directed his step to where he knew he would find a friendly face – the only one he could cope with in his anguish. He craved sane company. Worn out with the constant vigil of his mad wife he sought to avoid her for an hour and try to forget his troubles. Yet a nagging worry gnawed at his tormented mind – was Cannetta safe to be left alone? If he had locked her in would he have felt any easier? That he was responsible for her now as her husband he did not shirk from and yet the long years of facing and dealing with the insanity that loomed ahead of him filled him with horror. To send her away was unthinkable, to neglect her was callous cruelty and he could conceive of no way out of the trap he found himself in. The neglected warnings that had been flying around before he married her now hit him and he began to realise what a fool he had been.

"It is all they said it would be!" cried he, bitterly shaking his head. He passed fields of workers who looked at him curiously, seeing a broken man who walked with slow, solemn steps and whose sad visage was grey with pain.

"Fooled," he muttered at intervals. "Deceived." And the knowledge was all the worse because his own family had tried to warn him because they loved him but he had ignored them all and even taken against them for their comments. He had married her of his own free will and now he was forced to stay with her against that will.

The cherry pink cottage at Ardle was lit up by the early autumn sunshine, with occasional shadows skimming the roof as the pink, wispy clouds came and went. Upon the rooftop perched two white doves cooing and billing and the last blooming of the large garden was profuse and fragrant. The hum of busy bees filled the air as the insects came and went from the hives in their constant work, making the most of the final nectar from the flowers that year. John was uplifted by this gentle vision and remained looking at the peaceful scene that unfolded before him. After a while he directed his steps into the front path but his ears picked up the hurrying gait of another person and although he stopped to see if anyone appeared after a few seconds of waiting he shrugged his shoulders and walked on. Little did he know that this visitor had seen him, stopped dead in her tracks and then hidden herself in the scrub bushes that surrounded the property.

"Ah-ha," murmured Cannetta. "By my life, this is prearranged. He feels a passion for the cousin he saw yesterday. What time will show! Has he tired of me already? Does my husband seek other arms for his embraces?" Merging into the foliage she remained silent and seemed set to remain there and wait for John to quit the cottage for she had observed him enter and her hiding place afforded a good view of the door. She lingered there uneasily for a full hour, her eyes never leaving the dwelling although nothing showed itself beyond a fluttering of doves on the roof. A few birds hopped about the bushes by her, regarding Cannetta as part of the scenery, so still did she stand. A cold breeze raised its head and blew the hollyhocks and delphiniums in a wild dance but apart from that nothing stirred. Cannetta kept her vigil despite the chill air, the pink stain of the cottage's wash remaining imprinted on her retina. At length movement, and two figures stepped across the threshold, one her husband, the other his cousin, Connie. Cannetta blinked furiously and narrowed her vision to observe them closer. It was soon obvious they were very easy in each other's company and were well acquainted as she gazed at him almost tenderly and he laughed his feelings back. The watcher was enraged. The two drew nearer as they left the house front; John, carrying a strapped- up suitcase and a bag, whilst Connie held a small wooden box. As they approached Cannetta could hear their conversation and see the looks they flashed at each other.

"You must take great care," murmured he, in concern. "I would be very upset to hear that any trace of your illness returned due to overwork or neglect of rest. They treat you well at this place, I trust?"

"Fairly," returned Connie glancing up at the contours of his face in deep interest.

Cannetta tightened her lips and muttered a silent curse.

"The food is plentiful?" he continued.

"Oh yes!" assured Connie. "I find it more than adequate!"

"And the sleeping quarters are dry and warm?"

"They are tolerable - if a little cramped."

"Don't work too hard then, Con!" pleaded he, squeezing her arm and smiling at her.

She laughed at his serious tone and they moved off together and passed Cannetta so she lost the thread of their conversation. Eventually they went out of earshot completely.

Directly the contours of the land had hidden them Cannetta emerged from her hiding place and shook her leaf-encrusted gown free of vegetation. She gave the cottage a last glance then took to her heels and began running back towards her home along the lanes whilst the chattering couple kept walking in the opposite direction.

The sun had risen considerably and was sailing in the treetops by the time Cannetta reached home. By then her breath came in short pants, her side was aching and her eyes rolled wildly. Overcome with exhaustion she leant upon the topmost bar of the gate, her hand pressed to her stitch which raged in her left side.

"Oh, my love – my life!" panted she. "How can I bear it? That he has tired of me already after only days! Scarce a week-old bride and I have been replaced. What shall I do?"

She flung herself down in the rough grass by the gate and wiped her moist face. Gradually her eyes grew bright, her breath slowed and steadied and her heart resumed its regular beat. Only her mind raced. At length a glint of hopefulness came into her face and relief hit her so she stood up and went through the barrier in a calmer frame of mind.

"Ah-ha, my lady!" cried she aloud, a malicious sneer framing her lips. "I sacrificed much for you and this is how you repay me – you steal my husband! You have turned his heart away from my love to your weak charms! What were you to me? Nothing! I only did it for HIM. So, you have betrayed me. I will have my blood back." She slammed the gate shut with such venom that the hinges split so that the wooden barrier tilted at an odd angle. But she did not care for material things, her mind was forming another spell and this one reeked of revenge.

It was quite late when John arrived back at Fourbridges and he was very hungry, having neither drunk nor supped since the preceding evening. True

Shirley had offered him a plate of breakfast but today he felt uncomfortable in her presence and was glad that Connie was there, to whom he directed most of his conversation. He sensed that Shirley was just waiting for an opportunity to question him further regarding his revelation of yesterday and he felt uneasy and embarrassed. Thus he was glad of a chance to escape and help Connie into the bargain as she needed to return to the Hall and had considerable belongings to take back there. In Connie's company he experienced a gentle charm with no emotional ties such as bound him to Shirley and the girl did not condemn him or interrogate him concerning his sham of a marriage and for that he was whole-heartedly grateful. His walk and chat with Connie afforded him some much needed solace and an escape from the nightmare situation that awaited him at Fourbridges. Thus he lingered longer than he had intended at the Hall and only left when Connie's superior made it clear it was time for him to go.

Throwing open the door of his dwelling he entered the kitchen through the back door, thought painfully of his wife and called her. No answer, nor the stir of a figure, just silence. His heart beat fast with dread. Where was she now?

"Cannetta!" he cried again. The air hardly moved.

He ran through the hallway and entered the parlour where he was relieved to see his wife stretched out on the settle, appearing to be asleep. He crept up to her, observed her to be breathing deeply and fully, then the fresh shine of blood horrified him. Her wrist had a gaping wound upon it and he felt revolted by the gore, almost faint, so that he leant against the settle and awoke the light sleeper.

Cannetta stretched, yawned and sat up in one graceful movement, her eyes falling on the form of her brooding husband towering above her. She swung her legs to the floor and stood up.

"Where have you been?" asked she. "Have you been neglecting your wife for other beauties?"

"A man must work," replied he evenly, apparently unconcerned by the underlying meaning of her words.

"True – but he needs to play also," returned she. "And in regions away from home where other attractions draw him!"

He turned sharply at this, no longer indifferent to her accusations and cried, "To what do you refer?"

"Ah-ha!" enthused she. "I hear the first throes of guilt flung at my head. Why is it my fault that your cousin assumes richer beauties in your eyes than I now possess?"

John turned away and leant upon the nearby table. He felt suddenly faint and sick.

"My meeting with my cousin was purely business! It does not concern you in any way, shape or form!" he cried, in anger.

"Do not lie to me, husband!" flashed she, her eyes huge and furious with increasing rage. "If you preferred HER why did you ask me to marry you? SHE was free, and still is, but you are not! You are mine!"

Something in her tone stung him with its bitterness and he shook his head as if to dispel her negative emotions.

"Cannetta!" he gasped, turning to face her. "What nonsense is this?"

"It is the truth!" retorted she, with passion. "My eyes are not closed to the ways of men – wandering men, I should say. You hoped your dalliance would be ignored by me and hidden under the guise of cousinship. Have you lain with her, John? Was this going on before you took the vows? Come, tell me how it is between you and Connie; tell your poor wife and break her heart!"

In answer he stepped up to her, slapped her once across the face and turned away, every nerve in his body taut and trembling.

She took the blow as best she could and scarcely moved but her eyes were livid and a small rill of blood cascaded from her nose which she wiped with shaking hands.

"What a feeble answer to a question that you cannot frame a reply to without condemning yourself! Do you suppose I am going to drop this adultery charge because you are physically stronger than me and can beat me when you chose? Ah, I can destroy you by other means, should I decide to and then we will see who comes off worse! Come, I am waiting for an answer – have you lain with her before or after our marriage?"

"She is my cousin – nothing more," growled he, refusing to look at his wife. "My love for her is just what you feel for your mother, or should feel.. She is an innocent and shy girl so do not degrade the kinship we feel for one other."

"Damn you then!" spat she, wildly flinging back her tangled locks. "I curse you for loving her and leaving me! You'll both pay dearly for this – and right under my nose as well! Did you expect me to believe your story of kinship when I observed earlier on today the knowing looks between you both and the tender glances! They should have been kept for ME, and for ME alone! Come tell me, is she everything I am not? Is she innocent and shy whereas you find me coarse and loud? Ah, weeks ago you loved my spirit and wanted to be joined to me for life! Where has that desire gone? Damn you, John Straeton, for making a fool of me for all of Ardle to see!"

He was so angry he could not speak and he wanted rid of her company so he walked over to the door, flung it open, slammed it furiously shut behind him and then she heard him quit the house by the back door.

As he passed the window Cannetta became sensible of her loss and she banged on the pane and shouted,

"No, don't leave me! Don't! I am your wife and she is only a cousin! John, John, don't go!" But her words drifted unheard and unheeded on the air and he walked on and out of the garden without a backward glance. She fell upon her knees, totally prostrate, and exuded tears that flowed profusely, soaking

107

her dress and splashing onto the grey carpet. All outer sensations ceased and she was left alone with an overwhelming sorrow that engulfed her disturbed mind...

She cried until time became meaningless and every scrap of sanity was drained from her broken body. Then, sitting up stiffly, she rolled her eyes, gazed around the room, appeared not to recognise her surroundings and dragged herself over to the door. Grasping the handle she turned it and pulled but the huge barrier was firmly locked and after minutes of useless struggling she gave up and threw herself on the floor. Her hands plucked at the carpet's pile and she shredded vast quantities of wool which she flung about the room, laughing hysterically so that soon most surfaces were festooned with grey fluff.
"John Straeton shall not keep me in by a lock," cried she, some realisation returning to her muddled brain. "Ah! I perceive a window."
But the largest pane of glass could not be opened and the tiny top window would only admit or release a small dog or cat and not a human, however slim. Accordingly, Cannetta thrust her hand through the biggest sheet of glass, battered the remaining pieces until they lay in shining fragments on the path outside and then commenced climbing through. She did not sense the deep cut on her palm which ran freely with blood, so great was her desire to escape.
In the front garden she flung up her arms to the sky to celebrate her freedom, then skirted the lawns and reached the sandy path. Her feet were still naked and now muddy and grazed from her earlier journey but she felt no pain and the dripping blood did not cause her any concern at all. Rounding the side of the house she paused to get her bearings and listened, her wild bloodshot eyes rolling as she searched the scenery from side to side. Then she gave a scream of delight and made her way to the base of a young oak tree that grew sturdily in a corner plot. Around its gnarled roots it could be seen that the soil had been violently disturbed and Cannetta knelt here and began to dig frantically with her hands in the soft brown earth. Presently she uncovered a long, pointed object that she snatched up greedily to her chest and then concealed in the pocket of her gown. Scraping the soil back and flattening it out she glanced around her in fear of being watched but, when no onlooker was apparent, she got up and retraced her steps to the garden where many bees were busy at their last pollen gathering of the season. A furious rage kindled in Cannetta's dirty face, streaked with soil from her digging and marked with blood from her weeping palm, and it soon became painfully obvious that in her mental anguish she knew not what she did and insanity took over...

Meanwhile her husband, who dreaded returning to his abusive wife, wandered the lanes of Ardle and climbed the hills of Stackhouses until

108

exhaustion overtook him. He felt disgusted at his violent behaviour but, apart from a nose wound, he did not believe he had hurt Cannetta, at least not physically. That she was in pieces mentally he recognised and her insane jealousy aimed at his innocent cousin frightened and alarmed him. Luckily he had quietly locked her in so she could not follow him or, worse still, seek out Connie for retribution. Dusk began to roll in from the west and it grew chill and much darker. John knew he would have to return at nightfall as then his wife would be at her worst and God knows what she would do to herself or his property if left alone. But what could he do? Sit up all night restraining her? Tie her in ropes or chains? He shuddered. Thankfully he met no one he knew and only a couple of wandering vagrants who looked at him in sympathy, so desperate and pathetic a figure did he portray. He kept his head low and was totally unconscious of the scenery which he usually admired as fine. A deep sense of pride prevented him from journeying to see Shirley, and although he knew she would have evinced considerable sympathy such an emotion would cause him to break down completely, and he needed to keep his mental faculties in order to think. Besides which he could not endure her enquiring eyes that pierced his soul every time he beheld them. Why was she so totally in tune with him? He shook his head as if to dispel the comforting picture of his cousin that rose up to taunt him. No, he must fold his grief back into his heart and come up with a solution to his disastrous marriage. There had to be a way out or some course of action he could take that would mean Cannetta was cared for and he was free of her insane behaviour.

"Ah, for Scotland!" sighed he. "For the sight of a bell of heather, och, but it'll be dying in Scotland soon and the frosts blackening every stem! Yet I would fain be there, no matter how cold and lonely, away from this torture!" His eyes brightened at the thought of the country of his birth but all hopes of ever seeing her again seemed diminished by his rash marriage. He was no longer a free man. It seemed Cannetta's form trailed the paths and lanes with him, shackled to him in chains of blood – a mad Cannetta, growling and moving on all fours as he had seen her at night. He shuddered. Despite his fear of her his mind shrank from having her committed where he knew she would certainly die. And could he take the looks of smug righteousness that this act would result in from the whole of Ardle? It would mean he had failed. But was imprisoning her, the safe thing to do? He knew the loss of her freedom would seal her doom and then he would be responsible for her demise. He could not take that. Raising his head he found he had wandered to the path behind Fourbridges and, as he turned in at the gate, he noticed the dying sun was slipping down below the treetops and the twittering birds were seeking roosts for the swiftly coming night. The red glow of the sun hit the house as he gazed upon it and he noticed the reflections in the windows of burning fire, except in one space that remained in darkness. He drew nearer. Now it was obvious there was no pane of glass in that dark space for the curtain had blown through the gap and flapped gently in the rising breeze. He ran forward in alarm and perceived the entire pane smashed in fragments upon the ground which meant, without doubt, that the window had been broken from the inside. Little drops of dried blood darkened the path. John peered into the room cautiously but he knew that his wife was not there. Standing upright he ran a shaking hand through his hair whilst his mind raced.

"Oh God! I feared this would happen! Yes, she is free and God knows where. She can be left no longer. I must find her and bring her home." He crossed the sandy path with quaking steps and the darkness swallowed him up. His eyes grew accustomed to the blackness and his restless stare searched everywhere for a human form hiding in the shades of night. The sloping fields opposite where Cannetta had sleepwalked when the powerful harvest moon drew her were empty and the tiny wood likewise deserted. Could she have gone further? It had been several hours since he locked her in and he did not know how quickly she had gained her freedom. He returned to the house, unsure of what to do next and moved to the garden once more. Why did he feel she was somewhere close at hand? And then, suddenly, he heard a voice, the very voice he sought, coming from the front garden. The tone was wild and the words almost incoherent, interspersed with cackles of laughter. He was horrified to find his knees shaking at the thought of facing her and he could hardly persuade his legs to walk. Crawling to the source of the sound the singing became louder and even more raucous-
"Then go to your lover and give him the letter,
 For the dreams it contains will make him feel better;
 If you love me, if you love me, in the marshes so green oh,
 If you leave me, I will kill you after what I have seen oh!"
She sang this in a drunken lilt as he rounded the corner of the house to find her. The rising moon glinted on her form and something she held in her right hand which, as he approached, revealed itself to be a wide mouthed glass jar filled with a colourless liquid which he presumed was water.   As Cannetta had her back to him she had not seen him as yet and she continued to swish the liquid round in the jar and laugh piercingly. Suddenly she darted forward and enclosed her hand upon a flying insect, presumably a gnat, dropped it into the jar whereupon she shook the contents and giggled. John could see the inside of the jar was dark with an assortment of drowning insects – bees which she must have caught earlier in the day, wasps and many gnats and flies. The mad gleam in her eye when she turned to him, the exalted, trembling lip, the eerie laugh that emitted from her dark throat - it all sent a wave of terror over him and he felt sick to his stomach. He lunged at her and grabbed the jar from her hold.

"No," cried Cannetta, struggling fiercely to reach the container which John held high in the air, well away from her. "You shall not have it. What manner of thing are you that only comes with the setting sun and reveals itself, not in the throes of daylight, but by the moon's gleams?"

"Enough of this nonsense, wife!" remonstrated he. "You know I am your husband and you shall not have the jar!"

"No, no, you cannot be John!" screamed she jumping for the object and flailing her arms about. "I remember him but he left me for someone else whose blood I recovered this afternoon that she might die for her betrayal. Me – ah – you do not ask about me but I shall live for my sins!"

"Give over!" shouted he, trying to fight her off as she attacked him with her nails. "How can you kill the bees, Cannetta? They do you no harm – gnats and wasps will sting but these poor insects bring the sweetest of treats to our world with their honey. Yet you have caused many to suffer and die!"

"They mustn't do it!" Cannetta screamed back, still jumping at the jar which he held aloft. "They mustn't take anything from here! They are raping my garden and my power is going with them, leaving me helpless!"

They continued grappling for the vessel but he, being considerably taller, managed to elude her and keep contact too, so she began kicking him savagely which caused considerable pain to his shins. He tried to run off but she followed him, lunging at his arms in desperation and presently the jar crashed to the ground between her feet.

As the spattered contents oozed out she set up a loud wailing that only ended when she had run out of breath. "See what you have done," sobbed his wife. "How could you – how could you? Yes, you are John – you have just proved it as only HE would do such a thing to me! Everything is spoiled – and I ached for their power! How could you deny me the power their consumption would have brought?" She gave a last, wild gasp then turned from him and ran into the house, he following once his traumatised brain had registered her departure. He entered just as she bounded up the stairs, leant over the bannister and flashed him a look of hate and fear. Then she crossed the landing and disappeared from his view but he knew, by the crash of a door, she had shut herself into their bedroom. He ran up after her, made a dash for the door, perceived she had locked it against him and then heard her set up a hideous wailing. Grasping the handle he rattled it, threw his weight against it but failed to move it.

"Cannetta!" called John trying to sound calm although his mind raced. "Let me in!"

An echo of a laugh replaced the screeching and then she replied,

"No, not if you cry for eternity! You are not welcome here! We are equal now – yes, you sought to imprison me earlier so you could go to your cousin's bed. There is something very unsavoury about you with Connie do you not think? You crave admittance, John do you? Get down on your knees and beg!"

"Never!" he yelled, beating his fists upon the door. "I'll break down this barrier first!"

"And if you do that, husband, I shall throw myself out of the window and tell the angels you flung me out! Now what do you say?"

"I do not believe you," returned John. "You'll not destroy yourself for me. All of Ardle sees and knows you as a mad woman. Do you think it will be any different when you smash your brains out on the path?"

"Pah," scorned Cannetta loudly. "Do you really think I value my own existence? If so you are even more foolish than I thought! I am capable of great sacrifice, I have trained myself to feel no pain and I can endure things that would make you cringe and shake! If you come in and force me to jump, John Straeton, then my blood will forever be on your hands!"

Despite her ramblings he was somewhat relieved that she knew who he was but he did not want to take any chances with her personal safety so he backed off and withdrew into silence, leaning against the opposite wall, brooding on a solution to the massive problem before him.

No further sound came from inside the locked chamber apart from an occasional laugh which echoed eerily in the darkness. The moon rose, by and by, and flooded the landing with mystical silver streaks and a few drops of rain hit the window with rhythmic taps whilst the wind gathered power and blew around the house as if seeking admittance. Still John stood motionless in a strange wakeful kind of sleep where every sense was heightened and yet resting. A universal silence fell.

At length he moved over to the door again and, placing his ear to the wood, attempted to ascertain if Cannetta was still raving but he could hear nothing and retreating to another bedroom he picked up a sturdy three legged stool that he judged was strong enough to break the door down. Accordingly he raised this above his head, took a short run up to the barrier and flung the stool and himself against the wood. Luck was with him, the door splintered and broke and he gained admittance. Flinging the broken stool aside he gazed around the room hoping to locate a shadowy figure in the interior. He heard a noise to the left and turning, beheld her bunched up on the windowsill, the large window pulled up, her hands stretched out to warn him. In the moonlight he saw the fear etched on her face and stopped in his tracks.

"Come one step nearer and I shall jump," whispered she, deadly calm. "I have never been more serious about anything in my life, John. I don't give a damn if I jump. One step, my former love, and I will go." She glanced down to the hard path beneath her and the sharp stones that graced the borders which could easily break her body into pieces.

"A whole new world waits for me out there," continued she, gazing down with fascination. "I almost pray you will move...and end my torture."

She faced him again but he felt she looked through him and beyond him, seeing he knew not what, but definitely not her desperate husband. He observed she had torn the shoulder of her gown and a deep flesh wound showed in her white neck but she was oblivious of it. The moonlight came in

112

and flooded her face so that she smiled and thanked it in a silent soliloquy. John froze, conscious that his breath was coming in gasps, but unable to call her as his dry lips could frame no words. A light breeze stirred her hair and the tattered portion of her dress and gradually he observed she was losing her hold on the sill and slipping outward. He made a prodigious grab for her, caught her arm and pulled with all his might as she tried to spring from the window.

"No, no, let me go!" she screamed. "You can be free to marry Connie, your one true love, if you let me go!"

He continued to yank her back with superhuman strength.

"I will not be a murderer," he cried, between gritted teeth. "For that reason, and because, come what may, you are my wife - you must come back!"

Eventually he succeeded in pulling her away from the windowsill and, after fastening the frame and drawing the curtain with one hand, he flung her onto the bed and stood guard over her. But she lay there, gasping, motionless and prostrate, then she put her hands to her head, closed and opened her eyes frantically and asked,

"John – what has happened? Why am I lying here covered in blood? What have I done?"

He perceived her eyes were clear and lucid, that she touched him gently without her frantic grip of earlier hours and she seemed unaware of what had passed between them lately. He was unable to reply at first, so shocked was he at the change in her manner and demeanour. It was like a different woman inhabited her body now and the clutching screeching harpy had gone replaced by reason and passiveness. But she was very confused too and kept staring at him for an explanation. After a few minutes of silence she came and touched his arm as if seeking solace and comfort. Trying not to be repulsed by her John took her hand and led her gently out of the chamber and into a back room, much smaller, where there was a single bed made up as a couch. He bade her lay upon it and covered her with a blanket, putting two pillows at her head. Gazing into saner eyes he tried to speak to her and explain why she was here.

"You must sleep on this couch tonight, Cannetta. Believe me there is a reason and it is for your own good."

She gave a start at this and asked why he could not tell her but he remained grave and silent.

"Here alone?" she faltered, nervously. "Oh, John, I…"

"Hush," he replied, putting his fingers up to her lips. "Rest now and we will talk later. You have to trust me, Cannetta, on this one. I shall not be far away and I shall see you in the morning but, for tonight we must sleep apart."

She did not understand but she nodded, her eyes filled with tears.

"Trust me," he whispered again then he left, scared lest his newly-found compassion would lead to him taking her back into his bed. He felt numb and utterly drained. He waited at the door until he heard her breathing settle into the rhythm of sleep then he locked the barrier as quietly as he could and put the key under his pillow. Too tired to do any reasoning he could only be thankful that his wife had returned to the world of reality where he could cope with her. How long she would remain there only time would tell and what he would do when her insanity broke out again he dare not think…He flung himself fully dressed onto bed and immediately fell into a light yet restful sleep of complete exhaustion.

CHAPTER 11

Cannetta did not remain asleep for long. She woke suddenly with a start, just after midnight, and sat up in her unfamiliar bed, her figure stiff and erect; her mind racing. She clasped her hands protectively round her knees and every so often she gave a small sound that echoed like the whine of a distressed dog. Soon she began to rock herself back and forth, tears flowing down her face and soaking her dirty, torn gown. Feeling the sting of her open wound brought back memories of the night before and the thrill of pain spurred her on. She got up off the bed and removed her tattered gown, finding, as she did so, the sharp point of an instrument in the pocket which she drew out and gazed at in delight.

"So he did not take it after all. Yes, he took my nourishment but not my weapon! See how it shines in the moonlight!" cried she, turning the cruel blade to the window which was not obscured by curtains or blinds. Further memories hit her with a glancing blow.

"He has put me away in here that he might sleep with HER!" she wailed, fury returning to her dilated eyes. Turning the knife back towards her chest she nicked her flesh quickly and laughed.

"For him," she whispered, collecting a small quantity of blood on the blade. "Our blood shall mix then he will come back to me."

Approaching the door she discovered it was locked but that did not deter her. Did she not have a powerful weapon in her hands and the lock was old and rusty, like many things in the house? As yet John had not had time to repair these ageing doors. She applied the knife carefully, split the lock easily from the rotten wood and forced the barrier open, keeping her movements quiet and calm. Padding down the landing she stopped outside the bedroom that had previously been theirs and listened, her ears strained to hear if two breaths rose and fell in the darkened room. She could only hear one but the voices in her head told her two and, being totally controlled by them, she believed all they said. She tried the door. It was open.

Entering with considerable stealth the intensity of the darkness almost dazzled her and she took a moment or two to get her bearings. Yes, there was the large stalwart form of the wardrobe, there the smaller form of the cabinet, so where was the bed? She held the knife out in front of her as though it were a lamp to light her way and, by and by, her eyes picked out the bed. There was the long, silent shadow that was her husband; there was the impression of his head on the snowy white pillow.

Cannetta raised the knife and closed her eyes, just for a split second, as a small rill of blood stung her with its flow from her neck, down into her blue petticoat. She opened them again and struck but the blade pierced the mattress; no form lay incumbent on the bed and the knife was stuck in the material. She struggled to remove it, became sensible of a presence behind her and spun round, having freed the blade at last.

"I must cut the evil out of you that she has put in since she touched your life," she gasped. "When you married me you were turned towards ME and you were innocent but since SHE beheld you, as her love, you turned away from me. She shall not have you and since you persist in lying with her you must die at my own hands. Do you hear me?"

John wrenched her wrist as she lunged at him and succeeded in knocking the weapon out of her hand. In a thrice she darted forward to pick it up but he snatched at it and held it high over his head, out of her reach. She gave a scream of despair. John threw the knife into a nearby drawer, secured his wife's hands behind her back and then tied them with his belt which he took from his trousers. He shook terribly and his teeth chattered. Cannetta suddenly flopped and offered no resistance at all. Her head lunged forward on her chest and her plentiful hair covered her features but her eyes were closed and she leant against him as a dead weight. He flung her onto the bed, kindled a light and then finished tying her feet with another belt which he took from the wardrobe. Now, in the candle's flickering flame, he could see the dirt in her hair and on her skin, the huge wound at her neck still bleeding. She began to whine gently, as though in pain, but he felt no compassion for her. How nearly had he lost his life! His knees shook and he knelt upon the ground, suddenly weak and dizzy. Shock was setting in as he leant against the bed and covered his eyes, hating to look upon the prostrate form of his wife, even though she was now silent and still.

"Oh, Cannetta! Oh, my God, what am I to do? She cannot be left again. She must not be left again. Insanity has truly taken over and defeated the last grains of realisation she held onto. She is mad, completely mad and as such if she regains her freedom she will try to kill me again or, even worse, Connie. She must be hidden. No one must see her, only myself. The locks must be strengthened in every room and I must search her daily for anything she has concealed to use against me. Oh
God what a life we must lead now? No not a life, more of an existence. Yet what else can I do? Give her up to the asylum? I would rather kill her first!"

He found another two belts and used them to ensure his wife's feet and hands were securely bound so that he could leave her with some safety. Her eyes followed him now and she began to hum, as she lay there like a disobedient child he had caught performing a misdemeanour. Covering her with a fringed blanket, as the room was cold, he perceived she tore at the tassels with her teeth in an insane frenzy and he could take no more but hurried from the room in tears. The blanket could have been him.

A week passed away quietly in the district of Stackhouses and the winter weather asserted itself by thrashing storms, high winds and hail upon the village of Ardle. Pieces of ice the size of walnuts frequently rattled against the window panes and candles were required before the hour of seven o'clock rang out in the evening. Men going a-field in the morning did so in darkness and everyone complained they had never experienced weather like this in September. The last fragile links with summer were broken and the sun hid beneath thick, grey cloud refusing to leave her stormy bed. The trees began to lose their leaves and seemed stripped naked overnight, the occasional pine or holly cheering the woodland with some greenery. Great piles of dead leaves filled every available ditch, hollow and incline and blew about the land like demented fairies. The last of the summer migrants departed for warmer climes and the winter hibernators prepared themselves for a long, cold sleep.

To Shirley the approaching season promised nothing but hardship and, despite her husband's presence, loneliness too. Her love for John did not fade and she hoped, day after day, that he would visit but she saw him not, apart from in her dreams. Within her heart she felt his marriage kept him away but not because he resided in happiness, more because he was immersed in trouble. She longed for him to open up to her, who cared so much, but she knew it was not right to call on him and she feared Cannetta's anger if she did. She remembered the last time he visited and how withdrawn he had been; how he had ignored her and only spoke to Connie in desultory tones that were quite unlike his usual cheerful way of speaking. It showed he was greatly preoccupied by his change of state but his eyes were so low and sad she knew it harboured nothing good and the rumours concerning Cannetta and him still ran rife. That he had disclosed some of his trouble to her she appreciated but only if he were brutally honest and frank could she help him. She felt there was some reserve and discord between them over this, an awkwardness that had never been there before but surely existed because John kept his own counsel. And as Connie had left to go back to work Shirley was thrown into her own company and she yearned for the presence of another to end this speculation.

When the weather was reasonable Shirley spent long hours ascending and descending the hills to Stackhouses, traversing the paths and generally walking the tracks in the hopes of meeting her cousin. Before his marriage he had been constantly perambulating, latterly riding, about the district in his work but since he took Cannetta to Fourbridges he seemed like a hermit. Every churn of horse's hooves sent her heart racing but it was never the black gelding and she gave up expecting to see him. Enquiries told he was still treating the local stock but not as frequently as before and sometimes he stated he was indisposed, never giving a reason but just sending the farmers to other horse doctors for help.

Connie, meanwhile, was settling herself back into a working routine of rising every morning at five but she found it exhausting and far harder than before her illness. She assumed she had grown lazy and spoilt, having spent many weeks being cosseted by her stepmother, but after a while she lost her appetite, evinced a terrible thirst and lost the tiny amount of weight she had gained whilst at home. The familiar pain returned to her side, she coughed

117

long and loud into the night and struggled to lift even the lightest tray. Yet in all her suffering the one thing that comforted her was the picture of John, her cousin as such, helping her move her things back to her tiny room. Although she saw him no longer the memories of his kindness and concern cheered her and she began to understand just what her stepmother saw in the man. He was truly difficult to forget.

The autumn days wore on and the first white frosts covered the land, tinged the air with ice and bittered the running streams which were swollen with the heavy rains of summer. To Connie every breath was agony, the cold paining her failing lungs and freezing within her, although at times sweat beaded her brow and she felt the fire of fever burn in her body. A few dead leaves still fluttered against the panes and lay, rotting, on the verdure of the stately lawns. The gardeners raked them up and built bonfires to lighten the autumn evenings, sending the pungent smell of wood smoke spiralling up into the starry skies.

John, at first, became immured in his own self -pity but, at last, he recognised the nightmarish quality of his life was receding as a wretched, yet persistent hope entered his heart and beat within his brain. It could not always be this difficult. At some point in the future his life would have to improve and to that day he remained focused, especially when his wife bit and scratched him and seemed worse than usual. He vowed not to leave her for more than a couple of hours and generally remained constant to that vow but sometimes time ticked away and, treating a more difficult case, turned in to half a day or more. Then he felt the pain of guilt for neglecting her and he would try to bring normality to her world but she would repel him with her snake-like embraces and her rabid clutches that resulted in injury to his person. Constantly covered in bruises and wounds he hid them as best he could and wondered where it would all end. Rarely could he let her out of the chains he had forged for her and even then he shackled her feet so she could not run away. Most of the time she did not recognise him but when she did she pleaded with him to free her and he had to harden his heart to say no. Then, lo, the next time he visited her she would be totally immured in her inner world of madness and crawl on all fours, growling and snarling like some demented animal, that had she been a creature, he would have shot on sight. In vain did he try to encourage her to sew or stitch, she usually ripped up the material with her teeth and scattered the remnants with laughter. He dreaded nightfall as she was far worse then and he dare not go out of the house until the chains were in place and frequently he had to gag her to stop her screams from keeping him awake all night. Often, at dusk, she would hurl her meal at him, try to snatch the candle and only cease the restless wandering in her mind when he had given her a measure of laudanum or alcohol by force. When she slept he sat savouring the welcome silence and luxuriating in the knowledge that she could not reach out from her world of slumber and haunt him. But she knew he was afraid of her and she revelled in this at times, laughing at his discomfiture and trying harder and harder to bite and wound him. It was like dealing with a man-eating lion or tiger that he could never turn his back on without the threat of serious injury and he only had to be off his guard for a few seconds and she would attack him, enjoying the shedding of his blood and licking any cuts with great relish. She revolted, shocked and degraded him but he had no choice but to continue imprisoning her and caring for her in the very basic manner the situation allowed. Sometimes she would lie stiff and unyielding on her bed and he would creep in to see if she was still breathing but sadly she continued in rude health and he rebuked himself for hoping otherwise.

Keeping his counsel about her illness he murmured to others, if they enquired of Cannetta, that she was kept indoors by some lingering cold but that he expected her to be abroad again soon. To his mother-in-law he told the same lie, slightly more involved it was true, but he was relieved when Rose made no plans with him to see her daughter. In fact he only encountered his mother-in-law once or twice in his travels and she seemed almost careless of Cannetta's health. John assumed she was grateful for the peace that now reigned in her life after God knows how many years of coping with her daughter's growing insanity. Of course he knew nothing of the room hidden behind the arras and the chains that had graced the walls there for many summers and winters. But Rose was not a fool and she noticed the flame of fear and the light of terror in her son-in-law's eyes and she turned away, anxious not to get involved with the trouble that had surely descended on him when he took Cannetta as a bride. Rose consoled herself with the thought that she had attempted to warn him of what he was to become joined to but his adamant wishes to wed were his own choice.

"He has made his bed, despite what I told him as her mother, and he must now lie on it. God, if she is there at night, I do not know how he copes with her but it is there in his face...the sleeplessness, the terror, the shock of beholding, every day, Cannetta's insanity and, moreover, dealing with it," she mused.

October came – wild, wet and windy with days when the frozen ground did not thaw out and the black frosts remained victorious over the weak and feeble sun. Common ills raised their heads in Ardle and the surrounding areas as the cold took its toll, affecting the animals too. John was increasingly busy. The slow peal of funeral bells rang out for many of the old folk and the gravedigger rubbed his hands in glee at his constant work of digging in the hardened earth. Many days he had to wait past midday before he could begin his labour but the money spurred him on and he lived well that month. The skies seemed waiting for the first fall of snow – so pallid, empty and silent did they stretch as far as the eye could see, reflecting their colourless insipid light onto a winter landscape.

Connie was sent home in view of the return of her illness which now corrupted both lungs and meant she struggled to get her breath, even when sitting down. She gasped when she exerted herself at all and could do no work at the Hall save the simplest of tasks and her constant coughing kept everyone awake at night. She refused to have a doctor summoned as she fervently believed that the disease would pass, as last time, if she just rested. Thus Shirley was suddenly thrown from her dreamy, wistful existence to one where she was constantly busy, looking after an invalid who quickly became bed-ridden. In some ways she welcomed it as to think of John and Nurse Connie was nearly impossible and she tried to concentrate on her step-daughter. Connie's care kept Shirley from continuing her walks and she sat indoors, gazing out at the bleak scenery or sewing whilst Connie slept fitfully.

As the month passed away John became sensible of a change in his patient, which he welcomed gladly, although he could contribute it to no known cause. Gradually Cannetta stopped attacking him, seemed calmer and a little more lucid than she had. It gave him hope that she had turned the corner on her illness – if that indeed was what it was, and would continue to progress with no return to the violent, screaming harpy he had been forced to deal with in the past weeks. One morning she commented on the beauty of the bird song she had heard at dawn and the next she noticed the rare sunrise of gold and red in the morning sky. For the first time she ate, slept and sewed without resorting to her inner world of madness and spoke to him sensibly and lucidly. He relished the newly-found peace this changing situation brought but realised he must not be off his guard just yet. Accordingly he slackened her chains a little and did not bind her so tightly but still observed her carefully at every opportunity. Here, at last, was hope that they could return to some sort of normality after weeks of residing in a hellish life that offered no comfort. He encouraged his wife to read and sew and smiled at the improvement such activities brought her.
One morning, as he brought her breakfast Cannetta asked him if he would join her and he assented, they both sitting down to the first meal together since the week of their wedding. She thanked him sincerely for the food, said grace and consumed it with a good appetite. Usually she crammed the food into her mouth with both hands which revolted him, especially as most of it remained on her face and clothes, but today she used the utensils and ate calmly.
"Why can I not go out, my darling?" she asked when the meal was over and he sat with her still. "I could go out with you, my husband, and we could walk the lanes again. How I long to see them in their winter glory! Has any snow fallen yet?"
"No, the paths are clear but it is cold and the sky is full of impending flakes that will fall before long, I fear. But I cannot take you out there, Cannetta, at least not yet. By and by if things settle down I will see."
She bowed her head and murmured that she would be content with that.

"Please do not shackle me!" she begged as he prepared to put the chains back on after her meal. "Let me be free a little while longer. I promise all I shall do is my tapestry work until you return. Look at me John! Do you not perceive the change in me? Yes, you can wrap me in chains tonight – I will allow that with no complaints but for today let me be free."

Her tone was very persuasive and he was considering her request when a sharp rap at the door summoned him from the room. He thrust her into her chains as quickly as he could, locked the door behind him and ran down the stairs to his visitor.

Descending the slope towards Ardle some five minutes later astride his black gelding on an urgent call to a sick cow he observed, ahead of him, the hurrying form of a woman carrying in her arms a clothed bundle. She approached him rapidly and he reined his horse over that she might pass more easily for the track was narrower at that point. In doing so he believed he recognised her gait but his mind was elsewhere with the progressive change in his wife, which bemused him. The woman had a hood up which hid her face and as he mused inwardly on his situation she passed him and cried loudly,

"Oh John!"

He did not seem to register her call but gazed ahead of him, with a blank expression on his face, and when he did turn towards her it was as if she were a stranger.

When Shirley observed this she flung back her hood, allowing her thick golden ringlets to tumble out of her tightly gathered cloak.

"Do you not know me?" she asked, in a hurt tone. "See, I am your cousin, can you not remember me?"

John shook his head and, slowly, her facial features burnt into his mind and realisation hit him.

"Ah, Shirley," murmured he, somewhat confusedly. "You must forgive me – I am not myself at all and the troubles of my life rise up to choke my failing memory."

He perceived he had hurt her by his nonchalant behaviour but it was not intended and after a while he saw she forgave him and seemed pleased to behold him again.

"How are you, John?" she said, in a concerned tone, when it was obvious he was not going to impart any more information.

"Very well, thank you," he replied, putting his guard up at her intrusive gaze which seemed to pierce his soul.

"I am on my way to take Damion his forgotten lunch. He is working in Cooper's meadow, not very far from your house," she replied, attempting to get him to open up more.

"And I am off to Marlowe's farm to see a sick cow," he ventured, feeling he was on safer ground now. He picked up the reins and made as if to depart.

"John…" she laid hold of his horse's bridle, as if to stop his imminent progress. "John….how is she? You know who I mean - your wife. No one has seen her for weeks. You looked so happy on your wedding day and now you seem transparent, pale and miserable. I know 'tis not my business to ask but…"

John leant forward in the saddle.

"And it is not mine to tell, cousin," he whispered, as though fearful of being overheard. "Yes, at times I crave to tell someone and have the support of a sympathetic ear and there is none in Ardle that I love as well as yours. Everywhere I go the sky laughs at me, the wind mocks me. But what I have endured is fit for no human ear to listen to and no eye should ever behold what I have seen. The hills hereabouts have stood witness to far worse than my suffering and they keep their silence so why should I not keep mine? Yes, I was a fool. Do you not think I know that now? Now when it is too late? I would love to run away, run away and never look back but I am trapped until death overtakes me. Lately I have been led to hope things will improve but I own I cannot believe it - I will not, in case disappointment comes calling as she has many times before…"

He gazed into her beautiful blue eyes and felt mesmerised by the love they contained, spilling over in the form of cascading tears. She swallowed and tried to control her feelings.

"John, if I had been free you would not be in this dreadful situation now…"

He looked away to the distant hills and shook his head.

"There is no purpose in mentioning things that can never be, now or in the future," he murmured. "I must go. Goodbye, Shirley," and he urged his horse forward and left her.

Shirley watched him go. She yearned to go after him, take his hand and hold him to bring some comfort to his nightmarish world.

"Oh, God, how he suffers." she breathed to herself. "He is plagued by the ills of a bad marriage – lack of sleep, anxiety for the future and the constant pangs of loneliness. She has become a millstone around his neck as we all foretold she would and unless he cuts himself free she will utterly destroy him." She remained standing there, staring at the ground for a few minutes then she came back to reality, dried her eyes and continued on her journey.

Within the walls of Fourbridges a figure stirred, discovered her chains had not been fastened properly and that with a shake and a pull she was at liberty to roam around the room that had been her prison for many a long week. Cannetta was free. Her husband, in his urgency to answer the door and leave the company that he found so distasteful, had failed to lock the clasps on her shackles and with minimal movement the wrist irons fell away and she was able to rise and walk about. She tried the door, found it barred and went over to the window. John had not bothered to fasten this securely, knowing in her chains she was totally unable to leave her bed, let alone approach the window. With frenzied fingers and wild, delighted eyes she freed the large pane and scrambled out onto the windowsill. There, below her, was a drop that constituted a good ten feet and beneath her quaking form was the hard, white stone path bordered by rectangular flower beds. To fall on that would mean certain injury, maybe even death. For a moment she resolved not to care but her eyes darted on a tree close to the house, spreading its branches to the left of the window. The topmost bough was only about six feet away and would surely break her fall even if it did not take her weight. Moreover it had leaves which would afford her some protection from the pointed twigs that made up the bough. She executed her plan perfectly, dropped off the windowsill into the spreading tree, its bough buckled a little under her weight but allowed her to reach the ground with only a few scratches. She smiled in delight when her naked feet touched the earth for the first time in weeks and she stood there, savouring the contact before moving off.

Running swiftly down the white path she approached the young oak tree which stood stalwart and naked under the grey morning sky. Feverishly she began to dig in the same spot as before and this time she unearthed another object, thinner and longer than the last, which had a handle. Cleaning it on her dress she gazed around her, suddenly fearful of being observed but seeing no one she pocketed the item and began to cover her tracks by replacing the earth. When all was done to her satisfaction she stood up, ran back along the path and left the property by the side gate. The morning breeze fluttered the curtain from the open window on the first floor of the house and a couple of broken branches from the tree and a few impressions in the mud of the flower beds were all that remained of the prisoner's escape.

Cannetta ran onwards, never pausing in her flight, her bare feet sure of the track she found herself on. Running lithely along the back lanes of Ardle she encountered no one it being past nine o'clock and the men all a-field. Presently she reached the path she desired, gave a great scream of triumph and increased her speed as her feet struck its shale. The lose material did not slow her down at all or impede her progress but rather she ran faster as she neared her goal. Her mouth was set in a determined grimace, her eyes glassy and piercing, rarely blinking in their powerful stare. At length she reached the cottage that was her destination and approached the cherry pink door. A huge dog, shackled on a length of chain, stood up to greet her, but recognising her instantly, he merely whined and licked her hand when she came near him. Cannetta leant against the wall to recover her breath. Sweat trickled down her face, stung her eyes and matted her damp hair at the temples so she wiped her face brusquely. Then her sensitive ears picked up a low hollow cough that seemed to echo from the cottage before her and play about the winter garden. Cannetta stood up, quelled her restlessly beating heart, her hand tightening on the implement in her dress pocket. Following the side path that led to the back of the dwelling she surveyed the place and took in a partially open window which showed the interior of the kitchen. A rickety, three-legged stool stood by a scrubbed wooden table that was surrounded by three chairs and on one of these sat a young, thin woman whose pallid face was covered in perspiration. It was she who was coughing and presently, as Cannetta watched, she got up, fell against the table and moved round to the opposite side where a glass of liquid awaited her. She drank with great difficulty then remained sitting with her back to Cannetta, a dry rattle sounding in her throat leading to a spasm that allowed no breath and caused her to gasp loudly for air.

The watcher brought forth the concealed item and caressed it lovingly. She moved forward silently and pushed open the window to a wide semi-circle from the ledge, the space between being amply sufficient for Cannetta's slim figure to pass through. Grasping the sill with one hand she swung herself up as noiselessly as a cat and landed, without a sound, on the kitchen floor. Raising the item she carried to her eyes she put it out in front of her. It was a small yet extremely sharp curved knife.

Connie, whose senses were dimmed by her coughing and fever, had heard nothing to alarm her or cause her to turn her head. As far as she was aware she remained alone in the kitchen. She leant forward and drained the glass thirstily then coughed again and wiped her mouth. There followed a long, heavy silence during which Cannetta stood only feet from her victim, blessing the weapon she proposed to strike into her adversary.

Only a few minutes behind Cannetta, the stepmother of this lamb to the slaughter dawdled slowly along the track, her eyes sad and low her heart bleeding for her suffering cousin. Her mind had been searching for a solution to his problems or for any way she could help him in his troubles. Although she did not know the full extent of his grief she had felt it keenly at their meeting and she could not forget his grey, pain-twisted face. His eyes hovered in front of her, wretched, desperate and unhappy. Yet his pride was too strong to release him from his enforced silence and turn to her for help. What had he said? There was no ear he loved more than hers? But he had not sought her out; she had come upon him.

She turned in at her gateway. And there was Connie too, who was not getting any better but daily becoming weaker as her symptoms gained strength. That cough! To lie awake at night and listen to it, knowing she could not help the girl, was indeed soul-destroying. She approached the back of the cottage and passed the kitchen window where, by chance, she happened to look in and the scene that greeted her eyes froze her in terror. For there was John's wife, knife in hand, creeping up on her stepdaughter who remained oblivious to the danger. Shirley shook her head and looked again. The scene had not changed, except Cannetta was nearer her prey. The maniac had her arm outstretched, the knife in front of her the blade glinting in the light. Suddenly Connie became aware of her intruder, words were spoken and Shirley saw Cannetta lower her arm with the weapon in. Had the insane woman given up her threats? Shirley's mind raced. What could she do? To enter the kitchen and try to restrain Cannetta herself would put her life at risk as well as Connie's. She turned and ran from the terrifying scene, praying that she could find John and get him to come back and deal with his mad wife.

Connie tried to stand up from her chair but her legs almost gave way under her and she clung to the table for support.

Cannetta stopped waving the knife about and seemed confused as to who she faced. She stopped her progress and narrowed her eyes.

"Are you the girl whose life I once saved? I am not sure now. Do my eyes deceive me? You look like her but she was surely bigger and not wasted into death like you!"

Connie knew she had to deny her name and try to keep this woman talking so Cannetta did not use the weapon she held so lovingly in both hands. She caressed the handle of the knife and murmured words too low for Connie to hear.

Suddenly, catching the girl's eyes upon her, she bounded forward and cried, "He has chained me since he slept with - that woman, no, she is not a woman as I am - full-blooded, mature, lusty - she is a little girl. He has subdued me for far too long...long, precious weeks of my life have gone in his grasp...He has taken my freedom but I have claimed it back!"

"That is dreadful," gasped Connie, terrified at the nearness of Cannetta and her mad, wide bloodshot eyes.

"Yes," replied Cannetta. "Let me tell you about it. You will not tell him I can see as you do not know him. Do you know him?"

"No, I do not," assured Connie, keeping her eyes on the weapon that was still in the mad woman's grasp.

"Then you know nothing of his atrocities to me! Let me tell you he has for days kept me shackled and in chains in a mere box room while he sleeps in the master bedroom with HER. Ah, I tried to catch her but she was too quick for me! Now deliberation has brought me here, where I thought she resided. And he starved me so I was forced to live on flies and rainwater. He would not even allow the sun to shine on me lest I should defile it and he boarded my window up so I was a creature that crawled in darkness. The light of day never reached my face. He humiliated me, he tortured me, he neglected me, yet still a portion of my power remained and broke through. Well, do you love him now? Is you he loves? Has he thrown me over for this pallid, wasted thing I see before me? Do you love him enough to die for?"

"I am not she of whom you speak. She used to live here but she does not now. She resides most of the time at your dwelling. THAT is why you are locked away! She is probably there now....with him. If you return you could catch them both and surprise them," returned Connie, cleverly, thinking quickly as to how she could diffuse the situation which was becoming desperate.

"Hush. Do not invent falsehoods! I am sure I saw you walking with him, so it follows that you are laying with him too, and in OUR bed. Did he not carry your cases one day and you both smiled in easy conversation? I stood in a green bower and observed it all. Except that you look very different from that day...so is it....could it be you?"

"That was my sister he helped," Connie tried to assure her. "She is bigger and younger than me. At the moment she is at work at the Hall but she will be back later if you care to wait."

Cannetta narrowed her eyes and stared at the terrified girl before her. The grip on her knife tightened.

"I do not believe it," she cried. "Your lungs pump as though you are dying. Do you not feel it as penance for sleeping with a married man? Come confess to me how you enticed him away. Did you use magic?"

"I have no knowledge of spells or magic but my sister affirms she is a witch and has likely controlled him by some incantation. Surely you, as the greater witch, can break her spell and secure the man with your power."

Shirley ran as fast as she could. Her heart beat almost fit to burst and her side ached at the unusual strenuous activity. She turned in at the entrance to Marlowe's farm, paused briefly to catch her breath then set off again her eyes searching for John's horse. She prayed desperately that he had not finished here and gone on to another call, the destination of which she did not know. But the end of the sandy track revealed the stolid farmhouse and her cousin's black gelding tied up outside it. She slipped on the gritty track, righted herself and gazed around in anguish.

John and Marlowe were at present engrossed on a heated discussion on the merits of blistering swine's feet which was interrupted by a loud bark from Marlowe's lurcher guard dog. The farmer broke off conversation in mid-sentence and stepped hastily out of the barn to find the intruder. John followed him and the pair scanned the length of track that led from their location to the house. They were just in time to see a woman almost slip over on the path, regain her feet and almost fall again from sheer exhaustion. John sped away to her, took her in his arms and patted her back as she struggled to gain some breath and thus impart to him the urgency of her mission.

"Shirley," murmured he. "What ails you? See you have cut your temple and it bleeds! I am sure Mr Marlowe will not mind you coming inside to rest. Lean on me."

"No, no, no," stammered Shirley, hardly able to form the words. "I have not come for myself and I pant because I have run all the way from ours. Oh, John! Oh, my God...It is your wife - she has come to the cottage and has a knife at Connie's throat. I saw it all through the window and just fled here. Oh, pray we are not too late - you must hurry..."

His face grew deathly pale and a terrible fear came into his eyes and he shook his head incredulously.

126

"That cannot be. I chained her, I shackled her, I locked her in."
Shirley shook him.

"It is the truth, I swear it," she gasped. "Please, John, please, do not delay. She may have killed Connie by now!"

At her affirmation his eyes changed, he gazed about him wildly, dragged her by one arm to the black gelding and threw her on his horse's back, vaulting up in front of her with nimble strength.

"Hold on to me!" he cried, as he urged the horse into a gallop.

They passed Marlowe as a whirl of legs and hooves and he gazed after them in astonishment.

"By God!" swore he, "that's the fastest exit I have ever seen. And with Penlow's wife if I'm not mistaken!" He chuckled to himself. "I know he was losing the argument but really." He wandered into the farmhouse to soothe his nerves with some home-brew.

As they sped along Shirley, who had never ridden a horse before, did not know whether to be frightened or relieved at their mode of transport. She had expected John to gallop off, leaving her to follow in his wake but clinging onto him, in spite of the constant jolting, calmed her racing fears. He did not speak but just urged the horse to greater velocity every time the beast slackened his pace. John could feel her arms and how they melted into his body so he did not know what part was his and what hers. It was like they were melted and fused together and at every stride he felt more in tune with her, even in the midst of this tragedy. The high banks, fields and meadows whistled past them in their flight and they drew near to Ardle. Presently the pink cottage came in sight and the fear rose again in them both. What would they find? And how had Cannetta escaped from her bonds and a locked room?

The horse delivered them to the door. John reached up for Shirley and lifted her down as gently as he could.

"Oh my darling," he breathed. "In whatever follows you must trust me – you must have faith in me."

"Yes," faltered she "Yes, I do."

He grabbed her arm and they both ran round the side of the cottage, slowing to a walk as they neared the window. John looked in.

It was exactly as Shirley had said it was. Nothing seemed to have changed. He observed the menacing figure of his wife, still brandishing the knife but her face turned away from them as they watched. In fact she had her back to the window and seemed oblivious of anything except the prey she stalked. There, huddled in the far corner was Connie, trying to make herself as small as possible whilst her aggressor towered above her.

John took in the dreadful situation, slid to the back door, found it was locked and bolted, possibly from the inside. Shirley's eyes bore into his soul. How could he fail her now? He noticed the open window but how could he fit his six foot plus frame through such a small gap. He turned back to his cousin but her eyes pleaded with him and he resolved to try. Grasping the pane he forced it open to its widest gap, wrenching it even further by superhuman strength. He could hear Cannetta scolding in the tone that meant she was totally immersed in her inner world of madness. She could not hear him. Her whole attention was on the cowering girl before her.

John was surprised to find Shirley had joined him, ducking through the window easily as she was slim and shorter than he. But their entrance had been too swift, too sudden for Connie whose petrified eyes darted on her rescuers and she gave a little scream of mingled fear and relief.

Cannetta, whose attention was totally on her victim perceived the look and, following the glance, she spun round and faced the two intruders.

John, realising he had been recognised by the bloodshot eyes of his wife, advanced slowly and held out his hand, but Cannetta was not about to give up so easily and she darted the knife towards him so he was forced to withdraw to the window. He motioned Shirley to keep behind him.

"Ah-ha, John Straeton, you are come at last are you?" screamed Cannetta, relishing the power over him her position gave her. "Well, as usual you are too late. I neither want nor need you. Yes, you locked me up in chains stinking of your own cowardice because you could not face me since you had lain with her."

"Give me the knife, Cannetta," replied he firmly but quietly, advancing towards her once more.

"No, never," vowed she. "What, would you take away the one vestige of pleasure that is left in my life since YOU entered it? But I see all the evil ones are here." catching sight of Shirley cowering behind John. "She, that bitch you hide, she is guilty too of adultery. What, have you slept with them both? Oh my God, you are even worse than I thought! Now, who shall I kill first? What a choice! YOU, John Straeton, shall be last as you will give me the most pleasure but which of these two bitches wishes to taste the knife first? Come on, speak up!"

"Give me the weapon, Cannetta," repeated John, his eyes never leaving her face.

He continued to advance but very slowly and Cannetta retreated until she had reached Connie, still huddled in a corner, sobbing.

"Now," she whispered, rubbing the blade of the knife against the skin on Connie's arm. "Now 'tis time. No more delays, no more mercy. Did you show me any when you seduced my husband? No! Come any nearer and my knife shall pierce this colourless body and spill her lifeblood!"

John stopped dead but held out his hand, coaxingly.

"Come to me, Cannetta. You are still my wife. These two mean nothing to me, nothing to me at all beside you. Do you notice how pallid their beauty shines beside yours? Give me the knife, my angel!"

Cannetta threw back her head and laughed.

128

"You shall draw it out of her throat if you come a step nearer," she enthused. John put down his outstretched arm and stared at his delighted wife.

"Are our roles not completely reversed?" cried she. "Are you not shackled and imprisoned by my power now? But the difference is none of you shall escape. Ah, I was too clever for you but you shall not subdue me now!"

"You will never get away with this, Cannetta," warned he. "They will never rest until they have hunted you down and put you away for the rest of your life, not just days and weeks. Come to me now and I will get you the help you need. You will never be chained or locked up again."

"Do you suppose I value the worthlessness of my existence? You have been in league with my mother, she shackled me too. I would rather return to her cruelty than face yours!"

"That is not MY Cannetta talking," pleaded John. "She was good and kind and it is her I love, not this evil harpy I see before me. Ah, I would take HER back tomorrow and give up everything for her!"

"I was never yours!" screamed his wife. "You just used and abused me whilst sleeping with these bitches. It is these women that you want, not me."

"That is not true, my darling," soothed John, his eyes pleading with her to come to him. "Do you not fear eternal damnation for taking three innocent lives?"

Cannetta shook her head.

"You speak of my sins John Straeton, but what about YOURS? If you would hand out physical retribution then look to your own heart!"

An uneasy silence fell and John perceived that his wife seemed to be losing touch with her surroundings, as had happened before at night when she saw visions rise that bore no shadows in the physical plane. Her mouth drooped open and her grip upon the weapon was diminished as she stared, as one in a trance gazes with fixed, unblinking eyes and little comprehension of present reality. Quickly he darted forward and tried to grab the knife but she, returning to the world from her inner nightmare, closed her fingers upon it and with no hesitation plunged it into his flesh. He gave a short, sharp cry of pain, stepped back and clutched his arm where a deep, bleeding wound now lay after the blade's entry.

Cannetta held up the weapon, gazing at it quizzically, as though the knife had assumed a life of its own and had then attacked her husband. She gave a small scream at the rill of blood that ran down the handle and soaked her own fingers with gore.

"You should not have made me do that!" she cried, looking up with a maniac's fury kindling her furrowed brow. "It was of your own doing – I warned you enough!"

John swallowed his fear and tried to blot out the pain as he saw by the trembling of her limbs and the twist of her mouth that he was very near to subduing her. Watching her horror at the gore a gleam of inspiration came to him and he held out the dripping wound towards her.

"Oh my angel," he cried. "I know that was all my fault and that you are blameless. See how my blood gleams – it will drain and kill me now for sure."

"Don't show me," she sobbed, breathlessly. "I don't want to know! Be angry and furious with me – that I can take but I can't get any pleasure from your pain if you love me!"

"But I do," he entreated, letting the blood fall at her feet. "Do you think these two bitches around me mean anything compared to YOU? Cannetta, I would die for you and as you have almost achieved it I am happy to fall at your feet. But before I die I would like to get some pleasure from killing these temptresses. My blood drains fast away so I must be quick before my strength leaves me. Let me kill these bitches since they revolt you and the gore from them may splash upon your dress and stain your skin. Give me the knife that I may do it!"

Cannetta was revolted by the blood on her feet and she drew away.

"You would really do that for me?" she whispered.

"I would do it for US," he pleaded, holding out his bleeding arm.

His wife regarded it and shuddered.

"Let me kill them," wheedled he, slowly moving forward but keeping his eyes on her. "They deserve it – they are adulterers – they tempted me and now they must pay. You will not get the satisfaction I will get from plunging the knife in. Do let me do it, Cannetta and then we are rid of them and can be together for always.....always. I want you back in my bed and these bitches dead and gone!"

Cannetta seemed visibly moved by his words and he pressed his advantage home.

"Darling, angel, my own true wife, let me kill these temptresses now!"

He saw Cannetta's knees buckle at his words and the knife slipped from her grasp. It hit the floor with a loud ring and within a second he had pounced on it and had it in his possession. It was over.

For a full minute no one spoke and no one moved then John went up to his wife, perceived she neither saw nor heard him and took her arm. Her face was completely blank and she muttered some gibberish he did not understand. Slowly he guided her past Shirley, who had not moved from her place by the window and drawing back the bolts on the door he took her outside. Cannetta was beyond anything and she walked mechanically, as though in a dream, her lips twitching, her eyes glazed and turned inward to her world of torture.

"Can this really be the same woman that threatened my stepdaughter a few moments ago?" echoed Shirley when Cannetta had left the kitchen. She moved to the door and asked her cousin,

"John, what will happen to her now?"

John could not look at her but stared at his mesmerised wife, who clung to his arm despite the blood that dripped upon her. What did she see? he wondered. What did she hear? His eyes were full of tears.

 "Go back in and care for Connie," he whispered. "It is over now and she will threaten no one any more. Your stepdaughter needs you desperately."

 "And you do not?" replied Shirley, noticing his wet face and the shaking limbs he exhibited.

 "I helped cause this by my refusal to listen to sense," he said, in great sadness. "Therefore I must sort out my own mistake. It will all be done as tenderly and lovingly as I can...but be assured it will be done!"

Like a funeral procession they set off from the cottage, Cannetta walking with stiff limbs and in silence. John wept openly but he knew she did not hear him, or anything in their journey. They turned up the hill to Stackhouses, entered the district of the town known as Fourcrosses and were seen no more.

CHAPTER 12

Much later the same day John returned to Ardle alone, his head bowed and his eyes permanently lowered so his tearful gaze rested on the ground. He walked like a beaten man who had had every vestige of hope and faith snatched from him. Only negative emotions flowed from his heart and his mind received them with grief and despair. For him there was only the present moment; he could not conceive of a future, much less a life where he could recapture some happiness and status.

"I am no more than the smallest creeping thing that moves on the earth," murmured he. "Nay, I am worse than that, I exude evil, and I destroy all I touch."

Reaching the village he recalled his duty, turned into a familiar track and came upon a tiny, isolated cottage beside a gleaned field that had the first touch of winter about it. Passing through the gate he paused to remember how often her hand had lifted the latch. Alas, no more. He tapped upon the front door of the cottage, heard the sound of feet descending the stairs and waited till the barrier fell inwards, to admit him.

"Yes?" asked the auburn-haired woman as she gazed at him. "You look like my son-in-law, apart from the deep shadows around your eyes which were never there afore you married my daughter. You look like you regret not heeding my words and there is sorrow in your face, great sorrow, such as I have known when Cannetta was in one of her most difficult phases. Come, have you good news for me, although I doubt it – your face says otherwise."

John bowed his head.

"Mrs Hardy, the only news that I have come to impart is painful beyond belief."

Rose looked alarmed.

"Is it that bad?" she enquired. "Mr Straeton, you had best come in."

He stepped over the threshold with a sigh and faced her with tearful eyes.

"Yes, it is Cannetta I come about, Mrs Hardy. I wish it were not. I wish it were good news to make you proud but it is not. I do not know how to tell you. I do not know how to begin... It is too dreadful to contemplate - but I had no choice. You must realise that, I had no choice, there was no choice."

"Mr Straeton – you are making no sense. Don't tell me you are growing as mad as my daughter? Is it infectious – her insanity?"

"I was a fool not to listen to you," he murmured, casting his eyes to the floor. "Oh that I had heeded your warning! Then it would not have come to…this and she would be with you now and not – "

Rose gave a gasp.

"She is not - dead," she whispered, leaning upon the door heavily as her strength left her.

"No not in the physical sense. But...she has left Ardle."

"To go where? And why are you, as her husband, not with her?"

"Where she has gone...I cannot follow her."

"Mr Straeton – my patience is running out. Where is my daughter?"

John raised his head and gazed at the quaking woman before him.

"I tried, Mrs Hardy, I really tried, but she was too much for me. I was not safe in my own bed whilst she was there. She tried to stab me, she bit me, she scratched me; you name it she did it. I was shocked, I was disgusted so I resolved to hide her and hoped the madness would pass. I chained her and locked her in a room but I did care for her whilst she was there. Some days she was lucid then when I went back to her prison she would grovel on all fours like a dog. But exhaustion made me careless and she escaped - she got a knife...God knows how as I checked her daily for weapons since she would use anything against me. She stabbed me with forks and even flung her dinner at me...Oh God - it was unspeakable. But she escaped when I was out with this knife and she tried to kill my cousin, believing I was seeing her behind my wife's back – "

"And were you?" interrupted Rose, angrily.

John regarded the question as superfluous. He shook his head.

"Were you?" repeated Rose.

"How did I have the time to see anyone when SHE took up so much of my time and all of my energy? I had to try and work too, and make sure no one found out the painful circumstances of my wife's illness. I am a proud man, Mrs Hardy, or I was. Now I am degraded and I crawl, whereas once I walked with my head held high. But Cannetta nearly killed someone, a member of my family, and then I had no choice, no choice..."

Rose stood up tall.

"I know what you are trying to tell me," she cried loudly. "You have had her committed haven't you? You have had my daughter put away when, for twenty odd years I coped with her and never complained. You coped with her for a few weeks and you have put her away."

"I had no choice, Mrs Hardy," beseeched John. "I had no choice. Believe me, I did not want to do it - nothing was further from the truth but I..."

"Mr Straeton - mad or not - Cannetta is my daughter."

"And mad or not she is still my wife!" he pleaded. "But I could not cope; I could not rest ever again with her in my house."

Rose moved forward and pushed the desperate man.

"Get out, get out! Leave my house, Mr Straeton – I never want to see you again! Do you not know what you have done? She will die in there. No one comes out alive...Bedlam...Oh my God how will she stand it? She led a sheltered life here because she had to; there was no other way...I did my best but you took her and destroyed her. Get out!"

She pushed him to the door and opened it.

"Get out of Ardle, Mr Straeton, no one wants you here. Leave the village, leave the town leave the county. Go back to your wilderness in Scotland – you belong there. You have heaped havoc on my life since you came here and now you have all but killed my daughter. She might as well be dead to me as I will never behold her again. Do you not perceive that? She is lost, lost to us, lost to me!" Rose burst into noisy sobs and John tried once more to plead with her, but she thrust him out into the dusk and shut the door with a slam.

John stood there in the gathering dusk and sobbed. He banged again on the door.

"Mrs Hardy! Mrs Hardy! Please hear me out! There is no one that I can talk to but you! No one! Please! I cannot go back to my empty house with this burning in my mind. Please! I must speak to you!"

Eventually Rose opened the door again. Her face was wet with tears and her hands shook but she was adamant she wanted nothing further to do with him.

"What more is there to be said, Mr Straeton? You took my daughter away from her place of safety, despite my warnings, and now you have locked her up...forever. I cannot bear to look at you!"

John hung his head.

"Do you think I don't rue the day I laid eyes on her?" he replied. "But I was in want of a wife....and she seemed everything that was perfect - loving, gentle, beautiful. How could any man resist her?"

"Because her mind was not sound, Mr Straeton, her mind was mad, insane and she did things that you and I found impossible to cope with. But I did cope with it, I coped because she was my own flesh and blood and you should have coped because you were joined with her – despite my disapproval."

Silence fell. John was about to turn away when Rose seemed to evince a change of heart and beckoned him in.

"There are things you should see before you leave," she said, in a low, sad tone. "I have never shown this room to anyone. Only Cannetta's eyes have rested upon it but it was forged out of desperation and it did duty to contain her for many a year. And she would still be there now were it not for your interference. Follow me, Mr Straeton."

She led him up the flight of stairs and stopped on the landing by a large fall of arras, taking from her pocket a rusty key.

"Now," continued Rose. "What do you imagine to be concealed beneath this tapestry? What is the secret of this wall? Can you guess?"

John gazed at it but his mind was muddled with grief and he shook his head.

Rose flung aside the thick arras and revealed the handle of a small door, cut into the stone wall. She bent to unlock the door and the barrier fell inwards.

"Come," she murmured and stepped into the room, John following, fascinated by the nature of what lay before him. He was soon to know.

The room they entered was dull to the point of darkness with one tiny skylight set high up in an opposite wall. Rose excused herself for a moment, descended to fetch a light and left John alone in the eerie gloom that seemed cold and encompassing. On her return the candle shone and created huge shadows that moved in the corners of the room like living things, dancing and jumping as Rose's hand shook. John saw a pile of musty bedding on the floor, a pervading smell of damp, neglect and sadness filling the entire space that opened up before him. Upon the far wall he saw two long, rusty chains screwed into the stone about halfway up, ending in thick manacles which bore small keys projecting from the voids. Chains at the bottom of the wall flanked them and the room was undecorated apart from the flourishing spores of fungi that provided a range of green hues and the glisten of dampness. Slime dripped from the ceiling in one place and splashed onto the floor with continuous monotony. John felt he could hardly breathe. So this was what Cannetta had talked about when she said her mother hid her away! How could she have endured this for years?

"Oh, my God," he cried, falling back against the door. "And this is where you imprisoned her when she was beyond you."

"Yes, mostly at night, occasionally during the evening. In truth I have not really been in here since your wedding but, strangely enough, I had sought the key out today to visit it one last time and strip the walls of these fetters," replied Rose. "She will never need them again."

"If you had only showed me this before we were wed - well, we would not have and she would be with you now, not in some madhouse."

"Well?" asked his mother-in-law turning the light to him and illuminating his pallid face. "Have you seen enough? Do I need to explain anything further? This was my only solace when she scratched and bit me; my threat to get her to behave. But sometimes she could not help it – she knew not what she did...I tried things at first...opium, brandy but nothing subdued her apart from these chains. She was terrified of this room but she let me shackle her here as there was no other way. I could not let her wander abroad in the state she was in at night. I cajoled her, I pleaded with her, I begged her but I always chained her. There was no way I could have slept over the years otherwise. She was never like other children; she did things...eating worms, pulling flies apart, laughing hysterically at voices I could not hear. It was all in her head and that head got worse and worse and she became even more insane when a woman. What was I to do? I could not commit her – she was my own flesh and blood and it would have destroyed me. Even this torture chamber was better than handing her over to some country Bedlam where she would not have survived for long. And now you have come to tell me my daughter is committed and lost forever."

There was a heavy silence, full of sorrow. John did not know what comfort he could offer this devastated woman. Her child was gone.

"But for you, Mr Straeton, she would still be here. Yes, she would be chained at night but by day she had reasonable freedom. How can you face me? Get out of my house and never come back! I hope the picture of these chains haunt you forever! You are a murderer – do you not perceive that? Why should you be free while she is caged? Her blood is on your hands, her blood!" and she began to hit him, until he ran down the stairs and out of the front door. Then she collapsed, sitting curled up on the steps, the candle flickering out, so she was left in the dark, weeping...

John turned away from the cottage, struck the path towards Stackhouses and crawled, like a crippled man, towards his dwelling. The descending night covered his anguish, the rising wind blew his tangled hair and the whirling raindrops mixed with the tears on his cheeks and dripped in slow but profuse drops onto the cold ground as he walked...

CHAPTER 13

By the next morning a little composure had returned to John's life. True, it was only a vestige of hope but he remained convinced that he had done the right thing and that a major catastrophe had been averted by Cannetta's departure. He realised how close Connie and he had come to dying at the hands of a maniac; his own judgement, the reason for his cousin's suffering, hit him hard and he wondered if they would ever forgive him. His rash vow to care for a mad woman also caused him grief as how could he have believed he was strong enough to guard his wife twenty-four hours a day. And one lax moment had resulted in this horrifying situation. In some ways he felt a sense of relief but in others the memories of his wife's presence in his house brought fresh tears. He remained at home all day, fearful of wandering abroad in case he met anyone in the lanes of Ardle. What he would say to them if they approached him he could not conceive and he worried people would be abusive too.

 "Yet how can they blame me any more than I blame myself?" murmured he. "I must go forth some time and face the world but not today. I cannot face people today."

As evening approached he remained in the dark and did not think of food or drink much less lighting a candle or lamp. It began to grow chilly but John was quite oblivious to it. He walked to the window and leant his burning forehead against the cool pane, finding comfort in the cold touch of glass against his temples.

About eight o'clock there came a gentle yet insistent tapping at the door, followed by the clatter of horse's hooves which woke him from his reverie. He approached the barrier, his heart beating wildly and opened it with considerable trepidation. It was a wild and windy night with a red sky promising a fairer morrow but lashings of rain coming down now to greet the darkness. The growing zephyr thrashed the naked trees about in its fury and a few weak and broken branches whirled about in the gale.

Dimly, in the weird half-light, John could see a small blonde woman holding the reins of a dark horse. His horse! He gave a shallow smile.

 "John!" cried the figure, "I was not sure if you were in as the house was in darkness."

"Shirley," he replied, part of him genuinely glad to see her, part of him still wanting isolation. "How have you managed him in this wind? He can be a bit of a handful sometimes!"

"Oh, Damion led him here but he did not want to stay in case you were indisposed so he has gone for his nightly drink. He is coming back for me at ten but will be at the Resort by now!" She shivered in the keen wind.

 "And Connie?" enquired John, anxiously. "How is Connie?"

 "Better than you are, cousin, by the look of your face."

  John gave a wry smile.

"You always were too perceptive," he murmured. "Go in Shirley. I will not be long," and he took hold of his horse, glad to have him back although he had almost forgotten of his existence. Leading him round to the nearby stable he bedded him down, fetched him a feed and then returned to the house.

Shirley had wandered into the sitting room but found no cheerful fire or any source of warmth. The room felt cold and damp. She looked to the hearth and saw a fire had been laid but not lit so she began to kindle wood to get it going and, by the time he returned, a few sizeable flames were flaring up the chimney. The refulgence increased as Shirley found two candles to bring light to the dark corners of the room where fearful shadows played and caused her to bring to mind the picture of Cannetta with the knife. Was she hidden somewhere in the house or had he kept his word and had put her away? Shirley shivered. Despite the flaring warmth she felt cold and anxious so she was relieved when John came back and threw himself down on the sofa next to his cousin. He flung his head into his hands and did not look at her but she could hear the stifled sobs in his heart. She leant forward and stroked his chestnut hair. Eventually he lifted his head and gazed at her incredulously.

"How can you bear to be near me after the suffering I have put you through?" whispered he, his eyes full and brimming over.

"You speak of suffering," murmured she, "But whatever we have been through YOUR pain has been far, far worse! I cannot even bear to contemplate what you have endured all these weeks here with - HER. It is beyond comprehension."

He sighed.

"I thought you had turned against me when I saw the ire in your face at the cottage. I told myself, Shirley has had enough of me, and no wonder. But I felt finished. Your approval is more than life to me."

She smiled and continued stroking his hair.

"How could I turn against you? It would be like rejecting my own flesh and blood. If you saw anything in my face that day it was merely fear. If it was anything worse why am I here with you now?"

He nodded.

"But what does Damion say? Does he not damn me? I would not blame him. My stubbornness and stupidity has harmed a lot of people and almost killed one. I am conscious of that every minute of my existence now and it will not end as I know my wife would be with her mother were it not for me."

"Connie and I deemed it best her father knew as little as possible of the incident. Con was very anxious that things be left as easy as possible for you.
"

"And how is she?" asked he. "I am so sorry - wrapped up in my own troubles I neglected to enquire. Forgive me."

"She is considerably better than I believed she would be after such a trauma.....She does not seem to have suffered any shock. Indeed she is more concerned for you and encouraged me to come tonight. Damion was going to call and bring the horse but she insisted I come too and try and comfort you. How are you John - really?"

"I feel I have been standing at the gates of hell," he replied. "And I could even feel the fervid, burning breezes that came from Hades and blew on my face. Now it has receded a little but realisation sinks in and I find myself alone again. My pride has been washed out of me, all hope has been diminished but, yet, there is something to cling onto, but what it is I cannot say."

"Relief?" she suggested.

"The wounds are too fresh for that," he acknowledged. "They continue to bleed but I am conscious one day they will scab and then I shall just have the scars to deal with. Meanwhile I must live from day to day."

"But the dreadful pain of seeing her as we saw her - mad, frenzied and not knowing what she did! That is over. You will never have to behold that again," comforted Shirley.

But John did not see it that way.

"And I shall never see her again, apart from in my worst nightmares, when she will appear to rebuke me for imprisoning her, nay not just imprisoning her, but taking away the one thing she could not live without...her freedom. How long do you think she will survive…in there? You know where she has gone. No one comes out of there but in a coffin."

"But you would have been in that coffin had you not committed her!" cried Shirley. "And my Connie nearly ended up in one. You put her away to protect your life and the lives of other innocent people."

"Before I asked her to marry me SHE was innocent. She could not help what she did. She was not aware of her behaviour. Occasionally, when she was lucid, the puzzled look in her eye when I was afraid of her confirmed to me she remembered nothing of her madness. She was like two women and one of them I fell deeply in love with. And that woman was truly my wife and I love her still..."

"Then you love a dream...an enigma," returned Shirley. "How often was she that person? When you first beheld her, yes, but the wolf often appears in sheep's clothing. You were fooled."

"I did not listen to her mother. I will rue that to the day I die. I could not manage her. She tried to kill me, maim me and hurt me at every opportunity. I could never let my guard down with her for one second. And where did she get that knife from? It must have been a moment's carelessness on my part and look what nearly happened..." He burst into loud tearless sobs and leant on Shirley's shoulder, she putting her arm around him to comfort him.

"Hush! Talk no more of it. It is over now," whispered she, stroking his back.

"You are a great strength to me," breathed John fighting to regain control. "But for you the world would be a meaningless void and I would not want to live in it. My first thought when this was over was to leave and return to my ain country but a glimpse of your face again tells me I could not go and leave you here. And as you are not free to leave then here I shall remain and ride out the storms."

"We will ride them out together," she assured him. "And I shall start the healing process by making you some food. When did you last eat?"

He did not remember.

"How can I eat?" he cried. "Come to that how can I breathe, how can I live with what I have done? I went to see Rose - her mother. She showed me a room full of chains where she locked Cannetta up at night when her condition was worse. She has coped with her for many years and I gave up after a few weeks but Rose threw me out. It was no more than I deserved - I have ruined her life - taken her child away from her. And you tell me I must eat - all my stomach can digest is sorrow!"

But Shirley was adamant and prepared him a simple meal, standing over him as though he were a child until his plate was clear. In vain did he put his knife and fork down a dozen times, she picked them up again and at length declared,

"What? Must I feed you like some infant? If I must I will! You know I will do what it takes to put strength back into that gaunt frame, don't you?"

"You give me strength just by being here," he told her, catching her free hand and kissing it.

She smiled and he likewise managed a slight lifting of the corners of his mouth.

"There! That is better!" coaxed Shirley. "Your eyes have lightened considerably and you are almost the old John I met and immediately fell in love with!"

She perceived he gave a troubled start at these words and she lowered her head, knowing she had overstepped the mark.

"I am sorry, John," she murmured. "That sentence should have been for my heart alone."

He gazed at her with misty eyes and took her hand.

"You are beautifully honest," he remarked. "What man could ask for more? You know I am incapable of any decent emotion at the moment. Call it shock or call it distress, who knows, maybe I will end up as mad as my wife but one thing I am clear on. It is the nearest thing that I have had to heaven for a long while, to have you here with me...God, how I have missed you!"

He said it with such depth of feeling and passion she was reduced to tears and did not press him any further.

A bitter wind assailed the walls of Fourbridges and dragged its heavy fingers through the beds of reeds bordering the sluggish river behind the dwelling. Ere long the mantel piece clock rung out the hour of ten, as though alone, it remained calm and unruffled in a frenzied world of emotion.

Shirley sat up, glanced at the stern timekeeper, stirred the dying fire and murmured she must leave him.

"Don't go!" cried he, grabbing her hand as she stood up to depart.

"I must," she murmured," My husband will be waiting and I do not want to arouse his suspicions."

"Yes," said he with resignation, leaning back on the sofa. "There is constancy in those words – my husband – as though he will always be so. Do you want him to be?"

"You know the answer to that question so to reply would be unnecessary. My feelings have never changed since the first hour I beheld you but I was not free then and I am still a married woman. I may never be free in this life! But my feelings are free and the only one I love is you. But how can we be together at the moment? The tongues would pour forth poison and I would be shunned and named things I could not cope with. Besides there is Connie and she needs me more than you do!"

He shook his head violently at this.

"That is not possible," he cried. "It is not even that I want you...I am beyond wanting anything in this life at the moment but my need for you is immeasurable!"

"Duty calls me, John, and I must put my feelings to one side. It does not mean I do not want to be with you but, for now, I must return to my husband and stepdaughter." She pressed his hand, kissed it and then he heard her footsteps ringing in the hallway. A dull thud of the door announced her departure and he realised he was alone.

He turned his head from the pleasant fire, seemed glad the candles burnt low and waited for the welcome return of darkness to dull his sorrow. He craved to be cradled and swallowed up in the night. His thoughts verged on despair but he savoured the feel of Shirley in his arms, even though she had now gone. She had made no promises to return but his heart sung one song over and over again. Her feelings had not changed – she loved him then, she loved him now. It was all he clung to as midnight approached. But his conscience pricked him over Shirley, like it had troubled him when they first were together. She was not free! What had she said? She may never be free in this life and the shackles of duty fell heavily upon her. He could wait for her for thirty years and she would still be tied to that duty…His mind felt exhausted and he evinced a strong distaste for his present surroundings. How could he stay here, let alone salvage any happiness from his life while the memories of his wife rose up to strangle him? He had to get out of this house, out of this town. Maybe Rose was right. No one wanted him here, apart from one, who could not have him because of the circumstances of her commitments. Then he would not stay - he would linger no more in a foreign land. He could be packed and out of here very easily and he did not have to look back. England had nothing further to offer him but Scotland, Scotland, would always draw him. Every dice was loaded against him here and the bright jewels he believed he had found had turned into worthless glass and shattered. Sell up, get out, give up, he thought. What else is there to do to recover some of the lost pride and respect? Married to the local madwoman who everyone knew was insane apart from him. Could it get any worse? It was two o'clock in the morning and he had never felt so alone in his life...

Meanwhile, as John lay, waiting for darkness to engulf him, Damion and Shirley travelled the long, windswept path back to their dwelling. She was unusually withdrawn and silent; he was brooding over a story related to him in the Resort.

The trees rustled in the freshening gale and beside the tracks, the long grass whispered secrets and swept to and fro in a mad dance. The moon was obscured by high cloud, occasionally breaking free from her prison and flooding the earth with silver light. Shirley gave a deep sigh and pulled her plaid shawl tighter around her shoulders. A fine mixture of rain, hail and sleet hit the two walkers and dampened their apparel with cold fingers.

At last Damion, who lingered somewhat behind his wife, called to her to wait and catching up, told her,

"I have heard strange tales in the Resort tonight!"

"Oh?" returned Shirley coolly, her mind elsewhere.

"Yes weird tales that concern someone not unknown to us!"

"Well," replied she. "You must be careful of tales, Damion, and not repeat them, for that is all they may be – tales and no grains of truth present in their words."

"You should know," nodded her husband. "Since, for the last couple of hours you have been in the company of the one it concerns! I did wonder why he left his horse with us for so long. Come – is it true – he has had his wife committed?"

Shirley gave another huge sigh and replied,

"Sadly it is. I wish it were not." And she shut her mouth firmly.

But Damion was not fooled.

"I see by your silence that you know more than you are saying and that John has unburdened himself to you."

"He has - I own it but I am not at liberty to tell the secrets of a broken heart."

Damion looked pensive.

"The story was that she, his wife, flew at him with a knife and his hand was badly cut. They say he tried to chain her when her insanity reached its height but she got away and attacked him."

"True, sadly," admitted Shirley. "Have you heard any more?"

"Is there any more?" he enquired, stopping and staring into her face whilst the errant moonlight illuminated it.

"Not that should be aired by us but I saw hellish pictures in John's face tonight and terrible details that he strives to keep to himself since to air it will only increase its intensity. I did not question him further. It is not our business, Damion. I went to cook him some food as he is gaunt to the point of emaciation!"

"The talk is that he will not remain long in the district but will sell up and move back to the wilds of Scotland. I shall miss him greatly, not being awash with relations, as it were! His marriage is then over and there is no going back?"

"Yes, marriages do not always last," cried she, with painful irony but her husband seemed caught up in his own preoccupations and her words were lost on him.

It began to rain harder, a profuse blanket of wet descending on the tiny village of Ardle until the world echoed with the incessant drip, drip of water. Connie was soundly asleep when Shirley looked in upon her before retiring and the wheeze of her breath was scarcely audible so that her stepmother felt the nagging doubts surrounding her health recede a little. Shirley herself slept badly and, listening to her husband's snoring, she remembered the words she had uttered to John about duty, lack of freedom and her all-encompassing ties. At last she could lie there no longer so she rose quietly and dressed without disturbing Damion who snored on in a monotonous tone.

Leaving the room she crept downstairs and regarded the dark, wet world outside. The rain was ceasing and the wind seemed to have blown its power out so that silence reigned around the cottage. Was John sleeping she wondered...but she knew he was not. Was it true what Damion had heard in the Resort? Would John go back to Scotland? What was there to keep him here, she told herself. There was only her...and she could not make him any promises. She put some shoes on, flung a shawl round her shoulders and heard the deep, racking cough that showed, all too plainly, the sleeper rested no more. When the spasm was over and the house bathed in silence once more Shirley pulled back the bolts and stepped out into the dark night. She did not care where she went...all she cared about was that she left the cottage and her feet walked whilst her mind wandered in its own paths.

For over an hour she remained in this barely conscious state then the gentle rhythm of her steps soothed the fervent condition of her mind and she became conscious of her surroundings. She looked up, as though she had just awoken from sleep, and became aware of a thin line of silver birches, visible only by the gleam of their white trunks. The moon left her cloudy bed and shone on the cool surface of the river, beyond this the grim houses of Fourcrosses.

"Oh to be forever beneath those quiet waters and sleep." mused she. "Safe, tranquil and at peace after all the conflict of life! To be timeless, heedless and unmoved by the strongest agony the world can throw at us. To be perfect, omnipotent but moving in a spiral of eternity that only throws you higher and higher into your soul. Will I ever attain that? Will any of us?"

Nearby came a deep human sigh that was almost a groan which startled Shirley into action. She drew back a little, heard the groan repeated with indescribable sadness and ventured,

"Who is there?" in a small voice.

The shuffling of feet drew her attention to the left.

"Who echoes words that I crave as my destiny?" came the broken tones of a man. "'Tis poetry to my soul to hear such phrases and moves me to make that stream my final resting place."

"John!" cried Shirley, for she knew him at once.

"Aye – it is the broken down being you once knew as John. I could not stay in that house...I could not rest my head on the very pillow her teeth tore when she could not rip my flesh. Do you know she drank my blood and licked my wounds free of gore? And is it really you, Shirley? I prayed for you an hour ago but I did not expect to see you, let alone feel you in the flesh."

She hurried to his side and kissed his cheek then took his hand.

"Of course it is me. Did you think you dreamt me?"

"Dreams? It is a long time since I have had a dream. I have lived so long in a nightmare that THEY are my only sleeping companions and I dare not seek them tonight!"

He clasped her to his heart and they stood there, a shaft of silver moonlight illuminating their embrace.

"It is good to hold living flesh that does not coil round me like a suffocating snake," he breathed in her ear. "Flesh that does not repulse me or bite or tear at me, but reflects the warmth of a true embrace."

"There is love in that embrace," whispered she. "Whether you return it or not does not matter."

He lowered his head and sobbed.

"How I have wronged thee!" cried he. "I stand here with you and a wife in the madhouse and you stand here with a husband in your bed."

"Do not speak of that," murmured she, putting her finger to his lips. "Tonight there is only us and nothing else matters."

"But your husband, my cousin -"

"He might be in hell tonight for all I care. I left him snoring in a warm bed," she reassured him. "He will not miss me; he does not even notice I am there."

"He is a fool then," returned John. "Concerning you - at least. In other respects he is a good man and a much loved cousin."

"And I?" enquired she. "Am I a much loved cousin?"

He perceived she was smiling at him and he was loath to let her go.

"What will you do now?" asked she when they had embraced again.

He looked over to his house, sleeping in the infernal darkness.

"I cannot stay...there," he mused. "The house and chattels can be sold, I hope. My ain country is always calling me and this time I may heed her voice and go back. What else can I do? Where else can I go? Will I ever get her mad laughter out of my ears? It echoes constantly and sometimes I feel her nails in my back or her tongue in my wounds which have yet to heal."

"Damion said there was talk in the Resort that you would leave," Shirley replied, sadly. She drew off a little and made as if to leave him.

"I must go," she muttered. "Morning will be here before we know it and the light will catch us. We should not be together."

"You'll not leave me, just like that?" he gasped, deeply upset. He took her arm and embraced her again and although she tried to resist his caresses, she melted into him and all resistance was futile.

Nevertheless she struggled to get free.

"I must go," she repeated, as if to convince herself. "What more is there to say?"

"So you'll leave me to my fate?" bewailed he.

"Your fate is Scotland, John, and you've just said she calls you and this time you will answer!"

"But it is such a long way from you!" he cried. "Yes, I crave her beauty but she pales before YOU. And how drab she would be if you were not there! Don't make me go back to that house alone, Shirley – I can't bear it."

Shirley raised her head and looked at his terrified eyes, dilating in the moon's rays.

"Come back with me then," she whispered. "The parlour is free...and you may sleep there. Damion suspects nothing...but - one thing...do not look at me like you are now else all of Ardle will know our secret. Your face portrays your emotions, whether you know you are feeling them or not. You are numb with sorrow at the moment but not in your eyes - they portray love, even if you deny it."

"And yours?" he asked. "What do yours convey?"

"They say what they have always said, ever since you smiled at me," she replied. "They say my love is constant but yours! You left me once for younger beauty - will you not do so again?"

He turned away from her and seemed to be struggling to control his emotions. At length he shook his head.

"If you had been free I would have never looked at Cannetta. I thought I wanted a wife. I did want one but not her...I wanted you!"

"And you could not have me!" she cried, bitterly. "So what has changed? You cannot have me now!"

"But I can be near you. I can see you. I can talk to you," he begged. "For me - that is enough."

She considered his words, her head on one side as she deliberated.

"Very well," she returned. "Come back with me now before Damion awakes and Connie needs me."

"Then come with me to that haunted place and help me pack a bag for I am afraid to enter there alone. Her mad screams seem to whirl round me still and at every flicker of shadow I think I see her! Give me your hand - you must be an angel sent from heaven!"

She did as he asked but remembered, bitterly, how he had said this about someone else not so very long ago and it had hurt her...

They sauntered back to the dwelling, hand in hand.

"How menacing, how eerie she seems!" he cried, gazing up at his house with fear and in trepidation. "She wants to haunt me until I am as mad as that poor woman I committed. Only then will she be satisfied." Shirley perceived his hand trembled and she strove to reassure him.

"You feel like this because you are exhausted through lack of sleep and food," she comforted him. "Once you are tucked up on the settle at ours rest will revive you and you will wake a different man."

John entered the house, crossed the kitchen and climbed the stairs to his bedroom. Shirley remained downstairs but she felt the icy glare of the dwelling and the eerie silence that hung, stagnant, in every corner. She was glad when he emerged, bag in hand, and they were able to leave.

"I will return later to see to my horse," he murmured, as if talking to himself. "You have no stable at the cottage but I could bring a tether for him."

John locked the house up carefully, took one last look at the place that had seen his dreams shattered and turned into living nightmares, then he took Shirley's hand and they left, walking slowly across one of the bridges. The moon was more prevalent now and the cloud had decreased so that they walked by a silver light that was as bright as day.

"See she illuminates our way," murmured Shirley. "We shall be home before any one is up and no one shall see us." He pulled her closer and they strolled, side by side, she looking up at him every so often as if she feared he would vanish.

"This is our time," she enthused. "We must make the most of it. How beautiful the night is!"

"Not as beautiful as you!" he cried. "When I look at you, even in my despair, my heart sings and the more I see you the louder the song becomes."

Shirley smiled. They wandered on, she leaning against him, arm in arm along the silver highway. Their flesh cleaved together, their eyes shone only for each other and besotted and bewildered they struck the path to Ardle, turned across the field and entered the track that descended the long hill towards home...

Oblivious to anything else but her love Shirley chattered away to him of what she would do were she free and he joined her conversation with his hopes and dreams, too.

"We could leave Ardle and go where no one knew us and we could be Mr and Mrs Straeton, in name at least," she rambled.

"And I would buy you a fine hat and numerous gowns – one for every day of the week, my love," laughed John, carried away by her enthusiasm.

Neither of them saw the small, creeping figure at the bottom of the hill watching them. Suddenly John picked up the shine of a lantern close to them, the light suddenly raised to illumine their faces and then just as quickly withdrawn. John's heart raced. The owner of the light moved off and its shine diminished. Shirley cowered and tried to hide behind her cousin.

"Who is it?" she whispered, but he shook his head in ignorance.

146

"Perhaps 'tis only a traveller?" she suggested when he remained silent.

John walked forward.

"Who is there?" he cried, in a loud voice. "Answer directly – or you'll be sorry. Show yourself – and your light!"

Silence. The breeze whistled a plaintive lullaby in the trees but nothing else moved or uttered a sound.

"What can it mean?" murmured Shirley. "The moon has gone in too and left us in blackness. The light has been extinguished."

"I think it has been shuttered," he mused, looking around him but seeing nothing. "Do not be afraid, my love. It is surely some sneaking thief or vagabond. My patience is through with them since they will not reply so I shall leave my bag with you and go after them - just to be sure."

He dropped his bag at her feet, bade her remain there and ran forward following the path the figure had surely taken. It was someone who judged it was better to say nothing but draw off into the blackness but his heart sank and his mind told him it could be someone known to them who had seen their embraces. It could mean trouble if left to brew.

He hurried on, stumbling here and there as the path twisted but ahead of him he soon saw a figure, bent and running as best able. He slowed up, observed the figure and thought that he knew them from their pronounced gait. Suddenly the obscuring cloud released the moon's cold light and it shone full on the figure ahead of him and picked out her long auburn hair. He stopped dead in his tracks and gave a gasp of realisation. There was no doubt now that he knew the figure and that it was none other than his mother-in-law, Rose Hardy...

CHAPTER 14

Eventually a sense of reality came over John as he stood in the silent darkness, watching his mother-in-law disappear into the distance. He swallowed hard. He must get back to Shirley as she would be distressed if he did not return promptly. Turning abruptly from the field he made his way back to his cousin, his mind racing. The whole episode had unnerved and upset him. Just what had Rose gleaned, if anything, from her observation of the two of them? What would she make of it? And why, most of all, had she been on this lonely track in the early hours of the morning? He shook his head as if to dispel the trouble he feared would come from this. Shirley and he had never done or said anything in public to arouse suspicion and no witness had ever seen them declare their love - until now. Had Rose suspected something after he visited her? Had Shirley been careless in her talk when she spoke of him to people? He gave up analysing the situation and hurried back to his cousin's side. She was waiting for him, exactly as he had left her, but when she spied him she ran forward, anxiety etched on her pale face.

"John – who was it? Did you see anyone?"

He shook his head briefly, as though dismissing the picture of his mother-in-law from his mind. But his limbs shook and he felt faint so Shirley, who could see he was in a state of collapse, spread her shawl on the damp ground and bade him rest a moment or two. He did not look at her but hung his head as though dizzy or overcome with emotion. Shirley knelt down beside him and took his cold hand.

"He escaped then?" she asked, trying to look into his face.

"Yes," he replied, deeming it best to feign ignorance.

"And you did not recognise the man?"

Again the slow, solemn shake of the head for he only saw it as a half lie since she was mistaken over the sex of the watcher.

"Well," declared she, suddenly brave, "I think we can dismiss it as a wandering vagrant or tramp hoping for a picking at one of the cottages round about. You have seen him off nicely and fooled his plans of robbery! I am very lucky that you were with me and I did not have to face him alone!"

"Yes," muttered John between chattering teeth. "How...fortunate."

They started off again, John walking shakily with all his wits heightened in case Rose chose to make another appearance but they saw no one else on their travels. In a few tense minutes they arrived at the pink cottage, where silence greeted them and the parlour was cold and empty. John felt a partial sense of relief but knew they were still on dangerous ground.

Shirley hesitated by the bottom of the stairs and beckoned John to join her. "Hark how my husband snores," she whispered. "He has likely not even shifted position since I left his bed."

"I wish you would not call him that," returned her cousin, jealousy entering his face.

"Why? Is Damion any better? He is still...that - my husband. Do not forget you have a wife too...wherever she is!"

"God, that I could forget her," swore he, hitting his forehead in despair.

A new, louder noise broke the atmosphere and drowned the snoring. It was the rasping hack of a spasm of coughing. Shirley shook her head and her eyes filled with tears.

"Connie..." she murmured. "She does not sound good."

She led John by the hand back to the parlour and, raking through the ashes of the fire she rekindled the blaze and fetched fresh wood to fuel the warmth. John sat down heavily on the settle but said nothing.

Shirley regarded him quizzically.

"John, what is it that has suddenly put shadows in your face and darkened your eyes? You frown incessantly, too. Has something happened tonight of which I am ignorant?"

John did not look at her but he tried to sound nonchalant.

"What makes you say that?" he enquired. "Shirley, my love, I am exhausted with everything in this life but you. What do I care if some stranger saw us together tonight? Are we not allowed to be in each other's company since we are related?"

She kissed him tenderly and nodded, her suspicions laid to rest and her mind happy at having him under her roof again. As she covered him with blankets and rugs he murmured his thanks and heard her bid him be quiet and rest. She left him to return to her bed and, in his tortured dreams, he wished he possessed one quarter of the confidence he had exuded to Shirley.

Morning broke; cold, damp and bleak in her restoration of light to the pink, cloud-filled sky. A thick hoar frost had settled over the countryside and frozen the long grasses into stiff white tufts, the night wind dropping around the hour of dawn so the ice had been allowed to harden. High in the atmosphere a frugal sun was attempting to shine and raise the low temperatures that had engulfed the landscape during the hours of darkness.

The sleeper on the settle did not stir when, a little before the hour of six, a figure entered the room where he lay, pulled on his outdoor boots, dried brittle by the warmth of the hearth and winced when the taut leather bit into his chilblains. On seeing the lodger he raised his eyebrows, seemed sad rather than angry, and tiptoed out as best he could in noisy boots, calling for his wife at the same time.

Shirley descended the stairs to answer Damion's shouts, yawning and tying her robe as she came down.

"Wife, did you know John Straeton sleeps like the dead on our settle?"

"Yes," murmured she, keeping her voice low as Connie still slumbered.

"You are not angry, are you Damion? He came knocking late last night, long after you were asleep and, faith, I did not have the heart to refuse him entry. Besides you slept deeply and would not wake when I shook you so I sat up with him for a little while and listened to his tale of woe. He affirms Fourbridges is haunted and he cannot stay there, where he was attacked. He says he can hear the mad laughter of his wife echoing around the walls and - well he is our cousin after all."

"True, true!" owned Damion. "I am not against it – not one bit! Did he not live here before with little trouble for us? I hope he will not bother you if he stays. You have Connie to nurse but I know she is fond of him so perhaps good will come of it for he could help you with the girl if he is unable to work."

"Oh Damion, any relation of yours is welcome here! He may stay for as long as he likes. And I agree with you – much good may come out of it."

Her husband bowed and remarked she was all generosity with his cousin.

"I thank you, wife, for your kindness in letting him stay. I expect he will be off to Scotland as soon as he can arrange it but until that day he is welcome here!"

Shirley felt a little ashamed at her husband's praise of her when she was doing it purely for selfish reasons. And she had spoken the truth – much good would come from John residing here. But what would Connie make of it? Shirley wondered.

Damion threw on his old greatcoat, collected his food and went out into the chill morning air to begin work whilst Shirley finished brushing and arranging her hair before entering the parlour to wake John. But when she saw that he was sleeping sweetly she did not have the heart to disturb him and she knelt beside him, watching him as he slumbered. In the half -light he lay like some perfect Adonis – powerful, beautiful and almost Godlike to her. But her gaze eventually pierced his sleep and he stretched, smiled and squeezed her hand.

"Has Damion departed to work?" he whispered.

"Yes, a few moments ago," she replied, returning the squeeze and accompanying it with a kiss.

"You have told him I am here?"

"Oh, yes. He saw you when he came in to collect his boots."

"And?"

"He approves, John. 'Twould not matter to me if he did not but it is easier for us with his say-so. He thanked me for allowing you to move here but thinks you will not stay long as Scotland is calling you."

"He is right there, cousin. I fear I must sell up, pack my bags and go. I cannot stay in this district where everyone laughs in my face at my foolish marriage. Yes, I was an idiot but I do not want to be reminded of it by everyone I meet. Only by making a fresh start elsewhere will I recover some self- esteem and health."

"Don't! Don't!" cried Shirley her eyes pouring forth water. "Don't talk about going, John. I can't bear it. You mustn't think of leaving – you are needed here!"

"Time will wash away the pain of those memories," he comforted her, taking her hand. "What else can we do? What, are you saying you would leave all this and come away with me?"

She did not speak at first, so thoughtful was her face, but then she nodded and replied,

"I would forsake anything to be with you. I would go anywhere you go, be it the ends of the earth or the depths of the sea. Wherever you are, there I want to be. It is that simple."

He remained silent for a few moments.

"Well, I will not be able to go for a while so time may guide our footsteps into the same path as she did last night."

Shirley got up.

"Yes," she agreed. "Let us leave it there and trust to providence. We can ask no more."

The loud sound of coughing interrupted their thoughts and Shirley knew Connie was awake and needing help. John got dressed and completed his toilette whilst his cousin made food and took medicine to her sick stepdaughter. Connie, as usual, refused Shirley's help to dress but this morning she was so weak and shaky that it took her over an hour to get ready and her hands trembled as she fastened buttons and tied her simple gown. Every so often, when the cough came, she had to lean on the bed and with great difficulty she descended the stairs and went to sit in the parlour. By then she was out of breath, gasping for air and totally unable to greet her tall cousin who sat at one end of the settle, talking to Shirley.

John was appalled at the change in her. Last time he had seen her she was being threatened by his wife and he had taken very little notice of her illness, so anxious was he to get Cannetta away from the hapless victim. Before then he had carried her things to the Hall and she had seemed fully recovered, lithe and happy with glowing skin and shiny hair. Now her hair was thin and lifeless, her skin sallow and her temples soaked in sweat from fever and the constant coughing. She looked ready for the grave and he felt deeply concerned about her. Shirley's face portrayed her feelings all too keenly but she tried to smile at her stepdaughter and asked her if there was anything she wanted.

"Do think if any food whets your appetite, dearest," she murmured. "And I shall make it for you. You have John for a few days too so he will keep you company when I am forced to go out. Will that not be pleasant for you?"

Connie nodded but her wasted breath was difficult to draw and she could not speak much. Shirley decided to leave the two together whilst she worked in the kitchen, hoping that John would cheer the girl up with his stories and she, likewise, would pull him from his lethargy of spirit. Connie managed to hold a short conversation with her cousin but there were long gaps between her replies as she struggled for breath. John thought her thin almost to the point of emaciation and she, also, found him gaunt and hollow-cheeked. He noticed how often she held her hand to her side as if she had a sharp pain there.

"Are you in discomfit, dearest?" asked Shirley, coming in to bring some bread she had baked. "Shall I fill a stone bottle for you and you can apply it to your side?"

The girl nodded her thanks and tried to eat but she found it hard to breathe and chew so she soon gave up and left her bread in pieces on her plate. John tried to eat as Shirley had made an effort to bake for them but his heart was not in it. He ate what he could and then asked Connie what the doctor had said regarding her illness.

"I have only seen him once," she replied. "He gave me some oil to take but it makes me sick so I only consume it to please Mother, as she worries so. I hope that the disease will leave of its own accord as it did last time."

"Yes," he said,"I pray it will. Meanwhile you must keep warm and try to eat. You have consumed precious little for breakfast so you must try again at lunch time."

"I will," acknowledged the girl. "Mother tries to tempt me with little cakes and the like. She is kindness itself and I do not know what I would do without her. Father, too, relies heavily upon her and she is our personal angel, sent to keep us safe and well."

John evinced a sharp sense of guilt at this. It was obvious that Shirley could entertain no ideas of leaving whilst her stepdaughter remained so ill. But could he wait for her? It would take time to sell his house and pack so he need not think of that now but at some point a decision would have to be made.

"Are you warm enough?" he asked his cousin, concerned for her health and comfort.

She nodded and presently, by the light of the glowing fire, he saw her dozing off again, wheezing as she fell into a gentle sleep. He rose and went into the kitchen to find Shirley. She was brushing the floor and cleaning plates and utensils dirtied after cooking.

"She is not good," he whispered, his face expressing sorrow. "Can the doctor do nothing else for her?"

Shirley shook her head.

"Both lungs are badly affected. When I talked to him a few days ago he said it was only a matter of time. I have not told her this, of course nor her father, but I think they know."

"It is grave, very grave," murmured he. "She has fallen asleep by the fire's warmth so that may revive her but she struggles to eat and breathe."

Shirley leant against him and he put his arms round her and drew her close. It was a peaceful and tender moment, interrupted all too soon by a sharp knock at the door.

Shirley extracted herself, with great reluctance, from his arms and went to answer the urgent summons. A small boy stood outside holding a sealed envelope in his hand which he thrust at her. She perceived her name was inscribed on it and took it with a puzzled face.

"Please ma'am, a lady have just give me this and a penny to deliver it to your hands. She said no one else must take it only Mrs Penlow but I know 'tis you from your face at market."

"Who is this lady?" asked Shirley, taking the envelope from him.

"Excuse me, ma'am but she said I am not to name her or bad things will happen to me. I was half afraid of her as she looked raging but I wanted the penny so I have done her bidding and I know no more. Good day to you Mrs Penlow!" He touched his cap and ran off before Shirley could question him further.

Closing the door quietly to avoid waking Connie she took the envelope back to the kitchen, broke the red seal unfolded a single sheet of paper and read-

Dear Mrs Penlow,

No doubt you will be surprised to receive a letter from one hitherto unknown to you but the contents will not shock you, I am sure, because they constitute a tangible set of facts called the truth. I have, for several days now, been the silent observer of all that has occurred between you and John Straeton. In fact I have been witness to your meetings before then but only lately has it become painfully obvious to me that they are not innocent. I know John arrived late last night with your good self and that he occupies a downstairs room for the sake of propriety – and your husband, of course. What lie did you spin him? Did you lean heavily on the flesh and blood kinship and so blind Damion as to the true reason John is with you? What would your husband think if he read the contents of this letter or saw the things I have seen? You are a married woman and therefore not a free one. We must hope that my next letter does not have to be addressed to Mr Penlow.

Yes, I saw you last night and, whilst keeping my own identity hidden, threw yours – as lovers - open to the world. Cannetta was right with her suspicions of her husband's infidelity but she made one big mistake – she picked on the wrong cousin. It should have been your throat with her knife upon it, shouldn't it, Shirley?

If you wish to avoid further disclosures to wronged parties I suggest you come to the old gibbet site on Gallows Hill this very afternoon at four when all will be revealed to you. Come alone and with shame in your heart if you wish to keep your husband and your home.

She looked up from the terrible words and her face said everything to John. Turning away she handed him the letter and was surprised at his reluctance to take it.

"Yes," whispered Shirley. "Read it, read it. You must read it as it concerns you – you and I."

"It is not signed," replied he, glancing at the end of the letter to see who it was from.

"That, apparently, does not matter," said she, with tearful bitterness.

She stood silent and grave whilst he perused the note and then his face, too, mirrored her anguish.

"What can I do?" he asked.

Shirley shut the door in case Connie was stirring and shook her head. She sat down heavily at the kitchen table and looked again at the letter.

"Thank God Damion is not here," she breathed. "We have no choice – I must attend as asked."

"On your own?" replied John. "I think not. We do not know the sex of this observer and neither do we know if they are mad or sane. You would be in danger and I cannot have that on my conscience! I have too much already, concerning this family."

"No," said Shirley, firmly. "That cannot be. You must not be there. I must go alone. "

John saw she was adamant. But why was Rose asking to see Shirley, for it must be Rose? he thought. Why did she not want to see him? And what did she hope to achieve by threatening Shirley? Had losing her daughter sent her as mad as her offspring? The insanity must come from somewhere but he knew Cannetta had always named her father as being the disturbed one. He felt very uneasy. Here was Shirley, again, placed in danger and undergoing suffering for his dalliances.

"Very well," he said, at last. "But I am not happy with it, cousin. What will you do? What will you say to this person?"

"Hush! Hush!" cried she. "I hear Connie stirring. Please go and help her, John. I will burn this. And as I burn it a rash part of me longs to show it to my husband and say, yes it is the truth, and I love this man, far, far more than I ever loved you."

Just before the hour of four o'clock on the same day a figure appeared along the gravelled track leading to the earthworks known hereabouts by the grim title of Gallows Hill. It was more than halfway through October and the afternoon was already dusky due to a cloud-covered sky and a fading sun that had remained hidden most of the day. The location had, in the past, been the scene for public executions, a rotting pair of gallows reminding any traveller of its grisly purpose and, further on, at the acme of the hill, the rusted remains of a gibbet lay. It was said, on certain days, that the wind whistled through the latter object with music far more beautiful than any man could

154

produce in a church. Small burial mounds, dating back to before the gallows did their work, littered the landscape and gave rise to stories of ghosts and spectres. Horses would refuse to pass this way after dark and many locals said they had seen the old hangman's spirit rising from the gibbet with evil laughter. Free-roaming sheep and ponies never stayed long here, despite the lush grass that grew, but moved on swiftly to seek other pastures. Only the butcher bird frequented the place and enjoyed impaling his prey upon some of the smaller spikes that remained hidden in the overgrown vegetation.

The figure, who was aware of the rumours concerning the place, seemed very anxious as she climbed the hill and every so often she gazed round as if checking she were truly alone. Reaching the top she pulled her cloak around her tighter as the wind blew fiercely and turning to face the way she had come she stood and waited. A few spots of rain graced the air and were blown hither and thither over the hilltop but the figure never moved. Far away came the reverberation of thunder. The figure seemed oblivious to it and faced the wind in silence.

After a few minutes she began to gaze around her, pulling her hood up as the chill of the afternoon bit into her flesh. No sooner had she done this than she heard a heavier step behind her and, spinning round, she regarded the well-known figure of a tall, chestnut-haired man.

"John!" cried the woman, half in anger and half in relief at his presence. "I told you not to come! The person will be here in a moment and if they see you the next letter they write could be addressed to my husband!"

"And how could I remain quietly at home when I was in this torment – and I knew you were in danger, because of me, yet again? Do you think I have no conscience? Do I not love you more than life itself?"

"Hush!" she cried. "Someone may hear you! If you must stay then you need to find a hiding place where no one will see you!"

"My plan, exactly," he returned. "I have already found some scrubby bushes on the lower slope that will do office as a screen."

"Then go, go!" she fair screamed. "For I feel certain the person is almost upon us!"

He dashed off and she saw him vanish to the lower slopes. She remained standing there, facing the wind, feeling a little comforted by his closer proximity. The breeze flapped the folds of her garments and dampened her cloak but she did not feel it as her eyes were on a bent figure below her, climbing the hill and scattering a few fragments of shale and rock as she walked.

Eventually the well-wrapped figure arrived at the top, her breath coming in gasps, for she was no youngster. Shirley was surprised at the sex of the blackmailer.

"'Tis a woman," she murmured to herself. "A middle-aged woman." She let her eyes stray down the slope to the scrub bushes and wondered if John was as surprised as she was.

"Mrs Penlow?" asked the woman, when her breath allowed it.
Shirley confirmed it was she.

The woman flung back her hood, allowing her greying auburn tresses to escape. Shirley narrowed her eyes at the face.

"You know me?" enquired the woman, staring at her with sharp eyes. "Look again! I am no stranger to these parts!"

"I have seen you a couple of times, I am sure," replied Shirley, vaguely. She thought for a minute then realisation hit her. "You are Cannetta's mother!" she cried at last.

"You have spoken the truth – for once," answered Rose, lowering her piercing eyes. "I am - she. It is for that reason that I question your behaviour with my son-in-law."

"You mean that is the reason you blackmail me!" retorted Shirley, in anger.

Rose drew herself up to full height but she could not match Shirley's figure. "You are a brave woman, Mrs Penlow, a braver woman than I gave you credit for. Yet I am one who believes that actions speak louder than words."

"In that I agree with you," Shirley confirmed.

"Good! Good! We are settled on that then," Rose nodded.

A momentary silence followed. John, below, and surrounded by the sharp twigs of the bushes, felt a growing anxiety at what was to come. He had been prepared to see his mother-in-law but he knew Shirley would have been surprised at her appearance. The fact that the two had only seen each other as they both wandered round the district and briefly at his wedding and after he was aware of but exactly what blame Rose was going to heap on his head he did not know. He could see the scene at a distance from his hiding place but with the wind's strength he had no chance of hearing any speech.

"I do not doubt, Mrs Penlow, in my son-in-law's intimacy with you that he has told you of his harsh and cruel treatment of his wife, my daughter."

"Indeed, no, nothing like that has ever been discussed between us. In that much you are wrong."

"And the rest is right, then?"

"Certainly not!" returned Shirley, hotly flinging back her head in anger. "Your daughter was quite mad, Mrs Hardy, totally insane. If you have gleaned your information from her then you have wasted my time in coming here and yours, too."

"Ah, but my eyes did not deceive me, even if my daughter was mistaken in the identity of the cousin she believed was the adulteress."

"But was she so mistaken, Mrs Hardy? Maybe it is YOU who are mistaken."

Rose was confused.

"What do you mean by that?" she asked, her face wearing a perplexed look.

"Then hear me out. When John first arrived at Ardle, before he met your daughter, he formed a deep friendship with my stepdaughter."

"Impossible!" cried Rose. "How could he prefer her pale beauty with YOU about and so willing?"

"But I am not a free woman. I promised my husband when I married him that my days of dalliance were over. And, so far, I have kept my word. John is my cousin and that alone. I called on him recently because my stepdaughter is very ill, dying possibly, and I turned to him for comfort. Yes, it is no secret that I am unhappy with Damion but how could I risk losing my home and husband when Connie lies at death's door? She needs me desperately. I should not be here with you now but for your threats. I should be at home nursing her!"

"But John has been staying at your house!"

"Yes, as my husband's cousin. Damion is delighted to have found a relation as he has few others that own him."

"But you used to visit John and stay for hours at Fourbridges when your husband was at work," insisted Rose.

"Ah, it is a shame you did not consult your daughter in one of her more lucid moments, Mrs Hardy, as she would have told you John employed me as a housekeeper! Cannetta saw me there many a time and I served her tea and dinner. My husband knew all about it, of course. We were glad of the extra money, Connie being so ill."

Shirley could see the seeds of doubt planted in Rose's eyes and she pressed home her advantage.

"And John spent much more time with Connie than me. Your daughter saw them when John was helping Connie move back to her work. She put two and two together and got ten! So then she came upon a knife...somehow and came to kill Connie, despite the fact that the girl could hardly stand...Did you not know that?"

"Yes," admitted Rose, grudgingly. "But despite your confident words you have no witnesses to these facts."

"My husband was witness to my employment as John's housekeeper and he saw Connie and John go back to the Hall together. He approved of the friendship as I did. It was only your daughter who saw things that did not exist. And my Connie nearly paid for her cousin's company with her life!"

Rose shook her head.

"I do not believe you but time will tell if your words are true. Now I come to your part of the bargain. I must get at him through you, cruel though it seems."

"Ah," perceived Shirley. "Now we come to the truth that you prize so much. This has all been done for revenge. You seek to make John suffer because he did the decent and sensible thing and had your mad daughter committed!"

"Silence! You will hear me out!" shouted Rose, in fury. "From now on you will walk no more with John, unless a third party is there. And you will give up any thoughts of love for him, save in a cousinly sort of way. When you can you must avoid his company and regard him as a lodger in your husband's house."

"There is no purpose in such an oath since that is what I am doing at present. The circumstances you believe in do not exist in the first place. There is no affair, no dalliance, no love, only the feeling one cousin has for another. If that is the threat you have come here to play out then send a letter to my husband. He will not believe it. Especially when he hears it comes from the pen of the madwoman's mother. How do we know that you are not as insane as your daughter?"

Rose did not reply. She turned away as if giving up and Shirley called after her,

"Good day, Mrs Hardy. I would see a doctor if I were you in case Cannetta's madness was hereditary after all!"

But Rose was not about to go without a last word and she turned back to her adversary.

"Yes, I have made you suffer a little but he...why should he go unpunished? If he does truly love you then this will cause him some measure of grief although nothing could compare with the agony my daughter suffered at his hands and her suffering has only been multiplied by her present surroundings. And if this isolation from him breaks you then I will receive double the pleasure! So I am finished with you - for the moment. But for HIM - his interrogation is still to come. Tell him to come to my cottage silently by cover of darkness tonight at nine o'clock when the tracks are empty and every door is locked. He must come alone. And now I shall leave you to your conscience if, indeed, you possess one!" Rose pulled up her hood, stepped back onto the downward track and, after a few minutes, was just a speck on the landscape. Shirley watched, impassive, until the figure had vanished completely.

It was only a matter of seconds before John was with her. They embraced briefly and then stood, hand in hand, gazing at each other.

"Well, Shirley how do you feel?" he asked, with concern in his tearful eyes.

"Quite steady," replied she confidently. "Yet I would not crave such an interview again...Is the woman mad? Oh, John, she is a desperate woman!"

"Not only desperate but lying, deceiving and willing to go any lengths to extract her revenge if that letter is anything to go by. Did she break you down, Shirley?"

His cousin shook her head firmly.

"But I do not know if she believed my denials. I told her of my employment with you, sanctioned by my husband, and that obviously shocked her as she had no knowledge of that in her spying! And I heaped heavily on the kinship of cousins, saying that you were closer to Connie than me. Oh God forgive me for my lies. But I was desperate too, and like Peter I denied you and your love. If Peter was forgiven, in the sight of heaven, then can I not be stripped of my guilt too, for the sake of true love?"

John was silent for a moment. He felt the keenness of her anguish and knew it was due to his behaviour. If he had spurned her, promptly and continually, they would not be standing here now. But how could he reject someone who controlled his soul, even in the agony he lately felt?

Shirley continued, seeing as he did not speak.

"Your trial is yet to come. Rose wants to see you at her cottage tonight at nine o'clock. She was adamant that you must come alone. Will you attend?"

He nodded.

"How could I let you face this hell and then shy away myself from the trouble? Aye, she'll see me but she is not going to have it all her own way. We must stand firm, Shirley, on this."

She smiled, relief flooding her tense form. The wind blew heavy raindrops from the west and the two cousins ran from the eerie landscape.

John paused in his flight and let Shirley catch up.

"We must not be seen coming back together," he cried, above the tumult of the gale. "You run home first and I will tread these northerly paths and come back later a different way. Rose may be watching."

Shirley nodded willingly and sped past him, squeezing his hand as she went. Together, yet apart, they took separate routes off Gallows Hill and she arrived at her home first, John returning a good hour later affirming to Connie he had been to feed and bed his horse. Only a soft, glowing light present in their eyes showed their involvement and Connie was too ill to perceive that.

It was nearly quarter to nine and yet again John left the tiny pink cottage this time to visit Rose. His mind quivered with anxiety but he walked steadily, with his head held high. I have done nothing wrong, he told himself, and Shirley is totally innocent in all of this...If I am culpable then let me suffer...not her... He had no idea what he was going to say to Rose. All he could do was deny any claims of infidelity and certainly nothing at all had occurred whilst he was married to Cannetta. The fact that his love for Shirley had always been there, bubbling away like a fast flowing river, sometimes underground, sometimes breaking free at the surface, he would not reveal but he had rarely seen Shirley whilst Cannetta lay in his bed. He shuddered. The things his wife had done to him...they still came back to haunt him if he closed his eyes. So was it wrong to seek comfort with someone so different who had the power to bring a touch of happiness to his wrecked life? If so then he was indeed guilty and they could condemn him gladly.

He reached the outer gate, let himself into the garden and approached the cottage with a sinking heart. How much more unhappiness did he have to bear because of Cannetta? He knocked found he was a few minutes early and waited patiently in the porch. The evening had calmed down after a windy afternoon, peppered with squally showers. Now it was still and cold; there would be another frost tonight but possibly sun on the morrow, judging by the red glow in the west when dusk fell earlier.

Footsteps approached the door, waking him from his reverie, and the bolts were drawn back to admit him. A face peered out at him, recognised his features and bade him enter. He stood, awkwardly, in the hall watching his mother-in-law relocking and bolting the barrier. She turned to look at him and he saw, not only sorrow in the confines of her face but anger, too, and the twist of revenge. He looked away.

"Ah," she began. "You cannot bear my gaze because its purity highlights your guilt and brings the painful truth to the fore!"

"I feel no guilt," he replied firmly. "I came because you left a message with my cousin that you wished to see me. I hoped you had good news of Cannetta, my wife."

"Nicely side-stepped Mr Straeton.! As if you care one jot what happens to my daughter now she is out of your life. But a new woman has entered it has she not? Or was she there all the time?"

"I do not know to what you refer, Mrs Hardy."

"Really? Innocence does not suit you since you adopt it to hide from the lies Shirley has told me."

He shrugged his shoulders.

"I cannot speak for my cousin," he retorted. "What has she said?"

"That your relationship with her is purely that of kinship through her husband. But we both know different, don't we, Mr Straeton?"

"You seem to think otherwise, that I must say. But Shirley and I know the truth. Yes, we are close but not in the way you interpret things. Shirley's stepdaughter is very ill and she relies on me for help. Damion works long hours in the field to earn a living and supports me aiding his wife and daughter, whenever I can."

"It sounds so touching, this little scene you paint of the ties of your family and no doubt it has fooled Damion as he is a simple soul. But it does not fool me, Mr Straeton. I have seen too much with my own eyes. I knew you recognised me the other night. I followed Shirley from her cottage and saw you standing on the bridge, transfixed in silver light, embracing..."

"She was upset. Why should I not comfort her?"

"Because you have a wife whom you have locked away! You got tired of her mighty quick...or did the old love flare up again?"

"Mrs Hardy, your daughter did things to me that I shudder to name. She bit me, scratched me burnt me with candles..." and here he opened his coat and shirt and showed his mother-in-law several deep scabbed wounds, some just starting to scar. "Do you think I will ever get rid of these?" he asked. "And there are more...but the worse ones are on my heart."

"I don't doubt Cannetta was a handful but remember I tried to warn you! Did you heed me? No. I knew it would end in disaster but would you listen to my fears? Again no! And now you bear the wounds that come from ignoring me. Well, you deserve them. But my daughter does not deserve her fate; lying bound in a madhouse till she dies."

"Do you think I wanted to do it?" cried he, passionately. "But someone dear to me nearly lost their life. What would you have me do? Try and cope with her again then fail and let her escape to murder?"

"She neither escaped nor murdered whilst I looked after her," replied Rose. "I gave up years of my life to care for her when it was painfully obvious the only other place for her was the asylum. Do you think I even considered that option? Yes, she often bit and scratched me but I learnt to become stoic to it, careless even."

"Then you are a stronger person than I," he returned. "I have to work for a living so Cannetta had to be left with what consequences you already know. I could never relax for an instant. God, it was like being with a man-eating tiger and a snake all at once; if she wasn't biting me she was coiling her limbs round me to suffocate me! Mrs Hardy, I was not her husband, I was her constant prey!"

"She could not help it," shouted Rose, becoming very angry with his criticism of her flesh and blood. "She hated the fact that she injured me. She could never remember doing the dreadful things she did, so how could you blame her?"

"Mrs Hardy," continued John, trying to remain calm. "I do not blame her. During my time with her it was painfully obvious that she knew not what she did...I did not have her committed because I blamed her, I had her committed because she was a danger to others, and ultimately, she was a danger to herself. Can you not understand that?"

A heavy silence fell in the hallway and Rose stifled a few sobs but she carried on, bravely.

"Whatever you say, Mr Straeton, she was my daughter then, she is now and she always will be. It is distressing beyond belief to hear you say these things. But this does not help Cannetta. She has suffered enough but you - you seem to have escaped!"

"Believe me, Mrs Hardy, I have suffered far more than your daughter and I am still suffering now. Maybe I always will...."

"I doubt that, very much," replied Rose. "If you do suffer you have found relief in the arms of your so-called cousin."

"I have found friendship, support and a listening ear – nothing more."

"We beg to differ there, Mr Straeton. And because of that I will not rest until some sort of justice rears its head in this situation. Therefore it is up to me to administer it for the sake of my poor daughter."

"So what is your justice?" he asked, feeling suddenly nervous.

"My proposition is this – you must leave Ardle, leave Stackhouses, leave the entire area and go back to where you came from."

"And if I chose not to?"

"Then I speak to Damion and believe me I have more evidence than I am letting on and other witnesses who would come forward to corroborate my words. Do you want to take that risk, Mr Straeton?"

"But I cannot just leave like that. There is my house. I must sell it and get money to travel with. I cannot do it overnight."

"I am prepared to give you a few weeks before I make my disclosures. But make them I will, be assured of that, Mr Straeton."

He was silent for a moment then he nodded his head.

"Very well Mrs Hardy. I will put into place circumstances that will enable me to leave within a few weeks."

"Sensible choice. And, of course, it proves you are guilty."

At this avowal he shook his head.

"It proves nothing. If you must know I had already decided to go so it was only a matter of time."

"I do not believe you. You would not leave your rekindled love."

"Believe me or doubt me, Mrs Hardy, I do not care. I will be going whether you threaten me or not. And now I wish you good night and go to pack my things."

Rose saw there was nothing left to say, she had done her best.

"Good night, Mr Straeton. I trust, and hope, we shall not meet again."

She held the door open for him and he went through, trying to hold his head high. It was the final nail in the coffin over his departure and he went with mixed feelings over leaving a place that had defiled him, shocked him, devastated him and also led him to the most beautiful thing he had ever beheld in his life...

CHAPTER 15

Over the next few days John found it hard to look upon the suffering of his cousin and keep the tears from his face. Many a time he hurried from the room to join Shirley in the kitchen and unburden his emotions, returning to the parlour when he could control his feelings again. He excused himself to Connie, saying that shock, due to the failure of his marriage, still assailed him but he admitted to himself that relief was the lingering emotion he felt about Cannetta's departure. Unable to believe that Connie's situation was so hopeless John received permission to summon the doctor again and he duly came.

He arrived on the last day of October, a particularly bitter, blustery day when gales graced the region, roaring down the chimney and fanning the flaring flames. The fire was kept constantly lit and Connie soon found it impossible to climb the stairs so John carried her, so light had she become with illness. She had not been out of doors for many days and her wasted eyes no longer sought the pleasant garden visible from the windows. Most of her time was spent struggling to get her breath or consume a small quantity of soup or bread. Sometimes she did not even respond to her family and her terrible cough rang out all night and all day. Only sleep bought her any relief and that was short-lived.

The physician examined her carefully, grave-faced and silent. She struggled to answer his questions and seemed to shrink into herself but she had always been shy to the point of reticence, even when healthy. The doctor left the warmth of the parlour, shut the door and sought the girl's stepmother who was in the kitchen waiting for him. John stood by her, but not too close, after the fateful letter. The man came in, sat down at the table and shook his head.

"Alas," murmured he. "I can offer you no hope. It is simply a matter of time as I told you on my last visit. Both lungs are worse than when I examined them previously and the fever is higher. I wish I could give you better news but I cannot. You must prepare yourself for the worst."

Shirley nodded her head, her eyes full of tears.

"How long has she got?" she asked.

"It is difficult to say but only weeks, maybe a month...I do not know. She has a very strong and resilient spirit that I must say and she accepts my medicine gladly despite its foul taste but it will do little good. She is very emaciated and that worries me but she tells me she tries to eat but has no breath to do so."

Shirley thanked him for coming but her heart sank. She realised now that nothing could save Connie and no miracle existed, as last time, to bring her back from the brink. How would Damion bear the loss? He said very little to her but she knew he always kept his own counsel and had never opened up to her. Used to his secrecy and silent treatment Shirley poured out her heart to

John and he comforted her but they were both very careful not to appear in public together. Neither of them saw or heard from Rose again and she did not seem to go abroad much, although the inclement weather kept many indoors.

Fourbridges was put up for sale and a few viewed it but no one was moved to buy the damp, dark place. John tried to improve its condition but in the end he decided he was just throwing good money after bad and it should be sold as seen. He was prepared to make a loss on it providing it sold quickly but he said nothing to Shirley about his plans. She had asked what Rose wanted from him but he had murmured that it was more viscous scolding for his behaviour to her daughter and he had listened to her lengthy ranting and then left.

"No ultimatums then?" asked Shirley.

"No," replied he. "Just huge piles of blame heaped on my head for Cannetta's suffering. The woman is deranged with grief and although I tried to humour her I think it is best we avoid her at all costs."

Shirley agreed but they were still careful to keep distance between them unless they were certain they were alone. They obtained happiness just from being in the same house as each other and Shirley believed that one day, very soon, circumstances would throw them together and keep them there. She prayed for it nightly, almost as much as she prayed for Connie, and John was often the only thing that kept her going through the agony of watching her stepdaughter grow weaker and weaker.

It was early November. For days now a bitter east wind had frequented the district, hurling everything in its path into confusion and throwing squally showers like curses over the village. The elders found their aches and pains worse, their feet swollen with chilblains and their fingers stiff with cold. Men a-field groaned and moaned as they bent to top turnips and chop cattle feed for the ground was often frozen till late in the day and sometimes it did not thaw out at all. It had been a terrible year for weather and crops were poor in both yield and size. The farmers calculated they had lost money and were forced to lay men off until times improved. Luckily Damion was still employed and he threw himself into his work to try and block out the pain of watching his daughter fade before his eyes.

John resumed working spasmodically when he knew Shirley was there to sit with Connie but often he preferred to lose money in order to be with his dying cousin. He knew every day with her was precious even though it hurt him to view her pain, particularly as he could do nothing to assuage it. And what did one say to comfort someone who was dying? Was there anything that could be said? John felt inadequate and useless but he still craved to be there, if only to support Shirley. Connie made no comments to her stepmother about John but sometimes, when the two sat together, she would smile at them, as if she approved. Shirley said nothing to her either, anxious not to cause her any additional pain or worry. Shirley was very careful when

164

Damion was home to ignore John as much as possible and not even look his way in case her eyes reflected her growing love. But at night when both Connie and Damion were in bed and the blinds were drawn against the outside world they would give into their feelings and sit arm in arm, cherishing the comfort they received from each other. Then nothing else mattered and they both resided in heaven, although it was short-lived. But the memory of their special times lived with them until they could be together again. And all the time the promise John had made to Rose rang in his ears and he knew that this time with Shirley was precious because it had to come to an end.

On the fifth of the month, when huge bonfires graced the countryside, a small travelling fair arrived in Ardle and encamped on the tiny green, bringing bright sparks of colour to the drab winter scenery. When John related this to Connie, as a matter of interest, he was surprised that she hung on his every word and when he had finished she cried,

"But I must go and see them! Do you think I place any value on my worthless existence now? If I expired this very night viewing their wonderful array of colour and listening to the beautiful music you have just told me about do you not think I would die happy?" She panted for breath and, after a while, continued. "Oh I am so weary of these four walls. It is so drear to slide into death in familiar surroundings! Please take me to see the fair!"

John was shocked as it was the most she had said for a long time and he felt her yearning to be true but he feared it would be far too much for her.

"Darling," pleaded he. "You cannot even think of going out into the keen night air as its cold would stifle you at once and snuff you out like a candle in a gale! No, Connie, you must watch the flames of their camp from your warm and secure chair and be content with that!"

The disappointment showed in her face, she attempted to rise and shed bitter tears when she found she was unable to unless John's stalwart arm was aiding her. Her spirit was still strong and indomitable but her body was fading fast, slipping into the anathema of death. John knelt beside her and promised he would go and bring her back glittering descriptions of the fair plus as many souvenirs as he could carry. Connie regarded him with gratitude and nodded her head, her breath quite gone in her excitement.

"In order that you do not have to wait any longer than possible dearest, "he soothed. "I shall go this very night after tea and you shall hear all about it before you go to bed!"

She seemed very happy with that and hoped he would enjoy it too. For himself John would have completely avoided such entertainment as he felt no desire for merriment but he could do so little for his cousin that this gave him the chance to bring a vestige of sunshine into her dark world.

It was almost seven o'clock when John left the cottage and the winter darkness had crept up with a touch of moonlight illuminating the still, cold night. Small fragments of falling frost graced the fields and tinged the air

165

with ice so every breath steamed like dragon's fire from flared nostrils. John was glad to leave the stuffy parlour for the clear, fresh atmosphere outside but he knew that such air, although stimulating to him, would be death to Connie's corrupted lungs. He set off at a brisk pace along the footpaths that led to Ardle Green.

As he walked he encountered and passed couples or groups of villagers carrying slatted lanterns which cast a warm refulgence in the dark night. One or two nodded to him, wished him good evening and noticed that he barely spoke or looked their way. Reaching the small but brightly lit fairground he made a quick tour of the tiny stalls and kiosks that covered the hitherto deserted green. In the centre was a huge brazier that sent up sparks in a continuous flare of colour, lighting the dark winter skies and vying with the winking stars for radiance. The warmth generating from this large structure had attracted a group of people who stood luxuriating in the heat and catching up on gossip. Around them two or three brightly dressed individuals were letting off coloured flares of gunpowder in red, yellow and purple and John hoped that Connie could see the show from her chair by the parlour window. Further on an elderly woman was selling twists of sweets – peppermints and gaudy candies – so he went over to buy his cousin some, knowing that although she could not eat them, the striped decoration of the treats would please her and, besides, Shirley might enjoy them too. Next he journeyed on past a coconut shy to a paper stall where coloured lanterns were sold in numerous shapes, painted with strange animals and birds. Purchasing a couple of these he perceived he had spent most of his money and, as the night was cold, he moved back to the welcome warmth of the glowing brazier. As he toasted his hands by the leaping flames a figure stopped beside him, regarded him with interest and asked,

"You are Mr Straeton?"

John started and seemed troubled by this. The tall, thin gentleman who addressed him apologised for the abruptness of his words.

"Forgive me, sir," murmured he, raising his hat. "My eyes have seen things that no man should have to look upon. They are reserved for the world of nightmare and should be left there. Alas, I was witness to them and they have coloured my thoughts and mind causing me to speak sharply. I did not know such places existed before yesterday. Places where humans crawl and grovel on their bellies like demented animals, screaming by day and night so any lucid individual entering there would be as mad as the worst of them within a week!"

John put up his hand to stop this flow of words.

"What do you mean by talking to me in that fashion? What are you rambling about? Why collar me for your frenzied views? I do not know you, sir, and for that I am grateful. Move on and leave me, please."

The gentleman considered his words carefully.

166

"I agree you do not know me, sir," he replied, checking his emotions. "But I, after enquiries, know you and we both know someone who crawls in the filth of that institution I visited yesterday where her husband sent her because he could not cope with her behaviour. Rather I should say she crawled in the squalor but her lot was a happy one – she left it."

"For God's sake what are you talking about?" cried John, becoming angry. "Your words are like riddles to me and totally unwelcome. Pass by and pick another fool to rant at. You have got the wrong man!"

He made a motion to leave but the gentleman grabbed his arm.

"I think you had best stay, Mr Straeton, if not for your own sake then for the sake of your wife!"

John shook off his detainer but remained staring at him.

"Cannetta?" he cried, in amazement. "You are talking about...Cannetta?"

"Yes, your wife, no less. I heard about your wedding and the tragic events that followed so I made enquiries and found out where she had been sent. I went to see her...I only wish I hadn't. "

John gasped.

"What?" yelled he, jerking his head up with horror in his eyes. "You have seen her?"

"Yes. Cold and stark yesterday whilst all around her screamed and grovelled in the mire of that place! Have you ever been in an asylum, Mr Straeton? It is a visit that is calculated to give you eternal nightmares!"

John was struck dumb by the news. He shook his head from side to side whilst his eyes poured forth water.

"Come, "said the gentleman. "Have you forgotten her? Have you forgotten your wife, sir?"

A glance at John's face told him that his words had hit home.

"She will be here tomorrow," he continued in a softer tone. "Due to my intervening Cannetta's remains travel to Ardle for burial here. I have seen to that. I could do no more as she was dead the day before I discovered her. I wish I could have saved her, but, alas, that was not possible."

John came to life.

"And how do I know that this is not some sick joke that you play on me? You could be anyone! Have you come to mock me for committing her? You do not know what suffering she put me through."

"I can imagine, sir," replied the gentleman. "She was mad as a child...the last time I saw her and her father was insane too but she was still my flesh and blood and despite the animosity between her mother and I...well I made what enquiries I could to find my niece and rescue her from that hell hole."

John knelt upon the ground as his head swam and he felt dizzy.

The gentleman waited till he had recovered a little then he reached into his pocket and produced a long, white envelope.

"Take this, sir, and read it. It provides the proof you crave as to who I am and the sad fate of your wife. Be glad she died, sir. If she had lived longer in

167

that place her suffering would have been enormous. It was already very great but she did the sensible thing and departed. Alas, had she managed to survive the harsh regime another day I could have provided a more suitable home...I have come into money, you see. Enough to care for her without the provisions of chains and fetters anyway!"

John did not take the offered envelope at first. His mind wandered to his treatment of Cannetta.

"I shackled her," he whispered. "I plied her with brandy...even opium...but it did no good"

"She is beyond that now, sir. Her insanity can never hurt anyone again. Please read the letter."

John took it mechanically and opened it, bringing forth the single sheet of paper contained in there. He turned it to the blaze and with streaming eyes read...

Ledbourne

Institution

Dear Mr Hardy,

Yes, the lady you seek, whom you affirm is your niece, was here in this institution and being one of the more sane beings admitted to this asylum she was able to confirm her name and the fact that she was married when she entered here. The sign on her cage read Cannetta Straeton but she told me she was a Hardy at birth and that she had lived at Ardle prior to entering this establishment.

The details of this young lady's illness are strange to say the least. Sometimes she was totally lucid and would be able to hold a conversation, perform tasks and look upon the squalor she was forced to live in with the horror of a sane being. At times, however, particularly during the hours of darkness, she would crawl around on all fours, snarling and crying for her husband. Even in her maddest hours she called for him incessantly and whilst lucid she talked over and over of her love for him. Her sole wish was to be reunited with him but you know the situation here – no one ever leaves except in a wooden box and Cannetta chose this exit. She literally pined to death and though every effort was made to feed her with tubes nothing could be done. The worst thing was she was with child but the doctors here did not think the baby would develop due to her illness. They were wrong as the child continued to grow inside her but she did not; she shrank and declined. She died less than two days ago of malnutrition and wasting of the lungs, the child going to the grave with her sadly.

Come tomorrow, November the fifth, as early as you possibly can and bring the documentation you say you possess which will prove you are her father's brother – in short her uncle and the body will be released to you providing no one with a closer relationship claims her. You can then make arrangements to take her back to Ardle for burial. I know she wished to go back there fervently.

I am pleased to have been able to help you, and I remain, sir,
Your trusted friend,

Allen Bury

The letter fluttered down to the ground and John threw his head in his hands.

"Oh, my God," he said. "I did not think it could get any worse. My wife in an asylum...but it does. She died of a broken heart, carrying my child. Oh, God, how can I bear it?"

Mr Hardy patted his back.

"If you had seen the conditions she had to live under that would have made it infinitely harder to bear. As it is you rest in ignorance of her suffering but I saw it all...filth, rats, poor food and no sanitation. What do you think that did to her? She may have been mad but she had lucid moments and during that time she must have seen and felt the pain of existing in that hell-hole. She was a sensitive girl - disturbed, yes, but that did not mean she should have been abandoned."

John could not speak.

"And you saw her?" he gasped, at last.

"Yes, as I told you earlier, cold and stark lying on a plain wooden board with her name chalked on it like some animal. Do you know what that did to me? I remember her as a child so full of life. When my brother killed himself his wife Rose blamed me and we broke all contact...sadly. And then I hear of the tragedy from a friend in Ardle and lo, it is my niece who has been committed to an institution and left to die."

There was silence apart from the whirr of the fair in the background but John did not hear it.

"How did you find me?" he asked.

"I still have friends here with whom I keep in touch at the Hall. They told me and furnished me with a description of your good self. When I saw the height and the chestnut hair I thought there was a chance it could be my niece's husband. I had to tell you, Mr Straeton. You had to know. She will come back to Ardle tomorrow in a decent coffin and I will give her a Christian burial. I am staying at Mistletoe Cottage if you wish to contact me and see her. She will lay there from morning till her funeral the next day at eleven if you wish to attend."

John struggled to speak but could not form any words apart from stutters.

"I will leave you now, Mr Straeton. I can see my words have caused severe shock and I am sorry for that. When you come to terms with it you know where I am. Good evening." and he touched his hat and retreated, becoming lost in the crowds within a few seconds.

169

John, like a man in the throes of an intense agony, fell upon his knees again and covered his face with trembling hands. The crowds thronged around him but no one noticed him, bent and broken on the wet ground, so intense was their excitement at the wonderful jugglers and acrobats that ran forth from the darkness just like bright flowers exploding from the swart earth.

The night wore on. Ten o'clock came and went and the performers took a last bow and returned to their caravans. Stalls were taken down and put away for the morrow but still the chestnut-haired man knelt, frozen in his internal agony. The crowds thinned out and went home to bed. Gradually the huge flames of the brazier died and a warm glow remained, then, finally even that went out. The stars reclaimed their predominant shine and the whole green became empty and still. Eventually a little sensation returned to the man and he pulled himself up, gazing around him as though he did not know where he was. His feet slipped on the wet grass and he righted himself. Looking around him in fear and anguish he made off for a distant track on the other side of the green, stumbling as though great weariness dogged his footsteps. His hat remained on the grass and by its side the crumpled remains of the souvenirs he had bought with a light heart to bring a fleeting joy to his cousin. And, as the night wind gathered pace and flung the ruined gifts this way and that over the flattened grass the debris of his visit vanished into the darkness...

By nine o'clock, when her cousin had not returned, Connie grew anxious and attempted to stagger to the door to see if there was any sign of John coming home. Holding onto the handle and gazing out into the night she saw nothing but fleeing shadows and Shirley gently steered her back to the warm fire. It was turning bitterly cold and Connie almost fell as the rising wind hit her.

Back in her chair Shirley tried to comfort her.

"He has very likely gone on for a drink at the Resort seeing as he was out. I am sure he will return with your father very soon."

Connie tried to calm down but her disappointment showed in the tears on her cheeks although she had no breath to complain. Shirley squeezed her hand and wondered why John had stayed out so long. His mood of late had been sombre and grave, not one calculated to make him enjoy the spectacle and colour of the fair. In fact he had declared that he was only going because Connie could not and he desperately wanted to bring her back some tokens of his visit.

Eleven o'clock rung out and still Connie sat up, refusing to go to bed until her cousin was home. Shirley began to worry. When Damion came in, a few minutes later, he affirmed he had not seen John all evening. Shirley at last managed to get Connie to lie down, telling her that some emergency must have come up with an animal and he had gone to administer help. That went some way to soothe her stepdaughter and, when Damion had carried her up to bed she sank into a restless sleep.

Sitting alone on the settle by the glowing fire that she had banked up to last the night, Shirley listened to the other sleepers, one snoring and one wheezing, in their slumbers. Where was John? Had he planned this? She knew he still clung to the idea of returning to Scotland but Fourbridges was not sold, although one gentleman had expressed an interest at the reduced price. So had he really gone in order not to say goodbye to her? She gazed into the smouldering fire and saw pictures of a dark future, with her and Damion alone.

Suddenly she heard the latch of the door rattle and she jumped up and ran into the kitchen where her cousin was just entering, empty-handed.

One look at his face in the light of the oil lamp on the table stopped her in her tracks.

"Oh, God, John - what has happened?" she whispered, her legs losing strength to support her. She sat down heavily on a nearby chair and put out her arm to him. To her horror he moved back violently out of her reach and avoided her gaze.

"Go to bed, Shirley," he growled, motioning her away with shaking arms.
"But John, how can I leave you in a state like this? What has occurred to bring that look of agony to your face?"
"Go to bed, Shirley, as I asked you," he repeated. "I am in no mood for questions and I will furnish no answers tonight. Get to bed – and take that light with you. I desire darkness, darkness and nothing more than my own company."

Shirley was shocked at the venom in his tone but she rose, picked up the lamp, and left him in the isolation he so desired.

CHAPTER 16

The next day, before it was light, a succession of snowstorms hit the region and obliterated landmarks, drifting in the freshening wind to form huge walls of white against a pale sky. Cottages mirrored dark interiors against the dazzling purity of the snow and more threatened, coming down in spasmodic flakes of huge size. November held the world at bay like a stalking lion, and the earth shuddered at its breath.

To Shirley, watching the sullen, silent face of her beloved cousin over the breakfast table and hearing the dreadful rattle of her stepdaughter's breath upstairs it was hard not to lose every vestige of hope she clung to. Damion had gone to sew sacks in the farmer's barn and grade swedes since outdoor work was impossible.

Soon after breakfast John muttered some excuse of attending a cow and left the cottage without even seeing his sick cousin. His eyes were bloodshot and misty which told Shirley that he had slept badly, if at all. He had not spoken a word to her, apart from his leaving sentence and she rested in total ignorance of what had occurred last night. Had she done wrong, or had Rose resumed her threats? Her heart plummeted at the thought of more trouble. Did they not have enough? Facing the unknown was infinitely worse than anything she now dealt with and her mind raced in fear. Would John return, or was he merely going to collect his things from his house and depart on his horse? Was he going to give up on her and leave without one last embrace? She could not bear that, and sitting with Connie by the fire, gazing out at the white world, she felt despair creeping up on her.

Early afternoon saw a return of heavier showers and still John did not come home. He was then leaving his house, locking up and turning his footsteps towards Mistletoe Cottage in the grounds of the Hall. He felt alternately numb and frenzied and desired no company to converse with.. Words were useless since Cannetta lay in her coffin together with his unborn child...Oh God, to think he had to look upon her, silent and wasted! How would he ever get that picture out of his mind once he beheld it? But how could he leave her at her wake and not express some sorrow for what he had done?

"I had no knowledge that it would come to this, Cannetta," he breathed as he walked. "Do you really think I would have sent you there to lose your life and carrying my child too? But I did not know! I rested in ignorance and felt relief that you would not be in my bed to bite and injure me. They told me that you would be well cared for but I never checked...I never visited...I did not know what an asylum was. I visualised some clean, white hospital where you would be safe and we would be safe from you. Oh God, what a different picture Mr Hardy painted! Does Rose know? Is it my duty to tell her? Oh God, give me strength in what I am to undergo!"

By this time he had reached the grounds of the Hall and entering, he made his way round to where the small cottage peered out from behind the grand stable block. Knocking at the door he said to himself, I have kept my word to her this time, I have come... After a few moments the barrier swung inwards and his harbinger of bad news from last night stood there, hat in hand.

"Ah Mr Straeton. I was just about to go out, but please, enter." He sounded very sombre.

John stepped into the hallway.

"I have come to see...her Mr Hardy. I have not come to terms with it but seeing her may help that and I have things I need to say to her to ease my aching heart."

Mr Hardy bowed.

"I shall be but a short while," he replied. "She arrived just before the snow blanketed the region. I have laid her to rest in the parlour so you may remain undisturbed for however long you wish. No one will come in but me."

John nodded his head slowly.

"This way," murmured Cannetta's uncle, leading him down the hall and into a brightly lit room where a gentle fire burnt low in the grate. Numerous candles graced the table and upon it John saw a plain, dark wooden casket in teak, open to the air. He stopped dead, seemed unable to approach the coffin and bowed his head.

Mr Hardy patted his back.

"Take heart, Mr Straeton, she cannot bite or scratch you now and she looks like she has just fallen asleep."

John swallowed hard but did not move.

Mr Hardy withdrew and John heard the front door bang, then he was alone with his dead wife and the sleeping child who would never know his father. He gave way to huge sobs of agony and fell upon the carpet, clasping his hands together as if in prayer.

The silence in the room was heavy, stagnant and almost suffocating to John but he knew he had to get up and pay his last respects to Cannetta else what was the point in his coming? His legs seemed incapable of supporting him but somehow he managed to shuffle over to his wife's final resting place. He closed his eyes but he could still see the image of her, alive, laughing and teasing him in her lucid moments when all he was conscious of was her great beauty and warmth. Opening his eyes he gazed down at the wasted remains of his spouse, his heart pounding, his head racing.

"Cannetta," he whispered. It felt like she would wake up if he spoke too loud, so peaceful did she seem in her last sleep. She was much thinner apart from her swollen belly where his child had developed and now lay with her in a dream-filled trance.

"Oh, my God," he murmured. "You are still very beautiful."

He reached out a trembling hand and caressed her hair which was brushed and shone like silk. Her lips were full and, although pale, they were the very lips he had kissed with such great delight early in his marriage. Overcome with emotion he leant over and kissed them again. But how cold they were!

173

How lifeless, how clammy, how numb was the sensation of touching them! He brushed his lips as if to remove the unpleasant feeling of kissing stark flesh. Where was the Cannetta he had fallen in love with?

"I destroyed her," he mumbled. "I rejected her and sent her away for someone else to kill. Only they did not kill her, she decided to kill herself just days before her uncle came to save her. Oh cruel, cruel fate that could not keep her alive one more day so she could be saved!"

He touched her belly and felt the swell of the child – his child – within which was as cold and stark as she was.

"Oh, my darling – I have failed you," he sobbed.

Above her head a crude label was affixed which read-

"Cannetta Straeton nee Hardy. 22 Years of age. Documents attached. To be collected."

How horrifying that she had been trussed up like a parcel ready for transportation! Whatever she had done she did not deserve this end.

"My poor, poor wife," he whispered, stroking her cold cheek. Her eyelids were closed so softly, as if they had just fallen together in a light doze, and he could swear her mouth had opened slightly as he spoke to her, as if she murmured silent words to him. She was wearing one of the gowns he had bought for her just before they were married, a beautiful cream dress with a low neck and full sleeves. Her feet were bare and he wondered again at the length of each slim toe, likewise her long fingers that lay at her side. He picked up her flaccid arms and folded her hands over her chest. To his left he spied a vase of winter flowers – the last fading chrysanthemums in burnished bronze and these he laid round her head and put on her chest.

"They are not as beautiful as you," he sighed. "Oh, Cannetta, I have wronged you terribly but I did it through fear and with no evil intent. Had I known all that your uncle told me you would have come home immediately, whatever the consequences were! I wish you had known you carried my child as you would have received gentler treatment. How could I have sent you away knowing my son or daughter rested in your belly! I pray that you are both safe and happy in heaven! You have done no wrong. I knew you could not help your behaviour and were powerless to stop your ramblings. Oh God, what will your poor mother make of this?" He covered his face and let the silence of death wash over him.

The afternoon wore on. John remained with his wife, insensible to the passage of time until Mr Hardy entered the room with his sister-in-law who seemed shocked to see him with her daughter. They stood there observing him for a while and then John felt the power of their eyes upon him and he looked up.

"Rose…"

She stepped forward and bowed her head.

"This is no place for harsh words or arguments, Mr Straeton, so I would ask you to withdraw and leave me to spend some time with my daughter alone."

174

John nodded his head.

"Of course," he murmured. "I have finished here. I shall go."

He went to walk past his mother-in-law but she reached out and grabbed his arm, shaking him roughly to bring him to his senses.

"I hope you have looked long and hard upon your wife, Mr Straeton. I hope you have asked God for forgiveness for sending her to her death. She lies in her coffin because of you!"

John wiped the tears from his face.

"There will be no forgiveness for me, Rose," he said simply and left the room.

A minute later he let himself out into the snowy afternoon and turned onto the track that led back to the pink cottage where yet another loved one lay in the jaws of death.

The afternoon was already waning and the early winter darkness closed in as John arrived at his temporary home. Snow had drifted outside the front door and the garden was steeped in white splendour, broken only by his own footsteps and those of hungry birds and animals, searching for some nourishment in the vast waste. He entered quietly, took off his soiled boots in the kitchen and fetched some dry shoes which resided in a box under the table. As he did so Shirley entered the room, bearing a large ewer of water; he looked up and their eyes met. She never said a word but continued with her duties, ignoring his presence although it gave her great pain to do so. John stood silent for a moment and then extended his arm towards her. She regarded him coolly but did not take the offered limb.

"Shirley" he said, simply. "I have had a large sorrow placed in my path and I cannot overcome it. I do not have the strength to talk about it...yet. Give me one more day to sort out my feelings and I will talk to you and tell all. Will you give me the space to come to terms with it in my own time and then I will unburden myself to you? I have always kept my own counsel, for good or bad..."

"Mr Long called," she replied, trying to keep her own feelings in check, although her lips trembled. "It seems your house is sold, John, so there is nothing further to keep you here..."

He came closer and stared into her tearful eyes.

"I have upset you by my reticence, I can see," he whispered, suddenly aware of Connie in the parlour near at hand. "I am sorry but there are reasons for my silence which I know you will understand in good time. Once tomorrow is over I will open my heart..."

She did not look at him but gazed at the floor, her mind taking in all he had said.

"There is still no necessity for you staying once you have the money for your house," she replied, in a low voice.

"There is every necessity for me staying," he growled, firmly. "There is Connie and there is you."

175

She was close to breaking down so she left him, suddenly, and went back to the parlour where Connie was struggling to eat some food.

John followed her, troubled at her reaction.

"Hello, darling," he murmured to Connie, who looked up and smiled. He sat down beside her and took her wasted hand.

"Connie, something very serious happened last night when I was at the fair. I am not at liberty to tell you as yet but please believe me I did not want to let you down and return late and empty-handed."

The girl nodded.

"I understand but Mother was very worried and I hate to see her so unhappy."

John glanced at Shirley but she picked up some needlework to hide her confusion.

John turned back to his cousin.

"As soon as the snow is gone I shall return to the fair and buy you everything your heart desires," he promised.

"Do not worry," replied Connie. "Just sit by me for a while as I crave your company."

"Of course I will, dearest, "he murmured. "Shall I read to you? You like that and I see you have done well and nearly finished your soup. It will soothe you to sleep and that will refresh you."

"But you must eat first," said Connie, in concern for his welfare.

Shirley got up.

"I will fetch you some soup and bread," she offered.

John shook his head.

"There is no need," he assured her, lying valiantly. "I have already eaten."

Shirley did not ask any more questions but sat down and began to sew. John fetched some of his books and asked Connie what she would prefer.

"Poetry, please," she wheezed.

John opened a book and began to read -

"And he, who used to come, will come no more,
  Though roses thorn a pathway to my door;
  Though laurels weave a wreath of time and snow,
  And seasons scatter passion in their flow.

Though spring awakes the love in bowers green,
And summer shimmers heat in verdant sheen;
Though tawny autumn scatters fruit with gales,
My weeping heart can drown sad winter's wails.

And he, who used to come, will come no more,
Though suffering spilt my lifeblood on the floor;

176

Though nights of dreaming drew in hopeful light,
Alone, eclipsed, in this eternal night.

No sun can dawn to break this tortured sleep,
No moon can wax to pierce the shadows deep;
Long years of fruitless waiting gather gloom,
And at the end of time my prize – a tomb."

By the time he came to the poignant last verse he saw Connie was not listening but had fallen into a light sleep. He closed the book and remained gazing at her, deep in thought.
"If love could keep her alive she would not be facing the chasm of death!" he breathed, more to himself than Shirley, who sat at a distance, stitching quietly. Silence fell in the room and John dozed himself as sleep had eluded him completely last night. He did not even remember seeking the shelter of his bed on the settle so disturbed was his mind at what he had learnt. And every time he closed his eyes she, his wife, appeared to him, lunging at him, mad and screaming, then calming down into the very woman he fell in love with. He shuddered as he slept.

Next day the snow had receded a little and various features of the landscape reasserted themselves through the blanket of white. The hilltops were still covered thickly but the world ran with the melt of thaw water as the temperature had risen a few degrees. Connie groaned horribly in her sleep and Shirley shivered at the eerie sound. Still John barely spoke to her, reserving any speech he could muster for his sick cousin. About ten o'clock he went out, dressed rather smarter than usual, without any clue as to where he was going. Shirley watched him from an upstairs window. Was he meeting some one? Maybe it was innocent and just some business to do with his house sale. But her distressed mind automatically thought the worst.

John walked in stiff silence to his wife's funeral. The tiny church at Ardle was his destination and he hoped to reach it without meeting any one. In that he was lucky, very few souls had ventured out for the cold still held dominance over the landscape though the wind had dropped considerably. In arriving at the small place of worship, where he had been only a few times, he noticed two other individuals in the pews and recognised them as Richard Hardy, Cannetta's uncle and Rose. Apart from that the church was empty, though whether the snow or the fact that it was the local mad woman's funeral had stopped people coming, it was difficult to say. John nodded to Richard but Rose avoided his eyes and kept hers lowered on her hymn book. The vicar waited a few minutes to see if anyone else was going to attend but when the door remained firmly shut and silent he opened his Bible and began.

John found he was not attending to the words the vicar spoke but an inner dialogue consumed him concerning his future, if indeed he had one. He gazed round the little building and tried to find some comfort in his surroundings. But his lot here had been a very unhappy one and he craved to get as far away from Stackhouses as he could. Scotland was the only other place where he had ever been happy and to that country he now directed his thoughts. With his house being sold it would only be a matter of days before he could go. But the one thing that held him back was Shirley. There was nothing further he could do for Connie, except read to her, talk to her and generally care for her until death overtook her. That much he had come to terms with, hard though it was but what about her stepmother? Would she want to leave with him? Could she, in fact leave, with Connie requiring so much nursing? And then there was Damion – he was her husband after all. In the cold hard light of day would she really turn her back on him and follow John into unknown territory?

The service was over: John stuttered his way through the two hymns but never opened his book. Richard and Rose sat three pews ahead of him and only Richard seemed able to join the vicar in the singing as Rose was constantly wiping her eyes. John looked at her and at the coffin, now closed, and in the centre of the church. I have caused all this suffering, he thought. I must go away and the sooner the better. I should creep off in the night without telling anyone or saying goodbye. I have bought my family nothing but sorrow so they would not miss me. But he knew that was not true and that one would feel her world had collapsed when she saw him no more.

They moved outside and John was surprised to see that a grave had been dug for Cannetta, despite the lying snow and frozen ground. He realised it was in the pauper's plot where the sinners resided and he felt momentarily angry that his wife should be slighted in this way. She had not sinned – she could not help her behaviour and any God worth his salt and possessing an ounce of understanding and compassion would know that. Besides was He not omnipotent? Therefore He must have known how sick she was, in her mind. Why did He not help her? All these thoughts swum through his head as he stood by the open grave, preparing to say goodbye. Rose was almost uncontrollable and Richard had a hard job to hold her and keep her on her feet. John was horrified at the intensity of her grief and his guilt trebled. I am the cause of all this, he told himself again - I…me…no one else. Everyone tried to warn me but I would not listen. And because I took her away from the one place where she was safe tragedy loomed.

The funeral came to an end and the three people left the tiny church. John did not know what to do or say. He tried to offer some words of comfort to Rose but she refused to look at him or speak.

Richard pushed John away and asked him to go.

"It is better if we, as family, remain a little longer at the graveside alone," he whispered.

John nodded. Was he not family too, joined with Cannetta forever, by marriage?

He walked along the snowy paths and stopped by the church gate to turn back and look at the two people bent in their grief. His eyes flowed with water and he wiped them. No one else had come - no one else cared. He could not bear to go back to the cottage as yet so he wandered around in the snow and then went to take a last look at his house before it slipped out of his hands. He had lost a considerable sum of money in selling it but he just wanted it gone and what did money matter when he had lost so much already?

About three o'clock a bright gleam appeared in the sky and Shirley, who was sick of being indoors, saw Connie as comfortable as she could be made and then set off for a walk to Stackhouses. It was the first time she had been out for three days and the clear, cold air revived her a little. She wondered where John was and kept her eyes peeled for him but he did not pass her. As she approached Ardle church she met two people dressed in deep mourning with heads down and their slow, sad gait told her they had been to a funeral. As they grew closer Shirley recognised one as Rose, her blackmailer of earlier days, but the other, a tall, thin man she knew not. The man raised his hat to her and Shirley gave a small bow.

"Excuse me," she enquired. "Has there been a funeral here today?"

The gentleman nodded his head gravely.

"Yes," he murmured. "My niece has just been buried. She did not die here but I had her returned as she loved this place and desired to be interred here. We have just left her so please excuse us but my sister is extremely exhausted and needs to get home to rest."

"Of course," replied Shirley, feeling rather dazed. "I wish you both well and may God comfort you in your loss."

The gentleman bowed again and the couple continued on their way. Shirley remained static though, loath to move on. Her mind whirled. The man had said it was his niece who had died and the woman on his arm he had identified as his sister so that made the deceased.

"Cannetta," she said to herself. "Oh, my God, it is Cannetta they have just buried!"

She walked on to the church but somehow she could not enter the gate, so great was her grief. The poor, poor lass...she thought. She stood there while thick flakes of snow whirled around her, clinging to her hair and face.

Suddenly she knew what to do and turning she ran from the church, round the next bend of the path and to a small cottage that resided just off the path to Stackhouses. Banging furiously on the door she panted with her exertion and waited impatiently whilst the owner of the premises fumbled with the locks and, at last, opened the door.

"Why, Mrs Penlow!" he cried, saluting her with a toothless grin.

"Good day, Mr Edmunds!" she replied, in some anxiety. "Can you tell me whose funeral was held today at the church? I presume you are returning there later to cover the coffin."

"Aye," acknowledged he. "I had best be sharpish as the snow will fill the hole before I shovels the earth in at this rate."

"But who are you interring, Mr Edmunds?"

The man was silent for a moment.

"She is laid to rest in the pauper's plot, Mrs Penlow. No pride of position for her. Mind you there are some as say she should not be there at all! I don't think the vicar was happy but that Mr Hardy - well he has money and some notes waved at a funeral always ensures a good burial."

"Was it Cannetta Straeton? Cannetta Hardy as she was?"

The grave digger nodded.

"Aye, the local mad woman, that's her. Starved to death in an asylum so the story went. Too insane even to eat, they say. They tried to force some nourishment down her with some of them new- fangled doctor's tubes but she wasn't having any of it and vomited it all up. Sad, very sad, as she was a few months with child but that died with her of course."

Shirley wiped away her tears and asked the gravedigger if he could accompany her to Cannetta's final resting place.

"I will just fetch my spade and then I can kill two birds with one stone as it were," he told her.

Shirley stood on the doorstep waiting with considerable impatience whilst Edmunds donned his outdoor garb and fetched his tools. After a few minutes they departed. The snow had stopped by now and a little more brightness showed in the sky.

"Be showers of this all day and likely all night too," imparted Edmunds, who fancied himself as something of a weather-forecaster.

Shirley made no comment. So this was why John had been so devastated and distant.

Edmunds led the way to the side of the church where the sinners and those not calculated to find favour with God were buried. Shirley saw the open grave and gazed down into the dark depths.

"Poor, poor lamb," she murmured. "So this is where they have put you. It is only slightly better than where you were before. And your unborn child, enveloped within you, will never know the love of its father or mother. Oh God, how can this be right?" She knelt down and brushed the earth near the grave as if Cannetta could feel the comfort from her touch. Edmunds stood back and regarded the woman's anguish.

"I will leave you for a few moments to pay your respects since you did not know about the funeral," he murmured, bowing his head in reverence. "Mad woman or not, she deserves a Christian burial and proper mourners to feel sorrow at her demise. I can see you are quite overcome." and he wandered away to the church.

Shirley was left alone. She continued to caress the earth and talk to the sleeping girl below her.

"Did he come to your funeral, I wonder. There is one thing I do know, Cannetta, he did love you. Yes. I loved him...I still do and I know in that I am wrong but I cannot help it. There is a part of me in those blue eyes and that handsome freckled face. Oh, I know he was your husband and I did try to stay away. But my passion for him was too strong...it still is. I am so sorry, Cannetta, I am so sorry." She became engulfed with sobs and flinging herself down in the dirt by the grave she gave way to her feelings and let the bitter salt of her tears mingle with the sod that lay waiting to cover the wasted remains of John's wife. The wind raised its voice around her and blew upon the silent churchyard but Shirley's only thought was of her cousin and how he would cope with this tragic death that left him, not just an unrequited father, but a widower as well.

After a while she became conscious of the cold creeping up to bite her and she rose and brushed the dirt off her damp clothes. There was nothing left for her here. She walked over to the church gate and took one last, lingering look at Cannetta's final resting place in the gathering gloom.

"Be at peace now," she whispered. "No longer will the forces of insanity be able to torture and terrify you so you know not what you do. Oh, if only you had lived to bring forth the child you carried. The double loss must be tormenting John beyond reason! I must find him, I must find him!"
Anxiety took hold of her in a fearful grip and with one final look at the darkening scene before her she turned and ran off in to the bleakness of a snowy afternoon.

CHAPTER 17

When Shirley eventually reached home, dampened by a sharp shower of mingled hail and rain, she observed the cottage was in darkness and, apart from her sick stepdaughter, deserted. She let herself into the kitchen, pulled off her soaked shoes and stockings and changed into fresh foot ware. Connie, thankfully, was still asleep. Throwing a thick shawl around her Shirley made up the fire, saw that the invalid was deep in slumber, with no response to her stepmother's words, and sat down to deliberate on what to do next. She was extremely distressed and the fact that John was not here only increased her anxiety. She watched the flames roar up the chimney, then settle down into a steady burn. She leapt up, unable to be still and wondered where John was. In whatever location he found himself he was going through this tragedy alone that was sure. And where was her husband too? She looked in again on Connie, saw she had not stirred, and fetching fresh boots she quit the house and made her way over to Fourbridges. There was no containing her emotions and she could not wait for John to put in an appearance. How could they talk with Damion in the house? No, she needed to speak to John alone and that could only be done by seeking him out.

It was quite dark and she hoped her husband was on his way back to the cottage so that he could sit with Connie. She had no idea of when she would return but she could not rest until she had found John and talked to him. As she walked tears still dropped for poor dead Cannetta. Gone after only twenty-two years of life! Gone within a few weeks of being married and never to see the child she carried! She gave a small sob and carried on her way. It was bitterly cold but she did not feel the wind's blow or the piercing raindrops, laced with ice. She was used to walking in the dark and it did not frighten her. Beside the paths to Stackhouses were so well known to her that she could have found them blindfolded. As she neared Fourbridges she prayed, desperately, that John was there. If not, then where could he be? Lamenting over the grave at Ardle? That was very unlikely - with Rose about. Out on a call? Then she would sit and wait in his house if it were open or in the garden if she was locked out. She did not care. She had to see him! What he had been through this past two days she could only imagine. And, due to his reserve, he had faced it alone.

She ran across the bridge and saw, with great relief, a light shining in his house.

"Oh, God, thank you, thank you," she gasped, stopping for a minute to collect her thoughts. Then she plunged on and reaching the house, burst in without knocking.

"John! John!" she called into the dark hallway.

No answer, so she tried the sitting room where the light was burning but it was empty and no fire graced the deserted grate. Leaving the door open she ran up the stairs and into his bedroom where she observed him to be folding clothes and packing them into a saddle bag.

"John!"

He looked up as she entered and his eyes told her he had been expecting her.

"Shirley..." he said, in low tones.

She reached his side in three steps and took his cold hand.

"Oh, my darling, you are freezing!" she cried at the icy touch of his flesh.

He did not reply but stopped folding his clothes.

"I am going away, Shirley, once the snow has gone and I may not be back for some time."

She nodded her head but her thoughts were with his poor dead wife in her grave and she said, simply,

"I know, John, I know it all."

He did not reply to that at first but gave a very sad sigh and turned away from her. Eventually he murmured,

"And now you know why I have been so silent and withdrawn. How can I ever come to terms with –that - and what I have done, except by fleeing from the place where dark memories rise to strangle me? Every inch of this house screams at me; she bit you here, she scratched you there. Behold the bed where your child was conceived, never to reach full-term. How can I cope with - that?"

Shirley approached him but he swung away from her touch.

"Don't, don't," she whispered, tears spilling down her cheeks. "Don't reject me, John."

"I reject myself," he said. "I do not deserve your sympathy or comfort. It should be me lying in that sinner's grave, not her."

"You cannot think like that," she breathed. "How were you to know she would die in that place? And how could you know she carried your child - you had been married but weeks!"

"I had to go to her funeral alone," he sobbed, motioning her to keep away by his outstretched hand. "There was only me and her mother and uncle there. The village rejected her when she left as a committed woman."

"Why did you not tell me?" cried Shirley, putting out her hands to him. "I could have come with you." She yearned to comfort him but his eyes blazed to keep away.

"Ah, yes!" laughed he, bitterly. "It would have looked good if you and I had attended and shared a pew! Rose would have been delighted!"

"Damion would have accompanied me," she assured him.

"And who would have looked after Connie?"

She hung her head, knowing that she had come out today and left her stepdaughter alone.

A poignant silence fell then Shirley pleaded,

"You cannot...you must not bear this agony alone. I came to comfort you as soon as I found out from Edmunds that it was Cannetta - your wife he was interring before the snow obliterated her grave."

John was silent a few moments then he shook his head.

"I must go. I had planned to leave tomorrow, hence my packing now. We must say goodbye Shirley. There is no future for us here."

She understood his sentiments even though they ripped her heart out.

"But what of Connie?" she asked, trying to swallow the sobs that threatened her words. "It is days now before she leaves us and how am I to tell her you have gone away, just when she needed you most?"

He saw the sense in what she was saying and reluctantly he replied,

"Yes, I can see how upset she would be to wake and not find me by her bedside. A few days will make no difference to me but, during this time, Shirley, we must be as strangers to each other. To hold you and have to leave you will only prolong the agony. It cannot be done .I could not stand it..."

She felt a sense of mingled relief and sadness that he would stay until Connie attained her heaven but during that time his eyes would be for his dying cousin only. And then he would go.

"Will I ever see you again?" she whispered.

He shook his head.

"I do not think it likely. Scotland is a long, long way from here and I am not enticed to visit the south again. I must try my hand at earning a living where I was born and bred. At the moment the icy glens seem like paradise compared with my suffering here. If I do come back at all it will not be for many years."

"I see," she replied. "So I am doomed to a marriage with a man I do not love, and, worse still, despise."

"Damion is my cousin no matter what he has done and I shall be sorry to leave him."

"And me?" she asked. "Will you be sorry to leave me?"

He came forward and took her hand, then dropped it again as though it burnt him.

"God that I should never touch your flesh again nor see your beautiful face!" he cried. "How that is to be borne I do not yet know. I can deliberate on nothing but this sorrow at present."

"I will press you no further," she replied, seeing he was desperately fatigued and emotional. "I just came to tell you that I knew the painful details of Cannetta's death and I am here for you if you need me."

"I will always need you, Shirley," he acknowledged, tenderly. "That will never end but whether - with what has happened and is about to happen - whether in these sad circumstances I can act on that need. I do not know...I can say no more..." He sat down heavily on the bed and covered his face.

She perceived his confusion and knew if she stayed and talked more she would only make it worse so she murmured that she would leave him and go home.

"Will you follow me in a little while?" she asked, in concern.

He came to with a jerk, as if he had fallen asleep, and nodded.

"But it grows late and you should not go alone," he whispered, as realisation hit him. He walked to the window and gazed out at the dark, wet night that was, thankfully, obliterating the lying snow.

"I still cannot conceive of her in her grave," he murmured, to himself. "Even though I have seen her stiff and dead in her coffin, even though I have touched her cold flesh yet my mind sees her alive, dancing, screaming, laughing in every living position she can assume, except the correct one that reality reflects - silent and still."

"It is shock," she returned, preparing to leave. "It is shock, John, and it will pass. I will see you at the cottage. I must go alone. If Rose is out wandering and sees us, or we meet her brother it will not be good for us -"

"There is no us," he said, stonily. "No us, no we...anymore."

"I do not care for my reputation," she said, hotly. "That was in tatters before you came but I will have to live here when you are gone."

"Exactly! I have been a bad influence on you."

She shook her head.

"You have been my life," she murmured. "When you walked through that door and smiled at me I lived again and left the pathetic existence that had engulfed me since my rash marriage. I will live on those memories."

He did not reply, nor turn from the window, so she left quietly, descended the stairs and letting herself out of the back door she sought the paths to Ardle.

It was nearly seven o'clock when she reached the pink cottage and she could see lights flaring out from the interior so she knew Damion was home and attending to his sick daughter. Feeling relieved that Connie had not been on her own for too long she breezed in, called her husband's name and began removing her damp outer garments. Most of the snow had gone with the advent of the rain, apart from the huge drifts that had been blown to the perimeters of the lanes and lingered in the sheltered spots. It was less cold but she felt chilled from her walk and approached the fire to get warm. Damion had obviously banked it up and she heard his footsteps overhead in Connie's room, then he descended the stairs, calling her name in an angry tone.

Finding her in the parlour he grabbed her wrist and asked, in ire,

"Where the hell have you been? Here it is, past seven o'clock, and our daughter left parched and unable to get herself a drink – as you well know!"

"I am sorry - something serious happened and I was called away," she replied, feeling frightened at the red mist in his eyes.

"What is more important; your evening wanderings or our daughter's welfare?" he asked, shaking her roughly by the shoulders.

"I cannot tell you," she murmured. "It is John's business – not mine."

"Then you should have kept out of it!" he shouted at her, continuing to shake her violently.

Her teeth chattered together and by and by he ripped the shoulder of her dress and his harsh hands drew blood.

"Let me go, Damion!" she pleaded. "Have you been drinking? I have done nothing wrong."

"Not in my eyes, you worthless slut!" he screamed in her ear. "And if I have been drinking it is your bad behaviour that has driven me to it!"

Shirley began to cry, as he was hurting her considerably, and the more she struggled the harder he gripped her so that her arms ran with blood.

"You evil bitch!" he yelled. "How dare you swan off to gossip and leave my dying daughter on her own! I am ashamed of you! You deserve a good beating – and by Christ – you are going to get one!"

He began to hit her over the head and about the chest, the blows raining down on her and causing her to feel faint with the pain. She screamed aloud for mercy and then, suddenly, she heard running footsteps outside, approaching the cottage and the bang of the kitchen door.

John stood there, framed in the parlour doorway, with a lantern in his hand, his eyes wild with shock.

"Damion! Oh my God man, what are you doing?" he cried, stepping forward into the room.

His cousin dropped Shirley heavily on the ground and went out, climbing the stairs again, without a glance at either his wife or his relation. John waited until he was out of earshot and then he rushed to Shirley's side and helped her onto the settle. She gasped for air and her delicate flesh bled freely where her husband's rough and callous hands had grazed her. She was crying too with the shock and John took her in his arms and held her until the weeping ceased and she clung to him as though she would never let go.

"Oh, Shirley, Shirley, what has he done to you?" he whispered. "Oh my God, is this for my sake too?" He laid her down gently on the settle and returned to the kitchen where he obtained clean water to wash her wounds and a towel.

When he returned she was sitting up, looking pale and tearful but no longer trembling.

"Oh John, "she breathed. "You are covered in my blood."

He stared down at his soiled clothes.

"I do not care," he said. "It is your blood, so how can I not love it seeing as it runs in your veins?"

She did not answer him but seemed recovered from the attack.

"And is this what you have suffered before?" he asked, washing her wounds gently.

186

"Yes, when he drinks spirits...or I have displeased him."

"And how did you displease him today? My God, when I walked in I thought he knew - that he had found out - about us."

"There is no us, no we...anymore," she whispered, repeating his words of an hour ago.

He continued to dab her pale skin.

"I was wrong," he said.

"I angered my husband today because I left Connie alone and ran after you. She was sleeping sweetly and my mental anguish was great. John, I had to see you. I would have gone through this attack and worse to see you were safe. Of course I would never neglect my stepdaughter but she was only left for a couple of hours and, besides, Damion should have been home, not consuming alcohol to drown his sorrows. All reason flies out of the window when he touches whisky."

"He has no excuse. He should not treat you like this."

She did not reply but watched the care he exuded over her cuts and grazes.

"So, John," she whispered, taking his free hand. "Where is the vow you took to be as a stranger to me? Where has the agreement gone that we should keep apart?"

He tried to smile but his face was stiff.

"Gone to the Devil with one touch of your velvet flesh," he replied in a low tone. "Any vow would disintegrate into dust if it felt the joy of having you in its arms. You are meat and drink to me, Shirley, and the only thing in Ardle that keeps me sane. The broken promises made to my soul lie in a thousand pieces on the floor when you look in my eyes. I am quite powerless to resist you." and he kissed her shoulder with cold lips.

"And you are still leaving?" she enquired.

He looked at her and she saw the love and desire brimming over in them.

"I am still leaving," he said.

Another few drab and cheerless days passed each one marking a severe deterioration in Connie's condition. What little strength she possessed left her she could no longer rise and barely seemed able to swallow water. Remaining in bed she relied on her parents and cousin for everything and seemed happy to see them when in a conscious state. John, especially, she doted on and he rarely left her bedside, unless she was asleep when he would creep away and seek solace with Shirley downstairs whilst Damion drunk his reason away at the World's End Inn. No mention was made regarding the attack by anyone and the wounds began to scab over on Shirley's arms and shoulders. The cottage remained draped in sorrow and silence. The inhabitants wandered around conversing in whispers and the blinds were frequently drawn down all day. Damion talked to no one, not even his dying daughter, and he only looked in on her when she was asleep. He was frequently in tears which he could not bring himself to shed but they remained, misting his vision, for days. No apology was made to Shirley; in fact he rarely spoke to her except to ask for food or drink. Shirley was grateful for this and she and John comforted each other as best they were able.

The weather was a little milder and the wind swung round to the west, raising the temperatures and bringing some pale winter sun. After two days of not leaving the house John resolved to get some fresh air and visit his wife's grave. He gleaned a few winter flowers from the garden and set off with his heart in turmoil. As he drew nearer the church his step faltered and his eyes misted over but he pushed on resolutely, the handful of flowers creating a bright spot on a drab winter afternoon.

The little church was deserted and silent and the graveyard even more so. He went through the gate, round to the side of the plot and found the rough earth that marked where his wife lay. A small wooden cross had been erected in the centre of the grave and he assumed that Richard Hardy had placed it there, or Rose. He was thankful that neither of them were about today. Collecting some water and a jar from the end of the church his attention was attracted by the presence of two men carrying between them a large, flat object, wrapped in sacking. Behind them came a third man transporting a bundle of tools. John noticed they were bound for a grave near his wife's and when he returned with the urn for his flowers he found they stood at the very foot of his wife's plot.

"Can I help you?" he asked the man nearest him, who put down his tools and stared at him.

"Good day, sir," he replied. "Garfield's Stonemasons from Longbeck sir. Here to erect the stone to Miss Hardy for her uncle. The snow has delayed us I am afraid but I see it has quite gone from here. We've still a few drifts in our area."

John looked over to the church gate and saw a wagon and horses waiting.

His heart sank. Would he ever get any peace? And really he had come to say goodbye as he did not expect to be here more than another day or so.

He let the men get on with their job and retreated to the church where he sat on a bench sheltered from the wind and watched them as they worked. When they had finished one of the men approached him and bade him good afternoon.

"You bring flowers, sir," he said, gently. "Are you a relation, by any chance?"

John shook his head.

"No," he replied. "I am nothing to her. I am just here to pay my respects as I pass through. I do not expect to be here more than a couple of days and I may never visit the region again, so..."

"I see, sir," returned the man. "We will leave you to your deliberations and can only apologise for interrupting you."

John bowed and the three men wandered along, talking brightly. A few minutes later he heard the wagon drive away and he was left alone.

He went over to the grave and cast his eyes over the stone. It shone in its purity and his heart sank as he read the inscription on it

In This Grave Lie The Remains Of
Cannetta Hardy
Aged 22 years.

Thy Name, Oh God, Is Mercy.

There followed the dates of her birth and death but he did not see them, so blinded were his eyes by tears. No mention of him at all. She had died as Cannetta Straeton – his wife but Richard had obscured his presence in her life and wiped all trace of him away. It was like he did not exist in her world. But she had gone to her grave declaring her love for her husband and moreover she had died with child – his child. The hurt of it all crushed him and he felt it was the final straw in his relationship with Cannetta. He was excluded, forgotten, not even a memory in her life or her death. Turning away in deep grief he left the churchyard and vowed to return no more. Cannetta had never been his, wife or not, and he surrendered her to God and prayed for her soul. It was one more reason to leave this place of desolation and despair and never come back. Scotland suddenly shone with a bright light and he, weary and inconsolable, moved ever closer to her shine...

The next day Connie sank into a decline which the doctor confirmed she was unlikely to come out of.

"It is merely a matter of hours," he said, when summoned to examine her. "I can offer you no hope, only that it will be a release for her."

John and Shirley vowed not to leave her side but Damion was at work and his wife decided not to fetch him as there was nothing he could do and, besides, she craved the time alone with John, since he was to leave shortly.

John had said little about Cannetta's gravestone but Shirley, who was so sensitive to his moods, gleaned more by his silence than any words he actually uttered. She knew he was deeply upset over it and suspected that the inscription had annulled his marriage and left her to lie there as a Hardy. Very little was said between them but when they could they sort each other's arms for comfort and support. John told himself he was merely reassuring and aiding Shirley, since the only physical contact Damion made with her was with his fists. But the more he held her, the harder he knew it would be to leave her and the day loomed that saw him forced to commit her to her abusive and callous husband. Time and time again he wrestled with his conscience, and, deep into the night, he told himself, over and over again,

"She made her choice; she has to live with it and I have to surrender her to her husband and go alone." But he could not bear the thought of life without her and though he knew they must part every second in her company became precious and golden.

After the doctor had been shown out Shirley came back to Connie's bedroom and sat down beside John. Her hand sought his and fitted in it like a vital piece of his body. Neither of them spoke for a few moments then Shirley whispered,

"Do you suppose she knows we are here, loving her, and hoping she attains that paradise she so often spoke of at the start of her illness?"

John squeezed her fingers and kissed them.

"Of course she does, darling," he murmured.

"Do you not think it strange she never passed an opinion on our relationship since she became immured here, despite knowing how I loved you, and still do?"

He did not reply to this so she continued.

"My heart has always been so transparent and she saw my eyes seeking your face from the first time I beheld you. She told me to forget you and, believe me, I did try but the love was too deep for me. Over time she knew I could not give you up but she felt only sympathy for me. Even in her conscious moments she has mentioned nothing to me - no reproaches, no pity, no anger...Has she said anything to you?"

"No," he replied, in a low voice. "I am glad she has not as I do not know how I would answer her. In truth I know I have betrayed Damion, but, like you, I cannot help myself. Something in my soul called yours and the link was made, not even my love and marriage to Cannetta could break it. There is only one thing that will sever it - my leaving and that comes daily closer -"

She did not reply to this but squeezed his hand harder and turned her gaze to the grey face on the covers. Connie was stirring slightly. She put up a hand and brushed her face and Shirley darted forward,

"Dearest, we are both here, John and I. Do you want a drink, darling? Are you cold or hot?"

"No, Mother. I am very happy. Only one thing troubles me and that I must speak to John about - alone."

"Shall I leave you, dearest? I will only be downstairs in the kitchen but I understand." Shirley leant over the bed and kissed her stepdaughter with lips almost as icy as Connie's. Then she withdrew softly, smiling beautiful eyes at John, and he heard her light step descending the stairs.

The room became heavy with silence then Connie gasped for breath and said,

"Listen, John, I can hardly speak but I crave to write something before sleeps overtakes me again. I shall not come out of this next slumber here but will wake in a new world where all is bright, fresh and radiant. I can almost see the shadow of its luminosity coming to capture me in its rays."

"What do you want to say to me, dearest? I will do anything that you ask of me, you know that."

Connie tried to raise herself up on one elbow.

"Have you a pen and some paper, John?"

"I can fetch some darling, from my bag. Just wait a moment," and he darted off, returning swiftly with the desired articles.

Connie took the pen but her hand shook and she could not frame any letters on the paper.

"Help me John, please. If you guide and support my hand I can write what I need to."

"Why don't you tell me, darling? I will remember every word, I promise."

"I must record it because you will dismiss my words, cousin, but when I am gone you will have the paper and can read them time and time again until you know they are the only way of truth. Any other path will lead to great sorrow for you and Mother."

John felt very perplexed but he did as she wanted and she began to form shaky letters on the paper.

"Mother is an angel," she wrote. "She loves you, John, with a totally pure heart and you love her with the same purity. It does not matter she is married to Father – he does not love her as you do. When you leave you must take her with you. That is the oath of your hearts and it cannot be broken."

Connie fell back on the pillow and pushed the note into his hands. He read it with brimming eyes.

"I cannot do that, darling. I cannot! It will destroy your father."

Connie shook her head.

"No," she murmured. "It will destroy Mother, utterly and completely. Father will recover, but if you go and leave Mother here she will die. And you will suffer, too. You must be together..."

"Connie, you do not know what you ask. I cannot take another man's wife. Shirley must remain here to do her duty by Damion. She has already sacrificed too much for me, you all have."

Connie smiled like she saw a vision approaching.

"It has been revealed to me," she whispered, gasping for breath. "You will take her, John, you will..." Her face convulsed violently and John held her until the fit had passed but when he went to lay her down he saw, all too clearly, she had gone.

As he held her his eyes strayed down to the paper on the counterpane and, after covering her peaceful face he picked up the paper, read it again and then folded it up very carefully, kissed it and put it in his pocket.

It was the day after the funeral. John was packing his last minute things from the cottage, his heart heavy with sorrow. Damion was preparing for

191

work and Shirley was upstairs dressing. The burial had gone off smoothly enough with most of the village turning out to pay their respects to the young girl. John sat quietly in a back pew away from his cousins and watched the outer signs of grief. Only three people had attended the funeral of his wife but Connie - .she was well loved and people sobbed openly. There were many of her fellow workers from the Hall and the little building was crowded with scarcely a spare seat. Shirley turned to look at him once during the service and her eyes said a million things that he longed to forget. He looked upon Connie as being the fortunate one, swallowed up in the veil of death, unknowing, unfeeling and safe. How he longed to be there seeing as it was impossible for him to possess the one thing in this life that could make him happy! Instead he was forced to endure a span of years where all he did was exist. And regret. He listened to the drone of the vicar's voice and he became seized by guilt and despair.

So he was following his head now and leaving but his heart was saying – stay, stay!

He finished his packing and went to find Damion who was in the kitchen, putting on his outdoor clothes in readiness for work.

"I shall miss 'ee, cousin," cried the labourer, giving him a hug. "Faith, I am sorry you've had nothing but misfortune here but happen 'twill make Scotland all the dearer to you when you reach it. How long will it take you?"

"About five days. But I know places where I can stop and now I've got the cart life will be easier for me in my travels. I shall probably hitch up by the moors when I hit home territory and be quite cosy."

John had purchased a small cart for his journey and he thought it would help him get a foothold in his new job and, if his veterinary skills failed him, he could always become a carrier.

"You'll be back then, cousin?" Damion asked.

John shook his head.

"Not for the foreseeable future. I shall have to work long hours to set myself up again since I have lost much of my money here. Faith, I shall miss you too. Be kind to Shirley - that is all I ask."

Damion understood him at once.

"I shall not touch spirits again," he vowed. "My nightly half-pint is the only tipple I shall take then my temper will not boil over and my wife will be safe from my anger."

"But you do love her, don't you Damion?"

Damion shrugged his shoulders.

"After all the trouble emotions are worn out in me .I am a score older than you, John, and love does not really enter my world in the way you mean it. My body grows old and it is tired but I am content in her company and she keeps the house tidy and warm most of the while. Yes, she did stray when I first met her but no more. She has made her vow to me and I have made mine to her....I shall never hit her again...and she will never look at a man other than me."

John was secretly appalled. So this was what Shirley was sentenced to. A loveless marriage where passion had no place and affection never raised its unwelcome head. How could such a heart as hers...fiery, beautiful, fervent be content in the wilderness Damion had just painted?

His cousin shook John's hand and patted him on the back.

"I do not know how Shirley would have coped without you," Damion said. "Faith, I've no way with women, never did understand them but you John, why you might have been born one for your empathy with 'em. Shirley will miss you more than she's letting on, of that I am sure..."

John felt the familiar twinge of guilt assuage him.

"And I shall miss her," he replied, honestly. "But my path lies in a different country and ours may not cross again for a good while. Look after her, Damion."

"Aye and her chief pleasure in life will now be to take care of me, as a loyal wife should. I pray you will find another soul mate in that strange and alien land you come from!"

John could only nod. His heart was full to overflowing and he now had to say goodbye to Shirley...which was the hardest thing he had ever done in his life.

Damion quit the cottage and John stood at the bottom of the stairs. He felt lost and already bereft.   After a couple of minutes Shirley appeared on the landing and, looking down at him, perceived he was ready to go. She descended the stairs quietly and came to stand by his side, gazing up at him as if to memorise every contour of his face. He took her hand and kissed it.

"Is it time?" she asked, in a whisper.

He nodded.

"Yes, dearest, it is time to say goodbye."

"Must I?" she breathed. "Must I...?"

He tried to smile at her in reassurance.

"You must, Shirley. I must too. We must both say farewell..."

The gloomy day wore on and noon passed away. A bright gleam appeared in the sky around lunchtime and the workers saw it and cheered its progress for there had been precious few glimpses of the sun during the month.

Damion watched as the weak rays of light tried to break through the blanket of cloud. He cheered and encouraged them in their progress.

"When I was young my Scottish grandmother called them the eyes of God and said that they smiled good fortune on all they shone upon," he murmured to his companions. "It is misfortune that has frowned on John ever since he arrived here and I pray, wherever he is, that those eyes of God are smiling on him and will continue to do so for a very long time."

"Aye," replied his neighbour. "Buying a damp old dwelling full of fungus and marrying the local mad woman - you can't get much worse than that."

Damion finished work earlier than usual and hoped Shirley had a good tea ready for him. He had eaten very little since Connie's illness, and even less since her death, and the keen air had stimulated his appetite at last. Hurrying home to his cottage he was shocked to find no light streaming as a welcome refulgence to him on his journey. Was she out again? Had he not told her that behaviour must stop?

He entered and found the kitchen deserted. Shirley's shawl and bonnet were missing from the hooks behind the door so he assumed she was at the churchyard visiting her stepdaughter's grave. Well, she had been devoted to Connie and he must not begrudge her time alone with the newly- departed. There was no sign of cooking or food and no fire laid or lit in the parlour. He scratched his head. The place felt very odd; neglected, deserted, almost eerie. "A life has gone out of here recently," he told himself. "It is natural it feels like that."

He began to lay and kindle the fire. Once the flames burst into life, he thought, the house will be alive again. But it still felt heavy and dead.

After a while he went upstairs and found the door to Shirley's wardrobe open and most of her dresses and clothes missing. Damion was totally bemused. He called her name – once, twice but he knew it was all in vain. She was not here. Then he saw an envelope propped up on the dresser with his name upon it. Grabbing it in blind panic he ripped it open and with incredulous eyes read

Dear Damion,

By the time you get this note – the last I shall ever write you – John and I will be on our way to Scotland and a new life. Yes, I have gone with my cousin, but he is my cousin by marriage only, and that union was a rash mistake. I do not recognise it as existing any more.
I make no apologies for my conduct as in my own eyes I am no longer your wife and you are no longer my husband. We ceased to be joined when you laid heavy hands upon me and beat me. I cannot love, or be loyal, to a husband who does not respect me – and you do not love me, Damion, not in the way I desire to be cherished. John and I could not help our secret passion; perhaps if you had been a more attentive husband then I would be by your side now and not miles away entering a strange country.

Despite the fact I feel no guilt for leaving I do crave your forgiveness, if only for John's sake. He feels he has betrayed you but the passion began on my side due to your neglect of me. I am an ardent and intense woman, Damion, and I crave excitement – it is my lifeblood. With you I existed, with John I live and shall continue to live.

I wish you well. Look after Connie's grave for me. I shall talk to her often and I know she would want me to be happy. For the first time in many years I am. I wish you that happiness, Damion and a successful future.

Farewell,

Shirley.

The paper fell to the ground and then the man likewise. He gasped for breath. She had left him! He heard a sound downstairs and then a tap at the door. Pulling himself upright he descended to the hallway and went through to open the kitchen door. His heart had hoped it was Shirley back, meek and mild, asking his forgiveness.

But the doctor stood there, looking grave and pensive.

"Ah, Mr Penlow," he said, awkwardly. "Are you all right? I thought I had better come and see you and your wife after what has occurred to your family.....I am so sorry for your loss. I usually make a visit to the family of the deceased after a few days. Your wife, Mr Penlow, she was very distressed."

"Yes," replied the husband of that lady. "So distressed that she has run off with my cousin! They left this morning on route to Scotland."

"Oh my God! Then the rumour I heard was true. I am sorry, Penlow, but earlier on someone told me they saw Mrs Penlow about twenty miles from here in a cart with a tall, chestnut-haired man. They appeared to be...how can I put it? Intimately acquainted?"

"Yes," cried Damion, bitterly. "Very intimately acquainted! And I never had a clue that she felt anything for him that wasn't befitting a cousin. He comforted her when I lost my temper with her in my drinking and now I am repaid for my cruelty. I deserve it. I never loved her in the way she wanted to be loved. I was a disappointment to her and she regretted marrying me as soon as the act was accomplished."

"She is still your wife, nevertheless, Penlow, and it is not too late to stop them if you truly wish it. They have only been gone a few hours and could likely be brought back to justice before night fall."

Damion shook his head blindly.

"No – they went in freedom and in freedom shall they remain. It is my fault, as her letter says, I treated her so badly that I drove her into the arms of another man – and that man my cousin – my own flesh and blood."

He moved over to the kitchen window and regarded the winter garden.

"I hope in that strange cold land they will be entering a new life awaits them that is happier than either of them experienced here..."

It was four days later. On a stretch of wild and isolated moor just inside the borders of Scotland a man stopped his cart and put down his travelling companion, a beautiful, vivacious lady several years older than he. Then he jumped down too and became entwined with his woman, both of them turning to face the dying rays of the sun as it set in the purple sky.

Shirley stroked his face tenderly.

"And when you said we must say our goodbyes you did not mean to each other did you? You meant to Ardle and our old life in the south."

"How could I leave part of my soul behind?" he queried, in his gentle Scottish drawl. "Do you think I would survive apart from you for one day, one hour, one minute?"

She smiled.

"But you were so sure we must go our separate ways," she continued.

"Yes," he murmured, surveying the beautiful scenery that had always been a moving picture in his head. "That was before Connie spoke to me..."

"Connie? But you said..."

"No darling, she only talked to me the very day she died when she asked you to leave the room. Do you remember?"

"How could I ever forget?" she breathed. "It was the last time I saw her alive. What did she say, John?"

"She told me how much you loved me and she begged me to take you with me when I went."

Shirley shook her head.

"I don't believe you," she cried. "Connie told me I must struggle and contain my feelings for you. She even said I must forget you."

"Yes, I thought that too. But I did not dream it. And to prove it true Connie made me help her write it down in words for us to read now she is gone."

And he pulled the folded note out of his pocket.

"See, I have it here, and I do not think I shall ever part with it. It is the last thing she wrote and it was her most precious wish. Read it, darling."

He handed it to Shirley and as she perused it her eyes filled with tears.

"Oh Connie, Connie!" she sobbed, leaning against him for support. "I shall never forget you and what you did, in your dying hour, to safeguard my happiness. And you listened to her, John?"

"I have read the note many times since her weak and feeble hands inscribed it. How could I not act on her last wishes? How could I ignore her desire to see us both united? She said she saw it as a vision of the future and the way of truth."

"And is it?" she asked, turning to him again and smiling.

"You are my vision of the future, you are my way of truth," he said simply.

They held hands and watched the final glow of the sun as it sunk behind the impressive hills then they mounted the cart again and with renewed hope drove onwards to the turnpike road that led to northern Scotland and a better life...

Lightning Source UK Ltd.
Milton Keynes UK
UKOW04f1759041115

262108UK00001B/3/P